THE CURSE OF THE FALLEN

ABBEY FOX

THE WILD RABBIT LLC

This novel contains content that might be triggering, for a list of possible triggers please visit:
https://www.abbeyfox.com/the-wicked-kingdom-trigger-warnings

World map design: aaguirreart
Character and Cover Illustrations: www.camiladavila.com

"To my mom.
Thank you for being my best book pal during this whole process."

Obsidian City
Sable Forest
Iron Kingdom
Plume City
Leona Sea
Iron City
Rama Sea
Pearl Island
Tatum Ocean
Grey Island
Seems
Willowbrook

F Casztian
Alver Mountains
City of Casti
Bold Kingdom
City of Bold
Ender Desert
Ochre City
Eros Ocean
City of Milania
Ilian Town
Sien Forest
Sky City
Kingdom
Silver Kingdom
City of Silver
Rust Island
Briar City

THE
COPPER CITY
Society of Crows
Society safe's House
Society safe's House exit
Leela's house
The Lost Chariot Inn

Boar

SYNOPSIS OF THE PREVIOUS BOOKS

In the world of Caztian, soulmates exist. The catch is that, once they have met, one can't survive without the other.

In *The Curse of the Crow,* *Nava* and *Arkimedes* are soulmates. They meet when the Society of Crows sends him, alongside his adoptive brother, *Devon Black,* to kill her mother, *Celeste Forrest.* Stunned by the discovery that Celeste has children, and struck by the powerful force of the soulmate bond, Arkimedes convinces Devon to leave without hurting Nava, who is the one to greet them as Celeste isn't at home.

Nava doesn't see Arkimedes's face, but their brief encounter leaves them both with a soulmate mark in the same place above their heart. Her mother and father uproot their family that same day and escape to the non-magical town of Willowbrook, where the Society of Crows—an evil organization that upholds the unethical laws that force magic-wielders to train and serve the Crown from a young age—has less reach.

A decade passes. Nava is now a twenty-five-year-old woman who has been living a normal life without magic, taking care of her young brother *Cameron* and working in her late father's potions shop. She has regular dreams that remind her of the day she met Arkimedes—a consequence of being separated from her soulmate.

But Nava doesn't want her soulmate for two reasons. One, she is aware he's a member of the Society of Crows. Two, she wants the chance to fall in love of her own free will.

One fateful afternoon, Devon Black strolls into her potions shop. He has come to Grey Island to imprison deserters—runaway magic-wielders who ignore the royal draft. To Nava's horror, Devon remembers her. He asks her about his missing partner, who vanished the day they first met ten years ago.

That afternoon, Nava flees from her home in Willowbrook to prevent Devon from learning about Cameron's existence, and to escape the bounty hunters he sends after her. Her late mother's journal urges Nava to seek a man in the forest, supposedly the only person who can help her escape the Society. His name is Arkimedes.

Still unfamiliar with Arkimedes's face or his name, Nava remains ignorant that she is running straight into her soulmate's arms. In the forest, she encounters a dying Beekeeper, a creature made from wood who controls the bees. She uses one of her potions and her awakening magic to heal him. Later that day, Arkimedes saves her from the bounty hunters. He immediately recognizes Nava, but doesn't reveal who he is.

Arkimedes has been living alone in the forest since Nava's mother cursed him to become a crow every night. As he believes the only way to break the curse is to help Nava, he agrees to accompany her to the Northern Village, where the other deserters live. He assures Nava that, with their assistance, they can meet the threat of the Crows and fight Devon's army.

As Nava and Arkimedes travel across the island, encountering various threats, they slowly fall in love. Arkimedes encourages Nava to embrace her magic while she stubbornly denies it. The Beekeeper, *Aristaeus,* also comes to Nava's aid several more times.

Nava finds out about Arkimedes's curse, is kidnapped by Devon's people, and rescued by Arkimedes. They finally reach the Northern Village, where Nava learns that Arkimedes is her soulmate. She has suspected as much for a while, but was in denial. They fight about the secret, and Arkimedes leaves to patrol the area. Nava has her first dream about him since entering the forest. She realizes something terrible has happened to him and goes out to find him, just as Devon's army attacks the village.

Following their bond, Nava discovers Arkimedes, captured and injured after being betrayed by an old friend. She heals him with magic, then fights the guards keeping him prisoner alongside the Beekeeper, Aristaeus.

Aristaeus reveals that Nava is a Beekeeper herself—one of only two in the world—and that a larger destiny connects the three of them. When Nava, Ark, and Aristaeus return to the Northern Village, Devon's army has burned homes and imprisoned and killed many deserters. Amidst the final fight against Devon, they discover that Arkimedes's curse has been miraculously lifted. Nava also learns that Devon and Arkimedes consider each other brothers, since they were the only young children to be taken by the Society of Crows. Devon has been searching for Arkimedes for a decade when most thought him dead and is furious that he's been in hiding this entire time.

After defeating Devon, Nava reads the journal her mother left her, which she had previously avoided because of their complicated relationship. It explains that Arkimedes is her soulmate, why Celeste placed the curse on him, and that, in order to break it, Nava had to fully accept him as her soulmate.

Nava and Arkimedes return to Willowbrook to fetch Cameron. They plan to settle in the Northern Village permanently to begin a new life together.

In *The Curse of a Kingdom*, Nava and Arkimedes have been living a quiet, happy life for a year when Arkimedes is kidnapped by the Dark Ones, a race of fae that wield shadows like Arkimedes. Nava has to act quickly, as the sudden separation from her soulmate has immediate effects on her health. When the leaders of the Northern Village refuse to help her, Nava is forced to form an unlikely alliance with her enemy, Devon Black.

She offers to release him from prison if he helps her rescue Arkimedes. Nava knows she can't trust Devon, so she calls on the life debt Devon owes Arkimedes since the final battle in *The Curse of a Crow*.

Devon opens a portal to the Copper Kingdom and tells Nava that, in order to cross it, she must pay a price—usually a memory. During her passage, Nava meets a mysterious shadowy figure who knows she is a Beekeeper, right before another voice asks her for a memory. In her distress, she gives up the memory of her father and her potion-making skills.

The portal leads them into a castle, where they are quickly ambushed by royal guards and brought to the throne room. Beside the king of the Copper Kingdom sits Arkimedes, who has no memories of Nava or the last ten years of his life. He goes by another name, Orion, the prince of the Copper Kingdom. To save her from the king, Devon lies and tells everyone Nava is his fiancée. This cover story upsets Arkimedes, even though he doesn't understand why.

The king allows Nava and Devon to stay as Arkimedes's guests, but he orders them to wear jewelry that cancels their magic and tracks their whereabouts. Arkimedes is suspicious of Nava because he has been dreaming about her for the past four months but hasn't met her before. He believes she has put a spell on him and confronts her about it. Nava realizes that time works differently in the Copper Kingdom compared to the rest of Caztian. While it has only been a day for her since Arkimedes was kidnapped, four months have passed for him.

Nava attempts to regain Arkimedes's trust. During her time at the castle, she masters her ability to transfer with her Beekeeper power, which allows her to move from place to place as pollen and dust. When Aristaeus calls her into the forest, she leaves despite the danger. But Nava transfers inside the castle's library instead, where she overhears Arkimedes arguing with the librarian. It appears he is trying to unearth information about his mother, the queen, who died in a fire.

Nava and Arkimedes head to the forest together and fight a Zorren, the natural enemies of the Beekeepers, who have been burning the woods near the castle. Nava finally tells Arkimedes that he was kidnapped, and that they are all connected, although she keeps their soulmate bond a secret.

Arkimedes believes her and grows more suspicious of his father, the king, who must have erased his memories. During a masquerade ball, Nava and Arkimedes visit the queen's tree, which remains dead while the kingdom lacks a queen—only to find it flourishing. Arkimedes realizes Nava must be the future queen. They spend the night together, and Arkimedes spots Nava's soulmate mark, which matches his own. He realizes they are soulmates.

Afraid that his father might use her to manipulate him, Arkimedes pushes Nava away to protect her. Although the king doesn't yet know who Nava is, the sentient castle soon gives her away. On her arrival, it dressed her in blue clothes to signal her status as a guest, but now it transforms her attire into black—the color reserved only for the royals. When the king sees her wearing black, all hell breaks loose.

Nava, Devon, and Arkimedes retreat to his room to hatch an escape plan. Since both Devon and Nava are wearing the magic-suppressing bracelets, Arkimedes needs to retrieve the keys from the king's chambers. He orders Nava to transfer away, confident the guards wouldn't truly hurt Devon. Nevertheless, she stays to help Devon fight.

In the meantime, Arkimedes is attacked by the king and his concubines. They subdue him, intending to erase his memories again. Nava transfers in and places a dagger to the king's throat, demanding that Arkimedes be released and for the king to give them the keys to the bracelets. The king agrees, and Devon opens a portal with his regained powers, through which he and Arkimedes escape.

The king is surprised at Nava's transferring skills. He asks her who she is, and she informs him that the tree is alive, meaning she is the future queen. When Nava crosses the portal, the same shadowy figure confronts her again. He looks so much like Arkimedes that she is stunned by the resemblance. And this time, he attacks her.

On the other side of the portal, Arkimedes asks Nava if his father hurt her.

"It wasn't your father," Nava says.

It was you.

1
ORION

Few could escape a Dark One when they were out for blood, and tonight, the fae were coming for him and his soulmate. Orion tightened his hand around Nava's and sped down the narrow alleyway, nearly stumbling over a pile of scraps that blocked their path.

At this speed, they would never make it to safety before sunrise, and that meant capture. Devon was likely halfway to the safe house by now. They had foolishly split up after the guards ambushed them hours ago.

Tall buildings on either side offered them sufficient cover from the flying fae above. Even though Orion's feet ached, adrenaline and fear propelled him forward.

He glanced at Nava. Her skin glowed yellow with power. She was beautiful—and a beacon for their enemies to find them in the dark.

"Can you dim your aura? The guards can see better than humans at night." The air burned his throat with every word he spoke. He hadn't realized how out of breath he was.

Every gentle feature of her face had long since morphed into panic and exhaustion. They had been running most of the night, and they both needed a break. Yet the guards were relentless, flying low over the rooftops of the city.

Orion didn't want his citizens forced into choosing who to betray: their prince or their king.

Nava breathed raggedly. "How could they catch up with us so easily? We left the tracking bracelets near the castle. Surely they won't find us without them." Her voice wavered on the last word. Because much like him, Nava had a deeper understanding of their current predicament. The guards would never stop hunting for him, not when the future of the kingdom depended on him staying.

The castle bells had been ringing ever since their escape, echoing down the streets of the Copper City, a command for its residents to stay inside their homes, for the Dark Ones were hunting. Any poor soul who didn't obey their call would be the first to be questioned.

Was there something more leading the guards straight to them? It didn't matter. No need to trouble Nava unnecessarily when he wasn't certain himself. "It's not a large city to track when you can fly."

"But what if they can still track one of us?" Her soft tone pulled at his insides, her words echoing his own fears, almost as if she could read his mind. That thought alone was sobering enough.

Orion's muscles quivered with strain. Time to slow down the grueling pace he had been maintaining.

Nava's aura flickered as her boot caught on an uneven cobblestone. She stumbled forward with a yelp, and he barely had enough time to wrap his arms around her body before she dropped to the ground, dragging him along with the force of her fall. His wings, which he had concealed while crossing the portal earlier that night, reflexively popped out of his back right before he hit the pavement. The weight of her body sucked the air out of his lungs. Hot pain shot through him as a sharp stone dug into his body.

"Are you hurt?" She scrambled off him. Her icy fingers touched his cheek.

"I'm fine." He sat and drew a deep breath. They didn't have time for this. As much as he longed for her touch, he could dwell on that later.

His gaze stuck to the injury that branded her forearm. Someone had attacked Nava when she'd crossed the portal, and in the hours since, she'd refused to tell him what had happened.

"There is a possibility my father put a secondary spell on me so I wouldn't escape my duties again. I don't remember if he did." He brought both hands to his temples, massaging away a burgeoning headache.

"That would explain how they found us back at the plaza." She craned her neck to take in the grimy alleyway. "Do you know where we are?"

Debatable. "Yes."

She narrowed her eyes at him. "There is a myth circulating in Caztian that fae can't lie. You prove them wrong. Constantly."

"You forget I'm half human. Besides, I didn't lie just now. This part of the city looks different from what I remember." He shouldn't feel amused by the crinkle on her forehead or the way she pouted ever so slightly. This was not the time to want to kiss her, not when his father's guards were hunting them down like animals. Not when he was supposed to be keeping her safe but failing miserably at doing so.

He rose, dusting his hands off on his coat and then offering one to Nava. "We should get going. I understand you're tired, and so am I, but it's imperative that we reach the safe house before sunrise."

She opened her mouth as if to speak—but jumped toward him, pressing her hands over her lips. Her skin glowed yellow, and bees buzzed around her.

Had she seen someone? Another Dark One? Orion moved swiftly, pulling her behind him, expecting the shadows to morph into the shape of a fae.

Instead, a fluffy gray shape skittered across the rubbish-strewn ground, its long, pink tail trailing after it.

Every muscle in his body instantly relaxed. "A rat, really?"

"It crawled over my foot," she defended herself, and he could not contain the smile that spread across his face. "What? They carry diseases."

Orion chuckled, already peering through the alleyway into the larger road that lay beyond. He recognized that wooden sign hanging from the storefront… He'd been to this part of town before. When Fael had found him roaming the streets months—no, years—ago.

The safe house was five blocks south. Yet he hesitated to leave what little cover this spot offered them. Out there in the open, they would become easy pickings for the flying guards.

After the torture he'd endured earlier when his father's concubines attacked him, he was too tired to fight anyone. Especially since they had already encountered three sentinels in the plaza. Nava was probably feeling much the same.

"We aren't far from the safe house, but using the street is risky right now."

Nava chewed her bottom lip, as she often did when she was feeling nervous. "Why don't we wait here until we're sure they're gone?" She sighed. "I wish we could just sneak out during the day. Blend in with people."

"You know that won't work. I stand out from everyone, including my own kind." He caught her beautiful, strange-colored eyes as they traveled down his body. Nava had told him once she couldn't see the dark shadows that always accompanied him. Some comfort, at least.

"You're easy to see during the day, and I'm easily spotted at night." She sounded as tired as he felt. "I can't continue to run this fast without using magic, Ark."

"I know." Orion placed his open palm against her lower back. Hope blossomed in his chest when she didn't flinch away from his touch. For the last few hours, she'd avoided being too close to him, so this was a minor victory.

It was clear that she was angry with him after everything that had happened at the castle. Admittedly, he shouldn't have locked her inside his chambers and left on his own to get the key to free her from the bracelets. Of course she needed time to forgive that. But why would she seem *scared* of him after crossing the portal? He didn't like it.

"We have to reach somewhere safe before daylight. There is a large population of humans in need who live in this area. Knowing my father, he will issue a reward to anyone who turns us in. Come on."

They walked in silence toward the main street, shielded by the balconies that jutted from the buildings on either side of them. Orion tightened his hand on Nava's waist, stopping her as they reached the end of the alley. Wind moved the wooden signs of the shops, carrying loose debris along the grimy, open road. It lay dark and empty before them, barely illuminated by gas lamps. All was quiet. Until…

Tap, tap, tap.

A rattle from the rooftops above. Like small pebbles trickling down the terracotta tiles.

The hairs on the back of Orion's neck stood on end. His skin grew cold and clammy. He pressed his hand over Nava's lips and pulled her into the shadows of the alleyway. She tensed under his touch but allowed him to move them swiftly beneath the ramshackle balconies.

A shadow drifted from above, and a silhouette appeared against the backdrop of the moon's silver light. A guard knelt down like a six-foot bird of prey, scanning the streets.

Nava's breath hitched as she spotted him, too. Orion called for a shielding spell, and his magic poured from him, fibers of power weaving around their bodies and making them invisible to everyone. A frustrating, draining spell, but it might buy them enough time for the Dark One to leave.

Thankfully, the guard leaned forward, his wings flapping. Then he leaped off the rooftop and took flight, vanishing off into the night.

Nava relaxed inside Orion's embrace, and he uncoiled his arms from her waist. He hadn't even noticed he held her so close.

A thick mist rolled down the street and wafted into the alleyway. Nava trailed her hand through the humid air, which was thick enough to blur the lanterns' yellow light.

"Mist is common near the canals." Orion crept toward the main road, careful not to draw further unwanted attention. "I think we need to hide inside one of these buildings."

He pointed at the shut-down shops in front of them. Many of them were boarded up. The sign he'd spotted a while back hung crookedly in front of what had once been a glass display, creaking in the night wind.

"I thought you said we should get to the safe house tonight?"

"I did. But that guard will return as soon as the mist clears."

Unfortunately, many of the shops they passed were still locked, with thick chains wound around their door handles. It would create too much noise if they tried to break into one of them.

His father hadn't mentioned how terrible a shape this part of town was in—the rats and the filth littering the streets. A decade ago, all these businesses had been flourishing.

"What if they're waiting for us down the road?" Nava took a deep breath, clearly struggling to keep up with his long strides.

"I doubt it. The guards are aware I can conceal my wings to blend in with the humans." Orion shrugged, still keeping an eye out for somewhere to hide. He needed to get Nava to some semblance of safety. A place to settle for the rest of the night. "They also know that fighting me can be deadly, as I possess the Curse of the Fallen."

Or, as his father liked to call it, the Gift of the Fallen.

It wasn't how Orion saw his particular type of magic.

"Don't tell me there's another curse on you I have to break?" Her voice rose to a frantic pitch. Too loud.

He turned to her and pressed a finger to his lips, signaling for her to remain quiet. Nava glared in response. It was almost enough to make him smile.

"I'm talking about my ability to remove fragments of people's souls. My power is my curse to bear, if not an actual curse. But you're already familiar with it. My father's guards know that engaging in a direct fight with me means that could happen to them. So they will hunt me down from above and then signal each other to ambush us instead."

Nava was quiet, but her gaze still burned with fury. "Is that why so many of them came when they kidnapped you from our home?"

They hadn't truly spoken about that night since she'd found him. His father had sealed his memories with a complicated spell, and before tonight, Orion hadn't even wanted to unravel it. Funny how, only a few days ago, he hadn't cared about his old life at all. He wouldn't have dreamed of abandoning this kingdom.

His father didn't know that the reason Orion had left the Copper Kingdom in the first place walked beside him now. If he'd understood that, Nava wouldn't have survived this long. The thought made his stomach clench in fear.

Whatever reason his old self may have had to avoid telling her the truth about his lineage—it wasn't good enough. A part of him was thankful those memories were gone. No need to remember the stupid decision he'd made. Or the glaring fact that it had put her in danger.

Nava tilted her chin up. "And was that why your father's consorts attacked you all at the same time tonight?"

Although his father's concubines were Dark Ones like Orion, they couldn't steal fragments of souls. They could, however, drain his energy instead.

"Yes," Orion said. They really shouldn't be speaking out here in the open, even if they were barely whispering. But his body throbbed from the concubines' attack, and the sting of his father's betrayal burned too hot to ignore his need to open up to Nava. Her pain and anger sang through their soulmate bond, churning in the pit of his stomach and gripping his heart.

All of a sudden, she froze mid-step, as if she'd seen a ghost.

Orion followed her line of sight. There. Something moved behind a slightly cracked door to their left. The mist was thick enough to make it hard to see farther than five feet ahead, let alone across the street into a filthy, locked-up shop.

A pale hand emerged from the shadows, and then Devon Black's familiar features rose like a wraith in the mist. His lips were moving soundlessly as he beckoned them in. But Orion didn't need to know the exact words his brother muttered to know they should follow.

2
NAVA

Inside, the shop reeked of mildew and body odor. Nava climbed over broken furniture, taking in the wide room. A wooden counter with shattered glass ran along the back wall. It must have held loaves of bread once upon a time, like Simone's shop in Willowbrook. If Nava closed her eyes and brought it to mind, she could still smell the scent of freshly baked goods. Her stomach immediately rumbled. Gods, she was hungry.

Tears pricked at her eyes as a wave of emotion surged through her. She couldn't deal with this now. Not when her life had turned into this hide-and-chase game that didn't seem to stop.

"Took you two long enough. I almost thought you'd let yourself get captured." Devon closed the door behind them.

"You shouldn't have left us behind to deal with those guards alone," Arkimedes complained. In the dark room, his magical eyes shone with green light.

Heavy footsteps echoed toward them from the hallway to their left. They drew close. And closer. "Watch what comes out of your mouth, brother," Devon said. "We aren't alone in this place."

Arkimedes fell still, his aura darkening as he turned toward the sound.

A young man who couldn't be older than eighteen stormed out of the corridor. He lifted the rusty sword he carried with shaking hands, scowling at Devon. "Fool! You brought a Dark One with you. Now we're all damned!"

"I discovered that this shop had prior occupants," Devon said, ignoring the young man's outburst as if he were a puppy waving a stick instead of a sharp weapon.

Admittedly, the sword's blade looked rather dull.

"Get out, or I'll—"

"You'll what?" Devon's cynical smile raised gooseflesh along Nava's arms. There he was, the old enemy she'd almost forgotten. "What do you plan to do to us?"

Hesitating briefly, the man glanced at where he had come from. Was there a room? Nava couldn't see much other than crumbling plaster walls. Without a warning, he lunged at Devon, sword raised over his head.

Devon effortlessly grasped the blade with one hand, his fingers turning white as ice quickly spread over the metal's edge. Then he pulled the sword from the young man's grasp and tossed it aside. His tall frame loomed over the stranger. "There is only one fool in this room, and it's not me."

The coldness of his tone instantly transported Nava to the day Devon had first set foot in her shop in Willowbrook. He hadn't used it with her for quite some time. Alarming, how fluidly he could transition to villainy.

The young man stepped back with wide eyes. His worn blouse slipped off his shoulder, revealing his bony torso as it nearly fell off him. With such a skeletal frame, he couldn't have been eating much during his time in hiding. Whoever he was protecting was clearly a loved one.

The stranger's wary eyes darted from Devon to Arkimedes. Nava felt sorry for him, even though they'd done nothing to deserve his outburst. Fear could make anyone do foolish things.

"Stop," Arkimedes growled and rested a hand over Devon's shoulder. He looked at the young man with a stern gaze. "We mean you no harm, but we *will* stay here tonight."

The young man heaved a shaky breath, even as he crossed his arms in a vain attempt to appear larger. "N-no, you won't."

This wouldn't end well. If the child persisted, he would get hurt. "We will be gone by morning," Nava said, hoping her calm tone would ease him. Unlike the other two brutes, she was used to dealing with teenagers. "Much like you, we need shelter tonight."

His arms loosened as his shoulders dropped, and for the first time, his eyes landed squarely on her, taking in her dirty features. His face softened somewhat. Perhaps the person he was protecting was a sister. Or a sick mother.

Devon made a move toward the hallway. The young man attempted to step in front of him, although the fight had clearly left him. "You're always the voice of reason, Cat," Devon said as he pushed past the boy.

"Are we going to follow Devon to the back?" Nava asked Arkimedes. Did she even want to? The stranger had claimed this shop as his home, right? It seemed rude to impose like that.

"I know it seems wrong." Arkimedes reached for her hand, pulling her down the narrow corridor, the floor creaking beneath their feet. "But it's better if we keep our eyes on our new friends while we rest. I'm uncertain who they are and what they are capable of."

The room turned out to be a kitchen. It was larger than the front room, with a clay oven in the corner and a large sofa in front of it. Tables that must have once been used for making pastries and bread were now propped up against the walls, broken and with chunks of them missing.

A family lived here. Used these tables as kindling for fire. Two heads of raven hair peeked out from behind the couch, hiding away from their inquisitive eyes. Children.

Devon prowled to the far end of the room, ignoring the young man's protests. He shrugged off his coat and draped it over a pottery rack.

"They are very young." Nava's horrified tone matched Arkimedes's expression as he too realized what they had stumbled upon. "Hardly anyone we should worry about."

Why was man, no older than eighteen, alone in this place, protecting them? Were they his siblings—or perhaps his offsprings?

Her brother, Cameron, instantly sprang to mind. He wasn't so little anymore. At fourteen years of age, he was a young man who would try to protect her if he needed to. Oh, how happy she was that he wasn't here with her and safe instead, traveling to Pearl Island with her friends Gavin and Violet.

Tears blurred her vision as she took in the little ones. How could she help them? She stomped toward Devon, rage burning through her.

"Why did you do that?" she accused. "You *knew* there were children in here!"

"Don't look so alarmed. I never claimed to be a good guy." Devon's smile deepened, although it didn't reach his eyes.

Nava faked a laugh, a strained sound that echoed through the large room. "You didn't have to be the monster I thought you would be."

"If only I cared about what you thought of me, Kitten."

Maybe Nava would have believed him a month ago, but not anymore. Working together to save Arkimedes from his evil father had revealed layers beneath Devon's cold exterior. Devon desired to appear as an all-powerful villain, but Nava was no longer buying it.

"I don't like deserters." He ran one of his hands through his hair and glanced over her head toward the family, who were huddled by the warmth of the oven. "A household who run away with their young usually cause more harm than good to the innocents. That man's cowardice and selfishness have left them starving in this dump."

"You have it all figured out, don't you?"

"Yes, I do. Unlike you, I haven't lived a sheltered life. I've seen suffering like this before. Every time the Society of Crows takes a child for the Crown, the families get paid a handsome sum they can use to feed the rest of them. The Crown values all magical children, so they're fed and clothed."

"How do you even know that's what they are?" Nava narrowed her eyes. And where was Arkimedes, so he could talk some sense into his brother? "Being poor doesn't automatically make someone a fugitive."

"Use your eyes, Nava."

Nava drew a deep breath. Although she'd never seen his face so serious, she didn't want to get into a nasty argument with him—even if he was baiting her like this.

"I've set some wards around the shop's front. It should give us time to escape through the back if we need to." Arkimedes rejoined them, seemingly unaware of the tension brewing in the room. Or perhaps he was choosing to ignore it.

Nava studied the family more closely. A smokeless blue fire burned gently underneath a pot in the clay oven. The only fire with that color was the magical kind. She had seen it a year ago when Devon's army burned the homes of the deserters on Grey Island.

Was that how he knew what they were? The fire?

She swallowed, blinking away more tears. She wanted to go over there and promise help she couldn't offer. What would she have done if that had been her and Cameron? Would she have allowed him to live in these conditions?

And underneath all these what-ifs, another question arose. Had the city fallen into ruin because of Arkimedes's absence? Had the businesses failed during that decade he'd spent waiting for her, far away from here? Was this all her fault?

They were safe from the guards for now. But what about the male Nava had encountered in the portal, back when she'd escaped from the castle? He'd looked just like Arkimedes.

Steam billowed from her lips as she sighed, and the chill air burned her wet cheeks. She wiped away silent tears with her hand and sniffled quietly. For now, Arkimedes had given her some time alone and left with Devon to check for other points of entry into the building.

She dropped her gaze to her arm and probed the tender skin of the burn her attacker had left behind. The raised blisters had popped open during their flight to this part of town, and now an oozing wound remained behind, at risk of getting infected.

Biting the inside of her cheek, she rolled up the sleeves of her blouse, trying to keep the dirty fabric off it. Her attacker hadn't called her by her name, but he'd known she was a Beekeeper.

Hours ago, when she fled through the portal and got stuck in the shadow world, her panic hadn't allowed her to truly think about who or what he was. And seeing Arkimedes waiting for her on the other side had been too much. The similarities between them were uncanny. But surely the gods wouldn't have made Arkimedes the Beekeepers' protector, let alone her soulmate, if he meant to hurt her. She had felt nothing for the man in the shadows who looked like her mate, other than that he was her worst nightmare. No stomach fluttering, no heart racing. None of the sensations she felt when Ark was around.

She let her head drop and allowed the weight of her body to relax against the wall.

The lingering scent of magic clung to the fibers of her clothes, an insistent reminder of her run-in with the guards at the castle.

If she closed her eyes for long enough, she could still picture the way her power had come to her aid when the shadow man attacked her. How wooden branches crawled over his arm, subduing his power and buying her just enough time to escape.

It had been a first for her to grow a tree vine over someone's body and a self-defense mechanism she hadn't known she possessed. One more thing she had to learn to control.

After all that time in the castle, she wouldn't stay locked inside the

Society's safe house like a prisoner. Demons still wreaked havoc in the forest, burning trees and extinguishing life, hunting her fellow Beekeeper, Aristaeus, across the land. She should be out there with him.

With everything that had happened in her life, Nava couldn't brush off the connection between her and the shadow man, either. Why single her out when three of them had crossed the portal? It had to be part of a much bigger picture, right? She no longer believed in coincidence. That she was a Beekeeper seemed to be of importance to him.

Was it the Zorren?

"What are you thinking?"

Nava jumped, barely holding a scream. "You're going to frighten me to death."

"I've been sitting here for quite a while," Arkimedes said, sitting in the opposite corner, his long legs bent, his arms resting upon his knees. His green eyes dropped to her forearm, where the burn was clearly visible after she'd rolled up her sleeves. "Are you ready to tell me how *that* happened?"

"No." She swallowed the panic that rushed through her. It tasted sour on her tongue. "I don't want to talk about it."

"Nava..."

She needed time to sort through her feelings and thoughts before she told him. "It's been a long night."

Arkimedes was already teetering on the edge of self-loathing, of wanting to keep a distance—and secrets—from her. She didn't want to feed into that by telling him that his doppelgänger had attacked her.

"You're mad at me, I know that. I deserve it."

She tugged her sleeve down, covering her mottled skin. Thankfully, there weren't any tears left in her as she let out a shaky breath. "That's an understatement. You locked me inside a room with Devon, knowing the guards were coming to kill us. Then you told me to leave you both behind."

Arkimedes's gaze skittered away from her, toward the cracked tiles that had once made a beautiful design on the floor. "They wouldn't have killed Devon. A member of the Society of Crows cannot be killed by a kingdom's army unless they violate the rules of the treaty."

"Devon is a big boy. He can take care of himself," she agreed. Although him being roped into this situation was partially her fault, since she'd called upon the life debt he owed Arkimedes. "I'm upset because you made that decision for me. I get to choose whether I stay and fight for you, with you."

Arkimedes met her eyes. Even now, Nava wasn't sure he felt any regret. He looked completely unapologetic. "I knew you could leave that room using your power, and I hoped you would get as far away from my father as possible."

"And from you."

"I beg your pardon?"

"You wanted me as far away from you as humanly possible." If only the words didn't hurt so much. But her heart still ached inside her chest at his rejection, at the memory of the massive fight that had driven a wedge between them only days ago.

He didn't want her. He'd tried to get her away from him as soon as he'd learned what she was to him.

Arkimedes's forehead wrinkled, and he reached for her—then seemed to think better of it and pulled his hand away. "Nava, I was angry that you kept our bond a secret, but mostly, I needed time to figure out a way to reveal to my father who you are to me while you were out of his reach."

She swallowed the stone that had lodged in her throat. Gods, she was a mess.

His nervousness filtered through their soulmate bond, making her heart race. Was he afraid she wouldn't forgive him? That she would leave him? If he remembered their past, then he would know how impossible that was.

"When I locked you in the room, I couldn't think of anything else to prevent the guards from coming in and hurting you. I know it's not an excuse, and I shouldn't have done that. It will never happen again."

"You're damn right it won't," Nava said.

Arkimedes rubbed the back of his neck. The top button of his shirt came undone, revealing the angular lines of his clavicle, streaked with sweat, dirt, and—were those bruises? "Have patience with me, Bee."

Nava's skin tingled with the use of the nickname he'd given her a year ago, after she'd found out she was a Beekeeper. It warmed her from the inside out, bringing flutters to her stomach. She shifted on the cold, uneven floor. "Outside, you said this area of the city has changed since you were here last. Were the shops open ten years ago when you first came to the kingdom?"

"I bought bread in this bakery on my way to the Society's safe house," he whispered, glancing at the family who sat by the fire.

"Do you think it's because you were gone for so long?"

Nava wanted to believe that her mother hadn't known that cursing Arkimedes eleven years ago would condemn a whole kingdom. She'd been so focused on protecting Nava, who was only fifteen, that she hadn't asked any questions. And so she'd cursed him to become a crow every night until the moment Nava accepted him as her soulmate—of her own free will.

Arkimedes considered her words in silence, his face hard and lost in thought. He didn't need to answer for her to understand that he'd been asking himself the same question.

"I don't think I was the sole cause for this. I believe my father allowed the kingdom to harbor resentment toward humans, and so the wealth of these businesses flowed elsewhere. *Our* connection to the kingdom will allow nature's balance to continue. The crops will grow, and the animals will breed. This..." He pointed at the room, at the cobwebs accumulating in the corner above them, at the dusty surfaces everywhere. "Hate caused this."

Balance. That was how Aristaeus had described their role as Beekeepers. Their task was to create balance.

Small, shuffling steps drew their attention. A child not much older than her brother was approaching them with two steaming bowls. The girl wore a tattered dress and a wool sweater that was two sizes too big for her. "Would you care for a meal?"

"Oh! You don't have to give us your food."

The girl ignored Nava's protest and crouched forward, placing the small wooden bowls on the floor. The liquid inside them was still steaming.

"The broth will keep you warm at night. It gets cold in these old buildings." She stood and watched, as if she was waiting for either Nava or Arkimedes to accept her offering.

Nava reached for her bowl. It instantly warmed her stiff fingers. "Thank you."

"Kyle is just looking after us," the girl said, taking a long step away, her weary eyes bouncing from Arkimedes to Nava.

"You three are too young to be here on your own. Where are your parents?"

The girl flinched at the gravelly tones of Ark's voice. She moved back another few paces. "They are gone."

"How?"

"They came during the night, demanding that we surrender Caden, my youngest brother. My parents tried to fight since Caden is only seven. They said the Crown has no rights over us until we are twelve."

Arkimedes leaned forward, picking up the bowl near his feet. "Did the Crows come to take him?"

The old fear Nava had stopped feeling ever since she'd escaped Willowbrook flooded her in a flash. This was what Nava's mother had warned her would happen if the Crows ever discovered Cameron and her. The Crows and the Crown worked together in a way. First, the Crows tore young magic-wielders from their homes—usually between the ages of twelve and fifteen when they first presented their gift of magic. Then the kingdom's army took over the care and training of the children until they'd served the kings and queens for long enough to return home. But people died before that time ever came.

It was an abhorrent practice.

The girl nodded. "We heard they don't come to the Copper Kingdom, so we traveled here by ship, seeking refuge. But the Dark Ones are even worse. They hate humans."

"I'm half human," Arkimedes said with a curve to his lips. He took a small sip of his soup as he leaned against the wall. "Don't tell strangers about your story. It's true that Crows seldom come this way, but be wary."

The girl's shoulders dropped with a sigh, and a tentative smile lifted the corners of her chapped lips.

This. This was the Arkimedes she knew. How he'd been before his memories were taken. His good nature, forever masked by an indifferent frown and a scary aura, nevertheless shone through.

Her heart fluttered as she took him in: his long dark lashes and the straight profile of his nose. She loved him so much. Her earlier fears seemed idiotic now.

Nava glanced at the shop's door where Devon was taking the first watch. Then she looked at the children by the fire. Little did they know that a Crow stood right amongst them.

3
NAVA

"Is it true that you can speak to bees?" a small child's voice whispered through the webs of sleep.

Nava blinked, opening her eyes to a dark room and a stranger's face looming before her. The pungent smell of mold snapped her from a dreamless slumber, her body instinctively scrambling against the wall, trying to get away.

"What?" Blood rushed through her head, thundering inside her ears as she peered past the child's shoulder. Where was Arkimedes? Or even Devon?

"Are you looking for the large men?"

"Yes."

"They are in the front room." The boy moved closer. At this distance, he was close enough to count the freckles on her skin.

Nava eased him back by one of his bony shoulders and took a deep breath. Relax—she needed to relax. "You're supposed to be over there with your family. Are you Caden?"

"Did the bees tell you my name?"

Surely this was a dream. Right? How else could this child know that she could speak to bees? "No..." True panic settled in the pit of her stomach as the meaning of his words filtered through to her sleepy mind. "How did you know?"

"They tell you when danger is coming, right? Much like my dreams. Are they speaking to you now?" The child looked down at the ground, where three bees were crawling over her boots.

Caden possessed the very rare gift of the Sight. Was that the reason the Crows had murdered his family, even though he was so young?

"Why would they speak to me now? Are—are we in danger?"

As if they'd heard her, Arkimedes and Devon came rushing inside the kitchen, heading straight for her. Their eyes widened when they saw the boy still kneeling beside her. Perhaps, in her panic, she'd called Arkimedes through their bond.

The child's eyes glazed over as he looked at a spot on the crumbing wall above her head. Like he was lost somewhere all of a sudden. "The male lives in the shadows and lets the demons into our world. He is coming."

"What's happening here?"

Arkimedes's deep voice startled Caden out of his trance. He leaped away and scrambled swiftly around Devon, returning to his side of the room.

"Why was he here?" Devon asked. In the background, the family spoke in hectic, subdued voices.

The man lives in the shadows and lets the demons into our world.

Caden's words made her blood run cold. Did the child mean Arkimedes's doppelgänger? The man who had hurt her?

Was he letting the Zorren into this world? The shadow man had recognized her as a Beekeeper, the nemesis of those demons. Had he been working with them all along?

The first time Nava crossed the portal, the God of Shadows had ripped the memories of her father from her as payment and left her alone. She'd never even seen him. But he hadn't been alone that afternoon, had he?

Why was the other man—if that was even what he was—waiting for her in the portal crossings?

She stumbled to her feet, and a heavy piece of fabric tumbled to the floor as she rose. A black coat. She hadn't been wearing that, had she? The room spun around her as hundreds of bees suddenly circled her near the ground, expertly moving away from her clumsy feet.

Arkimedes tracked Nava's gaze, pausing as he spotted the insects, which were now crawling the walls and toward the ceiling. He picked up the coat from the ground and shrugged it on before reaching for her hand. "Let's go. The bells stopped ringing about half an hour ago, and the streets are full of people. We should leave now and take advantage the sun isn't out yet, and the morning mist is still thick."

Had the bees gathered around her because the man in the shadows was approaching, as Caden claimed? Or were they here because the guards were tracking Arkimedes across the city?

"Wouldn't they recognize you with your shadows—even if it's dark?"

"We are in the Kingdom of Dark Ones, and there are plenty other shadow-wielding-fae outside, I think the number of people outside will aid our cover."

Nava allowed Arkimedes to guide her toward the hall, feeling numb with cold and her rushing thoughts. But before they left, she turned and met the black gaze of the siblings by the fire. "Trouble is coming," she warned them. "Leave this place."

Arkimedes, Devon, and Nava walked for blocks in vigilant silence, filing past pedestrians who were setting up market stalls on the uneven cobble roads. The buildings' green copper rooftops contrasted with the terra-cotta color of their walls, made of bricks in varying shades of red, burnt orange, and ochre.

The people they encountered were obviously desperate for coin, selling a variety of knickknacks and dehydrated food.

Arkimedes tipped his head toward Nava, as if called by her turbulent thoughts. The endless questions running through her mind hadn't ceased since they'd left the shop. "We are close now," he said with a tentative smile.

He clearly meant to calm her down, but it achieved the opposite. Dread pooled in her stomach with each step that brought them closer to their temporary hideout. What if a group of Crows awaited them there? What if her enemy-turned-ally Devon Black betrayed them? After the way he'd acted in the bakery, she wasn't sure what to believe anymore.

Nava's legs burned as she attempted to match Ark's and Devon's pace. "If my mother were alive, she would die all over again if she learned I was marching into a Crow's safe house—willingly." She wiped off the sweat dripping down her temple. These giants had no sympathy for her much shorter legs.

Devon's smirk spread across his face as he turned the corner into a new, darker alley. "Do tell. What do you believe she would have said?"

"That I'm being reckless and foolish," she said, glancing at the sunrise peeking out from behind the roofs. It warmed her face despite the chilly morning air.

"Look at the positive side. We might find some of Celeste's old wanted posters in there. Perhaps you could take one back to your new castle as a keepsake."

"Hilarious..." Nava chewed at the inside of her mouth, trying to swallow the old grief that clutched at her heart as she remembered her mother's stern frown and the soft notes of her vanilla perfume. It wouldn't be so bad if she found something of hers in there, a little reminder to lend her strength. "What if we end up finding more trouble with the Crows instead?"

Arkimedes's dark gaze swept from Devon to her, his tall frame casting a wide shadow over them. "The Society hasn't sent the Corvus to the city in months. According to my father, none have come since my arrival."

What did he mean by the Corvus? It wasn't a term she'd heard before. She barely restrained a grunt of frustration. It was hard to make sense of what had happened when Arkimedes didn't remember the last decade of his life.

"So, has it been a decade since the Crows came here—or four months?" she asked. "Do you think the king lied to prevent you from coming here?"

"It's possible, although I keep hearing that the fae can't lie. So I assumed it's true..." Arkimedes's lips tilted into a wicked smile.

Nava smacked the side of his shoulder with an open palm. "Stop teasing me, Ark. I'm nervous. If you had asked me last year to walk willingly into a Crow's nest, I would have laughed and run away."

"I refuse to believe that," Devon said. "You crave danger. It's why you came to this kingdom to rescue Arkimedes with only me, your enemy, as your backup." He raised three fingers, counting out her recent questionable life choices. "Also, you're in love with a scary man who can rip people's souls away."

Nava's cheeks warmed. "That's not—"

Arkimedes's low chuckle cut through her words. "He's got a point."

"I don't crave danger!" Nava complained, though her tone lacked any heat. "I was *not* expecting you to be a prince without memories. Or that I would have to fight a mad king for your freedom." She cleared her throat, looking away from their irritating smirks. "In any case, what's our plan if the Crows do show up?"

"They won't. The safe house is the perfect place for us to regroup and plan our next move." The warmth of Ark's breath caressed her frozen knuckles, right before he dropped his soft lips to them.

Her stomach fluttered like dozens of butterflies had taken flight all at once. Arkimedes didn't blink or move, as if daring her to pull her hand back. Maybe she should, but she was having a hard time remembering why she was upset in the first place. Something about him locking her away somewhere.

Ah, there it was. The steady ember of her anger.

He smirked and let go of her hand. "Right now, the biggest threat to you is my father, not the Society."

Nava bit the inside of her cheek. Best not to blurt out her errant thoughts in the middle of an alleyway. Was the king truly her biggest threat? She was unsure who she should fear more, him or the Zorren. They were her mortal enemies.

If she were to believe Caden's words, the man in the shadows was coming for her and Aristaeus. She needed to return to the forest promptly.

Nava wanted no more secrets between her and Arkimedes. As soon as they escaped the streets, she had to inform him about the events in the shadow world—and about his doppelgänger.

Devon snatched a brown paper bag with roasted cashews from Arkimedes's hand. They'd bought them from a street vendor on their way. "Besides, the Society rarely sends the Corvus during the summer and winter solstice, for reasons the two of you are well acquainted with."

Arkimedes's cheeks burned red as he choked on the nuts he'd been chewing. Images of what had happened the night of the solstice flashed through Nava's mind, making her heart speed and blood pool straight into her core. The magically induced heat of the summer solstice had been sweet and hot, and the mere memory of it made her skin burn.

She stumbled, but before she could fall, Arkimedes had already grabbed her. He held her as if she weighed nothing.

"Watch your steps, Bee."

Their eyes met, and his pupils dilated. He must be remembering it, too. The way he'd ripped that ugly yellow dress off her body and made love to her after the masquerade ball. They'd discovered together that the queen's tree was, in fact, alive, signaling the arrival of a new queen. Nava.

If Arkimedes wasn't holding her so tightly against his chest, she would be dissolving into a puddle right where she stood. How could someone radiate so much heat in the chilly morning air?

Devon grunted in displeasure. The sound of his steps grew more distant as he left them behind.

Despite everything, this was where Nava wanted to be. Inside Arkimedes's arms. She pressed her open palms to his chest, knowing she had to tell him the truth about the man in the shadows. Trust that he wouldn't pull away from her, as he had done at the castle when he'd learned—rather abruptly—that she was his soulmate.

Admittedly, she couldn't truly blame him for being upset with her when he'd seen their soulmate mark on her chest after their passionate encounter during the solstice heat. She should've confessed their past long before, but her cowardice had prevailed.

Arkimedes released her and tilted his head to the side, studying her features. "Earlier this morning, you were afraid when the youngest child was speaking with you. Your fear called me. What did he say to you?"

Had he been waiting to ask until Devon gave them some privacy?

A renewed sense of dread clawed at her throat, and Nava scanned their surroundings, feeling it grow larger and larger the longer they stood there. "He had the soothsayer trait, and he knew about my connection with the bees—"

"What?"

"I'm afraid to tell you everything out here in the open." She pressed her lips together and eyed warily at the buildings surrounding them. They were alone in the street, but she wasn't foolish enough to think curious souls wouldn't listen in from the safety of their homes.

"All right. We can talk about it later. It'll be safer once we are out of here."

They resumed their walk, and soon they turned into a wide alley with uneven walls and deep puddles. It was eerily quiet. Not even the sounds of people buzzing about on the main road made it past the tall walls covered in ivy. There was only the heavy beat of Arkimedes's feet on the uneven ground. They followed a gentle curve in the alleyway, and the street behind them fell away altogether.

"There's something odd about these leaves," Nava said. She brought her finger up to the foliage, but right before she could touch it, Ark's hand closed around her wrist and pulled her away.

"Don't touch anything."

Nava met his gaze with growing curiosity. "Why not?" She could read the energy over the ivy. Pulsating waves of life gently enveloped each leaf, from the stems to the tips. A trail of pale blues and whites wrapped around each surface, the imprint of someone's spell. But unlike the flowers in the castle that spied on them, this energy was warm and vibrating with life.

"I don't know if it will consider you a friend or a foe. It's best to wait."

"Who…?"

"Not a who, but an it." He pulled her closer to where Devon was waiting for them. Arkimedes pointed to the barely visible sculpture of an old man's face amidst the greenery. A brass, deformed spout jutted out of his open mouth, and mold and algae hugged the porous texture of carved stone that formed a wide basin below. "We're here."

"Oh!" She studied the pipe once again. Contrary to initial appearances, the tube was actually a bird's head. A crow, to be exact, worn by age and decay. Its open beak served as a spout.

The Crow's fountain. illustration by Heather Souliere

Devon leaned forward and placed his hand underneath it. A gust of wind descended around them. "I nearly didn't wait for you two. I'm tired and hungry." He glanced at Arkimedes, before his black eyes cut across to Nava and narrowed into slits. "The question is, will it allow you to pass?"

Water poured freely from the beak now, steaming hot into Devon's open hand. The sculpture of the man screeched, transforming into an arched door.

As Devon crossed the magical doorway, the scent of roses and gardenias bloomed around them. Then, just as fast as it opened, it closed again.

"It's our turn," Arkimedes said.

Nava shot him a worried look. "Why might it not let us through?"

He rolled his shoulders, as if readying himself—for what? "I'm going to place my hand underneath the spout. It won't let you in, Nava. But you can transfer inside with me when I cross."

"What happens if it deems you a foe?"

"It will burn my hand off and alert the Society of a break-in attempt."

"Wait, what?"

Arkimedes placed his hand underneath the open beak without answering her, and water burst out, gushing over his hand and filling the basin. The clear, steaming liquid thickened, and then it turned red like blood.

4
NAVA

Nava's stomach rolled at the sight of the thick liquid covering her soulmate's skin. Wasn't red a bad color? What did it mean?

Arkimedes's face scrunched in pain, and Nava dug her nails into his arm, attempting to pull him away. But he was as immovable as the statue. "We'll find another way. It's not worth it. Is it hurting you?"

He flinched at her words, and his face hardened further. "The spell's not hurting me badly. It doesn't know what to make of me..."

"You left the Society of Crows more than ten years ago. What were we thinking? This was foolish and—"

The blood-like water turned clear liquid, and the groove of the arched door reappeared before them. Arkimedes let out a sigh of relief, quickly withdrawing his hand from the liquid and wiping it on his leg.

"I'm fine," he said tightly. "Transfer with me. It may not allow me back in if I have to come and retrieve you."

Instantly, her body lost substance, and she became pollen, dust, and leaves. Wind moved through her, and in this state, her senses sharpened. She could hear the voices of her bees, warning her about the danger of crossing portals in this state, telling her to stay with her soulmate.

Telling her that a storm was coming...

Arkimedes crossed, and Nava embraced his body like a second skin, floating from the misty morning of the Copper City to the chill space of an unknown garden.

Gasping for air, she transformed back and strained to see the alley they had left behind. But it was pointless, as the gate had already closed, shutting them in.

Inside, the same ivy wall rose before them with an identical fountain sticking out from its other side, and yet everything else was different.

A worn stone pathway led them to a narrow house that stood on top of a hill, surrounded by massive trees. Dozens of colorful globes hung from their branches.

Nava narrowed her eyes at the strange spheres. They appeared to be fashioned from blown glass that caught the gray light and cast an array of colors over the garden. What were they? Sculptural decorations? Birdhouses?

An icy breeze seeped through layers of her clothes and pulled her focus to the house. She needed shelter and somewhere to rest her aching body.

With its gray stone and tapered rooftop, the safe house appeared to be hundreds of years old.

"Is this place in the Copper Kingdom?" Nava whispered, studying the climbing roses that grew over the arch of a pointed window with detailed ornamental stonework. Plants shouldn't bloom at such a temperature. Not when her breath billowed in front of her face, and the chill burned her cheeks.

"The fountain is a gateway to a secret location in Caztian. Even the Society members don't know where it really is."

They walked the rest of the way to the house in silence, not veering off the crumbling pathway. The place had a hauntingly beautiful atmosphere. Every plant, rock, and sculpture seemed to be spelled to survive unnatural conditions. Somehow, even the butterflies hovering over the flowers *felt* wrong.

Devon had left the front door wide open instead of waiting for them on the porch.

"Do all portals lead to the same safe house?" Nava asked as their steps led them across polished tiled floors and into a circular room with a winding staircase.

"There are twelve portals that lead to six safe houses. There is only one safe house in the Copper Kingdom."

Were there any safe houses on the islands? Cameron was traveling to Pearl Island with Gavin and Violet, and the thought of him being exposed to Crows made Nava's blood turn to ice.

She hadn't considered how the Society moved from kingdom to kingdom so quickly without having to pay the price to the God of Shadows each time they needed to use one of his portals. It made sense now. They had used their magic-wielders to create twelve portals to specific locations. No need to travel through the shadow world at all.

The house smelled...pleasant. Like lilacs and something warmer—vanilla, perhaps? Not like a place that hadn't been visited in years. Memories of Nava's youth came to her in flashes, of the manor she'd called her childhood home. Of tending to the front garden whenever her mother left.

Of course, Nava had been forbidden from setting foot outside during daylight hours, but she'd done it regardless, craving the feeling of dirt underneath her fingernails, wanting to be close to nature. That was, before Devon and Arkimedes had arrived on horseback one fateful afternoon and forced her and her family to leave the Iron City.

She wrinkled her nose, although a smile threatened to break free.

Arkimedes snaked a muscular arm around her waist, preventing her from heading deeper into what she assumed was the parlor.

"Stay here while I check if it's safe." His words drifted through her mind.

Nava blinked, surprised. They had communicated like this before. Sometimes accidentally. Sometimes when they were practicing how to use the mental bond they shared to its fullest extent. But only ever before he'd lost his memories.

Was he truly embracing their connection now?

Either way, she stayed behind until Ark crooked a finger at her from the doorway.

In the parlor, Devon sat in a large chair with green velvet upholstery. The warm colors of the fire burning in the hearth reflected off the blue jewel shades of the wallpaper.

Devon swirled the amber liquid inside the glass he held in one hand with lazy movements. "The house let you in. I can't decide if I'm pleasantly surprised or disappointed." He tilted his head back and swallowed his drink in a couple of gulps.

Nava propped up her hands on her hips, tapping her foot against the plush rug. "What would you have done if the house refused us entry and called upon the Crows?"

Devon shrugged. "I would thank the gods I won't get dragged into whatever suicidal mission you're about to embark on. It will surely get *me* killed. Then I'd send a get-well-soon letter to Arkimedes."

Nava frowned. "Why a get-well-soon letter?"

"Because his hand would have been severed by the fountain's water if the spell thought him a foe."

Nava shot a murderous glare at Arkimedes, who at least had the decency to look abashed. "I thought you were joking when you said that." She stalked toward Devon, her blood boiling. "And you *wanted* the Society to take us?"

Devon's lips tightened into a fine line.

Arkimedes reached for her shoulder and squeezed it lightly. "I wouldn't have risked it if I thought my loyalty was genuinely in question. Being heir to this kingdom has its benefits. The Society can't take me—nor you—and Devon knows that." Arkimedes's frown deepened, and even though his voice remained level, she could *feel* that he was, in fact, peeved.

"Right." Devon shook his head as if he couldn't believe it himself.

Arkimedes's jaw worked, and he took a deep breath to calm his temper. "And you don't have to follow us into our *suicidal mission*. If you don't want to, we can call our life debt even now."

Devon straightened in his seat, placing his empty glass on the side table. "Really?"

The magical string that still tied Devon to Nava flickered, the life debt slowly withering as Arkimedes continued to speak. "You hurt my soulmate last year. While I no longer possess all of my memories, I do recall that."

The room fell silent, except for the crackling of the fire. Nava's skull prickled with nervous tension. Would they be safe if the life debt was gone? Or would Devon betray them?

"Ark..."

He raised his hand, and she closed her mouth. This wasn't her choice, nor her life debt. Not really.

"You helped Nava escape my father last night. You deciphered the prophecy in the book I brought you, and you searched for me across the seas, although everyone else thought I was dead." Arkimedes took a step closer to his brother, his face torn between anger and something softer that she rarely got to witness. "I would save your life again, Devon, because you're the family I chose. I'm not forcing you to fight demons, nor die for me."

The string pulled tighter and tighter, leaving Nava's stomach roiling just before it snapped like a rubber band. She wheezed with the force of the recoil, bending forward as pain radiated through her chest. Then it was gone.

"Damn you!" Devon barely caught himself against his knees, visibly shaken. He buried his face in his palms. "It would be much easier to leave if you were a coward."

"Are you going to?" Arkimedes asked.

Nava wrapped her arms around her midriff, trying to catch her breath as they waited for Devon's response. Would he? Did she even care?

For so long, she had hated this man. Then circumstances had forced them into becoming allies. When had he turned into a friend?

"Not yet." Devon rose from his chair in one fluid motion. If the dissolution of the life debt was hurting him as much as it was hurting her, then he was a great actor. He strode to the doorway, pausing briefly on the threshold. "After all, someone from the Society needs to be here and make sure nothing gets damaged or stolen while Celeste's daughter is here." His expression lacked the unfriendliness of his words.

Devon was a master at playing a part. But in the end, he *had* gone to the end of the world to find Arkimedes. Even a decade after his disappearance.

Nava resisted the urge to smile. Emotionally constipated men were so frustrating, yet entertaining to watch. Hopefully, this wouldn't come back to haunt them later.

Devon ran a hand through his wavy, black hair. "I haven't checked if the pantry is stocked. Let's just hope there's something to eat in this place, or this little adventure was for nothing."

5
NAVA

An enormous limestone fireplace dominated one side of the kitchen. Thick stone columns held up its high, vaulted ceilings, and Nava shivered in the expansive cavern of a room. Devon busied himself by tending to the fire, and soon, the space warmed.

"Are you still cold?" Arkimedes asked a little while later, placing a steaming bowl of stew in front of her. "Do you want my coat?"

The remaining chill she felt had nothing to do with the room's temperature and everything to do with her surroundings. This safe house was a vipers' den. She'd never truly feel at ease here.

Devon pushed away his empty bowl of potato stew, his unnerving black eyes resting on her. "You've asked her five times already if she's all right. I'm sure her answer will stay the same."

Nava glared at him and smoothed the messy waves of her hair. "I'm fine," she said and met Arkimedes's eyes in an attempt to reassure him. But whatever he saw in her expression clearly didn't settle his doubts.

Never mind. She returned to studying her surroundings instead. A large chandelier hung low above the table, elegant swirls sculpted into its iron shape. Its candles burned with eternal magical flames that cast an orange light over the room.

Devon slid off his chair, strolling to the fireplace and feeding it a new log. "So, are you going to tell us or not? What happened when you crossed the portal?"

Nava glanced down at her arm and the wound, now covered by the sleeve of her blouse, but the words stuck in her throat.

"Stop," Arkimedes said, a warning in his tone. He inched toward her, as if he could protect her from the sudden darkening of her mood. Perhaps he knew she'd rather speak to him alone.

"We can fill the silence with useless chatter about the stew you just cooked with those lovely dehydrated potatoes or we could make a plan? We can't stay here forever."

"No, we can't." Arkimedes sighed, placing the glass of wine he'd been nursing on the table. He didn't have to say a word for Nava to know he desperately wanted some answers as well. His feelings were pushing loudly through their bond.

Nava sank deeper into her uncomfortable chair. "I know who is letting the Zorren into Caztian. The child in the bakery told me."

"The child?" Devon scoffed. "Just when I thought I'd heard it all..."

"Caden had the gift of the Sight. It's why the Crows killed his parents. He told me the man in the shadows was letting them in."

"The man in the shadows?" Devon scoffed. "Do you know how ridiculous that sounds? Now we have to base our plans on some tall tale a child told us?"

"Why would you think he made it up?"

"Because all deserters have a sad story, Cat. I already told you who I think is at fault for their living conditions."

"You can lie to yourself about your precious Society, but he wasn't lying. Caden knew things very few people know about me," Nava insisted. "And he knew about the demons."

"That means nothing. A lot of locals attended the king's dinner where Arkimedes publicly revealed that the Zorren are burning the forests. By now, the entire city is aware of them."

Arkimedes pressed his fingers to the bridge of his nose with a sigh. "Stop making this about the Crows and deserters, Devon."

"Why? We could call on the Society to help us fight the demons. You were their golden boy. They will bend over backward to assist you now that you are the heir to an entire kingdom. I, for one, think the Corvus could be of great help to subdue the Zorren. After all, we are the most powerful magic-wielders in Caztian."

"I'm no one's golden boy. They have used me for as long as I can remember."

"And yet here you are, using them..." Devon raised his hands above his head, narrowly missing the chandelier.

Arkimedes's frown deepened. Then he turned to her. "Who is the man in the shadows, Nava?"

"I don't know his true identity—" she began, but Devon's loud grunt cut her off. Nava glared at him and rolled up her sleeve, revealing the angry blisters. "He did this to me when I crossed."

Arkimedes stopped breathing. His chair scraped over the floor as he stood and bent forward to better inspect the wound she'd been hiding from him.

The imprint in the shape of a hand stood out sharply against her skin, and Nava's heart lurched in her chest as she spotted the black veins that now extended up her arm. They flared out from the new blisters that had formed during the day. "I didn't see the veins before. Is it infected?"

"Did you encounter a Dark One when you crossed the portal?" Arkimedes's anger flooded through the bond and blurred the edges of her panic. Was he upset with her for not telling him sooner?

"Yes."

"Why didn't you say anything before?"

Devon leaned across the table, his brows scrunching as he, too, inspected her wound.

"Because—he looked like you!" she blurted out over the thundering of her heart.

In the ensuing silence, one could have heard a pin drop.

"What do you mean, he looked like me?"

Nava cleared her throat and waited for the room to stop spinning around her. The gentle crackling of the fireplace in the background wasn't helping. It only reminded her of the fires brought by the Zorren. "I've crossed a portal twice in my life. When we came to this kingdom to rescue you. And then yesterday. Both times, a man approached me in the darkness. I had a hard time seeing him the first time, but that changed last night."

"Go on," Arkimedes urged, his face drained of color.

Her stomach churned, but there was nothing for it. She had to continue. She'd promised to tell him the truth, even if it would be easier in the short run to hold it in. "When I crossed the first time, one voice asked for a memory, which I expected, but there was someone else inside with me. Devon mentioned back in the castle that he heard no one else—"

"True," Devon confirmed. "You told me about it during our first dinner with the king."

Nava nodded. "He knew I was a Beekeeper, Ark. And he hurt me because of it."

"You're a *what*?" Devon exclaimed.

Arkimedes didn't pay him any attention. His eyes zeroed in on her wound instead, although he raised his gaze to search her face before he spoke. "He looked like me—but did you *feel* it was me?"

She understood what he was asking. Underneath all the fear and confusion, their unique soulmate bond allowed them to feel each other. Their love remained, despite the weakened bond.

The similarities had been jarring, but… "No. He had your face, the same nose and lips. His armor resembled the Zorren's." If only she could recall more details to fill in the missing pieces of this puzzle. "His hair was white like your father's."

"You know I would never hurt you, Nava."

"I know that." She cradled her arm against her chest. "It shocked me when it happened. But I've never doubted that I'm safe with you."

In the uncomfortable silence that took over the room, it was hard to ignore her soulmate's harsh breaths or Devon's intense gaze.

After an eternity, Devon spoke. *"The child of royal blood came to this world sick, poisoned by evil, and was taken into the world of shadows, away from the land and our people."* Nava shot him a questioning look, but he was clearly addressing Arkimedes. "Those were the words I translated from that burnt book you brought me back to the castle."

"What are you saying, Devon?" The urge to climb over the table and choke him for planting a seed of doubt in Arkimedes's mind was strong.

"I'm saying Arkimedes brought me a recorded prophecy and was worried that it referred to him," Devon said. "Perhaps the Dark One you discovered in the in-between world resembled him because it *was* him."

Nava shook her head. Devon could go and cram his negativity where the sun didn't shine. While she'd been caught by surprise the night before, the answer was clear as day right now.

There was no chance the shadow man and Arkimedes could be the same person.

"It might have been, but it wasn't." Arkimedes's tone was stern.

"How do you know?" Devon drummed his fingers against the tabletop. "You were worried weeks ago. We don't understand how time works in the shadow realm. Perhaps you could be in two places simultaneously."

Arkimedes shrugged off his royal coat and tossed it carelessly onto the table. "Because I'd rather die than hurt Nava, and because my power doesn't leave these marks."

And he pulled the shirt out of his pants, revealing his abdomen to both Devon and her. His golden skin wrapped over cords of muscle, but that wasn't what sucked the breath straight from her lungs. The black veins that snaked up his back and over his ribs were a terrible sight to behold. She rose so abruptly from her chair that it crashed to the ground. Then she ran her fingers over the lightning-shaped marks left behind by the Dark Ones.

"My father's concubines left these markings last night when they ambushed me. I will get better in a couple of days as my body recuperates." He wrapped one of his large hands over hers, pressing it into his skin. "A Dark One's power leaves blackened veins behind, but mine doesn't. If it had been me, I would have killed Nava, and a part of her soul would haunt me for the rest of my life."

And since they were soulmates, it would be a very short-lived life, since neither could survive for long without the other.

"I can't take just the essence of someone's magic, like most of my kind. My power rips a soul apart, steals bits of a person's essence. Only my father and I possess the ability to do that in this world."

Devon settled in his chair, evidently appeased by Arkimedes's explanation. "All right. Who was the Dark One, then? A lost twin brother or a shapeshifting demon?"

Nava's breath caught in her throat, and her blood ran cold at the very idea. There were other types of demons than the Zorren? "Do they exist?"

"They do." Devon poured himself more wine. "The scriptures say they borrow the likeness of the one you love the most. But they aren't from this world." He shrugged and downed his drink in one gulp. "Nasty little things. It's why I'm not recommending we open a portal and take this fight to whoever is doing this."

"Maybe that's what he wants. He seemed to move a lot faster than I could while in the shadow lands. I just floated, unable to do much."

Arkimedes scratched his chin. "The gods' realms are a mystery. Only those with the ability to open portals, like Devon, can access them. There's no way for a mortal to stay there. So we can't bring the fight there, either way."

No mortal...

Nava gasped, her eyes darting from Arkimedes to Devon and back again. "Could he be an immortal? A god?"

"Let's hope for all our sakes that he's not," Arkimedes said.

Could Aristaeus visit the shadow world and fight there alone? Perhaps that was why the demons singled out the Beekeepers. She made a mental note to ask Ari the next time she saw him, whether he was, in fact, an immortal.

"So, what's the plan, brother? We wait until the Zorren come to hunt Nava, our precious Beekeeper?"

For the first time since she had met Devon, he didn't sound cold or flippant. There was a touch of reverence in his tone. "I'm still the same woman you imprisoned on the island."

"If I had known you were a keeper of life, I wouldn't have done that."

"Why does it matter? You just thought I was a dirty deserter, like Caden in the bakery."

Devon lowered his gaze, staring at the table. "I don't see how that's the same."

"That boy you were so cruel to warn me about who was bringing the Zorren into this world. He gave us a vital clue we were missing." Was Devon following her? He was completely avoiding eye contact. "He deserves the family he lost because of that gift."

Arkimedes had once told her that Devon's family had abandoned him when he was not even ten and that the Society of Crows had taken him in. It was rare for the Society to take responsibility for children. Usually, they went to the armies.

What if the Society had killed Devon's family, exactly like Caden's? Both Ark and Devon were children of the Crows. Both had immense, unusual powers.

"What if the Crows were aware of your lineage all along?" she whispered and met her soulmate's gaze from under her lashes. "You said not all the Dark Ones possessed the Curse of the Fallen, except for the king—and *you,* his heir. Wouldn't the Society know that someone with your power was the lost royal of the Copper Kingdom?"

Arkimedes drew a ragged breath and leaned against the table. His brows scrunched together as if he were struggling to find a response that made sense. Perhaps he was attempting to revive lost memories. "I'd always thought it strange. Devon and I were the only children in the Society. All the others were taken to serve the royal guards."

"That's an imaginative idea." Devon's voice shook, and he cleared his throat before he spoke again. "But I don't think so."

Obviously, her imaginative idea had cut them both deeply. Nava only had to use her eyes to read them like an open book: their hunched postures, how they were struggling to speak. And beyond that, she could tap directly into Arkimedes's emotions through their bond.

"The gift of opening portals is rare, Devon," Arkimedes said. "In fact, I've only met three people who've had it in my lifetime, and they are all members of the Crows."

Nava closed her eyes and tried to sort through her jumbled thoughts. Some magical gifts, such as being a soothsayer or having Devon's power to control storms, were rare. But portal making—she'd never known that even existed.

Her sheltered upbringing had caused yet another gap in her knowledge.

"Let's stop talking nonsense." Devon's nostrils flared as he lifted his head and struggled to mask his emotions with false indifference. "The Society of Crows is unrelated to the Zorren."

"They might possess knowledge we lack, although I'm not implying that they're connected to the demons." Nava glanced around the room as if she might find the answers hiding in plain sight or in some dusty corner. If only it could be that simple.

"Each safe house has an archive," Arkimedes said. "We can try to find out what the Society knows about the royal prophecy, or how we can stop the…*shadow man*…from opening more portals."

"What is an archive?"

"They're libraries that only Society members can access. Every year, the librarians catalog prophecies, new spells, historic events, and so on."

"And there's one here?"

"A smaller version, yes." Arkimedes shifted on his feet.

"We should not step one foot inside that place unless you want the Crows to come here," Devon said, a warning infusing his tone. He slammed a hand on the table, and Nava's half-full glass of wine rattled in response. "You can't seriously think that's a good idea, Arkimedes."

"Do you have a better suggestion on how to move forward?"

"Sure. How about we *don't* go in there?"

"Why not?" Nava clutched her stomach with her wounded arm. She already knew she wouldn't like the answer to that question. "Is it not just a place for books?"

A stupid thing to ask, judging by Devon's clenched jaw and Arkimedes's tightened fists.

"Not quite," Devon said. "All archives have a scrying mirror. I haven't been to the one downstairs, but there must be one. The Society hides the mirrors in many shapes, and they communicate directly with its headquarters."

Now she definitely felt uneasy. She moved toward her chair, reaching for her discarded drink. Alcohol would do wonders to make her forget about her anxiety and bone-deep exhaustion.

"But the mirror can also find information," Arkimedes said. "The books will contain knowledge about the portals, and using the mirror can help us locate the right source quicker."

Devon rubbed his eyes. "The Vulcan will alert them, Arkimedes. She is Celeste's daughter. It's enough of a miracle that the house let you through. I'm not so certain the mirror will think you're one of us."

"Which is why I won't be the one handling it."

"You want me to do it?" A rough laugh escaped Devon's chapped lips, his chair scraping over the tile floor as he stood in a jagged motion. His jaw tightened before he spoke. "I'm too tired for this shit, and I'm not talking any more about this until I've had a wash and a good rest."

He picked up his empty bowl and dropped it in the sink on his way out of the kitchen. "I'm taking the first room to the left. Good luck finding a clean place to sleep. This house is not what it used to be."

SOCIETY OF CROWS

6
ORION

The halls on the second floor were long and narrow, with dark wooden panels that extended from floor to ceiling. Orion much preferred the murals downstairs. They reminded him of the forest.

Beside him, Nava's heavy steps dragged over the worn rug as she studied the paintings on the walls. All of them were group images depicting members of the Society of Crows, their faces a familiar anchor to a time that felt like an eternity ago.

"Are you in any of these?" She slowed to a stop and rose on tiptoes, studying the largest piece of art. Her brows were knitted tightly together with concentration.

"I'm sure they removed the one with me in it," he said.

"Why would they do that?" She moved on to the next image without waiting for his answer, her brown and blue eyes bouncing over neat brushstrokes. "Do you think my mother is here?"

Her tired voice lit up with a trace of hope. Of course. It made sense that she'd want to see Celeste's likeness immortalized in oil paint.

"No." The finality of his tone made her expression fall. He cleared his throat to unravel the heavy knot that had formed there. "They don't keep any paintings with members who have died or those featuring traitors."

"But these are group paintings. What about the other people who haven't died or betrayed the Society?"

"They commission a new artist, and the painting gets replaced. They don't want any of us to be reminded of our own mortality."

"Or that people can change allegiance?"

"Exactly."

Nava froze in front of the next painting, her eyes narrowing in on a dark shape that took over the bright picture. It wasn't hard to find him amongst the group of Crows. "You're still here…"

Orion moved closer to take in the old picture. That was him at twenty years of age. A month ago, before he'd discovered that he'd lost his memories, the image would have appeared recent to him.

But now…it seemed like so long ago, and he could tell the difference in his youthful face. He'd even forgotten what these people's voices sounded like, although some of them had been friends.

"This particular safe house we're standing in front of was in the Gold Kingdom." He remembered the rolling hills with tall grass, where it was less swelteringly hot in the summer.

Nava squinted at the picture. "Is she holding your arm?"

Orion blinked and inspected the picture again. Who did she mean? Ah, the woman beside him. He hadn't been paying such close attention to her before.

"I'd forgotten Faria used to do that…"

"She seems rather friendly with you." Nava's cheeks turned bright red. The pit of his stomach suddenly churned with feelings that weren't his but burned through his veins like wildfire.

"You know you've nothing to be jealous of, Nava," he whispered close to her ear, enjoying the way her skin pebbled beneath his breath. Then he grasped her elbow and turned her away from the painting to face him.

"I'm not…"

He touched her flushed cheeks and pulled her bottom lip free from beneath her teeth. She always did that when she was nervous or overwhelmed. "Tell me what you're thinking?"

Nava sighed, glancing at the offending portrait as if it might come alive at any moment. "When we met for the first time—you were about the same age, then. I see this picture, and I can't help but wonder if I ruined a relationship you had before me."

"That's not what happened."

"You don't remember what happened." She turned away, clearly not wanting him to read her as only he could. "Maybe if I hadn't been out gardening that afternoon when you came to speak to my mother, you would have stayed with Faria."

"I was never hers to begin with." Orion lowered his face enough that his lips were a mere hairsbreadth away from hers. Nava's breath stuttered, but yearning softened her features. "I've been yours from the moment I first laid eyes on you. Since before I understood who you were to me."

Nava crushed her lips to his in a kiss that caught fire as soon as he got a taste of her. It was right—perfect even—to chase her lips and marvel at the way she gasped for air as they broke apart.

"Stop saying things like that," she whispered. "I'm supposed to be mad at you."

Orion grinned. It was as if the weight of all their lies and problems had dropped off him, leaving him lighter. He felt drunk on a feeling he wasn't used to, on his love for this beautiful woman who belonged to him as much as he belonged to her.

Nava's hand traveled across his chest, pausing over the spot where the soulmate mark rested. Her touch was light, but even through his clothes, it sent a ripple of energy dancing over his skin.

Judging by her shivers and how her lips parted, she felt their connection, too. But then she stepped away from him, breaking the spell, and continued down the hallway until she stopped in front of the first door to the left. "Is this where Devon is staying?"

The double doors of the room were shut, hiding away the huge chambers inside. "Yes. It's the best room in the house, normally taken by high-ranking officers."

"I heard *you* were pretty high up in the ranks."

A smile curved his lips. "Was I?"

"Devon calls you the golden boy, and Roman used to say you called the shots. But you've never told me much about...any of this." She shrugged one shoulder, her eyes darting away again.

"It's hard to feel proud of being part of the Crows," Orion admitted. He didn't like to see that frown on her face, knowing the sadness it was hiding—or that his actions had put it there. "What do you want to know?"

"How many times did you come to this house before Fael found you?"

Fael—the guard who Orion had once thought of as a friend. Who'd betrayed him.

"I came here just once. The Society didn't allow me to visit this kingdom. They sent me to other places instead..." He broke off. Now that Nava had planted the seed of doubt in his mind, it was blooming.

What if the Society of Crows had known all along who he was?

"It looks like no one has been here in a long time," Nava said, lifting her chin to point at the spiderwebs that stretched from the corners of the ceiling. She was right. A thick layer of dust covered the pictures on the wall as well, dulling the gold tones of the frames.

"I was not supposed to come here when I did," he admitted, swallowing the nervousness that rose alongside the words. He hadn't told a soul. "They approved my leave and gave me permission to go to the Gold Kingdom to rest for two months."

Nava watched him, unblinking, as if waiting for him to open up further.

Orion dragged a hand over his greasy hair. He desperately needed a bath. "I knew the Copper Kingdom was the place where my kind lived, and I wanted to know if my family was still alive. I needed answers about the shadows that always follow me."

He pointed at his aura, although he already knew that Nava couldn't see it. She only ever saw him.

"And when you got here, you found more than you bargained for?"

A soft puff of air left his lips. "You could say that."

"Do you think no Crows have come here since you left the Society?"

Orion met her smart eyes, and for the first time, he yearned for those memories. He wanted to know what had happened when he headed to the Iron Kingdom eleven years ago after learning the truth about who he was.

He pressed his hands to his temple, massaging away an impending headache. If the Society of Crows had known who he was all along, then it stood to reason that they were now protecting their members from his father, the king. "I think they found out that I came here and learned who I was, and my disappearance suited them better than if I'd stayed to rule."

"Well, if we focus on the positives of this mess, at least we know they won't send any Crows while we're hiding here," she said.

"And that buys us time to go through the archives."

She hummed and pointed at the bee that was crawling across the wall underneath the picture. Its brown body blended almost seamlessly into the brown shades of the wooden panels. "Even if they don't come, we have little time. We have to go back to help Aristaeus in the forest. He can't battle the Zorren alone."

"I know, which is why I need to convince Devon to use the mirror to reveal the information we need."

"Do you think he's right? That it will call the Society if one of us uses it?"

"Probably. Do you remember how the fountain outside dripped blood over my hand until the very end?" She nodded at his words. "Well, on reflection, I believe that was because my allegiance to the Crows was already so weak. Now that I know they knew my true identity all along, whatever shred of it remained will be gone. And the mirror will see me as a traitor."

"You agree then? That they did know?"

The hollowness in Orion's chest deepened, and the voice of a spirit in his aura rose to his ears, as though the despair churning within him had brought it to life.

"I knew who you were, Arkimedes Valeron. Princeling of the Dark Ones. And now I am part of you."

Orion flinched at the sound, so twisted and hollow that it was impossible to distinguish its origin. A male voice. A fragment of one of his past victims. Panic snaked its icy fingers through his blood. If only he could tell who that voice belonged to. Perhaps if he could remember the person —their face—then he might finally gain some clarity. But with the number of souls he carried and the holes in his memories, it would be a challenge.

When he'd been a young Crow, Orion hadn't asked questions whenever the Society sent him to get rid of a problem. He'd believed everything served a greater purpose. They'd used him, molded him into a killer.

Had his mother not thought about what would become of him if she abandoned him in the Iron City, a place run by the Crows? She should have suspected it.

He swallowed the sour taste in his mouth and opened the next door after Devon's, waving Nava in. "This is your room."

The same dark wood panels as in the hallway wrapped around the walls, and on the opposite side of the door, a large, arched window with black trim let in the last rays of gray daylight. The floors creaked under Nava's tentative steps. "My room? Aren't you staying here with me?"

"I thought you might want space, after everything..." Orion hated how uncertain he sounded. The last thing he wanted was for Nava to think that he didn't want to be with her. He cleared his throat and moved toward her. "Do you want me to?"

A wave of her mixed feelings swirled in his gut: longing, desire...and hesitation.

"Yes," she whispered. "This place feels...wrong. Like there's something haunting the very fabric of what makes up this house. Is it cursed?"

Orion stilled as the image of the locked door in the basement flashed through his mind. He would have to tell her about the cellar tomorrow morning when they went to the archives. But there was no need to frighten her further by mentioning it right now.

"It's not cursed," he said and cleared his throat. "Are you sure you want me to stay? There's only one bed." He pointed at the piece of furniture in question. It was still shrouded by white dust covers.

"Are you embarrassed about sharing the bed with me?" Her words took on a teasing note, but the blush in her cheeks betrayed her nerves.

"No." A soft chuckle escaped his lips, and he grabbed the sheet, tugging it off the bed and tossing it into the corner in one movement. "I thought you were still upset with me."

Dust bloomed from the billowing fabric and itched his nose. He strolled to the other side of the room and closed the curtains, which were made of thick fabric, a blue so dark it was almost black.

The color reminded him of the dress Nava had worn to his father's dinner the previous afternoon. How the castle's magic had shown the king and the entire kingdom that she was royalty—for the sentient pile of stone and bricks allowed only the royal line to wear black inside its walls.

"It seems I can't stay mad at you for long," she mumbled, scrunching her freckled nose. "Even if this place gives me the creeps, you don't have to stay. I can handle it."

"I suspect there's nothing you *can't* handle." A warm wave of pride filled him. Pride and something more. Fuck, he'd been so lost without this woman in his life. He couldn't believe he'd tried to push her away.

Nava challenged him in every way. Made him want to be better. She'd come to this kingdom to save him and hadn't backed down, even when faced with a bastard as scary as his father.

Orion walked to her with long strides, stopping only when she was close enough that the warmth of her body seeped through his clothes. Her chin fit so easily between his fingers as he lifted her face to his.

"I was trying to be a gentleman and give you space. Don't mistake that for me not wanting to take all you give me, Nava. I'm a greedy creature." He touched her plush, parted lips and dropped his hand to her throat.

"Stay," she said and took hold of his hand with icy fingers. Her nervous breaths washed over his arm. "But only stay if you won't change your mind tomorrow. You asked me to marry you one night, and the next morning, you were planning on sending me away after you found out I was your soulmate."

"To protect you from my father," he said. "I'd just learned my whole life was a lie and that he took my memories of a past that scares me. I was upset about the truth you'd kept, but not about you being my soulmate."

"I'm sorry I didn't tell you." Her lips pressed into a flat line. "When I realized you had no memories of me, I was afraid you wouldn't choose me. But I realize I wasn't fair to you. All this time, I've been upset about the things you chose not to tell me. But when things got hard, I did the same to you."

He didn't even care about that nonsense anymore. Not when fear had nearly crippled him the night before when he almost lost her to his father and his guards. Even if they hadn't killed her, King Oberon would have made Nava disappear right along with his recent memories of her.

"Did you hear what I said in the hallway? I'm yours, and I will not change my mind. I love you, Nava. If you'll have me, I will stay."

Her lips trembled. "You love me?"

"I do. And I'm sorry I ever made you doubt it."

7
ORION

Devon sped past Orion on his black horse, loose pieces of gravel spraying around him as he went.

Then he pulled on the reins and slowed into a bouncy trot, turning around to meet Arkimedes's gaze from underneath the hood of his cloak. "Be prepared for Celeste to run as soon as she sees us. Better remember why we are here, brother."

As if he could ever forget. The branded letter in his pocket had five words written in red ink hidden behind the hard wax seal depicting the Society of Crows' emblem.

Deal with the traitor. Discreetly.

Arkimedes clenched his jaw as claws of dread buried themselves deep inside his chest. He dug his heels into his horse's flank, urging him to catch up with Devon. How he hated that he was the one to be sent to the outskirts of the Iron City to find Celeste.

The imposing, ornate iron gates hid the beautiful stone manor from the street, and tall twisting trees cast shadows upon the path that led to its entrance. The ground was littered with leaves in all shades of brown.

Arkimedes jumped from his saddle before his steed had even stopped moving, ignoring the ache in his thighs as he leaped up the steps, two at a time.

His dread grew, urging him to turn around and flee. He was not one to fear his fate when it came to handling most of his tasks. However, Celeste was a magnificent spell caster, and dangerous with a weapon in hand.

And he didn't want her soul to haunt him for the rest of his miserable existence.

Devon walked to the main door, and as Arkimedes followed him, movement to his right drew his attention. It was a girl, kneeling before a garden bed. She was lithe, with dark brown hair that flowed in messy waves over her round cheeks.

He took a step forward, attempting to get a better look, swallowing past the knot that stuck in his throat, past the fluttering of his erratic heartbeat.

Celeste? No. The girl was too young to be his old instructor. Still, the similarities were impossible to ignore.

Then her beautiful, strange eyes met his, and time stopped.

The air fled his lungs, and sudden pressure constricted his chest, burning him from the inside out. His hands dampened with sweat, yet he forced himself to step forward. Since when did he find it challenging to talk to a girl?

"Excuse me, do you know if anyone is home?" he said in an attempt to distract himself. He didn't want her to flee the moment she realized who they were.

Her brows shot up, and her throat worked as she swallowed. "N-no," she stuttered, dropping the shears she'd been using to cut the plants.

His body still blazed with this strange fire. So much so he struggled not to lower the hood that covered his face to get some air. Why was he feeling like this? He'd never been so unsettled by meeting anyone before. What was going on? "Do you live here?"

"No, I'm just...the gardener."

Her words pulled a distinct snort from Devon's lips. The girl was far too young to be a gardener. And she was the spitting image of Celeste.

She pulled a dead plant from the ground. Dirt spilled all over the aged stone floor that she knelt on.

His heart fluttered as her gaze met his once more. What the fuck was wrong with him?

"You have peculiar eyes," Devon said.

Arkimedes's shadows instantly surged out of control around him, the voices calling to him in hushed tones.

"He can't hurt her," *one soul fragment insisted, raising gooseflesh across his skin.*

"She is ours," *another hissed.*

"I get that a lot." The girl's trembling voice gave away her nerves. Surely, she didn't think she could fool them.

Arkimedes was about to ruin this girl's life. If the Society wanted him to kill

Celeste, then they would recruit her daughter into the king's army without a second thought. That was, if she was fortunate enough not to suffer the same fate as her mother.

A new wave of dread crawled up his skull, chilling his body as the misty shapes around him grew ever angrier.

"You look too young to be a gardener," Devon drawled, and Arkimedes turned to meet his brother's perceptive gaze.

Devon had come to the same conclusion as he had: this girl was lying and was likely Celeste's daughter. Celeste's hidden child. If nobody knew of her, did that mean Arkimedes could help her vanish without facing consequences from the Society?

Either way, he doubted Celeste was here. She would never allow them to speak to her child freely. They needed to lie in wait for the traitor to return home. That would give him just enough time to convince his brother to let the girl go.

"Do you know when Miss Celeste will be back?" Devon asked.

The girl jumped, trembling like a rabbit under a predator's gaze. When she shook her head, her long, wavy hair stuck to her sweaty skin. "She's out at the market with my mother because we are the closest neighbors she has," she lied. "I can tell them—I mean, tell her you came around."

"Where did you say you lived?" Devon asked, moving forward. The look on his face only fed Arkimedes's rising panic.

What could he do? Push Devon away from her and give her a chance to run? Why was his chest burning like this, like a spell branding his skin?

"I didn't." The girl leveled them with a harsh look and placed her gardening tool inside the basket. Then she straightened her shoulders as if to make herself bigger. Brave and foolish, perhaps. It still warmed his dark heart either way.

Few dared to confront a Crow, let alone a Dark One like him.

"You aren't supposed to tell strangers where you live," she whispered. "I can tell Celeste you came by, or you can try to catch her at the market."

Arkimedes doubted Celeste would be near any market.

Devon moved toward the girl, but he froze when Arkimedes's shadows reached out for him, a silent warning to his brother to stay away from her. Devon glared at him from behind his hood.

"Not now," Arkimedes whispered to him.

His brother grunted his displeasure and turned around to head to the horses. It wasn't as easy for Arkimedes to leave, not with the way his heart suddenly ached. How could he even dream of leaving her here...

Arkimedes tightened his fists and shoved those unhinged feelings away. For crying out loud, the girl was too young to be anything other than a nuisance. And she would consider him a villain the moment he carried out the Society's orders. If he were a better man, he wouldn't return at all.

He turned away. Perhaps, in a few hours, this temporary madness would have passed. "Please tell her the Society of Crows came to see her."

Arkimedes descended the stairs, not looking back. That burning sensation seemed to be carving a hole in the center of his chest with each step he took.

Celeste had betrayed the Society. He had to remember that. She had brought this on herself.

"Why did you stop me?" Devon snarled at Arkimedes when he caught up with him past the imposing gate. "Since when do you have a vested interest in a random gardener?" Devon's last word dripped with sarcasm.

"I don't." If only he could explain it. The reaction of his aura had been purely emotional, almost instinctive. He was clearly tired from his trip to the Copper Kingdom. And losing his damn mind.

Why had the girl not flinched when she'd seen him? As if not even the curse of his power intimidated her.

"If you don't care, then we should go back. Take the girl and wait for Celeste inside the house."

Arkimedes knew they should take care of the problem like the higher-ups had commanded. Devon was well aware of their orders. And this would be Arkimedes's last task before departing for the Copper Kingdom forever.

But he couldn't simply kill that girl's family and condemn her to serve the people who'd ordered the execution. It wasn't the first time the Society had requested an assassination of him. Still, this time, there was one simple difference.

Her.

If they saw this through, she would become a prisoner of the king's army. Or worse.

He could at least buy her the time to escape a fate he wouldn't wish on his worst enemy. Fuck the Society. He was leaving after this mission, regardless. They'd been happy enough to withhold the truth from him for so long. He could do the same.

"Let's check the market first," he said and rubbed the center of his chest. It still burned with remnants of whatever that girl had done to him. Perhaps she could already wield magic. If so, that was another problem he

would have to deal with later. "We'll come at night when I'm harder to spot."

Devon narrowed his eyes and snapped his reins, signaling his beast to move down the road and farther away from the manor. "Don't tell me the visit to the Copper Kingdom has made you soft, brother."

Arkimedes's throat closed. All those truths he'd unearthed while he'd escaped to his birthplace for a few months... He'd promised his father, the king of the Copper Kingdom, that he would return as soon as he resigned from his duty.

A normal Crow might not have served enough time to retire, but as it turned out, Arkimedes was a prince, and that changed everything. Perhaps it was childish, how much he desired to see their faces fall when he told them he could leave.

He'd briefly considered not returning at all. Still, Devon deserved the truth, and this last mission together felt important somehow.

"Quite the contrary," Arkimedes whispered to himself. It had made him realize how petty the Society's actions were.

He followed his brother along the paved road that led them toward the center of town. With any luck, Celeste would be at the market. They would handle the problem, and he would never cross paths with that girl again.

Orion woke to the icy feeling of dread still crawling up his body. It invaded his head and transformed into a pounding migraine that rapidly grew in intensity.

He groaned, clutching his skull in agony as images from the dream continued to flood his mind. The scent of olive soap from the bath he'd taken last night lingered on his skin, and a steady warmth emanated from beside him.

His heart shrunk as he turned to Nava. She was still sleeping soundly, unaware of the state he was in. Even the tiniest detail of their first meeting rushed inside him, filling the gaps left behind by his father's spell.

He felt broken and unstable. A man caught between two minds...

He climbed out of bed, taking care not to wake her, and frowned as he took in the bees that were crawling all over the sheet and up his torso and arms.

Maybe a workout would ease the voices of his shadows. Maybe he'd even find Devon there—once upon a time, they used to train before sunrise on the regular. It was the perfect chance to convince his brother to help them with the mirror.

The solarium was situated toward the back of the house, on the ground floor. The rooms in every safe house had a similar appearance, regardless of where that safe house stood. It was a way for the Society to ensure its members always felt at home.

If his father had suspected the Crows knew who he was all along, then there was a possibility the king had watched Devon carefully during their stay at the castle. When they escaped a few nights ago, Orion had told Nava that the treaties between the Society and the royals would be enough to protect Devon. He'd been confident that his father wouldn't harm Devon when he'd locked them in that room and asked Nava to escape.

But Orion hadn't known all the facts then.

He stormed into the solarium, and its humidity wrapped around him. This was a place of life, with plants growing everywhere: an unseasonably warm spot of the house.

The faint scent of old magic welcomed him as he inspected the garden, full of lush greenery and blooms that wouldn't stand a chance in the cold outside. Here they thrived, aided by sorcery.

A crushed granite path led him to a wooden training deck, where Devon awaited.

His brother was swinging a longsword in an elegant arc with practiced ease. He froze in an attack pose as his black eyes fixed on Orion. "You are late."

"And you are shirtless."

"It's hot in here." Devon shrugged, then signaled for Orion to strike. "No magic. You know the drill."

Orion's magic tingled under his skin as it stirred, eager to be unleashed. "Why are you afraid? How long has it been since you've used your magic, Devon?" He smiled as he rolled up the sleeves of his shirt.

Devon glared. "A year, thanks to you and your wonderful soulmate." He tossed the sword onto the deck, and his aura bloomed around him, dark gray and sizzling with energy.

"You tortured her. Consider yourself lucky that it was only imprisonment..."

"So you remember?"

"Yes."

"All of it?" Devon's scaly tattoos moved down his arms like a real snake, slithering over his pale skin. They had both been marked as Crows on the same night. To assimilate into a fae-less kingdom, Orion had banished his wings with magic. He'd often longed for a symbol of them to remind himself he wasn't just human.

Devon's mark was a snake to represent his parents, who had given him away to the Society of Crows. After their discussion last night, seeing the tattoo sent chills down Orion's spine.

"I don't remember everything yet."

"Had I known she was a Beekeeper, I would have never harmed her."

Magical wind rushed through the leaves of plants around them, biting with unnatural coldness into their exposed skin. Devon's spell descended like a winter storm.

"You can help us and make it up to her," Orion said.

A laugh escaped Devon's pale lips. "Let me guess. You still want me to use the mirror?"

Orion dodged the ice spell, racing toward his brother. Frigid air burned down his throat. "You said it yourself. The house barely let me in. And we still need answers."

"You might not care about the allegiance we both swore to the Society, but I do." Devon's lips twisted into a snarl. "May I remind you that they protect the world from the very gods who sought to destroy us? Have you also forgotten that insignificant piece of history?"

Orion's back stiffened, his anger flaring. "We aren't talking about doing anything to harm your precious Society. We need to stop the demons from coming here and killing the Beekeepers. On our own, it will take us weeks to sift through the archives, and we don't have that time."

"Why not?" Devon raised his arms over his head. His alabaster skin glistened under the gray light. Frost or sweat? It didn't matter. "We're well hidden from your maniacal father here, and this place hasn't seen a Crow in ages."

"Because Aristaeus shouldn't have to deal with the Zorren on his own."

"Who the hell is this Aristes you two keep talking about?"

"Aristaeus," Orion corrected. "There are always two Beekeepers. You fill in the blank."

His brother's conflicted expression gave Orion hope. He stretched his arm across his chest, ready to get the training started. His stiff muscles really needed to unwind.

"What if it *was* you who hurt Nava when she crossed the portal? You were so worried at the castle about that prophecy referring to you..."

Orion stopped moving and met Devon's gaze across the darkness of his magic. "I would never purposely hurt my soulmate."

A cyclone of freezing air enveloped him not a second later, a wall of white blinding him as the moisture in the air transformed into snow that stuck to his clothes and body. He hissed and called on his shadows to shield him.

"Tsk. Getting sloppy in your old age, brother. No wonder your father's guards kidnapped you from the island. What was that thing you used to tell me? Rule one: do not allow your opponent to distract you. Not even if they're asking questions about your beautiful woman."

Heat surged within Orion's gut, and he raised both of his hands. His inky power exploded out of him in waves of faces and fierce voices that collided with Devon's stormy spell.

The glass above them shook with the wind now raging inside the solarium. Plants lifted from the ground and scattered dirt over the wooden floor beneath their feet.

Devon was right. He needed to get his head straight, or sooner or later, it would get him killed.

This round of training should at least help him release some of that pent-up tension and sharpen his priorities.

Protect Nava from his father. Find out what had happened to his mother, for her ghost still haunted him in this kingdom. And remove the Zorren from the land.

8
NAVA

Nava had been hovering on the threshold of their room for at least thirty minutes. Tapping the wooden doorframe with restless fingers, she studied the long hallway for any sign of either Arkimedes or Devon.

She'd woken up midmorning, aching from the fight with the guards two days prior, their evening of running, and the poor night's sleep on the bakery's floor. A yawn pushed its way past her lips, and she quickly pressed a hand over her mouth to mute any sound that might alert an enemy to her presence.

Gods, she was tired—and going mad with paranoia.

Rationally, she knew they were alone in this place. But the bees were her constant companions, a quiet warning that evil could be lurking behind every closed door. Since Nava was a child, her mother had instilled a deep fear of places like this in her, and she couldn't shake the undeniable sense of malevolence in the air.

A cold draft howled down the hall, making the hair on the back of her arms stand on end. She studied every inch of the space ahead of her. The bees were still with her, crawling over the walls and the clothes she'd borrowed from the set of drawers beside the bed.

She wrapped her injured arm around her grumbling stomach. Her burn had improved significantly compared to the night before, almost as if she'd used a healing potion.

Where was Arkimedes? Perhaps down in the kitchen having breakfast?

Her heart fluttered at the memories of what he'd told her last night. *"I will not change my mind. I love you, Nava. If you'll have me, I will stay."*

He loved her, even without the memories of their shared past. He was choosing to be with her, at least for now. They hadn't discussed their plans beyond defeating the demons and the man in the shadows.

Would he want to remain in the Copper Kingdom? Would she?

Her answer was simple. This wasn't her home, and she wasn't sure she ever wanted it to be. Why stay in a place that had only brought her pain?

She took a quick breath, shaking her head, and stepped out into the hall. She turned right and followed the path to the kitchen, tugging at the soulmate bond and letting it guide her toward Arkimedes.

The floor creaked and snapped beneath her feet. A sudden wind blew her hair into her face, just as the bees buzzed wildly around her.

Nava spun around, her heart in her throat. "Devon?" She hated how her voice sounded like that of a scared child.

The pads of her fingers prickled with nerves and magic. The hall remained empty, but one of the doors stood wide open, swaying slightly on its hinges. That had been shut before. Right?

"If you think this is funny, Devon, it's not. You're going to get stung," she called out, and her aura flashed bright yellow as bees of light joined their friends, wrapping her up in a cocoon.

There was no answer. Nava took a step toward the main stairs that would take her down to the ground floor. But…

Something called her to that room. And she couldn't resist its pull.

This was the kind of stupid behavior that caused a tragedy, and yet she couldn't force her feet forward. Even though she knew better. Even though she was hungry and wanted something to eat.

Her mother had loved to remind Nava that her childish curiosity would one day get her killed. And once upon a time, Nava had believed her. But now she was a powerful woman—not a frightened girl.

Sweat beaded on her temple as she crept to the mysterious door. If something or someone was there, they would regret trying to sneak up on her. And if danger awaited her, she could always transfer elsewhere and drag Arkimedes out of this hellhole while she was at it.

Her power surged through her veins, making her feet light. "Is there anyone here?"

An enormous window stretched across the far wall of the small room, flooding its wooden floors with gray morning light. Tattered curtains rustled in a breeze that whispered through shattered glass.

Nava's tense shoulders dropped as she breathed a sigh of relief. She had been ready to flee or fight for so long—the idea that a simple broken window might be the cause of this had never crossed her mind.

The room, similar to the one she'd slept in with Ark last night, held only a select few pieces of furniture: a small bed in one corner, a desk by the window, and a bookcase on the other side. Other than the mess of papers strewn all over the floor, it was empty. Chewing on her nail, Nava swallowed the remaining panic and edged closer to the table.

The scribbles on the yellowing parchment that lay on the desk were illegible. Nava skimmed the notes but couldn't comprehend them. Quickly losing interest, she moved on to a book with brown leather binding and uneven pages.

The gilded letters on it read: *The Book of the Dead. It's forbidden by the gods to kill a Crow.*

Its pages were thin and deceptively soft, the words inked with swirls of well-practiced calligraphy.

Gooseflesh raked over her skin. The Book of the Dead smelled like its name, and judging by the dust that pricked her nose, no one had opened it in a long time.

Delicate illustrations extended across each spread of pages, painted with burgundy ink that reminded her of dried blood. Roses framed the first image of a woman dressed in the Crows' black uniform.

She was beautiful, with light hair and youthful features.

Haerion C. Windsboe. Society of Crows member since the age of twenty-two. Killed by a deserter in the Iron Kingdom. Died aged thirty-four. No family survives her.

A heavy weight settled in her stomach as she turned the page, half expecting to see her mother's face next. Instead, she found one haunted-looking stranger after the other.

Page after page, portraits of dead Society members danced across her vision. The young and the old, each one remembered in detailed, etched drawings.

Nava closed the book with a thump when the scent of smoke rose to her nostrils. A cold draft slithered through the fabric of her wool trousers. She suddenly had the distinct feeling that she was being watched.

She turned slowly. In the corner of the room, a woman of nightmares floated above the bed.

Layers of a long petticoat moved in the air as if suspended in water. The figure was all black, with long bones for limbs that snapped about in jagged movements. She pointed at Nava with a gaping mouth and empty eyes.

Even though she wanted to scream, no sound left her lips.

She stumbled backward, hitting the table as the scent of burnt flesh and smoke clogged her nose. The spirit didn't move from her spot, but a bright string of magic shot through the room, straight from the center of her charred face and toward Nava.

The air crackled with energy, and the string cut through her shield of bees. Then it wrapped around Nava's skull, and images flashed through her mind, drowning her every thought beneath them.

Orange flames licked the bottom of the tree, red embers bursting into a flickering fire. She fought against the ropes around her body, trying to catch her breath between the sobs that tore through her throat.

"Please, don't do this. I love you," she called into the void, no longer able to see him behind the wall of smoke.

"Love? I wonder if you know the meaning of the word, Briar." His voice had once soothed her soul, but now it was cold and detached.

Briar closed her eyes and called on whatever strength remained inside her aching body. If this was her end, then she would die like the queen she was.

The smoke blurred her vision, and she choked on a breath. The flames licked at her skin, bursting it into blisters.

Her voice gave way, breaking with raw pain, and then there was darkness. For a moment, she floated above a dead tree in the forest, anger stealing her breath, but she couldn't even moan her lament.

The one she'd loved most of all had killed her.

Nava screamed until her throat was raw, her energy dwindling until everything went dark.

"Nava—Nava, look at me." Arkimedes's voice, smooth like honey, soothed her racing heart. She slowly opened her eyes and met a storm of green irises.

His muscular arms encircled her body, lifting her into the soft furnace of his embrace.

"Ark?"

"Yes, it's me." He cradled her tighter against his chest, and the quick thundering of his pulse calmed her. "What happened, Nava?"

His aura was so dark that she couldn't see anything else around her. Not even the spirit that had attacked her.

Her vision sharpened as she sat up straight, staring at the corner where the burnt woman had hovered a moment ago. "She was here," Nava said, twisting around in search of the spirit—only to find an empty room.

"She?" Arkimedes followed her line of sight, and his frown deepened. "Who was here?"

"There was a spirit in this room, but it wasn't a Neem. It was a burnt woman, and she attacked me with a strange spell."

Had it been an attack? It was hard to determine. Nava hugged herself tightly, trying to bring some warmth back to her body.

Ark's skin grew a few shades paler as he faced her. "What do you mean, a burnt woman?"

"Sh-she was wearing a long black dress and floated in that corner." Nava pointed to the spot where the spirit had been with a shaky finger.

Arkimedes's lips parted and then shut. He scrambled to his feet. "You saw her? Was she wearing a crown?"

A crown? In her panic, Nava hadn't noticed that detail. But…she had been a queen. That much had clearly filtered through to Nava while under her spell.

"How did you know about that? Is she the spirit that Devon claims haunts this house?"

"No." Arkimedes avoided her gaze and covered his face with his hand, rubbing it over his forehead again and again, as if he was trying to soothe himself. It left her concerned and curious in equal parts. "I didn't think she would follow me here."

"What do you mean?"

"That spirit was my mother. I'm not sure why she came to you. I'm the only one who has seen her so far. She doesn't reveal herself to my father."

"What do you mean, that was your *mother*?" The images of the woman dying still churned inside her. Nava leaned against the desk, lest she drop to the ground again.

A month ago, Arkimedes had shown her the spot in the forest where his mother had died. A centuries-old tree burned into lifelessness.

Had Arkimedes known how his mother died because she'd shown him, exactly like she'd shown Nava just now?

A long silence fell. Nava vaguely registered the sound of rain pattering against the broken glass of the window. As if this morning could get any gloomier.

Tears welled up in her eyes. "I saw her dying…"

Ark sucked in a sharp breath. "You saw the burning tree?"

"I did." Nava fought off a wave of nausea. "Has she been visiting you for long? How does it work?"

When Arkimedes told her how his mother had died that day in the woods, she'd never dreamed that he'd *seen* it. But if he'd witnessed the same visions the spirit had shared with her…no wonder he was fighting to find answers.

Arkimedes stopped pacing across the worn rug. "When I first visited the Copper Kingdom, Fael brought me to the castle to meet my father. I didn't know I was the lost prince. I thought I was in trouble somehow, and I put up a fight."

"Did you kill someone?"

"Initially, Fael and the other guards assumed I had abandoned my royal mandate." Arkimedes stared vacantly out of the window. "I already knew that using my power to kill would mean I'd hear their voices for the rest of my life, so I was trying not to use it. Still, the guard noticed that my magic was not like theirs."

"The Curse of the Fallen."

Arkimedes met Nava's eyes and nodded. "My father recognized me immediately."

Undoubtedly. Arkimedes was an exact copy of his father, down to the straight nose and full lips. And even though Ark was half fae, half human, he possessed that otherworldly beauty that only the fae could lay claim to.

Arkimedes walked toward the table, paging through the Book of the

Dead, although Nava doubted he was actually paying attention to the obituaries. "I wasn't sure I was ready to stay, and when he saw me hesitate, the king offered me information about my past. He also promised to help me get a better handle on my curse."

"What do you mean by that?"

"That my shadows speak to me, and I thought I was going mad." He closed the book with a thump and frowned. "Now I only hear them when I'm overwhelmed, or if I lose my temper."

"So, the king promising to help you is what made you decide to stay?"

"No, it was the mystery surrounding my mother's death that tipped the scales. When I inquired about her, I was told the same lie they spin to everyone else." Arkimedes gripped the edges of the desk so tightly, his knuckles whitened with the pressure. "That she stole me away when I was a one-year-old boy and took me to a place where my father couldn't follow."

"The Iron Kingdom. Because the fae are allergic to iron." Arkimedes was half fae, so he could live there. "But why would she return? Surely, she would have expected to get in trouble?"

"I wondered about that, too," Arkimedes said, and something dark flickered over his expression. "My father told me she denied what she'd done, but he felt like she returned for something. They had no proof, and she claimed that someone else had stolen me."

Nava tucked a few errant strands of hair behind her ear. "But everyone at the castle claims that she took you. And back on the island, you told me she abandoned you at the orphanage."

"She did, Nava. The records say so, and so does everyone here. The castle workers, the citizens—everyone hated her. Her official postmortem report states that a few disgruntled citizens killed her in a fire in the castle's library and then killed themselves before the king could get to them." Arkimedes dragged a palm over his face and pushed away from the desk, reaching for her hand.

She took it, knowing deep inside he needed the physical touch. "But that's a lie."

"The night I learned about her supposed death, my mother's spirit visited for the first time. She showed me the day they burned her alive in the forest." His voice cracked with emotion, and that alone nearly broke Nava.

She pressed her lips tightly together as a heavy sorrow swarmed through her—an emotion that belonged to both of them. It wasn't the right time to bring out the stupid rumors about the fae she'd been teasing him with lately, but it was the first thing that crossed her mind.

"If the fae can't lie, how is any of this possible?"

Arkimedes blinked. Then his stern features softened. At least he continued to find this amusing. "Contrary to what you believe, full fae can lie—just not easily. They have to spin this kind of deceit carefully."

Nava hummed, not quite sure she believed him. "What happened after your mother revealed the truth to you?"

"I snuck into the forest. It took me three days to find the tree." Arkimedes was pulling her toward the door. Admittedly, Nava wanted to be as far away from this room as possible, too. Even now, it remained colder than the rest of the house, like the places in the forest that were haunted by the Neems. "Although she abandoned me in an orphanage, I can't help but think that she was protecting me from something worse."

"Yes, I think you're right."

This was why he was so keen to stay and explore the archive. While Nava understood that he wanted answers, the why hadn't registered as important before. He'd never known his mother, after all.

But after seeing the spirit—her charred skin and hollow eyes—she needed to discover the truth every bit as much as Arkimedes did. And she'd stay here for as long as that took.

"You left me in the midst of a duel, and there are feathers all the way up the steps. And you broke the chandelier. You know you can't fly in a house with low ceilings…" Devon burst into the room, in the middle of buttoning his shirt. His hair stuck to his face—from a recent bath or from sweat? Who knew.

Nava blinked. She hadn't even noticed that Arkimedes's wings were extended, crowding the small room with their impressive size.

"I was in a rush." Arkimedes shrugged and met her eyes, right as his wings disappeared behind his back.

Devon glanced around the room with a growing look of concern. "Who broke the window?"

9
NAVA

"Where are the dungeons in this place?" Nava's voice echoed through the massive room. The ceiling rose into a vault-like dome, decorated with intricate molding and painted in mauve gray. She stepped carefully down the wide staircase, her feet slipping against the polished stone.

Black feathers floated over the steps, carried by the air of their movements.

"Dungeons?" Arkimedes's serious expression broke as he glanced over his shoulder at her. He raised a dark, bushy eyebrow in response. "Why are you always asking about dungeons?"

Her cheeks burned. How long had it been since she'd challenged him to take her to his dungeon at the castle? Somehow, it felt like years ago. Not weeks.

With a shrug, she reached for the banister. "Where else would they keep their prisoners?"

He scoffed, shaking his head but continuing on his path.

"Seriously, though—where are the weapons the Crows used to murder all these innocents? This house seems rather normal."

Apart from the whole spirit thing, the reality of their environment was rather underwhelming.

"*We* are the weapons," Arkimedes tossed back and carried on down the rest of the steps. He sounded so much like his old self. Her heart squeezed tighter.

Hadn't he said those exact words to her the first time they'd trained together?

"Your modesty is astonishing." She ignored the fluttering in her stomach and the hope that blossomed somewhere so deep it blasted away the chill left behind by her ghostly encounter.

"Modesty is a waste of time," Devon called from behind.

A large iron chandelier lay shattered at the bottom of the stairs, fragments of wax candles peppered across the cracked floor. How hadn't she heard this break in the middle of her spirit-induced nightmare?

They cut through several rooms on the ground floor. She hadn't been here before, had she? They were taking her somewhere new. Although, admittedly, that covered most of the safe house.

"Are we going to the archives now?" Nava followed Arkimedes down an eerie corridor that led them to the back of the manor.

"Yes." He opened the first door into an empty ballroom. White sheets obscured every inch of furniture, except for the grand piano. "We should see if there's even a scrying mirror in there."

"I haven't agreed to do it," Devon warned. But he hadn't said no either. Clearly, he was only dragging out the inevitable.

They walked past a locked chamber with wards buzzing around it that would probably call the entire Society if they tried to break in. Then past the infirmary, a smallish room with a cot on one side as well as shelves packed full of old potions caked in dust and covered in spiderwebs.

It all gave her the creeps.

"After what just happened, I want us to get out of here as soon as possible," Arkimedes whispered so only she could hear. He hadn't told his brother about his mother's spirit, and Nava had kept her mouth shut.

Finally, they came to a set of narrow stairs that creaked under the weight of their steps and led them underground. Here, the wallpaper peeled from the corners of the wall: the same sage-green tones and dark wood paneling as inside the rest of the house.

Didn't the Society believe in the power of the arts? Of how color could change a person's mood and evoke emotions? Her skin crawled in anticipation of what the archive might look like—and of the truths it might hold.

It was too dark in here to see far. A lingering putrid smell she couldn't place mingled with the scent of dust and mold. Devon snapped his fingers, and gas lamps roared to life in quick succession, illuminating a circular room with an enormous door on one side and a hallway with no end in sight on the other.

The air around them was thick and humid, as if seawater had filled this entire floor before. Nava hummed and made for the door, studying it with growing dread. The Society had painted it cobalt blue. Gold rosettes embellished the surface. In its center, the crest of a Crow perched on top of a scale.

The emblem of the Society of Crows. Even now, it made her heart climb into her throat.

Nava wiped her sweaty palms against her trousers and forced her eyes away from the bird, called to the dark hallway to the far left of the room. The magic emanating from it left the back of her neck tingling.

Gray and white magic combined—something familiar that pulled at her and made her heartbeat run wild. Was her need to flee because of the blue door or due to the feeling emanating from that corridor?

"Since you're interested in the subject, the dungeons are over there. Home of the traitors." Devon's pink lips tilted up on one side as he pointed toward the hall.

Her stomach sank further. A bitter taste coated her tongue, making it hard to swallow. Even her bees were in disarray, crawling everywhere and sending mixed signals she found hard to decipher.

Whatever was down here, it wasn't good.

"Maybe we should leave," she croaked, shifting her weight from foot to foot. After the spirit upstairs, she'd had enough for the day.

"Stop tormenting Nava, Devon," Arkimedes growled. He pointed at a couple of bees that were circling in front of her, called by her burst of panic. "If you get stung, it'll be your own damn fault. I won't warn you again."

"But I'm not lying…"

Arkimedes's expression softened as he reached for her hand, squeezing it softly. "The cellar *is* cursed, Bee. It's meant to make you feel uneasy, so you won't enter it."

"The cellar? I thought—never mind." She narrowed her eyes at Devon and then at the hall. "Isn't that where normal people store their liquor?

Why does it feel so wrong? Is the Society hiding something dangerous there?"

Arkimedes evaded her eyes, turning toward the blue door. "We don't want to release what's in there."

That must be where the actual spirit of this house was, the one Devon had hinted at the night before. Now that she knew, it made sense. Standing in this basement felt a lot like being in Neems territory. Damn, she didn't want to be here at all.

"Not such a boring house anymore, eh?" Devon ambled past her. Yes, she'd been naïve to make that comment earlier. This house was anything but normal.

Arkimedes inspected the emblem with a frown. "Let's just focus on one thing at a time. Our main goal is to discover what the Society knows about the prophecy and how the shadow man is letting the Zorren in."

His hand landed on her lower back in a comforting gesture. A spark of heat radiated from the point of contact, making her ache. His gaze was heavy as he traced the shape of her face, from her eyes to her lips. Despite her fear, their combined desire washed through her, leaving her legs weak.

Devon reached for the door handle, his lips peeling in a snarl, revealing straight white teeth. "If you want my help, then keep the—whatever you two do—behind closed doors."

The filigree Nava had initially thought a mere decoration moved across the painted panels. A mechanism that operated an intricate locking system. It rotated and clicked into shape. Metal scraped over metal as the spicy scent of magic wafted around them, mixing with the mustiness in the room. Then the blue door swung open.

Devon stepped through it without a glance back, leaving Ark and her alone outside. The dread in the pit of her stomach only grew. Her hands prickled with sweat. "Do you think he's going to help us?"

Arkimedes shook his head. "I don't know, but he understands what's at risk if he doesn't."

"What if one of us does it?" she asked, wetting her lips. "I know he said in the kitchen that the Vulcan will alert the Crows, but—"

"We can't. Like the fountain outside, they put a spell on the mirror to trigger a warning. If someone who isn't a Crow touches it, this place will be crawling with members of the Society before we know it. It will also poison whoever grabs it."

Her mouth went dry at his words. "Poison?"

Arkimedes nodded. "The Vulcan is a god's artifact. They say someone stole the first scrying mirror from the gods during the last war many centuries ago. The Crows split it into smaller fragments to use in the safe houses, but as with every artifact, you become poisoned if you hold it more than once—and if it considers you an enemy."

Nava almost turned around and headed the way they'd come, but Arkimedes cleared his throat and pushed her forward with the hand that was still pressed against her lower back. He'd read her emotions, her need to flee. And he was her anchor in a moment of weakness.

"When we enter, you'll find the Vulcan will call to you with what you want to hear. But it's not a call you want to answer, Nava."

"What will it say?"

There was something dark in his expression. "It's different for everyone. I don't know how this particular Vulcan looks, so please be alert and don't respond to anything that feels strange. Come on."

They walked into the archives, Nava's steps stiff, her neck aching from the tense set of her shoulders. Flickering candelabra on the walls illuminated the room with magical candlelight so dim that it was hard to make out any detail.

"Easy there." Arkimedes soothed her with a smile that didn't quite reach his eyes. His wide hands grasped her shoulders, and her quickened heartbeat eased to a pleasant drumming that made her skin tingle with awareness.

She took a deep breath to calm her heavy breathing. "I'm fine."

"You're glowing."

Nava looked at her arms. She was shining such a bright yellow she was easily the most intense source of light in this place. Her energy rolled like waves from the magical core beneath her skin, and she didn't even feel all that threatened now they were inside the room. The bees that had accompanied her from the castle still circled her body.

Something was wrong, and she couldn't ignore it any longer. Did it have anything to do with the mirror? Perhaps, perhaps not. She was just happy Cameron was as far away from her as possible.

The archive wasn't quite a library. Two of its walls held bookcases that extended to the tall ceiling. The other two were covered in large glass cases that contained old weapons and unfamiliar gadgets. In the center of the room, several circular wooden desks surrounded a mirror sphere that rested upon a limestone pedestal.

Any spot on the walls that wasn't hidden by books or artifacts was covered in beautiful landscape paintings and portraits.

Nava followed Arkimedes deeper into the room, glancing at Devon, who stood frozen before the scrying mirror.

A song flowed down from the ceiling, gentle like the buzzing of bees and leaves rustling in the open air. The globe in the center shone white and yellow, like her own aura. Ari's voice called for her to return. She only had to touch it, and she would be back in the forest with him.

The sphere's yellow glow flickered, and Ari's voice grew distant. He was asking for her help. He was hurting. The Zorren had returned.

She collided with a mass of muscle, and strong iron-clad arms wrapped around her body right before she could sprint toward the Vulcan. The warm air of Arkimedes's breath hit the side of her ear, and panic flooded Nava. She couldn't move.

Her body began to lose matter. She had to transfer... "I have to answer Ari's call!" she shouted, pushing against the wall that held her.

"Ignore its call," Arkimedes urged.

It took several long seconds for his words to filter past the fog in her mind.

This wasn't real—it was a trick from the artifact, designed to get her to touch it. Hadn't Arkimedes warned her?

She let out a shaky breath and sagged against his hold. "I don't know what happened to me..."

His hand caressed her arm in a soothing motion, before he intertwined his fingers with hers and pulled her in the opposite direction. "The Society trained us to handle the calling, but it's very hard to ignore the first time you experience it."

Nava's limbs felt heavy. She'd been tired ever since she'd woken up, but adrenaline had fooled her into believing she could push through. "Why is it called a Vulcan?"

"It's named after its creator, the god of truth and vision. He designed the mirrors to spy on our world."

Nava watched Devon as he threw his tunic onto the floor and rolled his shoulders. His forehead wrinkled as if he was sinking into a state of deep concentration.

"Is he preparing for a fight? Will the mirror hurt him?" Nava hated that she knew so little about all of this. It made her feel like a little girl asking silly questions.

"Devon has handled other Vulcans in the past. He will be fine," Arkimedes attempted to reassure her. However, the feeling coming through their bond didn't match his stoic face.

"I can sense you're nervous, Arkimedes. Why are you lying to me? And if he has handled a Vulcan before, wouldn't it poison him?"

A smirk tilted Arkimedes's full lips. "I didn't lie. Devon has handled the Vulcan before. The poison shouldn't be an issue because members of the Society use a potion that allows us to use it again—once enough time has passed. But I don't remember when he took the resetting potion, so..."

"You don't know if he'll be successful." She nodded, feeling dizzy.

"It'll be fine. Devon's not an idiot. And you know how much he values his life."

Nodding again, Nava stared at Devon as he reached for the orb. His hands glowed white as he clutched it. Energy buzzed through the room, making her hair stand on end with static.

Her skin itched; her stomach dropped. Ari's calls filled the air, much stronger now and so hard to resist.

Then Devon's deep rumble of a voice broke over Ari's screams. "Is Arkimedes B. Valeron the one opening the portals for the Zorren?"

Wait. That wasn't the question they needed answers to.

"No!" Nava screamed. The surge that blasted through the room in the next instant cut her words off, rattling the glass cases and blowing loose parchment from the tables.

Devon snarled, holding the glowing sphere aloft with both hands. His long black hair fluttered behind him, blown out of his face by the force of the magic from the artifact.

Arkimedes strode toward his brother. Was he readying himself to intervene if needed? The sphere's outer edges still glowed in a silver shade, but it was turning bright red at its center.

Nava didn't know how long they stood there, paralyzed by the intensity of its power. Of an old magic that smelled so similar to her own.

Then one of Devon's hands fell away from the glowing ball, dangling lifelessly at his side. His eyes glowed bright white. *"No mortal can stay in Dargan's world and speak the demon's tongue,"* Devon said in a distorted voice, and from a far shelf, a book flew out and landed with a bang on the floor.

Its pages flapped like a fan, moved by air that seemed to come from everywhere and nowhere at once.

Devon gasped, his body shaking.

Arkimedes's wings popped out of his back, and he flew forward just as Devon stumbled and placed Vulcan on its pedestal—and then dropped like a dead weight.

Time slowed as Arkimedes's immense wings closed in around his brother's body. He slid across the polished floor, barely getting underneath Devon before his head hit the hard ground.

For a long moment, the rustle of paper settling on the floor was the only sound in the room beyond the fast beat of Nava's heart. Then Arkimedes rose, carrying an unconscious Devon to a settee beside the blue door. He placed him against its cushions and turned to Nava. Shame twisted his features as he averted his eyes.

Anger bloomed hot in her stomach. How could Devon believe that Arkimedes had done it? They'd talked it through in the kitchen. This had *not* been the plan.

Undoubtedly, Arkimedes needed some space to lick his wounds and make peace with his brother's actions. Nava had to keep herself busy so she wouldn't swoop in and try to console him. To reassure him that she believed he was good...

She also needed to resist the urge to smother Devon with a pillow. So instead, she turned to the book that had fallen to the floor. This was the answer to a useless question the god's artifact had given them.

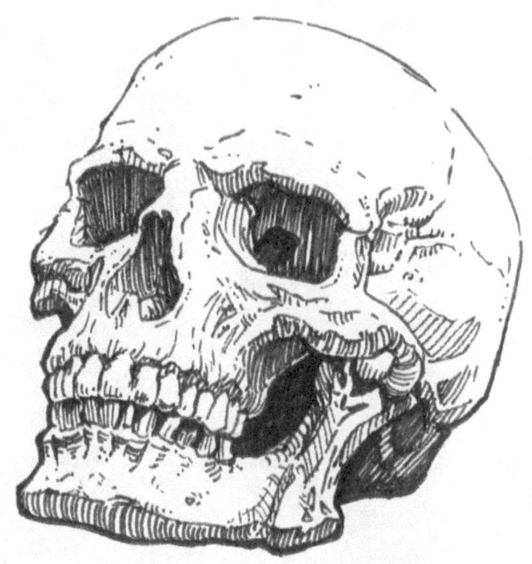

10

ORION

Orion didn't know how long he stood there, unmoving. He breathed deeply, trying to quiet the whispers from his shadows. To ignore the sting of betrayal.

A part of him wanted to give in to the anger simmering in the pit of his stomach, threatening to boil over. Why would Devon think he was capable of causing this disaster and hurting Nava or Aristaeus?

Orion always feared he was teetering on the edge of some wicked act. His nature demanded it. But he tried to rise above the darkness of his power. To not take life for granted, not for a moment.

And he loved, fervently. This world, and especially Nava.

He'd told Devon while they were training what they needed from the mirror: a way to shut the portals permanently. Devon shouldn't—couldn't—use the Vulcan again or it would poison him.

Even if they had access to the Society's potion, they wouldn't be able to ask another question for at least half a year. Fuck, they were in trouble. Orion dragged his eyes over his brother's unmoving body, and his heart ached. It shouldn't hurt this badly...but it did.

"Ark," Nava called from the other end of the room. She was kneeling by the book on the ground, her arms draped over her legs, not touching the pages.

He made it back to her in a few strides. Better to mask his disappointment with something that would bring her hope. "Is the book useful?" he asked, leaning forward to glance at the ancient book, its parchment thin and waxy.

She raised her head to meet his eyes. A crinkle appeared in between her brows. "It seems to be about the history of our world. Not sure how it can help?"

Orion grabbed the book, turning it around so he could read the elegant calligraphy.

The Creation of the Kingdoms:

The people of Caztian destroyed the land. They murdered and burned the land. The gods were angry and caused all that once was alive to perish.

The four leaders of the lands brought offerings to the deities to banish their ire.

The sorcerer brought mechanical inventions made of IRON. A gift of ingenuity.

The fae brought a creature of great intelligence and strength with a COPPER mane. A gift of creation.

The witch harvested SILVER and spun it like webs to link the magic of beings to the land. A gift of cunning resourcefulness.

Last, the creature of the night offered the gods their second-born. Her GOLD hair flowed like sand dunes. A gift of sacrifice.

The benevolent gods accepted the leaders' offerings, but they demanded one final gift of sacrifice from all rulers. In return, they would grant their bloodlines great power.

"What does that last part mean…about the gift of sacrifice?"

"Have you heard about the tithes?" he asked.

Nava pursed her lips and shook her head.

"It's said that the founders had to pay the tithes to the gods to save the world by forfeiting their second-born magical heir. Then, in their grief and to prevent the gods from waging another war we couldn't win, they mandated the creation of magical armies to fight the deities."

"Is that why families have to give away their magical children?"

Orion nodded, glancing at the pages that detailed a history he'd learned a long time ago. "At first, when the memories of the devastation brought by the gods were still raw, magic-wielders volunteered for the armies. And so did their sons and daughters, for a few generations. Then, slowly, they stopped, and the magic dwindled. First from families that held less power—out of four children, only two inherited the trait. After that, just one, and then an entire generation would go without magic."

Nava's frown deepened. "It sounds like the propaganda my mother used to tell me the Crows spread, so they could take the children away."

"The *kings and queens* set the tithe, Bee. The Crows uphold it. Every person born with magic needs to be trained to defend our world in case the gods come for us again."

Nava raised an eyebrow at that, silently challenging his words. "But how can we defeat a god? They can't die."

"They can, if you use the right weapons—or so the story goes." Not that talking about the gods would help them at all with their current predicament.

"So the founders created the Society of Crows to uphold the balance." Nava tapped her chin, but her voice turned high-pitched with irritation. "I don't like it."

Remnants of memories he still had to unveil tickled his mind, making the ghost of his headache resurface once again. He cleared his throat and rubbed his index finger over his temple. "Later generations forgot why the drafts happen in the first place, and it's the Society's job to keep records of those years of pestilence, war, famine, and death."

"Do all the kingdoms take tithes?"

"My father rarely does. He only demands that the Dark Ones join the royal guards. But there is no need to take them as children. Every Dark One born with enough power to wield it comes to serve the king willingly."

"I see how they serve him," Nava said tightly, shaking her head. "All the women ended up as his consorts."

Orion rested his elbows on his knees, meeting her unrelenting gaze. "They wanted to, Nava—they told me that much."

"I doubt they would say otherwise when the truth could get them in trouble."

He didn't want to get into this argument with her. Her hate for the king wouldn't allow her to see that some people regarded him as something close to a god. "I've heard the Gold Kingdom doesn't draft children either, but I'm unsure whether that's true or not. Their politics are complicated."

"How so?"

"For starters, they have two monarchies fighting for the same crown. The shifters who lost the last war and the vampires."

"Vampires?" She blinked rapidly. "Really?"

"It's not a place I would head to for a break, even though it's beautiful." Orion shrugged and continued paging through the book. Surely there was something in here that could help them?

"So the Society upholds the tithes, which keeps their armies strong with magic to fight the gods?"

"When I was a Crow, they taught us to be prepared for when the gods returned. They didn't teach us to harm people simply because they wanted the citizens of Caztian to suffer. Every family has given up something precious. The founders who became the royals paid the first tithe when they gave the gods their second-born child."

"But why does it have to be children?" Nava's lips flattened just as a wave of anger, mixed with sorrow, flared through their bond. "No matter how frightening the decline of magic is—or the supposed end of the world at the hands of the gods—a child should remain with their family."

"I agree." Orion nodded. "But if children stay with their non-magical parents, they can't be taught or trained properly. They might hurt themselves or others by accident. Some villages are so poor Nava, they lack education and sometimes they punish the innocent magical kids because of their powers, which they can't control." He'd prefer not to remember everything he had seen in his time. The innocents who'd suffered unspeakable torture. "It's hard to grow up when you're always the scary one. When people don't understand you."

Nava's expression softened, and she reached for his hand, pausing briefly before taking it. "You never told me about this..."

"It's not a good story to tell." Orion's chest felt tight all of a sudden. Why hadn't he shared any of this with her before? Regardless of the reason, he wanted her to know now. "Once, the Crows commanded me to check up on several families. The rumor was that they'd harmed their children because of their powers. When I found them locked in dark rooms, barely more than skin and bones, I nearly lost it."

"Gods..." Nava turned pale.

He ground his teeth. If only he could lose those memories, shake the echo of the rage that had consumed him, demanding he seek retribution. "And when I asked for the children to be released, the families demanded the price the Crown pays per head." Shame forced his eyes away from her compassionate gaze. "Of course, I also took some children who were loved because I thought I had to."

"And now you believe the drafts are wrong?"

"I believe the Crowns should invest in better education for their people. Also, I wish they wouldn't treat their armies like disposable human camps."

"I enjoy learning all this. It makes a bit more sense—I just don't understand why the Vulcan showed us this book."

Orion smirked, squeezing her shoulder. Nava was right. This was the legend behind the creation of the kingdoms. Not much use for closing the portals—nor for understanding who was sending the Zorren.

"Devon Black did this. Force him to hold the Vulcan again and get us the answers we need," one of his shadows spat, and its venom rushed through Orion's blood, awakening his power.

Orion took a breath to calm himself and clenched his jaw tight against the throbbing within his skull.

"I'm sorry about what happened," Nava said, as if she were reading him like the open book beneath his hand.

The crawling sensation under his skin intensified alongside the need to disappear into the shadows of the room. To hide and lick his wounds. "You've done nothing to be sorry for."

"Maybe I'm sorry for how you feel right now. Maybe it's time we show Devon who the wicked one in this relationship is."

Surprise pushed a laugh past Orion's lips. "You don't have a drop of blood in your body that's truly wicked, Bee."

"May I remind you that the life debt only existed because I almost killed him?" She let out a shaky breath. "Not that I'm proud of it. And I have grown to care for Devon—against my better judgment."

"I'm not angry about him wanting to make sure you are safe. He understands your role as a Beekeeper. You found a Dark One who looks like me and is letting the demons in."

"But we agreed it couldn't be you," she grumbled.

"Yes, and it hurts that he doubted me, but I would have done the same, and I will get over it. Devon needed to be sure he could trust me, and I understand that."

He was done talking about it, to be honest. He flicked back to the page the book had originally opened on and pointed to the line of text that mentioned the Silver Kingdom. "The witches tied the four rulers and their descendants to their new kingdoms. It's the very reason my father kidnapped me from our home on Grey Island."

She returned her focus to the book. "Because your magic feeds the land..."

"*Our* magic. You are the future queen, Nava." If only she didn't look so defeated. It tore him from the inside out. He reached for her again, as if one simple touch might revive him, but she turned her face away from him.

"I do understand that."

She hated it in the Copper Kingdom. How could she not? Everything she'd experienced here had been negative. The burning forests, the Zorren, the king—hell, even Orion had played a part in Nava facing trial after trial. The knowledge only made his stomach sink further.

"I understand why I chose not to come back of my own free will," he whispered, grasping her chin and lifting her face to meet his. The answer was simple. The Arkimedes from a year ago had known Nava wasn't ready for this. That she was too new to the world of magic—a world where her soulmate was a Dark One with a giant secret in the shape of a kingdom. "If you really don't want to be a queen, we will leave once all of this is over."

"Really?" Her lips parted, and she searched his face as if she was trying to find the lie there.

"Yes."

"What about the kingdom?"

"Perhaps we can live somewhere in our land but far away from the castle and the king." He paused, and the memory of a red-haired boy flashed through his mind. Cameron—Nava's little brother.

Another reminder of the family his father had stolen from him. He could keep the reality of him regaining his memories to himself, so it wouldn't detract from the bigger problems at hand. But he craved honesty between them. Her happiness was the most important thing.

"I bet Cameron will like it here. There are creatures neither of you have ever seen before."

Nava nodded and then froze. Her eyes widened as she seemed to realize what his words meant, but she didn't say a thing. Instead, she threw herself at him across the old book, barely giving him a chance to catch her.

She laced her fingers behind his neck and crushed her lips to his in a bruising kiss. He could taste the salt from the tears that were streaming down her cheeks on her tongue.

The kiss was too short. She withdrew and hiccuped before taking a deep breath. "How much do you remember?"

"Not everything. Just fragments. But they're coming back faster now that I'm away from the castle and my father."

She ran her hands over her face, wiping away all traces of her tears. Then she flashed him a blinding smile. Now they only had to defeat the man in the shadows before the Zorren destroyed the kingdom. It seemed easy enough, with her looking at him like that.

"When can Devon use the mirror again?" Nava settled on her knees, wincing as she spotted the wrinkled pages of the book wedged between them. She flattened her palms over them again and again, attempting to get rid of the creases, but all to no avail.

Orion sighed, glancing at Devon's pale form on the settee. His chest was rising and falling with slow, shallow breaths.

"We can't use the Vulcan again," he said, and the burning frustration returned like an old foe that had never left him. "It will kill Devon. Or hurt him very badly."

"So Devon ruined our chance to learn how to stop the man in the shadows and all we got out of it was a useless history lesson?"

Well, when she put it like that...perhaps hurting his brother wasn't such a bad idea. But maybe all wasn't lost. Devon had asked the wrong question, but the mirror had given them one useful answer. Even if it wasn't the one they'd been looking for.

"No mortal can stay in Dargan's world and speak the demon's tongue," he repeated.

It made little sense why this book had flown over to them when Devon had asked whether Arkimedes was the one opening the portals.

Nevertheless, the Vulcan had answered clearly by speaking through Devon's lips.

It couldn't possibly be Orion because he was mortal.

Whoever Nava had encountered in Dargan's realm was immortal, able to stay in Dargan's realm and talk to demons.

"He is an emissary of the gods." The words left his lips before the thought had fully formed in his mind. He looked up to see Nava's blank expression and grabbed the book from the floor, carrying it to the nearest table.

She scrambled after him. "A what?"

"Emissaries are the messengers of the gods. They walk both this world and their realms and deliver the gods' messages to the royals."

Orion found the sentence he was looking for. He reread it, his heart lurching in his chest.

> *The benevolent gods accepted the leaders' offerings but demanded one last gift of sacrifice from all rulers. In return, they would grant their bloodlines great power.*

"A gift of sacrifice." He pointed at the swirls of ancient calligraphy. "The Society of Crows believes the emissaries are magic-wielders. That families across the world offer sacrifice to the gods to gain something holy."

"So...you think the shadow man is a sacrifice to the God of Shadows?" Nava's voice came out strained, but she nodded as if it made sense. "If that's the case, then he has to be your kin, not a shapeshifting demon."

They stared at each other in silence. Orion knew with a terrifying certainty what Nava was thinking.

What if the man in the shadows was Orion's twin brother?

Maybe that was the reason his mother had whisked him away? Perhaps she hadn't realized what would happen until it was too late, and in her terror at losing one child, she'd wanted Arkimedes as far away from his father's reach as possible.

"If he's an emissary of the God of Shadows, Nava, it would explain why he was there each time you crossed."

"How are we supposed to defeat him if we can't kill him?" Her face twisted with shame, and she swallowed hard. "I mean...I don't mean we *have* to kill your blood brother, but—"

"He's trying to kill you," Orion growled. "I will do anything—and I mean that—to protect you." The words burned in his mouth, and dread squeezed his throat tightly.

But how? Without the Vulcan, they wouldn't be able to get a straightforward answer to that question, and finding another mirror was nigh on impossible.

"If we can't take him down, we might have to return to the castle and speak with my father."

But that would be the very last thing they would do.

11
ORION

By the time Orion got Devon into his room, night had fallen. It was particularly cold tonight, the chill sneaking past the thin windowpanes and creeping under the layers of his clothes. He threw a log into the chimney, and golden flames ate it up, roaring to life.

Devon lay on the bed, barely moving. He had said very little ever since he'd woken up.

Now he pressed his cheek against the pillow, his features drawn as he tracked Orion's movements with care. "If you're angry with me, Arkimedes, you can speak now or forever hold your peace."

"Peace?" Orion scoffed, straightening as he dusted wood fibers and ash off his hands. "We needed to know how to stop the Zorren, Devon. Not whether I was behind it all."

For someone so tall and strong, Devon looked frail now, weakened by the ancient magic of the mirror. "Just because you said you wouldn't do it, doesn't mean your blabber convinced me."

Could he storm out of this place like Nava had done mere minutes ago? Tempting. Still, deep down, Orion was glad Devon had tried to protect her from harm. Even if it felt a lot like betrayal.

"At least your question gave us something to work with." Orion headed over to the window and tugged at the curtain to shut it. This cold wouldn't do much to help Devon heal.

"Out with it."

"The one opening the portals is an immortal, and we have no idea how we will stop him."

Devon's lips parted in obvious shock.

"Unless you know how to defeat an immortal?" Orion crossed his arms.

"Of course I don't."

"That's the information we needed from the Vulcan. If we're to survive this mess, we have to work together, not against each other."

"She's a Beekeeper, Arkimedes." Devon slammed his open palm against the bed. Particles of dust rose, encircling him in a halo. "I want to protect her, and if you were destined to kill her in some strange twist of timelines, I wasn't going to make it easy on you."

"You knew as well as I did that we only had one shot at the Vulcan—"

Devon's harsh laughter cut him off. "Only weeks ago, you brought me a burnt book and asked me to translate it. When I told you the prophecy, you thought it referred to you."

Orion didn't need to hear his brother's justifications. In the logical part of his brain, he understood. But that didn't mean it hurt any less.

He turned his face away. "I'd hoped you'd believed me when I reassured you that I couldn't hurt Nava. Not in this lifetime, nor the next."

"You're in love now, but how many fall out of love?" Devon reasoned. "What if you stop loving her tomorrow morning and destroy the world by nightfall?"

Anger boiled over as he crossed to the bed with wide strides. Heat flooded his cheeks, and his shadows darkened, crawling over the bed. "That's not how soulmates work. I'd rather die than hurt her!" In fact, he would die, too, if Nava were to be killed.

"How would I know? I don't have a soulmate of my own for comparison. You have the girl and the father who wants you home. You have the kingdom, the power, and a life full of purpose."

"So what is it, Devon?" Orion narrowed his eyes. His shadows retreated, inch by inch, as his anger cooled, replaced by the bitterness of heartbreak. "Were you truly doubting my nature because you were concerned about Nava's well-being? Or were you secretly hoping I was going to be the villain all along because you're jealous?"

Devon's mouth opened, then snapped shut. His brows furrowed as he took in Orion's words. "You're twisting this..."

"Am I?" Orion backed away to the door. He just wanted to get out of here. To be alone. He swallowed a few times before speaking again to make sure his voice wouldn't crack. "Tell me it's not true, then. Swear it to me."

The silence was absolute.

Orion nodded and turned to leave, pausing by the door when Devon's breath hitched.

"I wanted nothing bad to happen to you, that I swear." His brother's voice was raw with emotion.

They both knew jealousy was a venom that could kill, even in relationships like theirs. "If you want to be the hero, I'd start by looking into what your precious Society is doing to innocents."

The creaking of the bedsprings made Orion pivot on his heel to meet his brother's haunted gaze. Devon was sitting up straight, his back like an iron rod against the headboard. "Don't bring them into our private affairs."

"I believe the Society knew who I was when they took me as a five-year-old boy. They kept me away from my kingdom."

"You don't know that for sure. Just because Nava whispers sweet nothings into your ear, doesn't mean she's right about everything."

Orion had neither time nor patience to get into this with Devon. He wrapped his hand around the handle and opened the door into the dark, cold hallway. "I believe they took your family from you, exactly like they did to the children in the bakery. I've been the villain to many, and I never truly questioned the Society. We were young and ignorant when we first met. But I don't have that excuse anymore, and neither do you. You don't get to blame me for the decisions you make when you continue to follow them blindly."

And without another look back, he left the room.

12
NAVA

Nava hated being alone, but especially so in this haunted place. With all that had happened three days ago with the Vulcan, tension had been running high between Arkimedes and Devon.

She hadn't left their room for fear of running into the spirit of Arkimedes's mother again—or, worse yet, meeting Devon in the hall and having to pretend not to be bothered by what he'd done.

She paced across the creaking floor, pausing by the window and peering outside. Mist enveloped the front garden, so thick she couldn't see beyond the rock wall that fenced off the manor from the wilderness outside. Her skin crawled with the need to be out of these four walls as soon as possible.

Where was Arkimedes? He'd said something earlier about catching some fresh air. She pressed her face to the glass, trying to spot him. Nava drew a fortifying breath. She had to leave this room eventually.

Venturing out into the haunted halls, she kept her eyes wide open and a shield of bees buzzing around her. The kitchen was empty, but there was hot coffee in the pot and porridge waiting for her on the stove. Wonderful.

She blew on the steam rising from her mug and closed her eyes as the bittersweet scent promised a boost of energy. If there was one thing she was grateful to the Crows for, it was the reserves of coffee beans they kept in this place. They could go to the shadow realm for everything else.

It didn't take her long to discover Arkimedes in the solarium. His bare, muscular chest came into view through its double doors, the glass distorting some of the detail. But what she couldn't make out, her mind filled in from memory.

Arkimedes stood in a wide stance, his charcoal pants slung low on his hips, showing off his well-defined abdominal muscles. He wiped his forehead. His skin glistened with sweat.

Nava swallowed against the sudden dryness in her mouth. Despite sharing a room, they'd been too exhausted for intimacy, except for the two kisses she had stolen from him.

She needed time to heal from the heartbreak of believing he'd chosen the kingdom over her. That wasn't the case, of course—but words only healed part of the wounds. Time and proof of his commitment would do the rest.

But it didn't hurt his case one bit that he looked the way he did. Heat rushed through her, coiling tight in her center. She rose up on tiptoes to catch a better view of her mate.

He bounced on his feet while rotating his shoulders. His power—rich and black—morphed into waves that swirled around him like a cyclone, shaking the wooden boards of the training deck. The shapes of his victims peered from the swirls. His aura was only visible to her when he was actively using magic, and perhaps it should have frightened her, but she loved that he was power incarnate. That he could choose to bring destruction but refrained from doing so.

He'd been coming here to train each morning at sunrise. Then he came to collect her for breakfast before they went to the archives to find the answers Devon had robbed them of. It was useless, as there were thousands of books to go through—and they didn't even know where to start.

"Are you going to stay out there or come inside?" Arkimedes's bright green eyes caught hers from across the solarium and past the dirty glass door. His gaze pinned her down like he was the predator and she was his prey.

"Hello." Nava scrambled forward, her heart beating wildly in her throat, and she lifted a hand in the most awkward wave any human could possibly give their soulmate.

He smiled, the sun catching the firm muscle of his abdomen, and the visual was so distracting that her foot caught on the step up to the training deck. She screeched as she fell forward, her coffee spilling everywhere.

His hands caught her before she could hit the ground. "Watch where you're going, Bee."

Nava met his knowing gaze, and her face heated. How could he still have the same effect on her after all this time? "You made me spill my coffee."

"What a catastrophe." His hands settled on her hips, the warmth of his touch seeping through the thin layer of her trousers. "You can always go back for more. I brewed you a big pot."

Desire rippled through her, making her shudder. "Apparently not enough if you're going to strut around the house shirtless," she whispered, her fingertips tingling as she pressed a hand to his chest. The touch alone sparked energy.

His laugh was breathy, music to her ears after he had spent the past few days sulking. "Are you here to train with me?"

"I don't know. You like to cheat."

"When have I ever cheated while training?" he challenged. His fingers dug into her flesh, and he pulled her forward with a sudden, possessive tug until their bodies touched.

"Please. Back on the island, you did all the time." Did he remember their training sessions again? Her heart was beating so fast, she could barely think straight. There was no greater gift than him regaining his memories.

"You're a sore loser…"

Nava pursed her lips. "I win if I reach the weapons rack first." Lifting her chin, she pointed in the general direction of the target. Her skin glowed yellow as a rush of magic came to her call, feeding the adrenaline already rushing through her veins.

"Since you're intent on tainting my name, I get to call the prize if I take you down." Arkimedes stepped away, depriving her of his nearness. He dusted off his pants and stalked around her like a predator inspecting his next meal. Oh, she wanted to be that. Badly. If only to forget about everything else.

"Do your worst." The challenge died on her lips when Arkimedes launched himself at her. She squeaked, darting out of the way of his shadows.

He'd always waited for her to attack first, and him making the first move unsettled her. But she transferred out of his grasp just in time. Her blood buzzed, warm with the delicious exhilaration of being chased across the wide expanse of this room, surrounded by tropical plants that lent their energy to her.

She laughed, half running, half transferring in a billow of dust and pollen toward the weaponry stack. Arkimedes's wings beat in sharp bursts as he swooped into the air and toward her like a bird of prey. She was almost there, but the reach of his magic was too great.

The air crackled with black particles that swarmed her. He was anticipating her moves, perhaps reading her emotions. Each time she appeared in a new place, he was almost there, ready to catch her.

The peppery scent of his magic brought tears to her eyes, blinding her and slowing her down. Through the gust of dark ink that wrapped around her like a secondary shield and refused to let go, Nava could see the shelves a mere four feet away. They beckoned her forward, calling for her triumph.

Suddenly, Arkimedes landed behind her with silent steps. Someone else might not have noticed, but Nava sensed the spike of excitement through the bond. Two could play the game of guessing where the other would go. She didn't need to see him or hear his steps to know he was running toward her.

He was close, too close.

She bolted in the opposite direction and reached for the shelves. Her fingers wrapped around the polished wooden handle of a dagger, just as his fingerlike mist grabbed her ankles and dragged her backward.

Nava kicked at the tendrils of magic and pulled the entire rack of training weapons from the wall to the floor. The ground shook, and Arkimedes tackled her from the side, emerging from the pitch-black wall of his power.

A scream escaped her as they tumbled to the ground, collapsing in a pile of sweaty limbs away from the weapons. Slowly, both their auras faded away to nothing.

"You're heavy," she groaned. Having the full weight of his body on top of her made her keenly aware of how perfectly it fit against every plane and curve of her body. Her blood sang with his nearness.

He lifted himself off her, although one of his hands lingered on her stomach, right over the spot where she could feel their bond the strongest, where his emotions blended with hers, intangible but real.

His need for her ran rampant, merging with her desire for him. She lifted the small wooden dagger she'd picked from the rack before Arkimedes had reached her.

"It seems you won. What's your prize, Bee?"

Nava dropped the practice weapon to the side and placed both hands over his sweaty skin. Gods, she loved the thundering of his heart under her palms. She trembled beneath him with the force of her craving. "I want you to touch me."

Arkimedes let out a low groan. His eyes darkened with something primal as he caressed the side of her face with one hand, before closing the gap that separated them with a kiss.

Their lips touched gently at first, but the kiss soon caught fire as he deepened it. His tongue traced her lips, then slipped inside her mouth, tangling with hers in an obscene dance that left Nava breathless. She shuddered, her entire body tingling with the need to feel him, to have him explore every inch of her.

She swallowed as his hand splayed over her stomach, traveling over her blouse, slowing down to trace her breasts, grasping the mounds and flicking a finger over her nipples.

"Devon could come at any moment." She dug her fingers into his scalp, pulling him closer.

"I don't want to hear my brother's name on your lips when I'm touching you like this." Arkimedes slipped his hand inside her trousers, and the breath caught in Nava's throat when his fingers met her aching center.

A gentle wind chime rang in the air, and his lips closed on her neck, sucking. His tongue lapped at her skin with the same intensity that his fingers danced over the point where she craved him most.

"Don't stop," she pleaded in a ragged tone, writhing beneath him as he slid a finger inside her, pumping harder.

Her hips moved of their own accord, rising and falling as she met each thrust of his hand until she was a tight coil ready to snap.

"Nava, I want to devour you whole."

Pleasure burst through her as her orgasm crashed down on her like waves, dragging another moan from her lips. He kissed her then, but unlike their previous kisses, this one was slow and languid, sweet.

Arkimedes pulled away and met her gaze. In his expression, she found love, desire—and fear. He pressed his lips to hers again, a gentle caress that made her heart stutter. She never wanted to be apart from him again.

The thought sparked the fire in her veins once more, and as it rushed through her, she reached for the strings of his trousers, eager to be rid of them. She needed to touch him...

The chime pierced the solarium again, followed by a loud ringing sound that echoed through the room.

"What's happening?" Nava blinked, dizzy as she tried to locate its source.

"Fuck," Arkimedes growled, and he was off her in a matter of seconds. His head snapped from side to side as he searched for the origin of the noise. "Something's triggered the alarm."

The fire raging through Nava's body died as if doused in water. He helped her up and hunted for his discarded shirt while she straightened her clothes.

"What does that mean?" Her mind raced as she looked around, half expecting to see a Crow bursting into the solarium at any moment. Had someone attempted to enter through the fountain? One of the king's guards, perhaps?

"It means the Society now knows we are here. We have to go."

13
ORION

The alarm rang louder inside the house. It morphed from a soft chime to a sound so high-pitched that it punctured Orion's ears and brought the remnants of the headache he had been fighting for days.

They ran to the entrance hall and the winding stairs that led to the second floor. "We need to get Devon before we—"

As if called by his words, his brother stumbled into the room from the other direction, clinging to the wall with trembling arms. His wide black eyes met Arkimedes's, bulging from their sockets as he gasped for air.

"Devon?" Orion rushed to him. His fingers went numb when he caught Devon's body just as he collapsed. He was cold as ice and soaked in a layer of perspiration that was seeping through his white shirt.

"I'm sorry, Arkimedes," Devon rasped. Whatever softness his cheeks had held before was gone now. His skin sagged over every bone of his skull.

Nava hurried to them, the glow of her body illuminating the dark room, bringing warmth to the greenish-gray shades of Devon's skin. "What's happening to him?"

Devon closed his eyes, his weight sinking more heavily into Orion's arms. "I wanted to get you the answers." He grimaced in pain as his body rattled with shivers.

Unease crawled over Orion's skin. "What did you do?" he demanded, fighting the need to shake his brother.

But he already knew the answer, even without an explanation. Devon had gone back to the archives and sought out the Vulcan once again. Orion pushed aside the anger that boiled within him and picked up his brother from the ground. Devon's weight was considerable. Even with the Vulcan's poison sucking the life out of him, he was still all thick bones and muscles.

Nava followed them into the parlor where Orion placed Devon onto the green velvet sofa. "What can we do to help him?"

The alarm bells were still ringing. They needed to leave. Orion turned to her and read the unspoken question in her eyes. *Is he going to die?*

Not today. Not if he had anything to say about it.

"We need to find a healing potion before we leave. It should keep him alive until we make it to the city." Orion rose, making for the small infirmary down the hall. The likelihood of discovering a non-expired potion was slim, but Orion had seen people perish under the poison's grip before. It was a fast and ugly death.

"I'll get it," Nava said, placing a trembling hand on his shoulder. "You stay with him. I know where the infirmary is."

Before he could argue, she was already transferring away, disappearing past the archway toward the long, dark hall. She could get there and back faster than he ever could. But it was too dangerous. He doubted the Crows would arrive so quickly, but she shouldn't be too far from him...

"I asked about the portal." Devon grabbed Orion's wrist, stopping him from dashing after Nava. His black hair stuck to the sharp angles of his pale face. "But I have been thinking about the children in the bakery a lot, and the thought sprang to mind."

Devon had triggered the alarm when his allegiance had changed while he was holding the Vulcan. Arkimedes squeezed his brother's shoulder.

The cold air enveloped Orion as he stepped out onto the porch after administering two healing potions. Nava awaited him in the front garden, both arms wrapped around her chest. She was wearing a Society ensemble today, with black pants tucked into tall leather boots—but the long dagger on her black belt was new.

Had he not allowed his nature cloud his mind while they were training, perhaps he could have stopped Devon from triggering the alarm and poisoning himself. He'd promised himself he wouldn't let things go too far with her, and he'd truly intended to kiss her senseless and nothing more—well, and maybe tease her a bit. But her beauty, how she'd glowed with happiness, had weakened his resolve.

He cleared his throat, descending the steps to stand beside her. He was still craving her warmth and her lips, but now they had to run and hide again. All he wanted was a warm meal and to take his woman to bed. To rest without having to worry about whether they'd have to fight for their lives and freedom. When would they get another reprieve like this one?

"How long does Devon have?" Nava asked, worry etched on her face.

"A couple of days. A week at most." Orion rubbed his tired eyes.

"We need to leave soon, don't we?"

"Yes. Soon. As soon as Devon is ready." Orion stared at the humming spheres that hung from the trees before them. Dozens of colorful globes spelled by the Society of Crows to act as alarm bells if someone broke in. The scent of magic swirled around them in a cloud of spice as they watched the chiming bells vibrate at a high speed.

"What if they get here before that?" Nava asked.

"They won't make it here so fast. We have at least a few hours," Orion reassured her, although he wasn't certain he believed it himself. "There are steps they need to follow before sending someone over. First, they have to find out which Society safe house was breached. This rarely takes long. Then they have to check what triggered the alarm in the first place. That way, they know who to send here. And then they need to travel, which will take some time…"

The movement of the spheres was far too rapid to be visible to the human eye. However, Arkimedes could trace its lingering echo, a faint blur that encapsulated each orb. The sound should have been one of breaking glass, but instead, it was the blaring song of wind chimes.

"How will they get here?"

"My father doesn't allow the Corvus to portal into the city anymore. They would have to come to the outskirts of the actual safe house." His ears ached from the noise that seemed to be building the longer they stood out here. "They have hidden passages all over Caztian." He sighed. "The truth is, I really don't know how long we have."

"You keep using that word. Corvus. Is it another way to refer to the

Crows?" Her voice managed to both soothe his growing dread and set his nerve endings aflame.

"The Society doesn't consider all Crows to be part of the Corvus. Think of them as the elite. They send selected members with enhanced skills to eradicate problems quickly. The hope is that the Corvus deals with it before they have to send a larger group."

"Enhanced skills?" Nava swallowed, fear clear in her eyes. "You mean they are more powerful?"

Orion tilted his head with a shrug. He couldn't lie, but he also didn't want to add to her nervousness.

Of course, Nava read him with ease. Her face lost its beautiful flush from before. She reached for his hand with clammy fingers. "How many Corvus do they usually send?"

"They usually sent us in pairs, Bee."

Her eyes widened. "You and Devon were Corvus? Was that why they sent you to my house ten years ago?"

"We were." Devon's voice came from behind them. Orion turned around to see him stepping out of the manor, bracing himself against the doorframe. "Once upon a time, before everything turned to shit."

Was he referring to their current situation? Or how things had changed after they'd found Nava?

"You shouldn't be up." Orion clicked his tongue. But if he was… perhaps that meant he'd gathered enough strength already to leave. Orion craned his neck, searching for the portal disguised as a wall fountain. He could have sworn it had been in that wall over there, surrounded by the ivy. Perhaps it was too far away to make out…

"I created this mess, so I need to get us out of it," Devon said. Some color had returned to his face. The old potions were clearly doing the trick.

Nava stared at the nothingness of the misty grounds around them, her eyes glazed over, as if she was stuck in her thoughts. "When you came to my home, back in the Iron City, did my mother trigger an alarm like this?" If her trembling lips weren't already giving away her nerves, the painful tightening of her grip around his hand certainly did a fine job of it.

"Celeste set off all the alarms. Her, your father, and their little team burned establishments from people who were loyal to the Crows. She killed members and freed convicted criminals." Devon wheezed before a cough rattled his chest.

"You are lying..."

Did Devon understand the concept of self-preservation? Clearly not, not even after poisoning himself. The distant buzzing of bees circled him as Nava's grip tightened even further.

Orion hissed in pain, pulling his hand from her grasp. "You're going to break my hand."

"Sorry," she said sheepishly. "So where do we go from here?"

Where was the gate? Orion walked along the path, toward the fountain they'd used to enter. There. What was that? The bowl that had previously jutted from the wall lay in pieces all over the pathway, partially hidden by the tall grasses around them. Gooseflesh erupted all over his skin as dread flooded him, overwhelming his senses with cold shivers.

"The fountain is gone. They've trapped us here." He kicked at the debris on the ground, his power surging in a bright flare. The piece of concrete bounced off the ivy-covered stone wall and landed somewhere he couldn't see. The edges of the safe house grounds wavered with an invisible shield of power.

Orion brought his hand to his temple and tried to massage the blinding pain away. Meanwhile, Nava inched forward, likely sensing the panic that gripped him.

"Don't get too close, Nava. We don't know what spells are circling the perimeter of the property."

"So what, then? We wait here to be captured?"

"No one is taking you from me again." The things he would do if that happened, and so soon after the debacle with his father... It didn't bear thinking about.

Nava glared at Devon. "Look at the mess you got us into! Why didn't you come and talk to us before—"

"I know!" Devon's voice trembled. He was hunched over with the cough still shaking him at intervals, and his eyes shone with remorse.

The need to leave grew more urgent with each passing second. The sound of the bells culminated in an ear-piercing crack of shattering glass.

"Ark?" Her voice boomed past the fierce thunder of his migraine.

"We can't be here when the Corvus arrives. We have to go through the cellar."

"The room downstairs?"

Devon magically seemed to regain some energy as he straightened to his full height, his eyes sharpening with worry. "You can't be serious."

"There are only two ways left out of this place. Now that the fountain is gone, that's not an option. The second is through the hills, and since we don't know where this house is located, we can't commit to traveling for weeks—months, even—back to the Copper City. Not with the emissary letting the Zorren in."

"You know we can't open the cellar. It's flooded and cursed," Devon said.

Nava's lips parted, but no sound emerged, although her growing anxiety pushed through their bond. She leaned against the wall, her gaze shuttered. "Why would the Society curse their only exit out of this place if a problem were to arise?"

Her eyes jumped from Devon to Orion. It had been difficult for him to wrap his head around the truths of the curse that lay underneath all the safe houses when he was young. He half hoped Devon might offer the information, but his brother remained quiet.

"So?"

"The Society did not curse the cellar, but what they did to its previous owners meant the spirits stayed." Orion got the impression she already knew what sort of spirits he was referring to. Neems were always the haunted, angry souls of those murdered on magical grounds.

"And it's flooded?" she asked.

Orion placed his hands on her hips, guiding her toward the house. "There is a spell on the cellar that allows for safe passage by loyal members of the Society."

Devon watched them approach, his face pleading. "Which we're not. They will kill us before we can get out of here. I can't be much help with the way I feel now. We should head the other way."

Taking the steps two at a time, Orion barely spared his brother a side glance as he crossed the front porch. "You know they'll discover it was you who held the Vulcan, which means they'll expect us to go through the hills. The Corvus will travel in that direction, hoping to catch us along the way. You know that."

Nava followed closely after him, the soles of her boots squeaking against the polished marble tiles. "How many spirits are we talking about? Two? Four?"

"The records don't specify the number, but the rumor is ten."

She lost her step, barely catching her balance as she stumbled into the circular entrance hall. Somehow, the house felt icy cold, as if the ground itself could read their intent.

Devon grasped Orion's arm, hard enough to send a ripple of pain through him. "You two should go without me, Arkimedes. Nava can transfer out of here, and you can fly. This is my fault. You don't have to go through the spirits to leave."

Orion's jaw ached from clenching it so hard. He shrugged off Devon's hand. "I don't have time to discuss this ridiculous notion that I don't care about what happens to you. I won't abandon you here, even if you've made some questionable choices. If you want to help, then find some more of those potions because you're going to need them."

Devon's lips thinned, and he nodded before shuffling down the hall.

"What if Devon opens a portal?" Nava's voice broke the momentary silence. "We don't have to go through the cellar."

Time froze as the image of her burnt skin and all she had confessed to him rose in his mind's eye. "No. Not after last time. The Neems are dangerous but mindless."

"I know what to expect now, Ark. And I'll be fine."

"You know what to expect, and so does the emissary. We aren't taking any chances, Bee. If he's working with the Zorren, he wants you dead. We can't risk it."

14
ORION

"I can't believe we're doing this. It's suicide." Devon stood in front of the cellar door, a monstrosity of aged, rotting wood.

If only he would stop pacing, then Orion could focus on something other than the crunching of broken tiles beneath his brother's feet. "Are you going to tell us how to open it or just continue to complain endlessly?"

Out of the three of them, only Devon had studied the languages of the old world, which meant he was the only one who could break the lock. Orion was fast losing his patience with his brother's lack of cooperation.

Devon sent him a withering look and stepped closer to the script etched into the wood. The Crows had carved magical runes into the doorframe and woven them into a powerful ward that prevented the room from being opened from either side. Magic was probably the only thing that kept this door standing.

Beside him, Nava was rocking on her heels. Her skin remained pale as she kept a respectable distance from the door. "I rarely like to agree with Devon openly, but this is suicidal."

The spell's warning compelled everyone to run from the cellar. They had been standing there for an hour, attempting to figure out how to break in.

"I'm not sure if the Crows are truly more dangerous than a room full of angry spirits," Nava continued, tapping her index finger against her lips.

Orion sighed, nodding curtly. "I know this is far from ideal, but we have no idea how many Corvus the Society will send. What we do know is that they're aware of who triggered the alarm, which means they might send multiple teams. The Neems are predictable, at least."

A crinkle formed between Nava's brows as she studied their surroundings. "It makes me sick to my stomach to think about this place. Why would they trap people in there to die?"

"The Crows aren't known for acts of mercy, and Neems are an effective security measure to block off the secret entrance." He swallowed thickly as her lips parted in indignation. Whatever else he could say would only anger her further and get her to feel more empathy for the spirits they would soon face.

"Or from breaking in," Devon said.

"They are using dead people as watchdogs?" Nava's nostrils flared. "You stood behind this society, even after knowing they would do something like this?"

"They were all I knew..." What more could he say? Orion stilled, his heart racing as an ache spread all over his body like a sickness. "They committed this crime long before I joined them."

"You were a five-year-old boy when they took you." She blew away an errant strand of hair that had curled around her chin, and her expression softened. "I feel like they lost their best member they had the day you left them."

"Careful there." It was a challenge to hold her gaze. "You're feeding my ego. I might start to believe that I'm worthy of you."

"You're more than worthy."

"Not of you."

Her lips curved into a sad but genuine smile that reached her eyes. "I think you are..."

The more time he spent away from the castle and his father, the clearer it became how much of an idiot he'd been to push her away. He brought his hand to her face, his heart still beating too fast. He hated the dark rings under her eyes from the lack of sleep.

"How are you feeling about being away from Aristaeus?"

"Tired." She glanced warily at the door. "If you're worried about me fighting the Neems, you can stop. I can do this."

"I know you can handle yourself."

"Useless," Devon muttered, moving away from the door. His skin was shining with sweat as he brushed his ebony hair out of his face. "I can't get close enough to see all the symbols because of the spell, and my Tharent skills aren't good enough to make sense of it."

Tharent was the old language of the gods, not spoken widely for centuries. Orion's father seemed to know it, and a lot of the old books in the castle's library were written in it.

"Is there nothing you can glean from it?"

Devon huffed and returned to his task. "Maybe. *We reclaimed our truth and stole your lies."* Devon pointed a finger at another line of runes, not quite touching it but tracing their shapes. *"Your curious mind won't get you through. Only those seeking balance will escape unharmed, or else they will face the wrath of the dead."*

"Perhaps it's simple. It won't open it if you're just curious." Nava stepped closer to get a better look. "You're always talking about balance, Devon. Maybe it will open for you?"

"It would have opened for me before I touched the Vulcan the second time." Devon drew a labored breath and pulled a small vial from his pocket, emptying it into his mouth. The healing potion brought some color back to his face almost immediately.

"And that made you not care about your precious balance...?" She matched his flat tone.

"You've figured me out, Cat."

Orion suppressed a smile. At least their banter was somewhat entertaining in such a grim situation. "It's simple. The door prevents any trespasser from leaving who isn't loyal to the Crows, and that's not us."

What if they didn't need a counter-spell to open the cellar? The safe house *had* to be in the Copper Kingdom, didn't it?

A kingdom connected to Orion's magic.

He stepped forward. The closer he came to the cellar, the more the wards pushed him away. He called on his magic, gathering energy from every inch of the building. The walls shook and crackled, raining dust over them.

"Ark, what are you doing?" Nava's wide eyes darted toward the cracks that split the ceiling apart.

Orion took another step closer, so close that the spell burned his skin. He pressed his lips together and pushed harder, reaching for the iron handle of the door. His misty aura rose, the voices of his shadows loud as they growled, lending him pieces of their energy.

He felt like he was stepping into a shield of hot coals or the embers of a fire.

Nava rushed up behind him, and the considerable weight of her magic warmed his spine. He pushed into the ward, and the house groaned. The land knew what it needed to do for its prince, and the Crow's spell crumbled.

"You two are sickening," Devon grunted from behind them, but he joined them a moment later. The air crackled with the energy of his magic, further weakening the shielding spell.

The burning sensation against Orion's skin eased, and the spell cracked further, right before popping like a bubble. Dread crawled up the back of his skull, increasing tenfold now that the protection had vanished.

Multiple haunted moans seeped from the crevices of the door, raising the hairs on his arms. He quickly pushed Nava and Devon backward, and they retreated to the circular room in front of the archives.

With the spell gone, would the spirits pass through the walls?

Orion waited until the first white hand pushed the door ajar. Five long fingers wrapped around the edge of the frame, skin tight around bones.

He stepped in front of Nava, shielding her with his body. Another hand, attached to a decaying arm, crossed the threshold. Then another. Devon cursed loudly and broke into a fit of coughs.

"Get ready," Orion warned.

Nava lifted her hand, her skin shining, and the bees that crawled the walls took flight all at once. They surrounded them in a cocoon of buzzing bodies.

"We are too large for me to hide us completely, but if they don't see us, they won't attack," she said.

"Cover yourself, Nava. Don't waste your energy on us."

She scoffed and continued to hold the shield around them, her skin shimmering with a thin sheen of sweat.

The first spirit that burst from the door had once been a woman. Her long hair stuck to her white face, the rest of her continuously decomposing. She resembled a walking corpse more than a spirit. Devon's magic flowed from the tips of his fingers, sparking with energy—and she was gone.

Two more followed immediately. Dark blood dripped from their faces, their jaws clanking open and shut. Their ghastly dead cries froze the blood in Orion's veins.

They fought them down the funnel of the hall, dissipating them, only for three more to emerge hot on their heels. He took a deep breath to calm his erratic breathing and regretted it immediately when the pungent scent of rot mixed with the spice of magic.

A small ball of light floated next to Devon. Where had it come from? Orion opened his mouth to warn his brother just as a Neem materialized out of thin air. Nava gasped, and Orion's head jerked to the side as another spirit rose from the ground. Its teeth dug into his hand, cutting through layers of skin and flesh. Intense pain shot up his arm, and he fought to pull his hand away, the ripping sensation bringing tears to his eyes.

He hissed, and the shadows of his aura snapped at the spirit that still clung to his body, its nails scratching his neck as it tried to bite his face.

He needed to focus. With a blast of energy, he dissipated the spirits until none remained outside the cellar door.

Well. Almost none. Devon was screaming as a spirit dragged him down the corridor, its thin lips opening wide as a ball of energy glowed in its pitch-black, gaping mouth. Orion flew toward his brother, his wings tearing as they collided with the rock walls around him. He bit his tongue so hard blood coated it.

He barely managed to grab Devon's flailing hand before the spirit dragged him into the cave-like cellar. Digging his heels into the ground, Orion found purchase. His throbbing hand spilled blood down his wrist and onto Devon's pale skin.

A ray of black magic snapped from his aura, and the Neem puffed out of existence, leaving them both gasping for air.

"Ark!" Nava transferred to them. She, too, was breathless. "Are you all right?"

Her face was scratched and bloodied. Fuck, he hadn't even noticed that happening. He stepped closer and reached for her chin, lifting her face to his to better inspect it. He traced every freckle, the curve of her lips, the long line of her neck.

Nava forced a smile, but the gesture didn't fool anyone. Then she glanced down. "Your hand!"

"I'm fine," Orion said past gritted teeth and pulled his hand away before she could grab it. It hurt too much, and they couldn't linger here for much longer. They had already wasted too much time.

She cleared her throat, clearly not happy at this turn of events.

Devon stood, winded and bloodied, much like Orion. The number of spirits had far exceeded their expectations. "Someone failed with the records they kept about this place," his brother choked out and spat blood on the ground.

The family trapped in the cellar had been a large one. Perhaps even their servants had suffered the same fate alongside them.

It gave him pause. What if Nava's family had shared their destiny? Would the Society of Crows have converted Celeste's manor into a hidden safe house?

The thought of her loved ones being cursed to be Neems for eternity crushed his heart. He felt for these people—now they were liberated from their haunted forms.

"We need to go," he said. Gods, he hated how his voice broke. He let go of Nava. He wasn't good enough for her. Not in this life. Not in the next.

Carefully, they crept forward. Brown water pooled in front of the cracked door. No more spirits emerged, but the air still crackled with angry energy.

While the Neems appeared corporeal enough to push this door open, once dissipated, they vanished into nothingness. Their true bodies rested inside the cellar they were heading into.

It took Orion only a moment to rip off a strip from the bottom of his shirt, and with Nava's help, they wrapped it around his bleeding hand to stem the flow. Then he pushed the door open. The light from the candelabra outside trickled inside the dark cave, illuminating rotten wooden stairs and deep green water beneath. The back of his throat ached, and his tongue tasted bitter.

His legs felt heavy—both from exhaustion and from the horror of stepping into that water alongside the corpses of those poor people.

"Do you think there are any more Neems down there?" Nava's voice shook, as if she was contemplating the same thoughts.

Devon brushed the long strands of hair out of his face. "I'm going to guess not." His mouth was set in a hard line. "They would kill us. They have no need to hide, especially since we've disturbed their haunting grounds."

Well. Wasn't it their lucky day if they escaped with only a few bites and scratches?

Orion moved down the first creaking step. It bowed under his weight. The stone walls were slick with algae, and the smell of seawater and rot was overwhelming.

His aura swirled around his body in a protective shield, much like Nava's did. The whispers of his souls warned him to stay away. He tested the second step before committing to the next. On his third step, the wood underneath him creaked and snapped, and he stumbled forward with the weight of his body.

Orion fought to regain his balance as his heart lodged in his throat. Thankfully, he steadied himself before he could tumble all the way down. The remnants of the previous step fell into the dark water beneath him.

Nava stood by the doorframe, illuminating the room more than any magical candle could. "Are you all right?"

"Fine," he breathed, trying to calm his erratic breathing. He didn't want to step into the water and walk over bones, but he had little choice. "Don't come down yet. It's all rotten."

The stale, humid air stuck to the back of his throat, tasting like old magic. If only he could be far away from it.

Shuffling forward, Nava moved close behind him, although she didn't follow him into the cellar yet. Surprising, that she wouldn't challenge his request when she usually enjoyed it so much.

Still, Orion knew her well enough by now to comprehend that she was one word away from transferring inside this hell and fighting whoever might harm him, before he'd even had time to inspect the place.

"I could transfer there…" she offered.

Hah. "Not yet. It's not safe."

"Why is it that you are so keen to believe you're more disposable than me?"

He glanced at her over his shoulder. His wing shrouded most of her body. Dammit, they had no time to get into this discussion. Still...he'd been trying to mend the rupture between them. Best not to aggravate her further.

"If you aren't safe, my head's not in the right place, which could get me killed. I want to protect you more than anything."

She didn't say a word but narrowed her smart eyes at him.

Devon, who had been too quiet ever since the Neems had poured out of the cellar, poked his head through the doorframe. "Do you need one of these?" he asked, dipping one hand inside his pocket, pulling out a healing potion, and extending it to Orion.

Orion shook his head. The bite had gone numb a while ago. Perhaps it was the adrenaline, or maybe the Neem had torn a nerve. Either way, he wasn't feeling much.

They had discovered a large stack of potions in the infirmary, but worry prickled Orion's mind. His brother needed too many of them, too quickly. He was weakening too fast for them to keep up.

Devon shrugged and emptied the potion into his mouth without preamble. Then he stared down at the cellar, his brows dipping. "Can you see a way out of this hole? Or did we open this place for nothing? Because if the bells didn't call the Corvus, opening this cellar sure did."

Devon was right. If they continued to destroy the wards, the Corvus might choose to break all rules and portal here against the king's demands.

The dark water mirrored the cavernous ceiling. Orion steadied the weight of his body with one hand against the roof and crept down a few steps. His fae eyes could spot more than any regular human. He rarely needed light to see in the dark. And whatever he didn't see, the souls in his aura would pick up. But they were quiet now...too quiet. It left him uneasy.

"The safe house must be near the coast. This is seawater," he said, finding a steady drip from a corner of the room. The waterline appeared to be three feet high at most. Shallow enough to wade through.

The cellar was about the size of the bedroom he'd shared with Nava for the past few days. Shelves extended on either side of it. They must once have been thick wood but now lay rotten and broken in the murky depths of the water.

The spell the Crows had cast upon this place must have resembled a typhoon, tearing this room to pieces.

Nava had finally had enough and followed him down the stairs. "If there's a way out, is it going to be a portal like the fountain that will take us back into the Copper City?" The wood groaned beneath her feet, and Orion's heart jolted as he waited for the next step to break underneath her.

"Stay up there," he growled as she propped herself up against the poor excuse for a banister. At least it was still bolted to the wall. Barely.

"Calm down—it's not that big of a drop. Can you see a way out?"

Orion stepped into the frigid depths. His teeth chattered, the water sloshing as he inspected every single fallen shelf and anything else that might cover a hidden doorway.

His mind was yelling at him to get out of there. A sense of pressure seemed to emanate from everywhere, suffocating him the farther into the room he went. Nava followed him on light feet, with Devon trailing behind her.

Magic pushed against the power of Orion's aura. Heavy, ancient, and furious. A gust of wind howled through a crevice behind a tipped-over wine barrel right before him.

"I think I've found it," he said and rolled it away—only to reveal the angry Neem of a child.

It hurtled toward him with a biting gasp, and he barely got out of the way in time before its nails sliced his jacket and shirt. The eyes of what had once been a little girl glowed brilliant white.

She launched at him again, and he was too numb to move—too tired. Too sad. Devon's magic dissipated her right in front of Orion's eyes, leaving behind the black tunnel her family had likely tried to hide her in, right before the Crows had flooded this place and drowned them all in it.

15
NAVA

Cold water sloshed around Nava as they moved through a narrow, winding tunnel. If it weren't for the warm glow of her aura, they would be in absolute darkness. They had been walking for at least five miles in the smelly water, and her toes had long since gone numb inside her old boots.

After the last Neem had appeared, the crime the Crows had committed by trapping a child and leaving them to this kind of ending had overwhelmed them all. The three of them had been quiet ever since.

"We are here." Arkimedes's voice made her jump.

Nava watched his hand as he trailed his fingers across a muddy wall. They'd hit a dead end, and in her daze, she'd barely noticed. Everything was wet, and water clung to every surface, dripping off the jagged shapes of barnacles.

There was no door, no handle—no light leading them to believe this was the exit. Only the walls closing in on her.

"Is there a door?" She swallowed around the thick knot in her throat. Had that child tried to escape through here and found no way out?

Placing a hand across her chest, Nava gripped her neck. With her other hand, she reached past Arkimedes to shove at the wall. There was no nature here, only death and despair. She was itching to leave this place. "Can you see a way out?"

His glowing eyes flashed to her. "Are you feeling all right?"

"Seems I don't like tight spaces."

Arkimedes swallowed. Maybe her panic was filtering through to him. "I can feel what might be a stone door, but it's concealed in mud..." he dug out the grooves of a clear rectangular shape, but in the narrow space, only he could work on it while she was forced to stand behind him and watch.

He leaned against the wall with one shoulder, pushing against it with the force of his full weight. It creaked and gave way by a fraction, allowing a ray of light to peek through its rim.

Nava's heart fluttered with hope, just as Arkimedes slammed into the door. Mud splattered against his face on his third attempt, and finally, the slab of stone fell beneath the weight of his body and a spike of his magic.

He breathed raggedly as he wiped streaks of filth off his skin with the heel of his hand. Traces of blood mingled with the mud. They really needed better wraps and something to disinfect his wound.

"I'll go first. Let me inspect the area before you come out," he said and dragged his entire body out of the narrow door, which hovered several feet above the stagnant water.

The light streaming through the gap blinded her, and the air held a stale quality she couldn't place. Nava climbed up to the hole, not waiting for Arkimedes's signal. She wanted—no, *needed*—to be out of there.

She waited for the warmth of the sun to hit her skin. For nature to recharge her depleted energy. But something wasn't right with the light. It was strangely cool.

Arkimedes's arms coiled around her as she hoisted her body up and onto polished white marble floors. Her heart slammed against her ribcage as he helped her out, like she was made from paper. She collided with the planes of his chest, and his breath wafted over her cheek.

"I thought I asked you to wait there?" he whispered in a biting tone. His annoyance pulsed in waves through their bond.

"It's safe enough." She pushed against his chest, although she was too tired to put any force behind the movement. It was hard to even find the will to argue with him.

Everyone was on edge after fighting the Neems and then being forced to crawl through their remains to this—

"...is this a mausoleum?"

The room's imposing vaulted ceilings curved into a large white stone dome. Immense pillars and crossbeams created the visual effect of a ribcage holding up the roof. Sun spilled through the windows, though judging by the lingering scent, the building was sealed.

Five urns stood on top of marble pedestals. The withered flowers beside them had dropped their brown petals to the ground a long time ago.

The walls were covered in writing, and coffins dotted the room. Nava looked down at the slab of stone Arkimedes had pushed off for them to crawl out. It had aged into yellow and brown shades. Etched into it in black lettering were the words:

Here lies Rudolph Abercorn,
Beloved husband

What?

She blinked rapidly. Had the Society of Crows hidden the secret exit of the safe house behind a tomb in a mausoleum? How fitting.

Devon exited the tunnel, sliding over the ground, wet as a newborn fawn. "This has to be a joke…" he said with a dry laugh. His face distorted with fury as he attempted to clean off the mud that stuck to his black trousers.

Arkimedes spared Devon a glance, probably to make sure his brother wasn't actually dying. Then, cradling his wounded hand, he moved toward the locked metal gate at the front of the tomb. "They made this an iron gate, probably to keep the fae away. I'm sure it has allowed the Society's entrance to remain hidden for longer."

He squinted at the bars and reached across to the padlock hanging from a chain on the other side. His aura became so dark it was hard to see the shape of his body, and the metal groaned and snapped.

Nava tilted her head. How much did it hurt him to touch the metal? The Society of Crows had kept a lot of iron at the safe house, but Arkimedes hadn't complained.

"Being a hybrid means I can hold iron without being burned," he said, looking over his shoulder as if he was reading her mind.

Wait, had he read her mind? Their mental link wasn't as strong as it used to be, especially after he'd lost his memories.

The cemetery lay quiet and empty before them. Here, the open air was warmer, and the scent of decay from their clothes was less noticeable.

The castle was a hazy shape in the far distance, looming over a city of small homes and shops. From this hill, Nava could even see a turquoise canal of seawater cutting through the city.

It seemed so long ago since they had all visited town together, right before the solstice dance.

They walked down a cobblestone path with golden grasses growing on either side of it. Even this small amount of nature nearby helped to replenish some of her lost energy.

"Now what?" Devon asked, trailing a few steps behind them. "This is clearly the Copper City. I doubt the Crows will give up so easily, which means we'll have to deal with the royal guards and the Corvus coming after us."

Arkimedes grunted, scratching one of his brows. "Give me time to think."

A wet cough left Devon's lips. "Well, hurry. We're at the mercy of your father out here in the open." He reached for another potion with a shaking hand. "Don't you have any friends that can shelter us?"

"I'm afraid you ran them all away." Arkimedes stopped Devon's hand before he pulled the cork out of the small potion vial. "You've got to pace yourself with those, Devon. We don't have any more."

Even in broad daylight, Devon remained as pale as the Neems they'd encountered. Not even the continual potions were easing his symptoms.

If only Nava could remember how to brew the potions, then maybe they could keep him going until they found a healer willing to help them. The thought made her heart ache with longing. If only their friends were here. Gavin, who was such a wonderful healer and human being, would have fixed them up in no time.

She peered at her soulmate's wounded hand, and her stomach dropped. The temporary bandage he had wrapped around it back in the cellar had turned a brownish red.

Devon shook his head and opened the potion vial. "I used too much energy fighting the Neems. If you want me to walk anywhere, I have to take it."

"I'll get you a fresh potion later today," Arkimedes promised.

Nava turned away from the pair. Where could they go? To the bakery

—or into any of these abandoned buildings? They would be right back where they'd started.

The memory of a fae with bright red hair flashed through her mind.

That was it! Leela, the maid who'd helped Nava during her stay at the castle, lived in this part of town. They had grown close, and Leela had even helped Nava alter her horrid yellow dress before the solstice ball.

"What about Leela?" Arkimedes's unyielding gaze met hers, making her want to squirm as butterflies fluttered in her stomach. Sometimes she was still surprised by how she reacted to him. Nava cleared her throat and reached for his bandaged hand. "I'm sure she would let us stay for one night to get our bearings. But I don't know exactly where she lives..."

Arkimedes's brows knitted together, his posture stiffening as she examined his injury. Her skin warmed, her magic humming to the surface as it called to him.

Arkimedes let her take apart the bindings. Although his wound was still fresh, it had stopped bleeding. Nava didn't want to further risk infection by keeping that filthy cloth pressed against it.

"I think I know where she lives, Bee. And it's not too far from here."

Unlike the cemetery, the streets were busy with fae going about their daily lives, bustling about. Some were cleaning their front steps while others fixed up the flower boxes underneath their small, uneven windows.

All seemed unaware that their prince was strolling along the streets, alongside two traitors of the Crown.

This area of the city differed from everywhere else Nava had visited in the Copper Kingdom. It reminded her a lot of home—of Willowbrook—when she was growing up. The homes were built close enough to one another that they appeared to be a single unit. The houses weren't extravagant, like the ones near the castle, nor dilapidated, like the ones near the bakery. Made of richly textured bricks and plaster and painted in a range of colors, they held the type of beauty that only came with age.

"At least nobody seems to be paying us much attention..." she mumbled as they crossed a bridge over the biggest water canal she'd seen. The rattle of carriage wheels and the cries of the seagulls drowned out the squelching noise of their hasty steps.

Somehow, the sounds of the city soothed her frazzled nerves. Finally, no alarms ringing in the distance—nor any guards flying above them.

"I think you need spectacles, Cat." Devon scoffed, shaking his head as he indicated a group of fae on the other side of the bridge who were pointing at them with wrinkled noses. "Look at them. If you read their lips, our appearance disgusts them."

Nava's cheeks warmed, and she glanced down at her scratched arms and filthy clothes. She could barely stand the scent emanating from them but doubted anyone that far away could smell them.

"Should we ask for directions?" Nava looked around the area, trying to find a place that would lead her to Leela and away from city folk. The longer they were out in the open, the greater the risk of someone recognizing them. Besides, they all needed a bath, proper healing, and a place to rest. "There!" Her heart skipped a beat when she spotted an old wooden sign bolted to the stone bricks of a building.

The name of Leela's partner stood out against the white background of the sign in green letters.

"Renna's Creations?" Arkimedes followed her pointed finger, his brow furrowing.

"Yes, I remember Leela saying her name. She's a seamstress."

They weren't far from the house, and the closer they got, the more Nava's heart sped up. What would Leela do when she saw the prince outside her home? What if she shut the door in their faces and refused to help them?

"Let me be the one to knock—you're too intimidating." She dodged away from Ark's hand, ignoring his complaint.

Leela's door screeched open a second later, and she peered through the crack. "Miss Nava?" She gasped and stepped outside. "You can't be here!"

She reached for Nava's arm but froze when Arkimedes cleared his throat. "Leela."

"Your Highness!" she screeched and floundered into a low bow.

"There's no need for formalities out here. I don't want to call too much attention to us." Arkimedes's eyes darted about, worry etched onto his features. True to his words, several people on the other side of the street were glancing curiously at them.

"Please come in." Leela's freckles were prominent now that a blush covered her face. A deep crease appeared on her forehead as she looked up at the surrounding rooftops. "We don't know who might be watching."

Her friend hadn't been at the castle on the night the king had sent his guards to apprehend Nava and Devon. Did she know everything that had transpired?

She led them through the shop, past a small desk piled high with knickknacks and pincushions. The back of the room was bathed in darkness, although Nava could spot large rolls of fabric lined up against the far wall.

Guilt churned deep within her. It was a good life the fae had here. And it might change forever if the king found out the palace's maid had helped them.

Why had Nava brought her into this mess?

Devon's harsh cough stopped her spinning thoughts. He needed more rest than what they could have found in a dusty abandoned shop on the other side of the city. This was by far the safest option for tonight.

Leela gathered her red tresses on top of her head in a messy bun. "I was not expecting your company. Although they came some days ago to ask me if Miss Nava came to visit me."

Oh no.

"Who came?" Arkimedes asked, striding across the cramped shop floor. A couple of wooden benches sat next to a large window, which was hidden behind thick velvet curtains. "My father's guards?"

"His ladies. Sir." Leela hastily added the last word and pressed her body against the desk, allowing them enough room to stand without touching each other.

Nava's heart was suddenly racing. In the absolute silence that fell, all she could hear was Devon's ragged breaths and the sound of crackling embers coming from the fireplace.

"Are they here now?" he whispered, low enough that only they could hear.

"They left that same night," Leela said, and her blue eyes dipped to take in Arkimedes's wounded hand and Nava's scratched skin. She frowned. "Nora said Miss Nava put a spell on you, sir."

"I knew this was a terrible idea," Devon said. "We should leave now."

Ark raised his hand to silence him and stepped closer to Leela, his voice gentle when he spoke. "Do you believe them? Do you think I'm under a spell now?"

Leela flinched, her eyes widening as she stared at what Nava presumed were Arkimedes's shadows. "I know Miss Nava was wearing the royal jewels when she was in the castle, and so was Mr. Black. There is no way she could've put a spell on you to betray us."

"This fae is lying, and we walked into a trap," Devon snarled, already shuffling toward the front door. Yet Arkimedes stayed right beside Leela, observing her quick breaths and studying her closely.

Was her friend lying? Nava didn't know what to believe anymore.

"Leela is not lying," Ark said. "Fae can't lie openly, Devon. You know that." His gaze flashed to Nava, whose mouth fell open at his words.

A flare of heat rose from the pit of her stomach all the way to her face. Fae can't lie... what ridiculous claptrap.

"If they can't lie, then how did they come here and *lie* to her about what happened?"

She hated to agree with Devon, and it pained her to think Leela would betray her—but she'd rather be safe somewhere else. This was a stupid idea. She shouldn't have brought them here.

Leela backed away behind the desk, paling further at Devon's sharp question and the wet cough that followed it.

"Nora *believes* Nava put me under a spell, which is why she attacked me in my father's room. It's also why my father's guards attacked me on the island and forced me back here." The tension in Arkimedes's face eased, and he nodded as if the pieces were falling into place. "They were convinced I was under a spell there."

Leela gasped, and the truth behind his words clicked for Nava as well. If the royal guards genuinely believed the heir and savior of the land was under the spell of an evil witch, then they would do anything to remove him from her reach.

Herous, the guard who'd hurt her the very day she'd arrived in the Copper Kingdom, had called her a witch. It made sense now.

"They all believe Nava has me under a spell." Arkimedes met her eyes, his expression heavy with meaning. "But Leela isn't lying because a full-blooded fae can blatantly not do so. They can bend the truth or avoid it."

Leela bowed her head, although her wary eyes flashed to Devon. Perhaps she was unsure what to believe.

Admittedly, there was some truth to it. Nava did have Arkimedes under a spell: fate had carved it into their skin and sealed it with a soulmate mark. They were magically bound and destined to fall for each other. No matter how much they pushed against it, that old, unbending magic always won.

"I would never hurt our prince. I know Miss Nava cares for him, and I don't think she's evil." Leela's lips thinned. "I don't believe she's forcing him to do anything."

Devon dropped his hand from the doorknob and pressed his forehead to the wooden surface. Then he reached for another potion with a shaky grip. This had to be the reason Arkimedes was choosing to stay as well.

"What else did my father's concubines say?" Arkimedes asked.

"They told me Miss Nava and Mr. Black wanted to kidnap you from our kingdom, which will make the land suffer."

The irony of those harpies blaming her for something they had done to him. They had kidnapped Arkimedes and taken him against his will.

Nava reached for her friend's hand. It was damp and cold inside. "Leela, we aren't leaving the kingdom. We need shelter in your home tonight, so we can figure out how to defeat what's causing the forest fires."

In the distance, thunder rolled, shaking the windows behind the velvet curtains. The gentle patter of raindrops followed it shortly.

Leela blinked. "The fires?"

"What Nava said is true." Arkimedes's expression sharpened with resolve. "We will have to go to the castle to speak with my father—eventually. But tonight, we need a meal, a place to wash off, and somewhere to sleep. We won't burden you for long."

Leela nodded and gestured toward the wooden stairs at the very end of the room. They were narrow and uneven, with metal spindles that swirled organically, like ferns.

Leela's home was a far cry from the opulent elegance of the Society manor or the castle itself. This was a working-class house, built with uneven materials. Imperfectly beautiful.

"My home is not fit for you, sir, but you may stay for as long as you need."

16

NAVA

They gathered around a small table on the second floor in front of a large, slender window with latticed metal running across its glass. Outside, a storm raged, blurring their view of the now-empty streets.

Their silverware scraped over ceramic plates, and the salty taste of buttery potatoes lingered in Nava's mouth as she chewed slowly. She was so tired. All of her itched to remove her stiff and filthy clothes.

"Leela, is there a potion maker nearby?" Arkimedes asked.

Yes, Nava wanted to say. *I'm here.* But the weight of the thought alone nearly brought tears to her eyes.

Leela took in Arkimedes's injured hand and Devon's general appearance. Then she shuddered and studied Nava's face. "There is no magic on the west side of the canals, sir. The potions available to us are only those of herbs and alchemy. If you require a true healing potion, then you must go to the center of town—or better yet, the castle's infirmary."

Devon's brows met in the middle, although he didn't lift his eyes. He'd been shifting his food from one side of his plate to the other, barely taking a bite. "You don't have to go anywhere because of me. I'll be fine."

Arkimedes dropped his cutlery on the table. "We both know what's coming for you."

Death by poisoning? A week, Arkimedes had told Nava as they escaped the safe house. Devon had a week at most if he didn't get proper help.

Nava cleared her throat, reaching for the blackberry wine to wash away the bitter taste that clung to her tongue. "Arkimedes also needs a potion and fresh bandages."

The silence grew thick. How much could Leela deduce from their conversation and appearance? Probably enough to grasp how dire their situation was.

Leela poured some orange and cardamom tea into a cup and pushed it across the rustic table at Devon, still quietly observing. "I—I could go to the center of town tomorrow and try to source you some potions. I'm afraid I'm unable to obtain one from the castle, as I'm no longer allowed inside the main walls. I would draw the attention of the guards if I tried to enter."

"Later today—" Arkimedes started with a smile, just as a flash of lightning cut through the sky, followed shortly thereafter by thunder. "Or tomorrow morning. I will be in your debt."

"I will, sir." Leela's face turned bright red, her eyes shining as she nodded. "Mr. Black, may I warm you up some stew? I know when I'm feeling unwell, it makes me feel better."

Devon leaned forward, interlacing his fingers in front of his face. Then he closed his eyes and sighed. "The food is not the problem, Leela. I'm not hungry. I'm quite spent and would like to retire for the night." He caught his breath as his cheeks turned a sickly green. "Can you show me where I'm staying?"

"I…I don't have a lot of space. Downstairs in the shop, there is a small room that we use mostly for storage. Mr. Black can use that one if he prefers. And there is a bed in there." She gestured to the dark hall on the other side of the living area, past the mismatched chairs and the narrow couch. "I suppose Miss Nava and I can sleep in the smaller room up here—unless she wants to share the downstairs with her fiancé?"

Fiancé?

"Why yes, where do you want to sleep, my love?" For someone as sick as him, Devon looked far too delighted. "Downstairs would be rather cozy for the both of us."

Heat pulsed through Nava's veins, flooding her cheeks as she stared at Devon open-mouthed. Fiancé? Gah! This was what everyone in the castle still believed them to be—the lie he'd told the king when they first arrived at the castle together.

"Stop, Devon," Arkimedes warned and flattened his palms against the table. "Since you are giving us shelter tonight, Leela, I will grant you some of my trust in return. Don't break it."

"Never, sir."

"Nava is not my brother's fiancée. She is mine."

"She is your—your fiancée, sir?" After a long, rather uncomfortable silence, she continued. "Is that why you escaped?"

It wasn't judgment that lurked behind her words, but an emotion Nava couldn't quite place tainted the inflection of her speech.

There was a vulnerability in Arkimedes's expression that he seldom displayed in front of others.

"Do you remember when I arrived at the castle and you kept saying the prince acted differently around me? You thought there was something happening between us," Nava said.

"Yes," Leela whispered. "He'd never invited anyone to stay in the green room next to his own..."

"Don't say it," Devon hissed at her, but Nava felt the rightness of what she was about to do in her gut.

Leela wholeheartedly believed in love and in Arkimedes's role in this kingdom. If she believed their story, she would guard their whereabouts. Maybe they could stay here for longer and find Devon some help.

"Well, that's because we are soulmates."

"Pardon?" Leela leaned forward, her eyes going wide as her gaze darted from Arkimedes to Nava and back again, as if she was trying to discover the hidden lie.

Arkimedes tensed at the revelation, his jaw tight. "Nava is telling you the truth. A few months ago, Fael and the other guards came into our home on the island where I was living with Nava and kidnapped me."

Leela reached for the steaming cup of tea she'd just poured and brought it to her lips with trembling hands. "But... you didn't know Miss Nava when she arrived at the castle a month ago."

"You don't need to know all the specifics. It's better that way. For your own safety." Arkimedes's displeasure rolled through the bond in intense waves.

Perhaps she shouldn't have revealed their secret without consulting him first. But Leela's loyalties seemed to be tethered to the king, and Nava needed her on their side if they were to rest safely in her home.

A drop of sweat trailed down Nava's neck, and she took another gulp of wine, hoping the alcohol would lend her some courage. "Do you know what happens to soulmates when they're apart from each other?"

Leela paled. "You… you die?"

"Nava…" Arkimedes warned in her mind. His voice was a growl that should have stopped her instantly—but she needed to drive her point home.

She avoided his burning gaze and the flare of anger that swept through their bond. "And yet the guards took him, and they left me behind."

"But that would have killed our prince! He is our only hope to breathe life back into our kingdom." Leela shook her head, placing her mug on the table. "The king wouldn't have done that."

"He didn't know I'd found her." Arkimedes rose from his rickety chair and slammed his hand on the table. "And that's the end of this conversation." He walked around to where Devon sat. His massive body filled so much of the space, it made the living area feel small. "Tonight, Nava and I will take the room downstairs. I want to trust you, Leela, but now you understand I would do *anything* to keep Nava safe."

"I wouldn't dream of betraying you or jeopardizing our future queen's safety, sir. You can trust me." Leela's lips trembled into a smile, and she bowed her head in their direction. "I knew Miss Nava was special from the very moment I saw her. I should have been a soothsayer." She scrambled to her feet. "I will get the rooms ready for you all and run the baths." She picked up the empty dishes from the table and hurried across to the small kitchen. Then she disappeared down the hall toward the bedroom.

Devon cracked an eye open, looking warily at the ceiling. "I can't believe you told her—"

"Leela and Fael were close, and I'm guessing she's also friendly with his sister, Nora," Arkimedes whispered.

"Exactly. So why did Nava think it was a good idea to tell her?" Devon got up on wobbly feet. "A year ago, I would have used that knowledge against you. In fact, when I suspected it, my original plan was to use the portal and take her to the Iron City to force your hand to follow me there."

A knot formed in Nava's throat. And he could easily have been successful if Nava's bees hadn't come to her aid.

"Because every citizen knows of the royals' connection to the land," Nava explained, rubbing her tired eyes. The weight of this truth being out in the open was frightening for both of them. "Which means that, as Ark's soulmate, I'm just as important to the kingdom's prosperity as he is."

"How can you both trust this girl after all the betrayals you've been through?"

"Girl? She's older than us." Arkimedes scoffed. "And I choose to trust, because the day I stop believing there is good in this world will be the day I become the monster you thought I was back at the safe house."

Devon clenched his teeth and faced the window. Outside, the storm still raged, with high winds slamming loose debris against the building. "I still think we should leave for one of those abandoned buildings—save ourselves the trouble."

Arkimedes shook his head, although he appeared to consider it for the briefest of moments. "You won't make it that far in this state. And even if Leela wants to tell my father where we are, she won't do it tonight."

"Is that the reason you're staying in the downstairs room?" Devon asked. "To block her way out?"

"We all need to rest, so let's take tonight to do that. How many potions do you have left?"

"Six." Devon coughed into a linen napkin. He quickly shoved it inside his pocket, but not fast enough for Nava not to notice the traces of blood on the ivory fabric. He reached for another potion, and as soon as the liquid hit his tongue, his skin regained some of the color he'd lost. "Call it five..."

Somewhere between their escape from Grey Island and Devon helping her rescue Arkimedes from his father, he'd become someone that she cared about. Nava hated seeing him this ill, even if it was his own fault for being so irritating.

Devon shuffled toward the door, following Leela's path, only to pause at the entrance to the hall. Darkness bathed half of his body, throwing the sallow angles of his face into sharp relief. "I respect that you can trust people after everything. I couldn't do that now. I will never forget what the Society did to my family—or the little girl in the cellar. I don't need to heal. What I need is revenge."

Leela hadn't been lying when she'd told them the room was tiny and disused. Nava's eyes prickled with the dust gathering on the sewing equipment and broken mannequins in the corner. Gauzy curtains did a half-decent job of covering the small window, which overlooked a dark alley.

The bed, which was considerably smaller than the one she had shared with Arkimedes at the safe house, had fresh linens and a patchwork quilt draped over the top.

Leela strolled out of the washroom, drying her damp hands on the skirt of her cotton dress. She jumped, barely suppressing a scream as she spotted Nava in the narrow, arched entryway. "Miss! You almost scared me to death!"

"Sorry." Quite the opposite of her intentions. She'd come downstairs so she could chat with her friend without the pressure of Arkimedes being in the same room. "I know it must be difficult to welcome us here, especially after Fael's sister visited you."

Leela walked over to a set of drawers, which leaned crookedly against the wall, and pulled out a nightgown. "My home is not fit for royalty, Miss Nava." She gestured at the surrounding mess. "Even less so this room."

"Ark—Orion and I have camped in a Neem-infested forest before, Leela. This is perfectly fine."

"Perhaps so, but I hate to make you both uncomfortable." The rain poured outside, and it was hard to hear her whispered words. "I—I can't believe you're the prince's soulmate. I mean, it makes so much sense now, why he looked at you the way he did. Why he defended you against our own, again and again, even though you'd only just met."

"What we told you today might put us in danger. Orion and I trusted you with our secret because helping us also puts your life at risk. But it's not something others should know."

It was still so strange to call him by his given name, but now that she'd been in this kingdom for a while, she was getting used to the idea of him being a royal and his connection to the land.

"Of course..." Leela shifted from foot to foot. "I'm afraid for you. What if the guards come while you're here? I'm—I'm not sure whether Nora has been watching over my house and waiting for you to come. She stays in the castle most of the day with His Majesty, so perhaps if we are lucky, nobody saw you come in..."

It was something that worried Nava as well—but surely if someone had been lying in wait and spotted them, they would know by now.

And even if the guards attacked them here, they would not hurt Arkimedes. After what she'd told the king before she'd left through the portal, he probably wouldn't hurt her either. Not if he knew the queen's tree was alive because of her.

The Crows were another problem entirely...

Leela laid the clean, lacy garment over the bed, before turning to Nava. "Mr. Black—is he cursed?"

Nava nodded and strolled toward the washroom. It was tiny, with limewash walls and a candle flickering on top of a rustic table. A barrel tub took up most of the space, and it was steaming with water full of salts and oils that made everything smell wonderful.

She almost moaned at the mere sight of it. Her aching muscles demanded she strip off her clothes and get in immediately.

"I used lavender oils to soothe your sore muscles. It seems like you need it." Leela hadn't commented on how battered they all appeared after their fight with the spirits, but they smelled and looked like death. "I also brought you my favorite soap from a local seller. I hope you enjoy it."

"This is perfect, Leela." Nava pulled the shirt she'd borrowed from the Crows over her head. She was itching to get out of these clothes. "Do you have anything I could wear tomorrow?"

"I'm sure I can find something for all three of you in Renna's shop. I'm afraid my clothes won't quite fit you," Leela said.

It was true. She was lithe and tall, while Nava had wide round hips and narrow shoulders.

"Thank you, Leela." Nava tossed her filthy clothes aside, then groaned as she dipped her feet into the milky water. Leela quietly disappeared.

It was easy to push aside the burning from her scratched skin or the ache from the bruises marring her thighs and arms. They had escaped the

Crows. They'd released those spirits from that awful place they'd been forced to haunt. Tears burned her eyes, and for the first time since they'd left the safe house, Nava allowed herself to cry.

"Nava?" Arkimedes's voice filtered across from the room next door. He sounded worried. "Are you here?"

"In the bath," she called, wiping her face. The water was still warm, and the oils were already doing wonders for her aching muscles. The only thing missing was a nice glass of wine.

She froze as Arkimedes stepped into sight, suddenly looming by the doorframe. His green glowing eyes cut through the room's darkness. A strong, gut-wrenching feeling took her by surprise. It was hard not to draw parallels with that night on Grey Island when he'd been taken from her.

"You disappeared on me." Arkimedes leaned against the door.

"I wanted to talk to Leela without you intimidating her." She hated that her voice wobbled, giving away her distress. Of course, it was silly of her to even worry about that. He could feel what she felt and was likely here because of that fact.

"What's happening? Your emotions are running wild." He pressed one of his fingers to his stomach, where she knew he could feel their connection. The floorboards creaked with each step he took toward her.

"Everything is overwhelming me," she said. "Then I remembered the night they took you from our home on the island. It was raining like tonight, and we were bathing." She glared at the soap that rested on the wooden stool next to her. "The scent of this damn soap is exactly like the one we used back at home." She almost tossed it across the room. But it wasn't Leela's fault.

Never again would she send Arkimedes away to bring her wine so they could relax in the bath. The experience had haunted her for almost two months and had forever changed the trajectory of her life.

"Ah. I regained that memory right before I showed Fael what happens when someone betrays me." Arkimedes rolled the cuffs of his shirt up over his toned arms and knelt behind her, dipping his fingers beneath the water's surface to caress the side of her arm.

She craned her neck to meet his eyes as he reached for the oil.

"We aren't on Grey Island now, but we are together. You came and saved me, Nava."

Tears welled up in her eyes as her throat constricted. "We are hiding in Leela's house from two different enemies. I can't claim to have saved you."

Arkimedes slid his hands over her shoulders, kneading her tense muscles. "I have regained most of my memories, and I'm closer to understanding what happened to my family, thanks to you."

He skimmed his fingers over her breasts, then along her ribcage. A light caress underneath her breasts soon dipped lower, bringing an intense flutter to her core.

Nava turned her neck to search for his lips. They were exploring the line of her jaw and traveling down her neck. "Are you going to stay there or come into the water already?"

"Where is your patience, Bee?" His laughter washed over her damp skin.

She twisted against the smooth surface of the tub, wrapped her arms around his neck, and pressed her lips to his. Their kiss grew to a languid dance of lips and tongues. Arkimedes leaned over the tub's edge, his free hand trailing down her spine and wrapping around her waist, pulling her closer.

"You know very well that I lack patience with everything, especially when it comes to wanting you," she said against his lips. She'd hoped to sound sexy, but her squeaky tone gave away her nerves.

Even after all this time, he still turned her into an awkward, fumbling mess.

"Good." He oozed the confidence she lacked. The bastard.

Nava moved her hands greedily down his torso, tracing the hard lines of his muscles beneath the wet fabric of his shirt. With his help, she pulled it free and wrestled it over his head. His pants soon followed, and then she lay back as he stepped into the tub.

Nava embraced him the moment he sat. She needed to feel his body. To silence everything sinister they'd experienced today.

Arkimedes's eyes darkened as his wet fingers crawled up her spine and wrapped around her skull. She settled her body weight on top of his, her knees falling on either side of his hips.

"Now I get to have you without secrets and without the *lies*," she whispered.

His eyes sparkled with mischief, and he tucked a strand of wet hair behind her ear. "I won't hide the truth from you again… I confess, I've been wicked." He trapped her face with one hand.

He had been. On Grey Island, when she'd first found out that he was her soulmate, Arkimedes had claimed that he never lied. But he could hide the truth. He could keep secrets and avoid questions by answering with other questions.

"All right, then no more of that fae wickedness. Not unless you're using it for its another purpose…" Her words brought those crinkles to the corners of his eyes he got whenever he smiled. Gods, how she loved them—how she loved him.

"And what, precisely, is that purpose? What sort of things do you want me to use my wickedness for?" He squeezed the round flesh of her ass, and his erection slid over her sensitive nub, again and again, pushing the air from her lungs.

Her insides fluttered with desire, and her skin grew warm at the huskiness of his voice. She rolled her hips over his, craving more friction against her aching center.

But Arkimedes held her tight, leaving her unable to move. Then he nipped at her neck and licked up the column of her throat until he was breathing against her ear. "Tell me."

"Ark," she whimpered. She needed more contact, but her words seemed to scramble each time she tried to find them. "I want you to touch me everywhere," she managed eventually.

"And?"

"I want you to make love to me…"

The moment she spoke the words, he slid inside her, kissing her hungrily.

Nava moved on top of him and found a steady pace while hanging onto his shoulders. She rocked against his body, until the water was splashing from the tub and his moans mixed with hers.

Her skin glowed as her magic soared through her veins. She was full to the brim, and pleasure ran through her body, making her toes curl. Goose bumps rushed over her skin as Arkimedes feathered his lips over her clavicle and up her neck and chin. The tension built, spiraling within her until she was about to burst, hovering right there on the edge.

She toppled over, her insides tightening around him as ecstasy pulsed through her. Arkimedes kissed her through it, lifting his hips from the tub's bottom and slamming into her with growing desperation. His movements grew erratic as he chased his own release, then he grunted, digging his fingers into her hips as he pushed himself deeper inside her.

For a long moment, they clung to one another, their ragged breaths easing slowly. Nava allowed herself to drift on the water until she could lay her head over his heart.

Now that they were separate beings once more, she felt empty—craving to be close and intimate again. But her mind was stuck between heated thoughts of repeating what had just happened and the weight of worry distracting her from her state of bliss.

The Crows were on their tail. The king was probably tracking them, and the Zorren were still wreaking havoc, assisted by an undying bastard. It seemed like the trifecta of trouble was intent on their ruin.

While they'd been at the safe house, for however short a period of time, at least they'd had a plan. Even if that plan was to find a solution. But now…

"What are we going to do, Ark?" Nava lifted her chin off his chest, studying the gentle flutter of his lashes as he closed his eyes.

He let his head fall against the edge of the tub, revealing the thick column of his neck as he swallowed. His hand drew lazy circles over the skin of her hip, and for a while, she thought he wouldn't answer.

"Be more specific," he said.

"Devon is poisoned and seems more ill with each passing hour. Then we have the issue with the emissary and the Zorren…"

"I don't want to talk about this right now." Arkimedes kept up his gentle caress.

Guilt swirled in her stomach, and she pressed her cheek against his chest, closing her eyes. If only she could push all her worries away. "Sorry. I just feel like we need to keep one step ahead of whatever is coming for us."

"We rarely get a moment of privacy where I can have you to myself, in peace." He sighed. "Right now, I want to trap you in this room where we don't have to worry about anything at all."

"Forget I brought anything up."

"Too late." He huffed a laugh and shifted, forcing her to sit up as well. The water had cooled down since she'd climbed into the tub, and unlike other washrooms, this one didn't have a stove to maintain the water temperature. "I've witnessed just one other person poisoned by the Vulcan, and the symptoms weren't as severe as Devon's."

"Why do you think it's different this time?"

"I don't know, Bee," he admitted and rubbed a hand over his face. "But whatever he asked hurt him badly. Or maybe he didn't let go of it in time."

"So tomorrow Leela will get us more healing potions. But do we need to find a healer?" She frowned. It didn't seem advisable if they wanted to remain hidden. "If only I could remember how to make a potion, I could sort this myself."

"You can relearn how to once things have settled."

She met his gaze, and hope blossomed. Perhaps she had given up on her old knowledge too fast. Why let the horrors of her circumstances defeat her? Why allow the God of Shadows to win when she could relearn what he'd taken from her? Sure, it wouldn't be her father's teachings, but she could regain that part of herself. In time.

Water dripped off Arkimedes's body as he stood and climbed from the tub, reaching for one of the fluffy towels Leela had set out for them on a wooden stool off to the side. Then he stilled, as if something had spooked him.

"Ark?"

"What if Aristaeus knows how to kill an immortal?" He turned to Nava, his eyes widening. "He's a creature of the gods. We lost access to the Vulcan and the archives, but we have a Beekeeper, and we can ask him things we don't know."

Her heart sped up as she thought it through. Unbelievable, that the answer might have been hiding in plain sight for so long. "Wouldn't he have told us about it the last time we fought the Zorren?"

"Not necessarily. Not if he hasn't seen the emissary." Arkimedes wrapped a towel around her body as soon as Nava emerged from the lukewarm water. "If the man in the shadows is opening the portals from inside the shadow world and allowing the Zorren into ours, then there is a possibility Aristaeus has never seen him."

He snaked both arms around her hips and lifted her with far too much ease, given her size. Then he walked her back to the bedroom, leaving a trail of wet tracks on the wooden floor.

"I guess that's possible. He has never mentioned who might be opening the portals." Nava steadied herself on his shoulders. Her heart was racing for an entirely different reason than the subject of their conversation.

Arkimedes's legs hit the side of the bed, and he lowered her until her nose was touching his. Her heart hammered in her throat as all her senses focused on her soulmate. What had they been talking about? Who even cared?

"Enough talking now," Arkimedes said and kissed her, before he dropped her into the bed.

17
ORION

Orion breathed a sigh of relief as the cool fall morning air hit his face the moment he cracked the window open. He studied the sky, still a deep shade of gray from the evening storm, and found nothing suspicious. No Crows appeared to be lurking on the streets, nor could he spot any Dark Ones flying above.

He shrugged off the long black coat Leela had brought him earlier and tossed it over a dining chair. Then he rolled up his sleeves while listening to Nava's gentle steps padding up the stairs to the second floor.

It was odd to sense someone without having to see them, but the more time they spent together, the stronger this bond they shared grew.

Nava walked into the living area, running her hands over the folds of an overly full, puffed-up skirt. "Leela's out of control with these clothes," she complained, frowning at the stairs. "Do something about it."

Orion grinned and headed over to her. "I thought you said I was *not* to scare your friend."

He reached for her waist and pulled her toward him to claim her lips. The gentle kiss lasted a few seconds at most—far too short for his liking.

"That was yesterday, before she turned me into her doll," Nava said and withdrew. She draped her arms over his shoulders. "I can't breathe in this." She pointed at her midsection, where a hidden corset cinched her waist behind the layers of silk and lace.

"I think she doesn't want her future queen to go out on the streets in anything but the best that she can offer." Orion fixed the suffocating collar of his stiff shirt. It was too warm in this place. "Even if it's ridiculous to wear it inside the house."

Nava pressed her lips together, clearly holding back whatever she was about to say. At a guess, it probably had to do with the notion of the royal title—and becoming his queen.

She changed the subject. "How is Devon this morning?"

"He was asleep when I checked on him earlier," Orion said. One day, they would get a reprieve from having to worry about their lives and Devon's. A moment to enjoy their togetherness without having to run.

But that day wasn't today. Not when the bees had been crawling over the ceiling of their bedroom this morning and were swarming all over Nava's dark dress right now. Had she even noticed? Or had she grown so used to them by now that it didn't seem odd anymore to be covered in insects?

"Has Leela left to get the potions?"

"Yes, when you were changing," he said.

He was just turning toward Devon's room when a sudden hissing sound called to him. It was an indistinct noise, so faint that Nava probably couldn't even hear it. Still, a chill instantly crawled under the layers of his clothes.

"You feel it too," Nava whispered.

Arkimedes nodded and crept along the corridor that led to Devon's room. The weight of a stone sat in his gut. There was no one else here—yet something was off.

"Devon?" Orion called. The hinges screeched as he pushed the door open, slowly revealing Devon's unmoving body on the rumpled bed. His chest was rising and falling with labored breaths, and his closed eyelids flickered as if he was stuck in a dream…or a nightmare.

Probably the latter.

"Is he…?"

"He's alive but not doing well." Orion knelt next to the bed and placed his palm over his brother's forehead. "He's burning up." He reached for the potions Devon had carefully lined up on the wooden nightstand. "We might need to take him to the healer in the center of town. I was being an overly optimistic fool last night."

Saving his brother was his priority. If he had to fight the guards to get him help, so be it. He brought the small vial to his eye. Were the potions spoiled? Too old, maybe? That would explain why they weren't working.

"I can fly him there, and you can wait for me here," he began.

"No." Devon grasped Arkimedes's arm with an impressive amount of strength for someone that ill. His eyes cracked open, and he stared unblinking at the ceiling. "It won't be my fault if you get caught..."

"You're dying, Devon." Orion pushed the words past the thick knot in his throat, resting a hand on his brother's burning skin. "The potions are doing very little. You need a healer."

"I don't. Want. It." Devon's chest rattled like a viper preparing to strike, and he shifted on the pillowy mattress. He looked so small for a six-foot man who was usually vibrating with life. "You've got to protect Nava. Not me."

"If only it were that simple to watch a person you care for die. Especially when you can do something about it."

"We must take him to the healer," one of his shadows insisted, becoming hard to ignore. *"We need his help to defeat the emissary."*

Devon's pale lips cracked and bled when he smiled, although the feeling didn't reach his eyes. Instead, he looked like a madman. "And what happens when the guards take you down? When the king wipes your memories again and you forget her and the emissary who is hunting the Beekeepers?"

Orion blinked away the images of that very thing happening. Perhaps his father wouldn't wipe his memories this time?

"I deserve this." Devon whispered. "I held the Crows in such esteem, yet they took everything from me."

Everything? Did he mean his family?

Orion remembered the day the Society brought Devon to its headquarters. Devon had been younger than him, and his body had been badly burned. He'd spent a month in the healer's quarters.

Devon shook his head, and blood pooled on the corner of his lips. "They told me my family dropped me on the Society's doorstep because they gambled their money away and couldn't pay for a proper healer to save me. I waited for months for them to return for me."

Nava covered her mouth with her hand and stepped forward from where she'd been hovering by the door. "They killed them?"

"I promise you, I asked the mirror about the emissary. But instead, it showed me what I *really* wanted to know. I didn't think it would take my wishes as a command, but it spoon-fed me my past like I was a starving man. I suppose in a way I always have been."

"Did they kill them because of your magic?" Orion asked. Devon's silence was answer enough.

"I'm sorry," Devon said to no one in particular, twisting to face Nava. "For the way I treated you in the past. For how I hunted you down like you were nothing but an animal. You were right all along."

Orion didn't know what he wanted more: to strangle his brother for reminding him of what he'd done, or to ask him to shut up and get him some help.

He handed Devon two new vials of the healing potion instead. Hopefully, Leela would be back soon with more.

Nava's lips trembled as she stopped beside the bed. "On the island, I healed Aristaeus and Arkimedes with an alchemist potion I brewed in Willowbrook. There was this warmth that came through me when I pressed my hand to your wound, Ark, and it helped you heal faster."

"You want to do the same with Devon?" he asked. Without warning, a tingling sensation clawed at his head. A sudden burst of images flashed through his mind, robbing him of his breath.

Orion leaned against the bed frame as the memories of the night Mortimer had betrayed him on Grey Island slotted into place, followed by a sense of foreboding. He relived it all in a strange time-lapse: Mort, one of the few friends he had—selling him to Devon by giving him spiked wine that made him pass out. How he'd stabbed Arkimedes in the side, so he couldn't escape.

Nava's face twisted with worry. "Is something wrong?"

He didn't want to worry her further. Trying to keep his face devoid of emotion, he handed Devon the potion with a forced smile. "No, I'm fine. It wouldn't hurt to use your magic…"

She leaned forward as the contents of the measly potion disappeared behind Devon's lips. Then she pressed her palms against Devon's chest and closed her eyes.

"This tastes like shit," Devon mumbled.

It didn't take long for Nava's palms to shine with white light—so different from the way her magic usually appeared. Perhaps some hope remained.

They stayed with Devon until his skin had gained some color, and his fever broke. When they returned to the living area, Leela had just arrived from her errand to the potion maker's shop and was fixing up some lunch on her small kitchen counter.

"Is Mr. Black all right?" she asked.

"He is doing a little better now," he said. "Did you encounter any issues while out?"

The fae's eyes crinkled with worry, and she glanced at the table. Orion turned just as Nava gasped, panic bursting through their bond.

"Ark..." She was holding a piece of parchment in one hand. The closer he came to his mate, the faster the dread pooled in his stomach.

It was a page of the *Russet Gazette,* the city's local newspaper. An illustration of a tree he knew by heart was etched onto the paper in forest-green ink. Above it, in printed letters, it read:

The queen has arrived in the Copper Kingdom.

"Leela, where did you get this?"

"The flyers were everywhere." Leela's face darkened. "They were on every lamppost, on all the shop windows. People were reading the *Gazette* and talking about it in the street..."

"Do you know if the king has announced anything?" Orion asked.

"No, sir." Leela shook her head and continued stirring her stew. "I asked the potion maker when the news came out, and he said they delivered it this morning before sunrise. I thought you might want to know, so I ripped the paper off a lamppost on my way home."

His palms dampened with perspiration, and he reached out for Nava. Did the king know the news had made its way past the castle grounds? Who could've leaked such information? Surely this wasn't his father's doing.

"Ark." Nava's small hand gripped his arm, but when he looked down, her lips shook as she pressed her palms to her dress, where her insects crawled all over.

So many more bees than this morning.

Orion frowned and stepped close enough that their bodies were almost touching. "Nava, what's happening to the bees?"

She lifted her hand, a pained expression on her face. A small bee was stinging her.

"I don't know," Nava whispered and then met his eyes with a wild expression. "It must be Ari. He needs us."

18
NAVA

It smelled faintly like a campfire out in the streets. On any other day, Nava would have thought it was the pleasant scent of firewood escaping through a chimney, but not today. Today it reminded her of destruction. Of death. The closer they got to the forest, the more nauseous she felt.

Of course, being this high up probably also contributed to the sick feeling in her stomach. They had left Leela's place a while ago, and now a mass of sepia tones blurred so far beneath them that she could barely distinguish a street from a building. If it weren't so dangerous for her to transfer to the forest on her own, she would have done it in a heartbeat. She'd prefer that over flying any day.

Her stomach was tied into knots as she snaked her arms around Arkimedes's shoulders, digging her fingers into the back of his neck to find purchase.

"You're going to choke me if you keep doing that." He glared at her, rolling his neck so she released him. "For the last time, Nava, I will not drop you."

"Sorry," she blurted, her cheeks warming as she moved her hands to his shoulders instead. "It's hard to hold on with the wings, and I don't want to rip any feathers and hurt you..."

He scoffed, tightening his grip around her and underneath her legs. "We're almost there."

They cut through the stormy gray sky. Thankfully, it wasn't raining as heavily anymore. Still, the icy drizzle remained, soaking her clothes and leaving her shivering. At least while it was so wet out here, the forest fire couldn't progress.

Arkimedes had taken the long way around the castle instead of flying over it to avoid any accidental encounters with the guards.

"It's been weeks since the demons came. I wonder if it takes the emissary this long to open a new portal or if there was something else holding him back?" If he needed time to regenerate his energy, that could be their saving grace.

"If a god owns his soul, then I'm sure he has other tasks that keep him from burning this world to the ground." Arkimedes's jaw tightened, and he brought Nava even closer to his body in a protective embrace. "Or from hunting you and Aristaeus."

Leela's home was a fair distance from the castle and even farther from the forest, so it took them a good hour to reach the trees. Arkimedes's aura helped him carry her all the way without stopping to rest.

Finally, he began his descent toward the immense block of greenery beneath them. The air whipped around them as gravity pulled them to the ground. The taste of smoke covered her tongue, although there wasn't a sign of flames to be seen.

"Fuck." Arkimedes opened his wings to glide over the treetops, his arms shaking with strain. "The air is changing. Hold on tight, Bee."

This time, he didn't complain when her arms wound around his neck like ropes. They were flying close enough to the canopy now that the leaves swatted at her dangling feet.

"The fires are over there." Nava pointed at the thick column of smoke that swirled angrily through the air, cutting the blue sky apart and casting a haze across the forest in the distance. "Ari has to be near the fire and the portal. That's where we need to go."

"I'm not flying you into the middle of a forest fire caused by your mortal enemies. We're landing in an unknown situation that could get us killed."

Nava thrived at solving problems as the situation arose, but perhaps this time she should put aside the need to find Ari immediately, for her soulmate's sake. Arkimedes was making sense, and if she expected him to listen to her, then she needed to do the same.

His wings beat steadily as he lowered them into the depths of the forest. Dry brush and leaves crunched under her feet as he set her down. Even this far away from the fires, smoke wafted over the ground.

The cries of nature resounded around her. The rumble beneath her feet as animals scurried through the darkness, invisible to their eyes but deafening to her senses.

"Let's find Aristaeus," Arkimedes said. Much like Nava, he didn't have a weapon to wield against the demons—and possibly the emissary.

All they had was their combined magic, and it had to be enough.

She closed her eyes and thought of Ari. His black eyes. The long trunks that formed his legs, permanently covered in moss and mushrooms. A gentle pull answered her, and Nava began walking—no, running—in its direction. Aristaeus was coming to her, and she needed to meet him.

She glanced at Arkimedes as her body shifted form. Her legs turned into swirling dust, her arms disappearing from view. "You can follow the pull of our bond. Find me there."

"Nava," Arkimedes called, wide-eyed, but he didn't stop her. "Be careful."

No mortal weapon could truly hurt an emissary of the gods. And with the demons he was letting in, the three of them might be the only thing that stood between this kingdom and certain destruction.

Nava flew through particles of ash, picking up speed as Aristaeus drew her to him like a magnet. She moved so fast her surroundings blurred into nothingness, until all that remained was the beacon calling to her. She could sense Ari, too: enveloped in a mixture of forest debris and blown across the place by a cyclone of ancient magic.

They collided in a cloud that momentarily pushed away the particles of ash raining down from above. And for a fraction of time, in the warmth of Aristaeus's embrace, Nava felt peace.

"Dearest one, you're back," he whispered inside her head. Oh, how she'd missed him. Then a burst of images flashed through her mind. A black portal opening in the middle of the forest. The Zorren passing through it, crossing the barriers between their land and this world.

Nava changed from air to flesh and bones, blinking away the daze left behind by the memories Ari had shared.

Ari popped into his own true form with the screeching noises of expanding wood. *"I feared the Dark Ones had imprisoned you, for I could sense you were alive, but I couldn't reach you anywhere."*

Guilt bubbled inside of her. Of course Ari wouldn't be able to locate her while she was in a strange safe house, guarded by spells and Neems. "I'm sorry. We had to escape the castle when my dress—" Oh, she didn't have time to go over the details. Not when a fire hissed so close to them, ravaging the forest. If only she could take her time to reconnect with him after this period of separation. "Are the demons nearby?"

Ari tilted his head toward the wall of smoke to her right. *"If you close your eyes and listen to the forest, it will tell you where they are."*

Nava clicked her tongue. Why couldn't Aristaeus give her a straight answer for once, instead of trying to teach her a lesson? They were already on borrowed time.

"I took care of the only Zorren who made it through the portal," he said, evidently sensing her frustration. *"Where is our protector? I sense him."*

"I came to find you first," she answered. The smoke burned her throat, and their bees flew around them in a shield of brown bodies, spilling from the hive on Aristaeus's head. The warning rang clear through their buzzing as a ragged line of flames pushed past the haze, crackling and reaching out toward them.

Behind the red glow of fire, black demons cast wide shadows over the area, watching, waiting—approaching with abrupt, broken movements across the land they hungered to destroy.

"Ari, I thought you said there weren't any demons," Nava gasped, jumping back with her heart suddenly in her throat. The imminent danger sharpened her senses.

"I closed the portal." Ari's voice lacked his usual calm. *"Another must have just opened."*

They looked at each other. They couldn't leave because this threat was coming for *them*.

"Listen to the forest, dearest, and follow its calling to the portal."

The changing wind blasted the fire through the underbrush. The dry bark on centuries-old trees caught on fire just as Aristaeus changed into his airy form and drifted away.

Nava closed her eyes, and the pained screams of the trees rang inside her ears. Tears sprang to her eyes at the sound of such devastation.

She needed to focus on her mission, on finding the portal. Like the air ruffling the leaves, she sifted through words in languages she shouldn't understand but did regardless. At long last, there was a clear call, beckoning her in. *There.*

She changed shape and followed their screams. Now that she was no longer in her human form, the smoke and flames didn't hurt her as she crossed the inferno toward the hum of the new portal.

Ari was already there, looming large like a magnificent tree. One of the four demons slipped straight through the fire. Its skull looked so similar to that of a human that Nava's hair stood on end. If it weren't for the small mandibles around the mouth that snapped in Ari's direction, she would have thought it was a monstrous human spirit.

Their shapes were all different. Some looked like a wasp and a human combined. Others had bones for horns, as if an elk had been stuck onto a human skull. They wore armor made of black metal—or dark stone, perhaps.

When they screeched, the entire forest fell silent. Nava swallowed the bile that rose in her throat, attempting to settle her nerves. The Zorren hadn't seen her yet, but they were attacking Aristaeus all at once.

Nava screamed and dashed toward them. Half of her body was still air, the other half human. She called on nature as she'd done many times before, and the earth beneath her rumbled, right before massive roots shot from thc ground, slamming into a demon and preventing it from hurting Ari.

It battled with the ropes of tree roots as branches dropped from above and pinned it to the ground. But the wooden prison wouldn't hold the demon for long. She needed to use her power to subdue it, like she'd seen Ari do before.

She rushed to the fallen Zorren and jumped on top of it, ignoring the blisters that formed on her palms as she clawed at its neck. Her stubby human nails grew into magical claws. It hurt like hell, but she persevered, digging them into its head, avoiding its sharp teeth.

The screams of the forest grew louder inside her ears, feeding her anger and lending her strength.

She dug into the creature's slimy throat until she met the gristle of muscle and bone. Her magic burned hotter, and the scream of the Zorren drowned out the cries of the trees.

Her magic flowed through her fingers, swirling over the demon's body like wooden vines. They charred but didn't break when they wrapped around its burning skin.

It bucked under her, nearly throwing her off despite her iron grip. Her aura glowed yellow, and she ignored the intense pain shooting up her hands and arms. Instead, she tightened her magical claws around its throat until she heard bone break and the demon slumped within her grasp.

Nava transferred away just as the forest rumbled beneath her in a furious call. It demanded to be fed by its enemy, and the dirt underneath the demon cracked open into a giant hole that swallowed the Zorren's body whole.

Fire rained down on them as Nava moved across the battleground toward Ari. Everything hurt, even in her non-corporeal shape. But Ari couldn't fight the remaining demons on his own and close the portal. There would be time to lick her wounds later.

All of a sudden, a claw reached out from the shadows of the forest, hidden by the thick smoke, and sank into her. Nails that shouldn't be able to grab at her when she was just air dragged her down by her ribs, ripping through layers of clothing, skin, and muscle.

The wound burned deep, and her body flickered into its solid form as the demon threw her forward into a pile of brush. Sharp sticks, fallen branches, and small sharp rocks dug into Nava's crumpling body as she screamed in agony.

The Zorren's claws had been knife tips, curling under her ribs and tearing her flesh. The demon snapped its mandibles in her direction, walking to her with an unnatural gait that made her blood run cold.

So much pain flooded her body in waves that she could no longer move her limbs. Her body became a dead weight on the ground. It was too hot here. Too suffocating.

She gasped for air. Her fingers and legs had gone numb. All she could see was the trees around her, moving in unison and swinging their long branches at the demon that was coming for her.

A rough, guttural scream echoed through the burning woods. The Zorren growled and surged forward, its claws glowing with fire as it moved to strike her down. The leaves in the canopy shifted above her just before her vision blurred and darkness welcomed her in its soundless embrace.

19
ORION

Orion followed the pull of their bond toward the fire, gliding over the treetops and across the column of smoke that stung his eyes. He couldn't just land in there, not when he had so little visibility and it could cost him his life.

Instead, he flew a league away from the main source of the fire. Twigs snapped under his feet as he landed as gracefully as he could, folding his wings between enormous trees. Then he ran like hell through the deep wall of smoke that burned his lungs like acid.

He pulled out the handkerchief Leela had stuffed in his pocket that morning and tied it behind his head, covering his nose and mouth. It was woven from raw silk, the weave so fine it would help filter the air.

An icy wind blew around him despite the fire, raising the hairs on the nape of his neck. A crackling energy that felt and smelled familiar, like his magic coming to life. Perhaps it was the filthy stench from the demons or the weird scent that usually emanated from the portals.

It didn't matter. He didn't have time to linger. Through the bond, he could feel that Nava was nervous—she was probably getting closer to the fire as well.

"A Dark One is hiding nearby," a soul in his aura whispered, pulling him back to the present with a sharp spike of adrenaline. *"It thinks we can't see it—him."*

Fear stripped what little remained of Orion's sanity as he followed the pull of his shadows, trying to find whatever it was referring to.

A Dark One? Could it be one of the king's guards had found him? He was closer to the castle than he would have liked, and they might well still be on the lookout for him and Nava. The tree where his mother died wasn't too far away, either.

The smoke hovering near a tree shifted ever so slightly, as if a large body had vanished from the shadows of two knotted tree trunks, leaving a gaping hole in the middle.

Orion's throat went dry as he discovered a trail of ebony mist crawling across the forest floor like tiny claws. To an untrained eye, it was almost imperceptible in the surrounding haze. But Orion was familiar with this form of disguise, only used by his kind. His father's guards had kidnapped him by shielding themselves in the same manner on Grey Island.

Whoever this fool was, he wasn't even twelve feet away from Orion.

He propelled himself forward using the element of surprise and the power of his wings. The souls of his aura helped him, preventing him from nearly hitting a nearby tree. His energy left him drunk on power, and he stopped feeling the paralyzing fear, funneling his magic into anger instead.

Why would a guard try to attack him now? What if the fire had been a setup all along? Somehow, something was telling Orion that this was a dangerous opponent, intent on harming him.

He struck the perfectly hidden shadow hard. All of his magic collected into his fist as it connected with a gooey substance that burned his hand.

"Poison!" a soul shouted in his ear, so loud it mimicked his inner thoughts at the burning sensation spreading across his arm. He wanted to yank it back, but he had to weaken the Dark One further.

Inside the dark void of the tree trunk, he grasped at the slippery shape of a neck and heard a distinct gurgling noise. He closed his grip around it and threw the figure across the clearing before the venom could cause him true harm.

A shadow without a true shape collided against a tree that exploded into fragments of pulp, bark, and coal.

Orion heaved, nauseated by the use of his power and the poison of whatever had been in that hole, waiting to strike him. He'd thought it was a royal guard, but he wasn't so sure anymore.

A black figure rose from the dead ground, almost seven feet tall, with disheveled wings that lacked the splendor of full feathers. His face peered through a crack in his black helmet, revealing skin as pale as flawless alabaster and bright red eyes. Orion went numb as the realization hit.

This wasn't a normal Dark One. This was the emissary of the Shadow God. Fuck, the bastard did look exactly like Orion.

He was everything Orion had expected, yet different. Taller by at least five inches. Slimmer, too. With long, pointed ears that peeked from his silver hair.

A full fae—not a halfling like himself. This couldn't be his twin, even though their faces were nearly identical. No wonder Nava had been a trembling mess when she'd exited that portal.

The emissary swiped his purplish tongue over his bloodied lips and reached for the hilt of a sword that protruded from a belt around his waist. The handle was shaped from polished onyx, catching the pale gray light of the darkening sky.

"I wasn't expecting you…" he croaked as he took in Orion's fighting stance with wide eyes. The metal of his long sword hissed as it slid from a scabbard made of smoke. "But I'm glad you saved me the trouble of finding you later, *princeling*."

That last word was spat out with such hate it gave Orion pause. Why would this emissary be looking for him? So far, he'd only targeted the Beekeepers.

Did he know Orion was Nava's soulmate?

Vines were wrapped around one of the emissary's arms, contrasting with the ebony of his armor. The wood appeared to be slowing down his movements.

"Why are you trying to hurt the Beekeepers?" Sweat beaded on Orion's brow as he sidestepped the emissary. He needed the freedom to escape if necessary.

The ground trembled under his feet. A call from the Beekeepers, a trace of fear, surged through their bond. Was Nava hurt? Had she found Aristaeus before the Zorren? Were they fighting now?

The emissary advanced with the confidence of someone who couldn't die. His aura swirled around him, black like Orion's, although it lacked the spirits. Which meant he didn't possess the power to take souls.

"The Beekeepers have done nothing to me. I've naught against them—but I'll do anything to get my revenge on you."

What revenge? "I haven't done a thing to you."

"Your existence is a reminder of what he did." The emissary's eyes narrowed on Orion, shining with hate. "And you look just like him, which makes it easier to get rid of you."

"You're mad."

"You will be dead before the day is over, and your bloodline will be gone soon. Then, and only then, will I be free." He swung his sword at Orion, and it rippled through space, a force of nature that bent the air.

Orion's power pushed him back, although he barely dodged the deadly waves that disintegrated the tree beside him. The sword held a devastating kind of magic he'd never seen before, much less on a weapon.

"If you're trying to kill me because I look like my father, remember, I look like you, too." Orion took a shaky breath. His power was burning hot, demanding he take a soul, even though this immortal fool had none to be taken. "And if you kill the Beekeepers, you will forsake this land and all its inhabitants."

"The land is already barren. People are starving, sick, or both." The emissary laughed, a rough croaking sound. "Your bloodline will only wreak destruction upon this kingdom. I'm merely fixing the problem."

Orion didn't think his body could react any more viscerally to the emissary. But now his blood turned to ice—the emissary's words were far too close to the prophecy Devon had uncovered.

"So you'll kill the king and me to free yourself from your ties to the god, and then what? You'll take the throne?"

Surprise washed over the emissary's features. Perhaps he'd never expected that Orion would find out what he was. "I don't owe you an explanation, but a monkey could rule better than you."

The emissary gripped the hilt of his sword with white knuckles, and black power licked over his fingers. The swirls of his sorcery were mere wisps compared to the raw power the king possessed, or even compared to Orion's magic. But unlike them, the emissary was an immortal with a powerful weapon Orion didn't know how to avoid.

Without another word, the emissary unleashed himself upon Orion. His strikes were so fast that it was hard to see, let alone run or fly away from. Each time Orion managed to dodge it, he landed on the scalding hot ground that burned through the soles of his boots.

Ash rained down on them as the fire roared closer, strong winds pushing it in their direction.

"Behind you," a spirit warned, giving Orion just enough time to move out of the sword's path. Still, the dark tendrils of its attack sizzled through the hairs on his arm.

Another strike and the pointed blade nicked his white shirt. Orion stumbled back and fell to the ground, crushing his wings beneath his body.

The emissary kept a large enough distance between them to prevent Orion from using the full force of his powers. That damn weapon was too strong to approach.

Suddenly, panic and pain flooded the bond in a fierce rush. Orion clutched his stomach with a scream and stared past the dark shape of the undying fae, into the thicket of trees and to a point where he knew Nava must be... Injured.

He jumped to his feet, ignoring the sharp pain that shot from his wings down to his shoulder blades. The emissary couldn't die, and he might possess a weapon of incredible destruction—but he probably couldn't fly with those mangled wings.

The air cracked around Orion as he called for a shield of energy to protect him. Then he flew to the highest branch of the nearest tree.

The emissary's sword chopped it off before he could land somewhere that would hold his weight. Orion pivoted, aiming for an even larger branch instead.

With the distance between him and the magical weapon, it became easier to find the perfect moment to attack. The sword was clearly heavy, and each time the undying fae swung it at him, it seemed to tire him.

It was a marvelous weapon, likely forged by the gods for the gods. It demanded a price in exchange for its use, and his opponent's strength was fizzling out. The emissary's skin was shining with sweat. He had completely underestimated Orion's power and determination to not die.

The next time the fae swung the sword to strike, it took him longer. Orion jumped off the tree he was perching on, his aura calling for blood, and caught his opponent by surprise.

His fist connected with the emissary's jaw, whose shocked eyes rolled into the back of his head before he fell to the ground like a dead weight. But Orion didn't stop hitting him. Not even when his vision grayed out and all he felt was bone breaking beneath his knuckles.

The sound of a portal opening barely registered. A sudden force shoved him off the undying, and he skittered across the debris-covered forest floor.

The emissary sat up a heartbeat later, like a puppet pulled from the ground by invisible strings. The broken bones that deformed his face snapped into place. Then his eyes blinked open, and he looked around in a daze, before they widened in understanding.

Mad laughter escaped his bloodied lips, and his shattered teeth healed right in front of Orion's eyes. He tried to jump the fae again, but some kind of shield held him back.

The emissary hiccuped, a rattle in his breathing. He rose on shaking legs. A red cape slowly appeared on his shoulders, fluttering in the high winds behind him.

The portal grew and sucked the emissary into its black center like a magnet. He clicked his tongue, and for the first time, he abandoned the mask of madness he'd worn before. "Be glad the God of Shadows called me, Prince—for I'm done waiting for my freedom."

The whistling wind of the portal formed a shield of air that nearly burned Orion's lashes. Then darkness swallowed the emissary's body.

Nava. He needed to get to her. Now.

Orion jumped up to the sky, not wasting another second as he followed the pull of the bond through the thick layer of smoke, to where the warm rays of Aristaeus's magic beckoned him.

Three horned demons remained in the chaos below. But Orion had no trouble locating his soulmate, who lay on the ground, clearly injured. A demon hovered nearby, waiting to devour her.

Orion called her name and jumped on top of the demon. His aura burst around him, and the wisps of his power captured the creature of darkness before it could hurt her further. It screeched, its flames failing as he grabbed the Zorren by its slimy neck, ignoring the burn of its venom against his skin.

All the souls in him feasted on the demon—soulless but so full of power. The Zorren collapsed forward, its body shriveling like dry flowers as Orion drained it until there was nothing left, replenishing the energy he'd wasted while battling the emissary.

He was ready to destroy them all. To make them pay for even dreaming that they could hurt her.

20
NAVA

There was no time to waste. Arkimedes came for her, had saved her, but they weren't out of danger yet.

Nava rolled over onto her stomach, pushing her body off the ground with trembling arms. Blood dripped from her lesion, leaving warm, sticky trails over her hand as she tried to stem the flow.

How badly hurt was she? She had seconds—minutes at most—to do… something.

If she didn't die from her wound and stayed here much longer, the smoke would eventually kill her. She limped toward the portal that still hovered in the air.

It pulsed like a festering wound right in the middle of this forest. The scent of ammonia wafted from it in waves, growing stronger the closer she got to it.

Was this what the shadow world smelled like?

She shot a look at Aristaeus. He was still fighting a demon, unable to come and help her close the portal. But Ari always told her to trust herself—that her instincts were there to guide her to uncover her potential. And it was true. Whenever she'd done so, destiny had always surprised her.

Still, there was always that small voice of doubt that clutched her tight and refused to let go.

Nearly doubled over with pain and ignoring the black dots that danced across her vision, Nava raised her arms toward the magical gate.

Weeks ago, she had closed another portal, together with Ari and Arkimedes. She hadn't spoken the language Ari chanted then, but had known what to say regardless. The spell had tapped into a piece of her soul that made her who she was. A Beekeeper.

Opening her fingers like Ari had done that afternoon, she closed her eyes and tuned out the screams of the forests and the growls of the remaining demons. Everything fell away.

Then the words came to her… first, quiet like a whisper, and then loud enough that she could chant them. They tasted strange on her tongue, but she chanted them, and the portal shrank right before her eyes. Yellow magic strings poured from her fingertips, beginning to seal the door to the shadow world shut.

Something landed at her side, but she didn't even blink, for she knew who it was.

Her heart soared as Arkimedes placed his hand on her shoulder, and his energy bled through her, intensifying the spell. The portal became smaller, condensing into a dot of ink—and popped.

"That was—" Pain cut her off. She doubled over, clutching her side with both hands, putting as much pressure as she could on the wound. But her body had turned cold, and she was trembling even though flames still burned all around them.

Arkimedes's arms wrapped under her legs and behind her back, and the air shifted as he took flight with Nava in his embrace, carrying her away from the inferno and, hopefully, somewhere safe.

They landed in a meadow. His limbs were shaking. He was probably exhausted. She was, too.

"Don't go to sleep, Bee," Ark pleaded as he set her down. The ground was so soft and pillowy. Covered in moss.

It was still drizzling icy water. She was so cold.

"Tired." She hissed when he lifted her arm to inspect the area the Zorren had dug its nails into. "Don't do that. Hurts."

"You're bleeding a lot." He shrugged off his coat and untied the green handkerchief he wore around his neck, folded it a few times, and pressed it against her stomach. "Hold it tight."

Then he pulled his shirt from his pants and tugged at the edges. The scent of spice filled the air, followed by the sound of fabric ripping.

The world spun around her, the treetops swirling above her. She tried to speak, but no words came to her lips, only senseless whimpers.

How bad was her wound? Did she even want to know? Ark looked paler than she'd ever seen him before. He wouldn't even meet her eyes.

"Sit still," he said in a clipped tone, and she obeyed. Who cared anyway? All she wanted was to go to sleep.

Arkimedes wrapped his shirt around her ribs tightly enough that it resembled a corset. When the white fabric turned pink and then red in a matter of minutes, he paled further.

"I need to get you to the city."

"Can't transfer anywhere." Nava's voice broke, her throat raw from inhaling so much smoke. She cleared it, wincing as she sank against the tree behind her. "And you're exhausted."

"I will take you to a healer even if it kills me."

She exhaled a shaky breath. No energy left to put up a fight...but she didn't want to move an inch either. "You'll kill us both. When you drop me."

"For the last time," Arkimedes growled, "I will not drop you."

A steady creaking sound alerted them to Aristaeus joining them in the meadow. His gentle voice was a whisper inside her mind. *"There are no demons around us now. I killed the last one, and you closed the portal. Well done, dearest."* His brows dipped slowly as he shifted, tilting his stiff neck forward to inspect her bloody shirt. *"Your body will heal faster if you remain here, close to nature. With your soulmate and me at your side."*

Would she heal? Or was Ari just trying to soothe her because he knew this was the end? If so, how long would that take? Surely blood loss would take her much faster than infection.

"What did he say?" Arkimedes asked.

"He said I'll heal f-faster if I stay in the forest by his side. And yours." She groaned in pain. Her skin felt so hot, but the heat didn't reach her.

"She needs a healer," Arkimedes argued, looking straight into Aristaeus's eyes.

"You are a Beekeeper with the gift of healing. When we met, the Zorren had hurt me, and you were the one to heal me. No human potion, healer, or fae could have saved me that day. Only you, dear one." Ari paused and glanced at

Arkimedes. *"It's why you could heal your mate back on the island when he was a prisoner."*

"Ari says I'm able to heal." Could it be? That it had never been the alchemist potions her father had taught her, but always her magic? She'd denied it for so long.

"You're like Gavin?" Arkimedes blinked rapidly and pressed his hand to her wound, making the sharp stabs of pain worse.

She swatted his hand away. "I don't know."

Arkimedes's frown eased. He settled into a crouch and opened his hands, closing his eyes. His magic swirled, as she had seen thousands of times before, and a small wooden box materialized on his outstretched palms. What could it be? Her mind was too sluggish to ask.

He opened the lid, huffing as he removed a curved needle and rummaged through glass vials that clanked against each other. "If that's true, then we need to close the wound now, and then go there." He shot a cautious glance at the clearing over his shoulder.

"What's happening?" she asked, although she already knew. Before her, Arkimedes lit a dry branch with a fire spell and used it to sterilize the needle.

Then he dropped the contents of the potion—no, alcohol—on her wound without warning. Nava screamed, her heart hammering in her chest. She scrambled for his arm, stopping him before he could lower the sharp point to her injured skin.

"What the hell are you doing?" She swallowed, searching his panicked face.

Arkimedes caressed the side of her face. "You're losing a lot of blood, Nava. I've seen this kind of wound before. It will hurt just for a bit, but this way we can carry you to safety."

He peeked over his shoulder again when the wind rustled the leaves around them. The rain was falling harder now. Thunder rolled above.

"Why do you keep looking back there? Ari said there aren't any demons left?"

"It's not the demons I'm worried about…" He shook his head, and then without pausing, he pierced her skin and looped the first ring of black thread, pulling her skin tightly closed.

Nava barely suppressed another scream.

"The forest is not a safe place during the night." Ari knelt by her side. The

absolute blackness of his eyes distracted her from the pain. He studied Nava like she did him, inspecting her for any other hurts the Zorren might have caused her.

Soot and mild charring darkened the bark of his body. The moss, once green and alive with mushrooms, had turned brown and now stuck to his side, shriveled and dry. *"I have a home of my own. It will keep us safe. "*

"You h-have a home?" Her breath stuttered as Arkimedes closed two more stitches.

Ari tilted his head, and while he lacked any human expressions, she could have sworn he raised one of his wooden brows at her. *"Where else would I rest and recover?"*

Damn. Of course. She'd always thought he slept in the trees.

Soon, her wound was closed and tightly wrapped. Aristaeus picked her up, and they set off for safe shelter.

This was an older part of the forest, untouched by civilization, and with trees so enormous that she couldn't see the tops. Not that she could make out anything clearly right now. Her vision was far too blurry. All she could focus on was the bandage around her ribs and how it kept slipping with each step Ari took farther into the forest. Nava pressed a hand to it to hold it in place.

Stray rays of sunlight filtered through the leaves, dancing like the sparkles on precious stones over the moss-covered ground. The trees looming over them rivaled even those on Grey Island.

Arkimedes trudged behind them in silence. He didn't need to say a word, for everything he felt howled at her through their bond. All his worry. All his love.

"I'm fine..." she slurred, cursing her stupid mouth and tongue. "Ark, I'm not even in pain."

The words wouldn't ease his concerns, and her rough voice did little to sell the lie.

"I met the emissary when I was trying to get to you," he said.

"What?" She raised her head from where it rested against Ari's chest. "You should have told me!"

"When, exactly? A demon nearly eviscerated you, Nava." He pointed at her bloody bandage, but his tone lacked any heat. He looked so tired and frightened. It broke her heart to see him like that.

"I'm fine," she whispered, and this time, she believed it. Although she was still in pain and weakened by the blood loss, she did feel more like herself.

Aristaeus was right. Being together—the three of them—helped her.

"I thought I was going to lose you." Arkimedes's voice cracked. He cleared his throat and continued. "It didn't matter that I found the emissary when your life was in danger."

All right. He had a point. If their roles had been reversed, she would have done the same. "What happened?"

"He was hiding in the shadows near the Zorren. I confronted him, and we fought. But then he got called away."

"What emissary is he speaking of?" Aristaeus asked, tilting his head to the side with a creak.

Of course Arkimedes couldn't hear him, so he continued. "I asked him why he was trying to hurt you two. From what he said, it's about earning his freedom. It made me wonder whether he's working with the demons as part of some kind of deal."

Nava covered her lips with a hand that smelled tangy and coppery, like blood. "He helps the Zorren come here to kill us, and then they help release him from his service to the god?"

"He wants to kill my father, too." Arkimedes hesitated. "And me. He wants revenge, although he didn't specify what for. But clearly, my father did something to annoy him."

She couldn't really blame the emissary. King Oberon knew how to make enemies.

"Ari, when I first found you—the day we met—there w-was another Beekeeper with you." She wished her voice didn't sound so weak. And that the throbbing pain would stop bringing tears to her eyes.

She swallowed heavily, trying to ease the knot in her throat as the memories caught up with her. The second Beekeeper had been dead and fading away into the ground. Smoke had lingered in the air that afternoon. Ari had told her that the Zorren had attacked them. But what if it hadn't been just the Zorren?

Arkimedes lengthened his strides to catch up to them. "What if the emissary killed the other Beekeeper?"

"His name was Illaris," Ari said and continued walking. *"I don't remember who or what struck him. But we were surprised by a large group of Zorren that day,"* he admitted in a sorrowful tone.

Could the demons come to this realm on their own? Or had the emissary been letting them in a year ago, too?

"They shouldn't be able to come to this land on their own. Every time we fight them, it's in the Beekeepers' realm."

Exactly as she'd feared. The Zorren, Ari, and Illaris—they'd all set her destiny in motion that day. Nothing was a coincidence.

"I don't know if the emissary can come into Caztian unless he's on a mission commanded by Dargan." Arkimedes shook his head, raking a hand through his hair. "Each time you've encountered him, Bee, has been in the shadow world."

That was true… Which would make defeating him that much more difficult because she couldn't move in his realm.

"I still must know about the emissary. This is confusing to me," Ari said.

Where to begin? It was such a long tale, and she was nearing the end of her reserves. Even with nature supporting her, the pain was becoming too much to bear.

"It would be much easier if I could share what happened with you—like you've done with me."

Ari inclined his head and reached for her with his empty hand. Without hesitation, she placed her much smaller hand inside his. *"Think of what you want to share. The clearer the image you gather, the better the picture I will receive in return."*

Nava brought her mind to their escape from the castle. To Devon opening the portal both times. To the Dark Fae approaching her. That he knew what she was and hurt her because of it.

She didn't want to remember that night or how afraid she'd been when she exited the portal.

Ari blinked those strange, beautiful eyes before glancing at Arkimedes. He could see the image of the man in shadows from her memories, and no doubt he was comparing his likeness to her soulmate. *"He looks like our protector—but is not."*

Undoubtedly, he could sense the fear that had gripped her then as well. It felt so long ago now. Such a silly thing to fear. "I know that."

"He wouldn't hurt you."

"What is he saying?" Arkimedes asked, peering at them with a frown.

"Open your mind. It will make communicating much easier." She repeated the words Ari had just whispered in her mind and pressed her cheek against the rough texture of his chest. "He saw my memories and what the emissary looks like."

"He isn't my twin brother, which is what I suspected him to be. But he was a full fae, unlike me," Arkimedes said. "The Vulcan showed us those scriptures from the earliest days of Caztian. About how the gods and the founders struck a deal of sacrifice. It could be that this emissary is my blood but from long ago. He certainly looked ancient."

"The Vulcan?" Ari brought his hand to Nava's arm, poking at the healed scar in the shape of a hand. *"Who used the god's artifact?"* Ari's alarm rang clear in his intonation, and the bees surrounding them buzzed into the air all at once. He studied Nava's body as if she might grow a second head at any moment. Then he did the same to Arkimedes.

"Devon did, and he isn't doing well," she said, wheezing a little. The air had turned so cold, like on a winter evening. "I healed him before we left. Perhaps he will be fine?"

Ari remained quiet. The wood covering his body creaked as he shook his head. Then his gaze swept to the tops of the trees above them, following the wind that moved them to and fro. *"No mortal magic can truly heal the poison that comes from a god's artifact. Yet I cannot understand why we ought to heal him. I thought he was our enemy?"*

She'd thought so too, and if Ari had asked her that same question half a year ago, her answer would have been very different. Now the man was not only Arkimedes's brother but also her friend. And after all that Ark had lost, it would break him to lose Devon as well.

"We shall go inside. It's not safe for you to be out here." Ari paused in front of the largest tree Nava had seen in this kingdom. Mushrooms and ferns grew aplenty, sprouting from the crevices in its bark and from in between the rocks at its base.

The massive roots of the ancient tree moved aside like curtains, revealing an entrance to a deep cavern. Giant fireflies hovered before her face, at least as large as her palm. The gentle but uneven flutter of their wings matched her erratic heartbeats.

A cackle of laughter cut through her sluggish thoughts as the brightly lit shapes snatched her hair, pulling it gently and exposing her ears to the bite of the chill night.

Wait. Had she completely lost her mind? Nava blinked raindrops from her lashes and focused on one of the fireflies as it tugged at the bloody bandage around her ribs. It had long, black, human-like arms and even tinier hands. Its elongated face had large, slanted eyes that shone with eagerness.

"Be careful with the pixies." Arkimedes brushed away the one on her stomach, his voice deepening with his annoyance.

The pixie flew off, screeching in offense, then promptly tried to bat at Arkimedes's wings. It quickly changed its mind as the shapes of his aura appeared by his shoulder.

"Your soulmate is right. They are the worst nuisance. They eat the nectar in my hive and torment the bees." Ari sounded unlike himself as he swatted at a few pixies darting around them. Their golden glow left shimmering trails behind them when they flew to the ground after his wooden palm caught them.

They couldn't be that bad. Right? They were tiny. Nava wanted to laugh, but she couldn't seem to muster the energy. She hadn't been that cold until now. Perhaps Ari had been keeping her warm with magic, and their conversation had been keeping her awake.

Now her eyes were drooping, and it was a task to keep them open. Nava couldn't force another word to her lips. Sleep was pulling her under.

"Bee?" Arkimedes's palm pressed to her forehead, wet with sweat and rain.

"Mmm..." A clattering sound echoed around her. Wait. Were those her teeth?

"She needs to be out of this rain," Arkimedes muttered. "Now."

If Aristaeus answered, she didn't hear it. She floated in and out of a drowsy state as they moved swiftly into the cave. The roots shut behind them, leaving them in complete darkness.

Ari's aura illuminated the wide entrance. Huge crystals jutted from the ground and ceiling and began to glow with an orange light as he passed them.

It smelled of dirt and minerals down here, and fresh energy soared through her. Whatever this place was...the magic clinging to every speck of dirt around them helped dull her pain just enough.

She slept.

21

NAVA

Nava filtered in and out of a dreamless slumber for hours, perhaps even days. Who knew how to tell time inside a cave?

The first thing she noticed when she woke up was that her body was swinging in the air. Then pain ricocheted through her from the cut in her abdomen. She groaned.

Her agony meant she wasn't dead, and that was something to be grateful for.

"Ark?" Her mouth felt drier than ever before. Hadn't Arkimedes brought her water at some point? Or perhaps she had dreamed, after all.

When no answer came, Nava slowly sat up, swallowing the bile that rose in her throat as she shifted her body across the woven surface. Where was she? Ah. Inside a hammock of sorts, strung up in between two tall gem pillars—and far too high for someone like her to sleep in.

Gods, she hated heights.

"Ari?" she called into the nothingness but received no answer again. Worry prickled her mind as she struggled to the edge of the hammock. It was only five feet high at most, but the ground was spinning slightly, and she had to take a few deep breaths before she managed to climb down.

At least she'd regained enough strength to use some of her magic. Around her, magical crystals gently illuminated the cave. Their energy hummed like a heartbeat, gentle and soothing.

Ari's home was beautiful in a raw sort of way. Dozens of trees dotted the place, many still seedlings, judging by their size. It was like the forest aboveground but on a much smaller scale. How could a tree live here without daylight? She touched the bark, and it trembled under her fingertips.

She withdrew her hand with a gasp. Before her very eyes, the tree trunk grew a new branch in response to her touch, purple flowers and deep green leaves sprouting from it in an instant.

"The crystals mimic the sunlight and give life to the trees." Ari's voice in her mind made her jump, and a scream tore past her chapped lips, echoing off the vast ceiling.

She pressed her hand to her heart, taking deep gulps of air as she met his dark gaze. He was hunched over next to a crystal, his wood still charred from their fight with the Zorren. He tilted his head, probably puzzled by her human reactions.

Could she surprise him like that? Or would he feel her approaching?

"These are my sun stones." He pointed at the crystal by his side, choosing not to comment on her appearance or ask whether she felt better. He had never been one to waste time with small talk. *"All Beekeepers possess a different gift that gives life. Much like you can heal, I can create these."*

"Where do you sleep?" Nava turned around to inspect the place, noticing the hidden stones tucked in between trees, rocks, and even growing from the ceiling. This was not what she'd expected his cave to be like. The trees and the crystals divided it into discrete areas and made it feel like an actual home.

"I rest amongst the trees," he said, pointing up to the very top of the cavern, where a hammock was strung from one side to the other.

Nava limped toward him, her bare feet cushioned by moss. Where were her boots? "How long have I been out?"

"A couple of days," Ari said. *"Your mate is out hunting."*

"Isn't it dangerous for him to be out there alone?"

"It was dangerous for him to be here with me," Ari snarled, a rumbling sound rising from his chest. *"He kept pacing around my cave, worrying about you, even though you are healing. Then he worried about his human friend, who burned the forest back on the island. I had to send him out for both our sakes."*

She battled a smile. Ari was right, and he didn't need to forgive Devon for the damage he'd done to the people of the Northern Village or to the forest when he'd brought his army there.

Now that Aristaeus mentioned Devon, it left her wondering, though. Was he all right? Would the healing she'd bestowed upon him keep him well for long enough until they returned? She could only hope so.

Nava stretched slowly. Her body ached everywhere, even in places she didn't know existed. "Where did you find the hammocks?"

"I made them for myself and Illaris when we first discovered this place." His smile displayed many sharp teeth that would make a more reasonable being run away.

But Nava had never claimed to be such a thing. Instead, all she could focus on was the sadness in the Beekeeper's gaze.

Ari picked at a charred layer of bark on his torso and ripped it away, revealing honey-like dew below.

"Ari!" Nava's scream bounced off the tall rock walls. But he remained unbothered, bending down to the nearest tree trunk and digging his iron claws deep into the pulp. Then he ripped off a long sheet of bark and stuck it to his newly opened wound, patching himself up like a patchwork quilt.

"I can't believe you just did that." Her stomach revolted at the images that kept repeating in her mind. Was that what Ari looked like in reality? A pale body covered in goop on which he stuck layers of bark, wax, moss, and everything else the forest offered?

"The layers protect me against the weather and fires, and it helps with camouflage," he said, reading her thoughts.

"You could have told me..."

"Why?" He blinked in confusion. *"I can't teach you how to do this on your frail body. You are one of us—and yet you are still human. A new creation I have never seen."* His body glowed in the same shade as the crystals, and his fresh layer of skin merged with the other parts, bit by bit, until it blended in seamlessly.

Well. He probably had a point. "You said these hammocks belonged to you and Illaris. Did you make this place together?"

"Yes, we built it decades ago. When the forests called us here for the first time. We suspected the Zorren would try to break into the land. We didn't find any demons then, but we found an underwater pool. It has magical properties that

make it impossible for the demons to bridge in this area and a perfect home for the Beekeepers."

Nava straightened at the revelation. "You suspected the Zorren would come into this land decades ago?"

Ari tilted his head forward in acknowledgment, and Nava's heart raced while her tired mind grasped at the fickle details floating inside her head. Something was missing. "Could that have been thirty years ago? When Arkimedes was born?"

"Perhaps...perhaps not... Time works differently for me. I don't track it like you humans do."

Maybe she shouldn't ask all these questions. Not when it might bring back painful memories for Ari. If Illaris had been as important to Ari as he was to her, then she could understand how devastating it would have felt to lose him.

She glanced at the crystals, which were flickering like candlelight. "Can I have a small sun crystal? I would like to keep it with me when I return to town," she said, and he went still for a time, as if processing her words. Maybe he couldn't understand that she would like to maintain the connection to him and nature, even when they weren't together. "I'm sorry that you lost Illaris, Ari."

"There is no real life without death." Ari placed one hand on Nava's shoulder, squeezing gently. *"The immortals crave its finality—obsess over it. Even the trees die eventually, so a new one can thrive in its place."*

"Still..." Tears pricked at her eyes. Why was she about to cry when she hadn't even met the other Beekeeper? All she'd seen of him was his quickly decomposing body—and how pained Ari had been.

"Don't think it a coincidence. You crossed the edge of the Grey Forest and were called to me just as the Zorren took Illaris's life. I'm happy you are my companion. There is no need to be sad. The pain of abandoning these bodies we occupy is fleeting. I will meet Illaris again."

Was that true? Would she meet them once she died? Or was she different because she was human? If she went to the Beekeepers' realm, what happened to Ark's soul? Would they be separated?

The question brought such intense pain that it took her breath away.

"Arkimedes told me his magic came to him when he was five," she said. Hopefully, the change of subject would ease her panic. "I'm five years younger than him. Do you think the gods chose me to become a Beekeeper because I'm his soulmate? Or..."

"Yes?" Aristaeus narrowed his eyes as he tried to make sense of her questions.

"Was I always destined to become a Beekeeper and that's why Arkimedes is my soulmate?"

"The gods don't choose soulmates at random." Ari inspected Nava's changing emotions. *"Does the order matter?"*

Sometimes it was easy to forget that Ari's emotions worked differently than hers. "I—I guess I'd be disappointed if they chose me to be who I am because of who my mate is and not because of *me*." She leaned against a tree for support and lowered herself onto the ground.

His movements were slow as he took a seat next to her. *"I will not claim to understand the emotions you feel right now. The gods picked you to be his—just as much as they chose him to be yours. You're from the same soul, equal and perfect for this task."*

For a while, they sat in quiet companionship as his words settled inside her. He was right, of course. It didn't matter why or how, for she wouldn't change a thing. Even if, at first, she hadn't wanted a soulmate or a kingdom to rule. And definitely not the huge responsibility of defeating an immortal.

A year ago, all she'd longed for was to be free to choose her future. But that was precisely what she was doing now. She loved Arkimedes and fought for him. She could have stayed in a home in this kingdom, lived a quiet life alongside her brother, and allowed Ark to continue his royal life on his own without remembering her.

Having a soulmate wasn't what defined her choices—it only brought clarity to what she really wanted. Their love was a partnership. The gods had woven them together, but nobody was forcing them to remain committed to each other.

It was them clinging to each other that would shape the future of this kingdom. And she was ready to fight for the people who lived here, too.

"Wait, did you say there's an underground pool here?" she asked, perking up. She desperately needed to be out of these bloody clothes.

"Aristaeus told you about the pool?" Arkimedes's voice floated toward her, and he stepped around a crystal a mere moment later, carrying two dead rabbits over his shoulder. He set them aside and crouched beside them.

"Have you seen it?" He nodded, but Nava could have answered the question herself. He didn't look half as filthy as she did. Even his clothes lacked the gray tones of ash and soot. "I want a bath."

"How are you feeling?"

Like demons had tried to kill her and almost succeeded. "I've been better."

Arkimedes grabbed her hand and pulled her to her feet, guiding her away. Ari stayed, quietly watching them sidle past fruiting trees.

Nava's breath caught in her throat at the beauty that greeted her past the tall rock columns that held up the cavernous ceiling. The pool was bright turquoise and smelled strongly of minerals. Its shape extended like a winding serpent, far beyond what her eyes could see.

She'd never witnessed anything so magical before, and she'd visited many places.

A small island jutted from the center of the pool, made of white rock. On it, one lonely tree grew. Above it, a giant hole in the ceiling let in the morning sky.

Nava was undressing before she could think of a reason not to. "Do you think there are beasts under the water?"

"No." Arkimedes laughed, gaining a glare from her. "The only thing you have to worry about here is me. Now, let me see how your wound is healing."

22
NAVA

Nava hated worrying about everything and the powerlessness that took over her body whenever she did. It always began as a rolling ache in the middle of her chest that felt a lot like heartbreak.

Arkimedes handed her a piece of rabbit meat speared on a stick. The delicious smell called to her with a promise of warmth and savory goodness, but she struggled to find her appetite.

How was Devon doing back at Leela's house? Arkimedes had been fretting about it for days… Fine. She had been worried, too.

He refused to return to check on his brother if it meant leaving her there, although she doubted the emissary would come to hurt her so soon after the attack. But of course, she couldn't be certain.

Arkimedes had shared everything he'd learned from the emissary with them, and now, as they all sat around the fire in silence, the question circled her mind again and again.

How were they supposed to kill an immortal?

"There's no pattern we can use to predict when to expect the emissary next." Ark reached for a piece of dry kindling and fed it to the magical fire that raged hotter in return. "I'm concerned about both of you going out there to heal the forest. He was there recently."

The licks of the flames from their campfire were blue instead of orange, and yet they reminded her too much of the hell they'd just escaped. After what had happened in the forest, sitting by the fire should prove an impossibility. Yet here she was, soaking in its warmth on this chill autumn morning. They had chosen a spot close to the pool to make the most of the natural light since Nava missed it so much.

"Why do you think so? Surely if he could come back that easily, he would have been here the entire time." Nava rubbed her tired eyes. Ari often said the crystals would help with her exhaustion, but healing this kind of wound took it out of her.

"We don't know that. You want to go out to the forest and bask in the sun"—Arkimedes paused his poking of the logs with his stick, sending her an all-knowing look—"but it's too dangerous."

"We can't hide here forever. You've been wanting to go to the city, and we should. If only to make sure Devon is alive."

Arkimedes opened his mouth but closed it again, clenching his jaw as he narrowed his eyes at her.

Sure, she'd played a little dirty by mentioning what he needed to hear, but there was no use in being afraid right now.

"If what I suspect is true," she continued, undeterred, "then the emissary can't come into this realm without the command of a god. He is probably on duty right now, and that's why he got called away."

"I believe you're right. Unless the emissary is on a mission for his god, he must not be allowed to come into our world. I hadn't seen him before."

Nava rubbed her chest, attempting to relieve the pressure that collected deep inside it, as if the forest was beckoning her to come and help. She'd taken so much of its energy, it was only fair to repay it, even if she was still healing. "Perhaps my need to leave the cave is because of the forest calling to me?"

She glanced at Ari, who inclined his head in confirmation. He looked so out of place in front of the campfire, with his massive tree-like legs bent at angles no human limbs could comfortably—healthily—achieve.

"The call is strong once you connect with your powers and the nature that surrounds you," he said.

Nava pulled at the bandages around her torso, which had gone brown with dried blood. No matter how much she'd washed it in the pool, the stain remained.

The gray morning light trickled over the water, bringing a gentle breeze that seeped through the thin layers of her clothes. Thank gods for

Leela and the wool coat she'd insisted Nava wear. It was burnt in places, but it kept her warm.

Hopefully, her friend was all right. And she was still helping Devon heal.

"All right, let's assume the best. The forest is calling you because it needs you." Arkimedes tapped his fingers against his thighs, but his expression was strained. "Let's prepare for the worst, regardless. What are we going to do if we get there and the emissary attacks us?"

"What if we call upon Dargan?" She scratched her arm as the crawling sensation under her skin worsened. "Each time someone crosses a portal, they meet with him to pay the price. We can ask Devon to open a portal and tell the God of Shadows his emissary is attempting to break free. Perhaps he will want to get rid of the problem for us?"

"The gods have been fighting their own war for decades, dearest. They don't care enough about Caztian to intervene, not when they have bigger problems to attend to." Aristaeus looked somber.

"I heard that." Arkimedes straightened, his eyes growing wide as he stared at Ari.

"You heard Ari speak?" Nava asked. She would have smiled if the information being shared was about a happier subject.

Arkimedes nodded and placed his half-eaten meal aside, looking dazed and a little horrified. "I felt this pressure in my head and assumed more memories were coming. I haven't been pushing them away for a while now, so I let it through..."

"He let me in. At last." Ari's expression softened. *"I would assume Dargan is aware of what the emissary is doing. Even if he believes he is fooling the god."*

"How can we kill him?" Arkimedes asked.

"Only an immortal can."

"Isn't your soul immortal—couldn't *you* do it?" Nava asked.

"My soul, yes. But my body is as mortal as the tree standing in the middle of this lagoon." Ari pointed at the aforementioned tree. The morning mist covered its roots and part of the trunk. It lost its leaves long ago, although Nava could see the ribbons of life weaving around it, even at this distance.

Well, that brilliant plan lasted about two seconds.

"You could search for a god's artifact," Ari added, although they could all hear the doubt in his inflection. *"At the beginning of time, many Caztanians stole these items from the gods. They soon learned that most mortals can't wield*

godly weapons, so they perished, and the artifacts went missing. Some deities have sent their emissaries on a hunt to collect them. Yet some remain."

"Why does everything have to be so difficult?" Nava groaned and stabbed the fire with the stick holding her food until its embers were dancing and sweat beaded on her temple. "Does the Society of Crows keep artifacts in the archives?" she asked, looking at Arkimedes. Because if so, she would gladly crawl back down that long tunnel of nightmares to retrieve one.

"Not in the Copper Kingdom. Perhaps in its main headquarters. But even if they do, Nava, we can't touch them without triggering an alarm. They will send the Corvus, and we can't win against the entire Society on our own."

The sunlight changed from silver to pink as morning fully embraced the forest. And they still had no clue how to move forward.

"It's rumored that the founders kept some artifacts hidden from the deities. Your father might have one inside your castle."

Arkimedes's breath caught. His eyes fixed on a spot in the distance, almost as if he could see it—feel it, even. "My father wouldn't give it to us even if he had it. He's mentioned nothing about the prophecy of our bloodline. He kidnapped me and lied about my mother's death."

"What are you saying?" Nava asked.

"I wonder why the emissary is letting demons into the kingdom to get revenge against my father?" Arkimedes's gravel voice trailed off as he reached toward the fire, opening his palm. The flames slowly suffocated, leaving behind a thin trail of smoke that dissipated into the open air.

Nava stood, dusting her pants off with more vigor than necessary. She needed to vent some of her frustrations. "You've said many times that the fires started right as you came to the kingdom. But what if they began before and that's the reason the king had you taken from our home?"

Arkimedes nodded. "When I went into his study to get the keys to free you from the bracelet, I saw a piece of art that depicted a king tossing a babe into a cloud. It looked ancient, like something that recorded history. I believe the emissary is my father's brother and that he wants to take the throne."

"And if there aren't any living members of the royal line, then the God of Shadows would release his emissary. It's a failsafe to protect the godly magic they gifted to the founders."

What Arkimedes was saying made sense. It would be a good enough reason for a mad fae to try to kill the prince as well. He needed everyone from his bloodline gone so he could be free from his ties to the god.

"Do you think they are twins?" she asked.

"Yes," he said with enough confidence that she believed it.

There was bad blood between the twins, and whatever had caused it, it had roped Aristaeus, Ark, and Nava into this mess.

"Why not ask the king himself?" Aristaeus reasoned, and his confusion was plain in the way he tilted his head to the side. *"If he possesses the artifact, then he can part with it for his own benefit."*

"I've been dreading having to go back to the castle and ask for help when he is far from an ally. He's all I have left of my family, but he wants to hurt Nava." Arkimedes shook his head and rose from the ground, shrugging on his coat, and offered Nava his hand. It was probably time to go and heal the forest. But then he carried on speaking, avoiding everyone's gazes. "I remember why I stayed away from here and why I didn't ask Nava to return with me. My father can't be trusted. I was gone for thirty years, and he didn't miss me. It seems odd that he is suddenly interested in being my father."

True.

"It's the nature of the fae to be cunning," Aristaeus agreed with a quiver in his voice that hadn't been there before. *"But your power has connected with the land. You are one with it, like the king. If I can sense the shift, so can he. I don't believe that putting you in danger benefits him."*

"Sure," Arkimedes agreed. He sounded stern. "A few days ago, I would have marched right in there and asked him if he has an artifact."

"So why the change of heart?" Nava asked.

"After finding out the emissary is after him, it gave me pause. What if he always wanted me to come back to deal with his brother? Just because he shouldn't hurt me doesn't mean he won't hurt you. He can keep you away from me and make me do things I don't want to—just to keep you safe."

Her mouth felt dry all of a sudden, and she fought the urge to wrap her arms around herself. He was right. They should try to defeat the emissary by themselves before attempting to forge an alliance with the king.

Ari shook his head, causing pieces of moss and bark to fly off him. *"If you're the heir, then she is the heiress. I'm not a human, nor a fae, but I know that much."*

"The king doesn't want a human queen, Ari, and neither do the citizens. Not since Ark's mother betrayed them."

Nava had tried not to think too hard about the spirit that had haunted her at the safe house, but now, the memories she'd shared that afternoon clicked into place, bringing with them a sudden burst of clarity.

The queen's final thought before her death had been that the one she'd loved the most of all had killed her. She'd told the man who'd tied her to a burning tree that she loved him, and yet he hadn't even flinched.

Nava had asked Arkimedes before, and he'd been adamant that his father hadn't been the culprit. "What if it was the emissary who killed her?"

Arkimedes froze and met her eyes. "My mother?"

"Yes. What if she was the first one to die in his quest for revenge?"

23
ORION

Orion followed Nava as she wove through the skeletal trees that remained after the fire. She glowed beneath the ash that streaked her skin, and the bees that always accompanied her seemed unfazed by the steady patter of rain. He'd grown used to the sight of them after they'd been in peril for so long, but that didn't ease his anxiety.

Mist billowed out of his lips as he exhaled. They were definitely heading into fall now, and with it came much shorter, colder days and the changing leaves of a new season.

"Stay near me," he said and turned to check on Aristaeus, who was too far away for his comfort. He had been using his Beekeeper magic to bring back some life to a large tree specimen. It had taken him an entire hour thus far, and he had still not moved away.

"It's cold out here." Nava blew some warm air into her hands and rubbed them together.

"Our coats have seen better days. It doesn't help." He poked at a hole in the fabric left behind by the fire and peered up at the husks of the trees. There was little left to shelter them from the weather, and lightning crawled across the dark, stormy sky, followed by loud thunder.

The weather was getting worse, and they were far from town.

Now that they'd left the sacred ground Aristaeus had built his home on, Orion couldn't wait to get back to Leela's house. He needed to make sure Devon wasn't dying. He'd barely slept during the past couple of nights, sick with worry.

Even though Aristaeus's home had offered them a semblance of safety away from his father's guards, the Crows, and the Zorren, they couldn't stay here another day.

"We must return to the city before nightfall and strategize about how to obtain the artifact. That's one thing we can't find in the forest."

Nava sniffed and shuffled close to him, seeking shelter under his wing. She cast a knowing look at him. "Do you know where we can start?" At least she didn't mention Devon again.

"No."

"Seriously, that's all you're going to say?" She pursed her lips. They had turned a light shade of mauve from the cold. Orion had to get her out of there, even if she needed to heal the trees. They'd endured hours of relentless rain with no end in sight, and he was done.

"While I was working for the Society, they used to hunt for smugglers around the ports. People frequently come here to poach rare animals and sell them to other kingdoms. Sometimes they trade in magical weapons." Orion wrapped an arm around Nava's slim shoulders and extended his wing to shelter her further.

"Like a god's artifact?"

"It's unlikely, but they might tell us where we can find one, for a price."

"So… our plan is to find a smuggler in the ports and hope that they'll give us the information we need?" She huffed a laugh.

"I know how it sounds." His face grew warm. "And no. They won't exactly give it to us willingly…"

That sobered her up. She blinked rapidly to banish the raindrops that had accumulated on her lashes. "It's just me and you, Ark. How are we going to fight anyone?"

"And Devon, too. If he is well." A heavy knot formed in his throat, and it took everything he had not to grab her and rush back to his brother. "We can offer them money, and if—when—that fails, then…" He didn't need to say the words.

Nava nodded, and her face set into a resolute expression that showed him how fucking brave she was.

Fighting pirates was less risky than going into the castle to take part in whatever game his father was playing. He couldn't take the chance. Not when Nava's and Aristaeus's safety was at stake.

He studied the surrounding area, his heart drumming in his throat. His fingertips prickled as his power awakened. What if the emissary heard them discuss their plan? Was there a shadow lurking nearby? A portal?

Nava's hand wrapped around his wrist, squeezing it gently. "We're safe. The forest and the bees would alert us otherwise."

He glanced down at her and the small smile that pulled at the corners of her pillowy lips. Then she pointedly glanced at her feet, where moss and grass were sprouting from beneath the ash.

The demons had taken life, and the Beekeepers had brought it back. This power was how Aristaeus had disposed of the Zorren weeks ago when he'd turned one of their bodies into a tree.

Orion had never noticed Nava doing anything like this on Grey Island when she'd called upon her power, but he had seen the signs of her magic crawling all over the emissary's arm.

She was sprouting life from death.

"I haven't been able to replicate this—this spell, or whatever you'd call this. I did it to him after he attacked me when I crossed the portal. While in the cave, I could only grow lichen over the rock." She stomped her feet over her newly made grass and smiled so wide he almost forgot all about the horrible destruction around them.

Meanwhile, Aristaeus seemed to have finally given up on the dead tree and was heading over to them. *"The life you give the forest will return to us when the Zorren strike again."* Aristaeus's eyes softened as he took in Nava's work, which continued to flourish a few feet away, returning color to the ashen tree trunks nearby. *"Mastering it is the quickest way to kill the demons. Practice using it even when you are away."*

Another peal of thunder rang through the air before the skies opened up and rain pelted them so hard it became difficult to see.

"I'm taking Nava to the city. We need to find the artifact. We'll be back when we have something." The rain rolled off Orion's feathers as he shielded Nava's shivering body from the worst of it. Still, flying in this tempest would be tricky.

"The emissary is on borrowed time for this world. We have time," Aristaeus said in their minds. The bees, which had been flying around them, rushed

to hide in the hive on his head, disappearing under its protective cover. *"No demon can cross into my home. I shall wait there until I sense you've returned."*

Nava stepped out from under Orion's wing and wrapped Aristaeus in a hug that looked far from comfortable. Aristaeus seemed surprised but awkwardly patted her shoulder until she was ready to let go.

"I hope it doesn't take me so long to see you again," she said.

"Let us hope that when we meet, it's not because of another attack on this forest. Not even Beekeepers can bring back life once it's left for good."

Orion and Nava arrived at Leela's house at nightfall, chilled to the bone by the cold front that had descended onto the city. It was far too early in the year to be that freezing.

The silver lining on flying through a storm was that none of the guards or the Crows would bother to keep an eye out for them.

The wooden awning that covered Leela's front door sheltered them from the downpour as Orion knocked on the glass. As soon as he could, he shoved both his hands inside his wet pockets.

The hinges screeched as Leela's red hair popped out to greet them, and a sudden wind slammed the door against the wall. "Your Highness!" she gasped and reached for Nava's wrist, dragging her into the house. "You can't be outside in this storm!"

The inside was much warmer than the cave had been and smelled of sweet tea and pigments used to dye fabric. He turned toward the closed door and placed a hand over it, whispering a warding spell that locked into place.

When he turned, Nava was standing beside Leela, speaking in hushed tones as her friend fretted over her wet appearance.

"Is Devon upstairs?" Orion asked, already ascending the narrow staircase, two steps at a time.

"He's fine, sir, just warming up by the fire. We've had quite the storm today."

Orion needed to see him with his own eyes, to hear his voice… To make sure his brother was actually alive and doing well. They'd left in such a rush, and Nava's healing had only just set in—there had been no way to tell how long it would last.

They'd been gone for far too long.

"You're alive." Devon's voice broke over the sound of a hissing teapot by the fire. He uncrossed one long leg, clad in elegant, wine-colored pants, and stood from the chair. It seemed Leela had found him a new set of clothes.

"I should be the one saying that," Orion said, fighting a smile.

Behind him, the stairs creaked under Nava's feet. She entered the room moments later, wringing out her long hair, and a mixture of rain, ash, and dirt dripped onto the wooden floor. "Devon," she greeted. "I trust you're feeling better?"

"Perfect, as always. You two, however, look like drowned rats and are making a mess of this wonderful place." He stretched like a cat, extending both arms over his head. "I take it you encountered demons?"

"And the emissary." Orion helped Nava remove her coat. It was so heavy with rain it nearly swallowed her whole. He draped it over the balustrade and peeked over it to see where Leela had gone.

A distant rustle of fabric emerged from the seamstress's shop. She was probably looking for dry clothes.

Devon was right. Perhaps they should have cleaned up and changed downstairs to avoid getting the floor dirty. They had inconvenienced Leela enough.

As if called by his thoughts, she bustled up the stairs not long after, piles of clothing stuffed between her slim arms. She dropped the lot on one of the empty chairs.

"I know I shouldn't interrupt." Leela patted her forehead with her arm, drying a thin layer of perspiration that clung to her skin. "You three are always talking about such pressing matters... But it's so cold outside, and I don't want you—nor Miss Nava—to get ill. I brought everything I could find that might fit you, sir. My partner doesn't sew for males as often as she would like."

"These will be fine." Nava joined them and began rifling through the pile with a smile. "I'll be glad to be out of these clothes, even if I have to wear a potato sack."

"Who hurt you, miss?" Leela's fingers reached out to touch the scars left behind by the demon's claws. The wet, white shirt stuck to Nava's ribs, revealing the darker color of her skin and the makeshift bandage Orion had created beneath.

"The Zorren," Nava said in a soothing tone he remembered her using with her little brother. It didn't work with Leela, whose face twisted with fear. "I'm fine. I'm desperate to change and toss these clothes. They smell like smoke no matter how much I wash them."

Orion wanted to see the back of them as well. They only reminded him how close she'd been to dying—an inch more and she wouldn't be here. They'd almost lost, and all before they'd even given that bastard emissary a good fight.

Leela took a few steps away, her eyes still wide. "I will run you two a bath. I got some new oils from the market a couple of days ago that will help with healing."

She was out of their sight faster than Orion thought anyone could move with the layers of her dress. No matter how all this ended, Leela deserved some reward for helping them without asking hard questions he wouldn't be able to answer.

When he turned to Devon, his eyes were trailing the curves of Nava's body with far too much interest. Her breasts were now visible under the layers of her sheer, wet shirt.

Orion stepped in front of Devon's line of vision and glared down at him.

Nava covered her torso with the item of clothing she was holding, but it did little to help matters—it was the type of frilly thing he'd rather Devon *not* see in the context of wherever his mind had clearly just ventured.

"I'm going downstairs to get clean," Nava announced, picked up a few things from where Leela had dropped them, and followed her friend to their room below.

"I wasn't looking..." Devon said, and his face turned bright red as he glanced away toward the fireplace. He took a quick breath before reaching for the tea. "Not like *that*. I just realized why it took you so long to get back here."

Rubbish. But Orion wasn't about to get into this fight, even if his blood was rushing wildly within him. "The demons hurt her, so we stayed until she was out of danger and could fight if we encountered trouble in the city."

"And what happened to the second Beekeeper—Arisfaeus or whatever?"

"He is fine." Arkimedes rifled through the clothing, trying to find something large enough to fit him. The awkward silence extended. "I see you're feeling better."

Devon shrugged, his face still hollow. The shadows under his eyes were more pronounced in the flickering light of the fireplace. "Better, but not great. The potion and whatever Nava did helped. I improved within a day." He refilled his mug and sat down in the chair. "Leela went and bought more healing potions today since I ran out and my energy has been dwindling."

"It wasn't the potion that helped you, Devon, it was Nava's magic." Orion shrugged off his shirt and reached for a black one. It was at least a size too small, with ridiculous billowing sleeves.

Devon settled against the chair's backrest. "I thought I'd dreamed that. Her healing me."

"No. The other Beekeeper confirmed she has the gift of healing—which is why she's walking around right now instead of fighting an infection back in the forest." Orion sniffed at the clothes. A mild scent of mildew and dust lingered on the fabric, but it was dry, and that was an improvement.

To his surprise, Devon didn't comment at all about Nava's powers. Instead, he sat quietly for a while, observing the hissing pot hanging over the fire. "What happened with the emissary?"

Orion told Devon all that he could, leaving out only the details about Aristaeus's cave and the magical pool inside it. He hooked his fingers under the waistband of his trousers as he spoke but stopped when he thought better of it. While he had no qualms about undressing in front of his brother, he was not about to get caught in the nude by Leela.

"Let me get this straight. You want us to find some pirates and make a trade for an artifact? Have you lost your mind? They kill for those." Devon laughed, although the sound lacked emotion.

"I'm well aware. But it's either that or going to my father and asking him if he has an artifact we can use. We have better odds with pirates than with escaping my father a second time."

"I'm not insinuating we should go back to the castle."

Orion's shoes squeaked as he made his way toward the couch. "If it were up to me, we'd leave this place and never look back."

"Isn't it interesting how the mind works? Last month you were moping about it, and now here you are—making strides to become the old you. I bet Nava's happy."

Devon was right, much to his chagrin. Orion had groveled about the man he'd been without his memories. But as appalling as his actions had been before, things had changed. His father had attempted to hurt Nava, and nothing else mattered as much as she did.

"Let's not pretend you care how happy I make her and move on to what we need to do next." Orion pushed the words past stiff lips. Who could blame him for wanting to punch Devon's shit-eating grin off his face? Especially when he'd caught him gawking at his soulmate mere moments ago.

"It's been a while since we've tracked illegal trades in the ports." Devon stared past Orion's shoulder, out of the large window above the dining table. Perhaps he was remembering all the times the Society of Crows had sent them to fight pirates. "Are you expecting us to recognize some of the old crews from the Iron Kingdom? I'm confident they aren't running the black markets anymore."

"The life of those who live at sea is fleeting. We both know that." Orion sighed, rubbing the exhaustion from his eyes. Had he secretly been hoping for that? Finding a familiar face would save them time from sorting out the pirates from the regular sea merchants, but he wasn't that naïve. "I'm just grasping at straws, really."

"Even if we stumble over someone we know from the past, I doubt they'd be happy to see us, let alone work with us. They will never forget the Reaper."

Orion let his head fall back, suppressing a groan. "I know they'll remember me. Perhaps that'll give them an incentive to offer what we need, though."

"So, you want to go on the offense from the very beginning?"

"Do you have any better ideas, Devon? I'm all ears."

"Any suggestion is better than that. Nava just got hurt. I'm slowly dying, and you look like shit. No offense."

"Go on."

"What if we let *her* deal with them?"

Orion stiffened and frowned at his brother. "You want Nava to speak to the pirates? She's powerful, but I want her as far away from them as humanly possible."

"I know it sounds ridiculous, but hear me out. She has that newness about her that would allow her to get close enough to ask the questions we need to answer." Devon took a sip of his tea, placed the cup on the side table, and leaned against his chair. "We can count on them underestimating her. We've all made that mistake."

"So, your idea is, we go to the ports, track a ship, and send her in there to ask questions?"

No one parted with a god's artifact without bloodshed, and Orion sincerely doubted the bag of gold he carried inside his pocket would be enough to buy them one.

"We go to the bar they frequent at night. Nava heads in, disguised as a deserter, and lets it slip that she has something to trade for a ride out of this place."

"That sounds vaguely familiar..." They had done that same stint several times in the Iron Kingdom.

"And it always works. A pirate overhears that she has money, and it gets her a one-to-one meeting with the captain—or second-in-command."

"Fuck, I don't know if I can stand back and watch her go in there on her own."

"She won't be by herself. We'll be in the tavern, also in disguise. There will be blood eventually, and I doubt they'll even have what we're looking for, but that's our best option."

Orion hated to agree, but the odds of them getting closer were better if the pirates didn't see either of them. "Does Leela have anything stronger than tea in this place?"

"She offered me some sort of fae honey wine. I passed, of course. I wouldn't have benefited from being completely out of it for a day." He tapped his bottom lip with a long finger. "I always wondered, does the wine affect you like a human, or are you immune because you're also a fae?"

"You've asked me this at least a dozen times."

"I keep forgetting. So, what happens if you drink it, would you get all... loose and relaxed?"

He narrowed his eyes at Devon and stood, moving to the kitchen to search for that wine. "We will head to the port tomorrow and see if there are any merchants around."

"Merchants? What a boring way to describe them."

True. But Orion didn't want Leela to overhear any more than she probably already had. There was some movement downstairs, faint noises traveling to his ears. He opened a cupboard and discovered a large bottle full of amber liquid. Honey wine. If Nava knew what he was about to drink, it would horrify her. He poured himself a glass and downed half in one gulp before walking to the living area.

Leela greeted him with a nervous wave, peering at the glass in his hand. "I see you've found something with a bit more punch to it. It's the best in the kingdom."

"It's the best I've had," he agreed and returned her tentative smile.

"So, what's the answer to my previous question, brother? Is it just liquor, or are you drinking it to get heated with your soulmate?"

"Mr. Black!" Leela exclaimed.

Orion maintained his flat expression and raised his glass in Devon's general direction. "Be ready first thing in the morning or we will leave without you." And he made for the stairs, plucking a pair of pants from the pile on his way.

24
NAVA

Pirates, fae, and sorcery—those three words would never have crossed Nava's mind a year ago. Alas, this was what her life had become. She pulled the metal stamp from the black wax, revealing an uneven seal stuck to the parchment.

"Everything will be fine. I just have to play the part," she repeated to herself for the hundredth time. Maybe this time she would believe it.

Arkimedes's voice carried through the floorboards as he called to her from downstairs. He'd been on edge ever since they'd woken up before sunrise and gone over the details of their plan. A plan that sounded completely ridiculous, given how awkward she became when she was nervous.

Even Arkimedes hadn't seemed convinced it was a good idea, so why should she be? It wouldn't surprise her if he changed his mind and demanded that she stay behind while he took care of the rest with Devon.

Nava handed the letter to Leela, who'd been waiting by the bedroom door. "Are you sure it's not too much trouble to take this to the post?"

"Not at all. It's near the house, and I'm glad to help."

When they arrived the night before, the first thing on her mind had been Cameron. What would happen to him if things went awry and disaster struck? She could have lost her life in the fight with the Zorren and he would never have known.

Nava had no home to return to on Grey Island, even if they succeeded—because she'd freed their prisoner and that would never be forgiven.

So she poured the truth about everything that had happened onto pages.

When her parents died, she'd promised Cameron the truth. Her little brother deserved that much, and the situation was dangerous enough now that, if she died, she wanted him to know what had happened. In the end, Cameron would never forgive her if she'd kept it all from him.

Leela tightened the strings of her tunic around her neck. It was the same color as Nava's, a deep shade of green that brought out the blue hue of her friend's eyes.

Nava reached inside her coat pocket and grabbed the sun stone. Its warmth seeped through her cold, clammy fingers, lending her some strength to move forward. At least she had this small piece of Ari coming with her.

Devon and Arkimedes were waiting for her outside the shop. Both leaned against the wall, talking in hushed voices as they watched the fae pass up and down the busy street. Arkimedes's eyes settled on her as she exited the building, and Nava's heart jolted, butterflies flying in her stomach as she took in his handsome features. The chill of the morning did nothing to cool off the heat washing through her body.

"You've got everything you need?" he asked, and the intensity behind his eyes told her he was having the same reaction to her.

She nodded. The gentle hum of the sun stone inside her pocket comforted her, even in this dreary weather.

"You won't return?" Leela asked, locking the door of her shop behind her.

"Not tonight," Arkimedes answered. He offered Nava the crook of his elbow. "It's best if we don't stay with you for long stretches of time. We have imposed for long enough."

"It's not a problem, Your Highness. Please come back if you need a place to stay." Leela bowed, clearly missing Arkimedes's sharp exhale as he attempted to stop her but wasn't quite fast enough. "I will deliver the letter, miss. Good luck with what you're doing tonight."

"What letter?" he whispered to her as strolled down the wide street.

"I wrote to Cameron. To let him know about what's happening here..."

"Cameron?" Arkimedes's brow arched, and he brought his face closer to hers, so Devon couldn't catch what he said next. "You think it's safe for him to know you're here? What if he comes and we're in the middle of fighting the demons?"

"Well, I don't know," she mumbled and focused on their surroundings instead of Arkimedes. Of course, she didn't want her little brother to come to this kingdom when they were under attack. But what else could she do when she didn't know what would happen to her next?

If she didn't do this, what would become of him? While Violet and Gavin had taken him along on their journey, it was too much pressure to expect their friends to care for a teenager indefinitely.

Never mind that he was mature beyond his years—he was *her* family and responsibility.

"I hope he won't receive the letter too quickly, and we'll have some time to deal with this." She gestured around them. The town was alive with flower carts on the sidewalks, and large carriages pulled up and down the streets by orrus. She'd only ever seen these beasts in the Copper Kingdom, a strange blend between a buffalo and a horse.

Arkimedes nodded. "Even if the worst comes to pass, he won't be left penniless, Nava."

"Our old property in Willowbrook is still there, but I don't think he'll live there."

"When I stayed at the castle, I discovered that I inherited a large estate from my mother, and I also have some gold stowed away from my time with the Crows. It'll be tricky to access right now—but not impossible."

Nava nodded, tightening her fists as a rush of adrenaline surged through her. Overwhelm didn't begin to cover how she felt at the thought of leaving Cameron with all that, without him understanding why or how to manage it.

She cleared her throat and focused on the odd behavior the citizens were displaying instead. Why were they all dressed in white and yellow?

"I don't remember exactly where Cameron is and why he's there," Arkimedes admitted, scratching his forehead with his free hand.

Had he noticed the change yet? Or perhaps this wasn't a change at all, but a regular occurrence. Nava hadn't been in the city long enough to fully understand its customs.

"He's with Gavin and Violet on Pearl Island. Violet needed to go there to research something about how to prevent the drafts of children for the armies—I think." Her friend hadn't been exactly specific about her aims, and Nava hadn't asked too many questions. "Cameron wanted to go so badly and see the largest library in Caztian. We were in Willowbrook for so long. I didn't want to force him to stay behind with me—but I also couldn't just leave Aristaeus."

"He's always wanted to be a librarian," Arkimedes said, his eyes turning glassy, right before he brought his hand to his head with a grunt. Another headache, perhaps? "I don't know how long it will take for the letter to reach him, Nava. I understand why you want them to know, but it's risky. It could be intercepted."

She knew that, and still, she didn't regret sending it. "We can't go up against the Zorren and not tell Cameron he might lose the only family he has left. I also needed to tell Gavin and Violet that I released Devon, so they know not to return with my little brother, just in case Roman gets any ideas. Devon hurt all of us, and not everyone is ready to forgive."

"I heard that," Devon said from behind them.

"It's not untrue." Nava huffed. A part of her would forever be unhappy at having released him—not continuing to hate him like she should.

But she now also understood the other side of the story. How desperate Devon had been to locate Arkimedes at any cost. How angry and betrayed he'd felt when he discovered Ark alive and well, hiding in the forest.

She couldn't forgive him for what he'd done or how many people he'd hurt… but she *understood* him. And now she had to explain her reasons to Cameron and her friends, just in case the emissary won.

"I didn't know the kitten had a baby brother. What a revelation."

Arkimedes glanced over his shoulder and shot Devon a sharp look that would quieten almost everyone. "Don't say another word."

"You two need to lighten up and stop treating me like I'm the villain. I'm heading into a pirate lair with you because I want to help." Devon's face lacked any of his usual mischief. He was serious now. His black eyes met hers, and he placed his hand over his heart. "I would never betray your brother's existence to the Crows if that's what you're concerned about."

Strangely enough, Nava wasn't. Not now that he was aware of what the Society had done to his family. "Devon, to earn our trust, you've got to work for it. Not so long ago, you went against our request and asked the Vulcan the wrong question."

Devon's cheeks flushed as he averted his eyes and shoved both hands inside his wine-colored coat. It matched the striped pants he was wearing.

Leela had been fussing over all of their clothes for the better part of the morning. Little did she know they would have to change into less elegant attires soon enough.

Arkimedes placed a large gloved hand over hers. "Have you considered what might happen if Cameron, Gavin, and Violet come here before we defeat the emissary?"

Nava chewed her bottom lip. Her insecurities grabbed her in a chokehold. "Then we will ensure his safety."

If only she'd mastered her long-distance transfer before all of this. She could have simply visited Pearl Island and spoken to them there. But she'd just begun to hone her skills, and it was impossible for her to travel to the forest in one trip, let alone to an island far across the world.

"We'll work it out," Arkimedes said. "It would be nice to see them again."

"Even Violet?" she teased with a grin that widened as his expression sobered.

"No, just Cameron and Gavin. Violet can stay there for all I care."

They crossed a large bridge made of worn stone. Aged copper railings lined the sides, painted in green and white shades that matched the turquoise water in the canal below. A trading vessel was crossing beneath it right now, sporting impressive gray sails.

The seagulls squawked in the skies, circling the bridge and flying too close to their heads for comfort in their search for food. This part of the city differed from all the other areas Nava had visited. The road led them to an open plaza with the biggest fountain she'd ever seen, sparkling right in the center of the square.

Although breathtaking, it wasn't the beautiful sights that called to her. It was the flags hanging from every streetlamp and balcony above a shop. A black tree rose against the golden yellow background, framed by white trim. The fae walking about were all dressed in similar colors, and they were heading toward a stage right next to the fountain.

Was that the queen's tree? Were they wearing masks? Was this another celebration, like the solstice?

They approached cautiously, sneaking through a crowd surrounded by the loud chattering of people as they awaited the play.

"What's this celebration?" Nava asked Arkimedes, taking in every detail—from the street seller waving golden feather masks, to the small children in white, waving bouquets of equally white flowers.

"Not sure..." Arkimedes whispered, but his emotions were tumultuous. Which meant he was lying at least a little bit. Even if he still claimed that he couldn't.

Three-foot-long banners were draped over either side of the stage. In the center of its wooden deck, a table stood, covered with white linens. A fae sat on a throne, dressed in white and wearing a golden mask. He had huge black wings—evidently fake, as they hung crookedly over his shoulders and didn't move.

The fae's costume was eerily similar to what Arkimedes had worn on the night of the masquerade ball during the summer solstice. Nava remembered it vividly. Especially after she'd removed every item of clothing from his body during their mating heat.

Her throat went dry at the same time that Arkimedes stiffened beside her. This was a reenactment of that night. She knew it like she knew her own name.

A bell chimed once, twice, thrice, and the audience fell quiet as another fae actor entered the stage. He was wire thin, sporting pale wings with gold tips and a silver mask, the same color as his hair. He stayed near the side of the stage and bowed to the false prince sitting at the table and then to his audience.

"Gentle fae of our city, thank you for joining us in celebrations of *The Solstice Queen*." The host's voice projected widely across the plaza, carried by magic and echoing off the buildings behind them.

The audience clapped, and laughter rippled through the crowd. The actor's voice was deep and pleasant, but nothing could lift the sinking feeling in Nava's stomach.

Arkimedes's breath caught in his throat as a woman in a canary-yellow dress stepped out from behind the curtains. The crowd howled.

Fuck. They'd even gotten her dress right. It looked so close to the monstrosity they'd forced her to wear that night.

"It looks like you two got caught," Devon said with a chuckle. His black eyes twinkled when they landed on her. "This should be interesting."

The narrator cleared his throat and silence fell once more. "Many of you saw a bright beauty on the night of the solstice, and no one could ignore how she captivated our prince." The female fae prowled across the stage, flirting with several of the dancers before crooking her finger at the prince.

What? Nava had never done that. She hadn't flirted with *anyone*. And Arkimedes had come to her on his own.

"My prince, would you care to have some wine?" the woman purred and traced a finger over her large bosom with one dainty, gloved hand. The fake prince followed her moves with false interest.

Something hot and feral flared in Nava's stomach as she watched them. How dare they make a mockery out of that moment—out of her and Arkimedes.

"We should leave before someone finds us here." Arkimedes's breath hit the exposed skin of her neck and raised gooseflesh wherever it touched. "We don't need to see this."

"I disagree. This is quite entertaining," Devon said. "I don't remember Nava being that…sultry, but I might be remembering it wrong."

Arkimedes glared at Devon and reached for her hand. He lowered his face to hers, and when their eyes met, the crowd disappeared behind them. "We know what truly happened that night. This is just going to upset us."

"But what if they overheard our conversation?" she breathed in a panic, right before his lips met hers. The gentle kiss wasn't enough to douse the sudden heat that swept through her. It was almost as if they were back to that night, when her skin had burned and desire for her mate had become too much to ignore.

Her chest tingled as Ark traced his tongue over her bottom lip, and the sensation traveled down to her core, leaving her wanting more. But he pulled away from the kiss before it caught fire. His pupils swallowed his irises, leaving behind only a trace of green.

"I don't want to lose my temper and hurt them. It will be worse if I give away who we are in the middle of the city. We have to blend in tonight to get the artifact."

The artifact—right. Nava nodded and kept her eyes glued to him, allowing Arkimedes to be her anchor. It was wise to escape from here. There was no point in getting overwhelmed by her need for him in the middle of a crowd.

"Devon?" Arkimedes studiously avoided looking at the play, although his gaze had turned more serious. Even Nava could see a flick of his power emanating from his skin.

Devon shook his head and pointed at the stage. "I'm staying to *mingle* with the good fae of this town… Perhaps I'll take a stroll around the piers later."

Arkimedes frowned, and he reached for his brother, draping an arm over his shoulder. "You're feeling fine to do that on your own?"

"Indeed."

"What do you mean by mingle?" she asked.

"He's going to find the location we need for tonight. It's easier if only he looks for it," Arkimedes whispered into her ear. His voice was so soft she could barely hear him through the loud clapping around them.

Then he led her away from the crowd and toward a large building near the edge of the town square. *The Lost Chariot* read the sign above the inn's door.

Arkimedes had already informed her that they'd be staying here tonight. Close enough to the docks but far away from the unsavory *merchants*. Nava's natural curiosity had replaced the fear she'd felt for most of the morning. The more she kept hearing about the pirates, the more she wanted to see what all the fuss was about.

"At least now we know how they found out about me," she said. It also explained the pamphlet Leela had brought with her when she went to the potion store a week ago.

The waves of laughter called her attention to the stage. More and more spectators were gathering to witness a moment in their lives that was supposed to stay private. "Do you think your father knows?"

"Let's hope for the safety of these fools—and for the sake of our plan—that he hasn't learned of this play yet." His brows scrunched in the middle as he glanced to where his brother stood. "But the distraction will serve as a good cover for what Devon has to do."

25
NAVA

Nava stopped in front of a black door. The paint had peeled around its edges, and time had faded the gold numbers on the black plate in its center. 211.

The keys jingled inside her grasp as she unlocked the door, feeling Arkimedes's body pressed against her back as he leaned over her. Her grip trembled when he wrapped his fingers around her hand.

"Let me go in first. I want to make sure the room is safe."

She met his bright gaze over her shoulder. "How can it be dangerous inside? We just got here."

"Indulge me," he pleaded, his tone rough. His grin did little to calm the speed of her racing heart. She dropped her hand from the doorknob and stepped aside on wobbly legs.

That play had left her in a tangle of heated thoughts and immense want. With the reminders of the solstice dance swirling around her head, it was hard to stay focused on their reasons for being here.

Arkimedes soon waved her inside. Nava eyed every corner of the small space, from the cobwebs accumulating in one corner to the lantern hanging from the wall, which lit up as she wandered past it. The room was empty and musty, with a bed that would barely fit both of them.

"It will do for tonight," Arkimedes said and tossed the brass skeleton key onto the stiff mattress. Dust billowed as it bounced over the edge and clanked onto the wooden floor.

"I guess it's not too bad, since we won't be sleeping much tonight." Her cheeks warmed as her mind caught up with her words. "Because of the night we have planned. I meant nothing else by that—though I wouldn't oppose it either, I guess."

Arkimedes's grin widened as he grabbed her by the waist and pulled her close. "Are you nervous, Bee?"

"A little?" She craned her neck to meet his gaze and pressed her body to his.

"Devon and I will go to the tavern first to make sure it's safe. You can follow our bond to find me. Once we are settled, I'll let you know if we've found some pirates."

"How are you going to talk to me in there if we aren't supposed to know each other?"

"I'll find a way." He traced her cheeks with his rough fingertips. "We have our mind connection, too."

"I like that." Their mind link didn't work all the time, but it was an option. She nodded, and her eyelids drooped as his caress traveled to her neck, making her stomach flutter and her insides melt. "If you've already spotted our target, then I won't have to ask the bartender for a ship to take me out of the city. I'm not the best of liars."

"If they hear a new deserter is offering gold for a chance to leave this kingdom, it will get you noticed."

"And not all traders are pirates—I get it."

"And not all pirates deal in magical artifacts. Don't trust anyone in there. From the bartender to the old hag drinking ale by the bar."

"The old hag?" She chuckled, pleased that he was trying to ease her worries.

"There is always some crummy-looking woman using her fragility to steal from you. They are the worst of all." The air of his breath washed over her face, warm and inviting. And now her heart was beating fast, too —not from fear or nerves but with anticipation.

"Are you trying to distract me, Arkimedes?" She walked her fingers up the lapels of his coat and wrapped her arms around his neck.

"Is it working?" he asked and kissed her, stealing her answer. His demanding lips and expert tongue were fuel for her desire. Nava dug her fingers into his hair, giving in to the heat running through her veins. The little intimacy they might have for a while.

She trailed her tongue over his lips, rejoicing when he met it with his own in a slow, languid dance.

"You're going to kill me if you don't kiss me again," he whispered against her lips. He sounded drunk on the same desire that churned inside her, his body warm and hard against hers. Gods, she wanted to throw caution to the wind and allow herself to let go.

The background noise from the play seeped through the crevices in the walls. The glass was thin enough that it rattled with the wind, letting in the icy air. Outside, the crowd erupted with laughter, presumably about a particularly funny punchline she wouldn't have found funny at all.

"Bee." Arkimedes pulled away, tracing her face with his hand again. "Are you still with me?"

"Yes." Nava frowned. She hated the people of this town all over again —and herself for allowing them to get under her skin. "But I can hear everything happening out there. And Devon could come at any moment."

They had informed the innkeeper that someone else from their party would be joining them. They'd left no key behind, so Devon would have to knock on the door to be let in, but Nava really didn't want to get caught making love.

"We can't get carried away," Arkimedes agreed and shrugged off his coat, tossing it onto the bed. Even with him gone, she could still feel the ghost of his lips against her own. "But we need to change out of these fancy clothes."

"Let me help you." Her fingers untied the cravat around his neck, and she swallowed against the rock that lodged in her throat. The afternoon had come too fast, and he had to leave first, to make sure everything was *safe,* whatever that meant. There was no safety out there for either of them.

Arkimedes kissed her again as he loosened the ribbons of her complicated gown with needy fingers, giving away his lack of control. Whatever she'd been thinking before no longer mattered.

He cupped her left breast, then looped his other arm under her ass and lifted her in one fluid motion. Pressing her to the wall, Arkimedes devoured her neck, licking all the way down to her clavicle and up again.

The lamp trembled, its light flickering with the movement of her body colliding with the cool surface of the wall. Nava wrapped her legs around Ark's waist, momentarily struggling with the thick layers of her dress.

She squirmed, stuck in between him and the wall. A mewl escaped her lips when two of his fingers snaked their way over the thin layer of her drawers, pressing against her center, which throbbed with need.

"These won't do," Arkimedes breathed. The air rippled with his magic, and her skin felt cold and hot right before the distinct sound of ripping fabric filled the room. He exposed her to the cold air just as he bit and licked her neck.

"I don't think this wall can hold us—" Nava began, supporting her entire body weight on his shoulders as he roughly pulled down his pants. She couldn't see him, but she could feel the warmth emanating from the bare skin that touched her thigh.

"Not another word, Nava," he growled and resumed the path his hand had followed before: up her thighs and toward her aching center.

The strength of his kiss and the rough texture of his stubble bruised her lips. Her body coiled tight with want when he touched her where she needed him most.

"So wet," he purred. His fingers moved in maddening circles over her clit, and he trailed his other hand down her neck and chest, over the peak of her nipple.

The touch drove her wild, and she struggled to find purchase on his shoulders as her pleasure built. He kissed her again, hard. She would never tire of his taste.

Continuing, he moved two fingers inside her, pumping in and out. How he managed it with the little space left between their bodies was anyone's guess.

Her hips jerked, and her pleasure neared a crescendo. She trembled as a loud moan escaped her lips. Any second now. Gods, she felt as if she might break.

"Ark."

"Come for me, Bee."

Nava cried out as the tension built until it snapped, and the orgasm swept through her body in waves while she rode his hand.

"Good girl," he purred, removing his hand and taking a firm hold of her ass. She felt him line himself up against her entrance, and then he pushed into her in one fluid movement.

His groan of pleasure was all she could hear, and the lantern on the wall rattled before falling to the ground. The sound of breaking glass didn't stop them, not even as darkness bathed the room, except for the trickle of gray light that filtered through the thick velvet curtains.

Arkimedes's punishing rhythm extended her pleasure. Time slowed until only the two of them remained, until her skin went tight again and she shattered into a million pieces. He slammed into her one last time and followed with a grunt, letting his body weight rest against her.

The world slowly returned, blurred at the edges of her vision as Arkimedes withdrew and set her down on trembling legs. The long skirts of her dress fell around her as she dropped her head to the firm planes of his chest, waiting for her breathing to calm down.

Her heart was so full, and her body ached in the best possible way. "I love you."

"And I love you." He pressed his lips to her head and held her tight for a while until her blood stopped rushing inside her ears. This felt right. It was worth fighting for.

"It held up fine," he whispered at last, a hint of smugness in his tone.

"What?" she croaked, still in a daze.

Arkimedes stepped away and tucked himself back into his trousers, tidying up his black shirt and messing his hair. Now he looked properly rumpled in his fine clothes. Then he tapped the wall with one hand.

A cough from the neighboring room answered him.

Horror cooled Nava's heated flesh as she stared at the wall with wide eyes. "Do you think they could hear us?"

"I would assume so," Arkimedes said with a rakish smile.

"Why aren't you more disturbed by this?" she accused, horrified, and paced around the pile of broken glass left on the floor. At least now that the room was dark, she couldn't fixate on all the suspicious stains the cleaners had missed—if anyone had even attempted to clean this room, that was.

"Where are my undergarments?" she asked. She'd smelled magic and heard her clothes tear, but surely Ark hadn't destroyed them. Right?

Sticky wetness clung to the inside of her legs as she kept hunting for her clothes without success. She couldn't possibly head out to that tavern wearing nothing under the dress.

He looked away sheepishly. Oh dear gods. He had.

"Ark." She glared. "I don't want to take a bath in this place—much less go out there without underwear."

"Let it be. It will send a message."

She gaped at him. "Arkimedes! Did you ravage me in this dirty room just so you could leave a mark on me like some sort of animal?"

A smile tugged at the corners of his lips, and at his shrug, her face warmed. "I never claimed not to be. The fae in me demands things from me humans don't do. But make no mistake, you are mine, and I intend for anyone out there to know."

Nava crossed her arms, flaring her nostrils. "And you are *mine*."

"Yes, and now when I go to that awful place, I'll get to smell you."

Thankfully, a tiny washroom adjoined their chamber. Arkimedes left to gather some items for the night while she cleaned up a bit. By the time she was ready, he'd returned and was standing by the window. He'd opened the thick green curtains, allowing daylight to pour into the room.

"I got you a new dress," he said and pointed at the garment lying over the bed. He was wearing different clothes, too. Black and a hooded tunic that hugged his wide shoulders.

Nava joined him, glancing outside. The play had ended, and the crowds were dispersing, leaving rubbish strewn across the wide courtyard.

Who'd dared to spy on the prince of the Copper Kingdom that night? They clearly had been an eyewitness. The costumes were too accurate for anything else.

She dragged her fingers through the messy waves of her hair before braiding the sides tight to her scalp and tying it all behind her neck into a low bun.

"When do you think you'll leave?" she asked, hating how worried she sounded—and felt. Her nervousness wouldn't help with their task.

"When Devon gets here and tells us what he's found." His eyes moved up to the sky. It had darkened considerably. "If he isn't here by sunset, we will both leave together and make sure he hasn't got himself in trouble."

Nava rose on her tiptoes, trying to get a better view of the square below. "How can Devon mingle with the fae and gather information when they all seem to hate humans?"

"Not all do. Although I'm sure meeting Devon won't help their views on humankind." Arkimedes smirked. The playful expression made her stomach flutter, and the need that should be satiated began anew. He arched a brow, and his smile grew. "Are you all right? You seem flustered."

"Oh, hush."

He huffed a laugh with a shake of his head. "To answer your previous question, Devon is good at intimidating people, and he uses as many tactics as he needs to make them believe he is someone to fear."

True. Nava still remembered the afternoon Devon Black the Crow had walked into her potion shop in Willowbrook. He'd put the fear of the gods into her and sent her into a frenzy to escape the threat of imprisonment and protect Cameron. He'd set all of this into motion.

Damn him, but she loved him for it.

"I remember him doing that… He did it to me," she said. And to think it was all a mask Devon wore to get the job done. Much like the indifference Arkimedes hid behind. It was all to show the world that he didn't care about their judgment of him.

"Most fae out there possess little magic. Having someone like Devon ask them questions will force them to answer if he displays just a small fraction of his power."

"Do you think he's going to get in trouble?" And if so, with whom? The royal guards, the Society of Crows, or the pirates?

"If he isn't indulging in frivolities and is, in fact, scoping out information as he's supposed to, then no." His growing frown did little to calm Nava's dread.

"How often does he indulge?"

"Enough for me to be concerned."

Great.

Arkimedes cleared his throat. "In the meantime, I need to get some things to prepare for tonight. You should call upon your daggers."

"Which one? The one I left on Grey Island or the one your father's guards took from me?"

It had been a year since Nava had learned to use her magic and to accept it. She hadn't used the spell to portal the things she owned often enough. It took a lot of energy, especially if the items were far away.

"Not the dagger the guards took. While that one is closer, they might track it to the inn. You'll have some time to recover your energy this afternoon."

Arkimedes sat on the bed and opened his palms to the ceiling. He closed his eyes, and his shadow power deepened, extending like a halo of darkness around his body. Swirls of magic began to resolve into the shape of a longsword in his grasp until the substantial weight of his weapon filled his hands. The air vibrated in response to his power.

He'd done the same in the forest when he'd called upon his first aid kit, but that time, she'd been too out of sorts to really grasp what he was doing.

His sword from back home had made it all the way here. The sweat beading his temple and the fact that he remained seated told her all she needed to know about how much the spell would take from her.

Nava dragged her finger over the cool metal of his blade and shivered when she traced the etched shape of the naked queen's tree. Her tree. The first time she'd seen this sword, it had been hanging from Arkimedes's cabin wall. Now she understood the meaning behind the symbol.

Had he known the tree would bloom if she made it here? When she was snooping through his things that afternoon, Arkimedes had been well aware that she was his soulmate—and what the tree meant.

"Why do we need weapons if most people are without magic?" she asked.

"Because of where we are going. We might encounter the blinding spell."

"I don't like how that sounds."

"The Society of Crows crafted it to daze magic users for a short period. Just long enough to allow them to deal with a problematic magic-wielder." Arkimedes paused and shook his head, as if getting rid of a bad memory. "Years ago, someone leaked the spell, and now it's available on the black market."

"And of course, we are going to deal with pirates..."

"Many pirates are deserters, Nava. Former magic-wielders. But the ones that aren't usually carry crafted spells."

"Well, on the plus side, I miss my old dagger," she said with a weak smile and sat on the bed beside him. The light from her spell blinded her, and the familiar cool metal of her mother's dagger filled her palms a second later. It felt like forever since she'd seen this weapon—let alone held it.

A rapid knock on the door startled them, and Arkimedes was up on his feet, sword in hand, and across the room before her mind had caught up to the fact that someone was there.

"It's me," Devon said.

The room spun when she stood on shaking legs, her blood rushing in her ears—a clear sign of how much the spell had drained her.

Arkimedes cracked the door open, and a moment later, Devon strolled into the room.

"I'm not sleeping in here." He whistled and glanced at the broken glass on the floor and then up at the ceiling. "Seems you two have been busy…"

Nava's cheeks warmed, but she didn't dignify his comment with an answer. It was true either way, so she couldn't exactly deny it.

"Did you discover anything useful?" Arkimedes asked.

"Lots." Devon paused a few feet away from her and turned to face Arkimedes. He coughed, but the noise wasn't as terrible as it once had been. "It seems someone followed you two into the castle's garden the night of the solstice, but they didn't listen to anything important—or they are smart enough not to divulge it to the crowds."

"What about the ships?"

"There are a couple of promising leads docked nearby. When I inquired with the local fishermen, they said they'd been docked for a week already, which means we don't have long to get what we need."

"Did you see any familiar faces?"

"I'm afraid not." Devon took a deep breath and promptly choked. He pulled a handkerchief from his pocket. Then he coughed loudly into it.

"I thought you were feeling better?" Nava stepped toward him, studying his pale face. It wasn't odd for him to look like this. Nava had met no one as fair as Devon Black.

"It's dusty here." He met her gaze evenly, but worry was etched onto his features.

"Don't lie to her, Devon. It won't help you." Arkimedes dropped his sword on the bed before he brought over the sheath and a long, aged black belt.

She sniffed. It was true that the air was musty here. "I can try to heal you once more before you leave?"

"No, save your energy. You aren't mentally ready to deal with the shifters and the lowlifes we are going to encounter. But you should at least be prepared by keeping some energy."

"Suit yourself," Nava said with more bite than she'd intended. But she hated the feeling of not being prepared and knowing less than everyone else in the room. It was how she'd felt for months after first being thrust into this dizzying world of magic.

Ark eyed her knowingly and reached for her hand, squeezing it lightly. "You'll be fine."

Was he trying to reassure her or himself?

"We should go soon. The sun isn't too far away from setting, and Nava shouldn't be walking the docks on her own at night."

Arkimedes nodded and knelt in front of her. "Here, let me get this ready for you."

She stood still, watching his hand trace the shapes of her legs underneath the skirt of her dress. Up and up they traveled as he met her gaze with a defiance that made her heart skip.

Devon walked toward the door, muttering something under his breath.

Nava's heart nearly leaped out of her chest. "Stop that." She slapped his hand away, even as her stomach twisted in delight.

Arkimedes chuckled and finished strapping the dagger belt around her thigh. Then he whispered, "You smell delicious."

"Did you know there's a blade with your name on the bed?" She narrowed her eyes at him and stepped away. She was half ready to stomp on him for teasing her—or push him into the bed. To hell with their mission.

Devon popped his head back into the room from the dark hallway beyond. "The name of the tavern is the Flying Boar. Don't leave this place after sunset, Kitten, or you will be sorry."

26
ORION

"It's not looking promising. Where are the merchants in this place?" Devon took a sip from his second pint of ale.

They had been in the Flying Boar for at least a couple of hours, although it was hard to tell the time when the windows were closed with wooden shutters and the walls were a uniform shade of brown.

Everything was dark in this place, undoubtedly to hide the layers of filth caking the floor and every sticky surface. Orion couldn't see the sunlight from where they sat at the far end of the room, but he hadn't felt Nava approach yet.

She should have left the inn by now…right?

"You should pace yourself with the drinks," he said as Devon gulped down his drink almost without breathing. He wasn't sure if his brother was drinking this much to take the edge off or to dull the pain he was under because of the Vulcan.

"I'm fine," Devon assured him, although his eyes were starting to glaze over. "Maybe you've forgotten I can handle my liquor."

"Everything but fae wine, apparently," Orion said with a smirk, bringing his own drink to his lips. Gods, it was terrible. Bitter and way too yeasty.

The dip in temperatures and the constant rain seemed to be driving everyone into this establishment. Most were local fae. The few traveling merchants Orion had spotted when they'd arrived all looked unfamiliar.

He sighed, rubbing his brow and trying to swallow his discomfort. Most pirates were shifters, humans, or former magic-wielders. He couldn't blame them for not wanting to come to the Copper Kingdom when the fae held a grudge against their kind.

Nava was right. He should have known this trip would be in vain.

"There is no one here to trade with. It's why so many shops have shut down," he whispered, unsure if Devon could hear him through the roar of drunken laughter and singing from the stage at the other end of the room.

Devon reached for a buttery roll in the center of the table and pulled a sizable chunk from it before dunking it into his broth. "You got your work cut out for you, brother. Fixing this place once the ol' man croaks won't be easy."

That almost made him laugh, but Devon was right. Orion's father's complete disregard for the human population that lived in the kingdom had proved atrocious for the economy. Perhaps that had been the true reason behind the kingdom's decline instead of his absence.

Then again, if he'd stayed, perhaps he'd never have allowed things to become this bad.

Even though the king rarely enforced the tithes, he'd also done little to provide for and protect the humans in his kingdom who lived in poverty.

The hair of Orion's arms suddenly stood on end as strings of energy rose from the ground. It was the same power that had come to help him when they'd escaped the safe house, but it felt different, too. Like a warning.

He shifted on his chair and secured the hood over his head, making sure none of his features peeked out.

"I doubt any of the fools dining here are trading on the black market. Look at them, they're happy and drunk. Perhaps we should check the rooms upstairs?" Devon pointed behind Orion's shoulder, looking grim.

Orion glanced in the direction his brother indicated, up the narrow steps that led to an open second floor. Even in the darkness, Orion could spot doors up there. A woman exited a room, wearing nothing but a sheer slip, her tits bouncing for everyone to see. Someone nearby howled at the sight of her, but she didn't pay them any heed as she fanned her shiny face. She looked utterly fucked and rumpled.

Orion raised his brows and looked back to Devon. "Do you think the rooms are rented by the hour?"

"Indeed, and I think sailors traveling across the sea for months can get awfully lonely. I wouldn't put it past the worst kind of *merchant* to be up there. Which could explain why there's no one down here—" A cough tore past Devon's lips, interrupting his speech. He took a deep breath and reached for a new potion from his pocket, avoiding Orion's eyes when he took it. "Perhaps you and Nava can accidentally stumble inside one of those rooms? It might be a way to discover if a pirate is exercising up there."

"*Exercising*, really? What are you, twelve?" Orion scoffed. "Either way, we shouldn't be calling more attention to ourselves than we have to. Coming here is already a risky move."

"I guess you're right. Sometimes I forget you're important."

"It's not about being important, Devon. But we are on the run." And he was feeling so on edge already. Like the tavern was telling him someone watched him. But there weren't any Dark Ones here, and everyone else was too drunk, dirty, and definitively not paying attention to them.

"Isn't being on the run and being important the same thing? I'm just fed up with hiding away from everything," Devon said in a pensive tone. "It must be nice, being in this kingdom where you actually fit in." He turned and patted the wooden backrest of his chair. "I've noticed the chairs here are designed for people with wings. Even the coat Leela gave me has discreet slits all across the back. It would accommodate someone like you, so you don't have to hide your true nature."

"I do like that," Orion admitted. "Here, I'm not an outsider simply for being a fae."

He paused and studied their surroundings again. Nothing had changed, but the anxiety within him was ramping up. It wasn't Nava who needed him this time, but something else. The same old patrons he'd become familiar with over the last couple of hours sat around them. The same band played a merry tune.

Where was the source of danger?

Devon ate his meal without a worry in the world. Pottery shattered as a scuffle broke out to their left, the stranger's drunken yells muffled by the general noise of chatter.

Most people ignored what was happening, but Orion couldn't.

Instead, he was inspecting the very shadows of the tavern, half expecting a royal guard to emerge from them to drag them away. Or perhaps it would be a Crow, blending into the busy night, much like the two of them were doing.

"You look tense. Talk to me," Devon said.

"Something is off." And there wasn't a point staying here waiting if Nava could arrive in a potentially dangerous situation at any moment. "We're being watched."

"Now?" Devon stilled. His dark eyes darted from side to side as he slowly placed his spoon on the table. The air shifted with the spice of magic, and his fingers whitened with shimmering ice. "I see nothing."

"I don't think it's anyone here, but I can't be sure." Orion stood, leaving his untouched meal on the table and closing his coat. "It's like the city is telling me something is coming. We should search the area."

Devon not even questioning how strange that sounded was perhaps even more unsettling than the fact that Orion was connected to the very land they stood upon.

"You check from the sky, and I will take the streets around the tavern. We'll meet in the side alley in an hour. If you don't come, I'll assume something happened to you."

"And if that's the case, make sure Nava stays safe."

"I swear it."

From the sky, the ports looked small and the streets eerie in the wet night. Nava should've been here well before dark, and it complicated matters that she hadn't arrived. Judging by the pull of the bond, though, she wasn't far.

There was movement down in the streets, the sounds of footsteps amplified by the puddles on the ground. Women in ornate gowns clutched their parasols close to their bodies, taking refuge from the early evening drizzle. Their silhouettes moved beneath the gaslight, casting long shadows over the wooden planks.

Orion didn't know how to explain the odd feeling he had. At least not without sounding like a madman, for it churned inside his blood, nearly suffocating him. But he'd learned that he needed to trust his gut, and if the land was speaking to him, then he would listen.

The cold bit at his cheeks as he circled the block around the tavern, inspecting the shadowy gable rooftops with care. It was unlikely that anyone would be able to stand on slick terracotta tiles. Not unless they were fae that hid in the shadows. Which could be the case…

He followed the instinctive pull that had led him here and landed in a crouch on one of the building's rooftops. His feet fit inside the terracotta tile grooves as he stabilized himself low to the surface. The clay was still warm from the afternoon's sun, and mist rose from it, warming his hands.

"Come out now. I know you're there, and I'd rather not have to hurt you," Orion said to the nothingness. He didn't want to harm a guard. Many of them had become friendly with him over the past five months he'd spent in this kingdom.

He focused on the chimney that jutted out of the building, where the shadows shifted with barely perceptible movements.

After the emissary's attack, the only thing consuming Orion's mind had been to find the artifact. His father and the guards had been the last thing on his mind today. How foolish of him, to walk around the place without a proper disguise.

Slowly, a winged figure appeared from the darkness, wearing copper armor from head to toe.

"Your Highness." The fae dipped his head as a sign of respect. His gravelly voice was one he recognized. The crashing waves rumbled in the distance, just as Cyrus's wings materialized on his back. They were as black as Orion's, not something common in their kind. Right now, it helped him blend further into his surroundings.

"Are there any more of you here?"

"No, sir. It's just me. I didn't mean to bother you."

Full fae couldn't lie outright, which made Orion inclined to believe him. The real question was, how much of the truth was he hiding? "Did you just find me this afternoon, and have you told my father?"

Cyrus tilted his head forward in acknowledgment. Something the fae usually did when they didn't want to answer straight away. Cyrus's armor screeched with the movement as raindrops dripped over the curves of the metal. "The king has sent two sentinels to watch over you ever since you escaped. We found you when you left the Crow's nest, sir."

Orion blinked rapidly as his mind caught up with Cyrus's words. "You have been following me all this time?" He couldn't believe it. How had he missed this?

But the guard nodded. "We have, Your Highness."

"Where is the second sentinel?"

"He's back at the inn, guarding your mate, sir."

Fuck. "If either of you hurt her…" Orion snarled. His wings fluttered up and down, sending debris flying off the roof as he readied himself to take off and return to Nava.

"The king commanded us not to harm the future queen, nor to be seen by either of you." Cyrus's voice held shame as he looked down. "Which I failed to do tonight."

Orion's chest tightened. After what had happened in the castle, his father had put it all together. He clearly understood Nava's importance in this entire story, so much so that he'd commanded a sentinel to stay with her.

Yet Leela had said that Nora, one of his father's concubines, had told her everyone believed Nava had put him under a spell.

Did his father believe a soulmate bond was a spell that clouded a person's judgment? A weakness? Wasn't Orion's mother rumored to have been the king's soulmate?

His throat went dry all at once as Orion focused on the bond he shared with Nava. Thankfully, she was fine, for her overriding feelings were nerves about their assignment—not fear or anger. And she was getting closer.

"My father commanded you to leave us alone?"

"That's correct, sir. We are here to secure your safety."

There was something not being said here, and Orion knew better than to fully believe all that the guard shared. "So long as we don't leave the kingdom?"

"If you remain in our land, sir, then we are supposed to stay in the shadows." The guard hesitated in silence, then pulled off his helmet, revealing bright blue eyes that shone in the night as they met Orion's from across the rooftop. "We lost track of you for a few days, and we feared you'd gone into the forest to fight the demons on your own."

Ah. So they'd known the Zorren were attacking but hadn't come to help? "Why didn't you come to my aid if you thought that was the case?"

"The king commanded us to report back if you left the city. I attempted to follow you while Eris went to the king. But with the storm, I lost your scent, and by the time I reached the fires, there were no demons, and you were gone."

Somehow Orion doubted his nervousness was the city warning him about the guards. Especially if this had been going on for so long. Was he feeling watched because something had changed with Cyrus, or was it a warning about something else entirely?

No matter what Cyrus had said, Orion had to ensure Nava was safe. "Don't follow me anymore," he commanded.

"Your wish shall become my command, Your Highness," Cyrus said after a long pause. He put his helmet on, beginning to fade back into the shadows. A well-considered choice of words. For in the future, Orion would come to overrule everyone else. But tonight, King Oberon still had the final say.

Cyrus was smart enough to know to give Orion space, and he wasn't ready to get into a fight and harm this guard because he was following orders. Not unless either of them hurt Nava.

Intent on following the soulmate bond and intercepting Nava as she approached the tavern, Orion leaped off the roof.

He found her fast. Her steps clicked against the wet stone, speeding up as she shouted over her shoulder at a nearby man. Her gown was puffier than what she usually wore, adorned by a corset that shimmered beneath the gaslight.

He could stop her. Tell her all he'd just learned. Then they could leave, still with no idea of how or where to get an artifact. Trouble seemed to pile higher with each passing day, but the threat to the world and the Beekeepers remained.

Now more than ever, they couldn't go to his father for help.

Orion landed on the cobblestone and rushed into the alleyway where Devon awaited. He'd allow his mate to go into the tavern on her own—for now.

"You come empty-handed. Does that mean I left my perfectly good meal inside that hole for nothing?" Devon asked in a flat tone, mist billowing from his lips.

Orion opened his mouth to tell him everything and promptly shut it again. The weird vibrations continued, coming at him in waves, rising from the ground.

"I take it you found nothing strange either?" Orion clicked his tongue and walked to the end of the alley, all the way up to the tavern's back door, where old produce crates were stacked against the wall.

"Of course I didn't. Have I mentioned that I hate walking in this muggy place when I can barely breathe?" A cough rattled past Devon's lips, as if to drive his point home.

His hair was sticking to the sides of his sharp cheekbones. He'd lost considerable weight ever since they'd escaped the safe house. Perhaps Arkimedes shouldn't have stopped him mid-dinner.

"It's probably a pirate who followed me when I returned from the piers. I haven't done this for so long now. I'm rusty."

It might be—or maybe not. "My father's guards have been trailing us ever since we left the safe house."

"What?" Devon looked up to the sky and the empty balconies that jutted from the surrounding buildings. "How do you know?"

"I just finished talking to Cyrus, a sentinel." Was Eris still with Nava?

"Well, that was it, no? You were right to feel watched. What are we supposed to do now?"

"I don't know if it was my father's guards triggering this feeling or someone else," he whispered. "Nava is in the tavern. We should head back in."

"So we continue with our existing plan?" Devon pushed off the wall, his brows dipping over his black eyes as he crept toward the back door.

They were soaked from the gentle but steady drizzle of rain by now, and the cold had snaked its way through all the layers of Orion's clothing. "I don't trust my father, even if for some strange reason he has known where we were and has done nothing about it," he admitted. He ran a hand over his hair.

"Do you think he commanded Leela to house us all this time?"

"It stands to reason he would," Orion said.

Devon cursed. "If I were the king, I wouldn't want either you or your soulmate harmed. Especially if it's true that the health of the kingdom depends on your bloodline." Devon's lips pressed into a fine line. "But I wouldn't trust him any further than that."

Exactly. Orion sighed. The air was thick with the rich scent of coal smoke and dampness. The distant rumble of a carriage in the distance drowned out the obnoxious laughter from the hansom cab drivers who were loitering outside the tavern, waiting for customers to drive home.

Orion opened the door that would lead them back into the warm hellhouse they'd just left, but he paused and studied his brother for a moment. "How are you truly holding up?"

"Still dying," Devon said. "And fine to do whatever needs doing today."

27
NAVA

Nava dragged her sweaty hands over the bodice of her dress for the tenth time in a row. By this point, if any crease remained, it was meant to stay. It was a full moon tonight, not that anyone could tell with the stormy weather.

The ocean waves crashed against the barrier of stone beside her, sending droplets of salty water into the air.

It had been drizzling ever since she'd left the inn, and it was far too cold to get wet. Would her dress allow her to blend in with the other patrons at the tavern, even if she turned up looking like a drenched animal? She'd hoped at the very least she wouldn't stand out as the only human in a crowd of fae. All she had to do was play a role and gather information that might save the kingdom. No pressure.

Rolling an errant curl of hair around a finger, Nava prayed that, for one night, she'd manage to put on the best act of her life instead of ruining it all with awkward comments. She was a deserter on the run, and she needed to act like it. She'd fought far worse battles than this.

"My lady." A tall man shifted under a streetlamp, tipping his head in her direction with a feline smile. His hair was thick and plastered to his skull with grease. Light golden flecks lit his eyes, brought out by the warm tones of the lamp. "Do you need a ride tonight?" His tone alone raised gooseflesh across her body, an excellent incentive to quicken her steps.

Was he offering her a ride home—in a carriage or on a beast—or was this an offer of another type of ride?

"No, thank you," Nava said, while her stomach revolted at the stench that emanated from him. Alcohol and a general lack of hygiene.

The faster she was out of his sight, the safer she would feel.

His eyes brightened in that unnatural way that was neither human nor fae. A shifter. "Are you sure? I could keep you warm."

"I'm not interested," Nava said in between ragged breaths and felt for the pommel of the dagger Arkimedes had strapped around her thigh earlier. Hopefully, the shifter wouldn't chase after her.

The noise in the busy area in front of the tavern swallowed his distant growl. Devon had been right, as much as she hated to admit it. She was completely inexperienced in dealing with shifters. It had been silly of her to fall asleep earlier today when she should have left earlier.

People dressed in their work clothing were strolling along beneath the streetlights, but most of them looked too drunk to pay attention to her. The women wore bright-colored dresses, their skirts wide with wire petticoats underneath them, and tight corsets. Fashion from another kingdom, for the fae's fashion was much simpler. Yet the dress Nava wore was similar in many respects, except not as bright.

Were all of them shifters? They must be. They moved in a sinuous, smooth way, unlike any human she had ever seen.

She shivered and nearly ran the rest of the way. The ground changed from thick wooden planks to cobblestones, and she was now close enough to the building she could make out every detail.

Outside it, carriages with enormous horses and orrus were waiting. The few footmen lounging about in this weather sat on a bench, smoking and laughing at the poor soul whose task it was to clean up the beasts' droppings.

A wooden sign hung above the worn double doors, reading, in black letters, *The Flying Boar.*

There wasn't any reason to be this nervous. Not when she'd fought in magical wars, defeated demons, and escaped the king. She could do this.

Nava took a deep breath and went in.

Ale, roast pork, and odors she'd rather not identify greeted her as she entered the establishment. Circumstances stacked the odds against her favor, as she had rarely attended places like this, even before joining the world of magic.

She studied the wide space with dozens of small wooden tables, where customers gathered, eating, drinking, and playing games.

Across the room, a long counter stretched, tended by a woman with black clothing and thick rings of kohl around her eyes. Nava cleared her throat and forced her heavy feet to move forward. One step, two steps, and she rounded the first table.

"Look at this gorgeous creature that's just joined us," a male voice said, and a strong arm snaked around Nava's waist, gripping her so tightly she lost her balance. The man pulled her onto his lap a split second later.

His large group of friends howled loudly, banging their fists against the rickety table, almost like a song. Nava met his brown eyes, glazed by alcohol. Her stomach twisted, and she pushed off his chest and stumbled back onto her feet.

"Touch me again and you will lose your hand," she snarled and pulled out her dagger so quickly her mother would be proud.

"I meant no disrespect, magic-wielder." The man shrunk so far into his chair that it creaked under his considerable weight. The laughter around them died away. His eyes were wide, although he wasn't looking at the tip of her blade, which was so close to his throat. Instead, he stared at her glowing skin.

Nava could feel Arkimedes's anger brewing through their bond, blending with her own. He wasn't far and was likely watching and getting ready to intervene. Dammit all, she'd almost ruined this entire quest by not properly avoiding these drunken fools.

It was too dark and busy to find either Ark or Devon amongst the patrons. If she closed her eyes for long enough, she might be able to pinpoint exactly where Arkimedes was, but this wasn't the time to hold back and allow another of these men to touch her again if it risked blowing their cover. She straightened her clothes and headed toward the bar without another glance.

"Ya aren't from around here," the barkeeper observed. She was wiping a tall clay mug with a brown towel that had been clean once upon a time. Then she stacked it into the neat row of similar mugs behind the counter.

Liquor and ale jugs lined the wall all the way up to the high ceilings.

Like most establishments in this city, they were evidently set up to accommodate the winged citizens.

The bartender turned to Nava with a steady gaze. "This not a place for a dame like yarself to come alone."

"I'll survive for one night." Nava sheathed her dagger in its strap. Good thing her dress had a side slit or she wouldn't be able to access her weapon so easily. "Can I have a glass of something other than fae wine, please?"

The woman raised a thin brow and tilted her head forward. Pointed ears peeked through the waves of her ebony hair. She had peculiar wings coming through the suede vest she wore, transparent and glass-like, like those of Nava's bees.

"Yar afraid of the fae wine?" She smiled knowingly and pushed a short cup over the smooth counter, filled to the brim with amber liquid.

"I'd rather keep my head on my shoulders tonight." Nava nodded and took a tentative sip of her drink. Smooth and bittersweet, with a smoky aftertaste. It burned down her throat and warmed her gut, right before it sent a cough rattling past her lips. The alcohol threatened to come back up.

"What on earth is this?" Nava pressed a hand to her lips, attempting to drown out her wheezing. This was not the way to blend in with a drunken crowd! She glanced around, hoping no one watched her almost spit up her drink.

"Not used to amber whiskey?" The fae continued drying mugs with the same towel, peering at the other patrons sitting at the bar. "It's two gold coins."

For one drink? Nava craved something to wash away the grit on her tongue, but this was not it. She studied her mostly full glass with a frown. Even though she was inexperienced with this general lifestyle, she knew this was very little liquid for such a price.

Still, her body had warmed significantly, and with one sip, she instantly felt less tense. This was no wine—nor any whiskey she'd had before. "Is this going to make me lose my mind like the fae wine?"

"Nah. It's what we serve the humans when they don't want ale."

Nava hummed and tapped her fingers against the surface of the bar. It had once been polished wood but now was stained with moisture rings and scrapes from the odd blade. "It's true I don't belong here, which is why I'm looking to leave."

"Leave the bar or the city?" The fae's tone filled with curiosity, although her bright eyes remained glued to her tasks. Then her expression changed to a conspiratorial look, and she rested her narrow hips against the edge of the countertop, finally looking up to meet Nava's gaze. "I saw yar doing magic back there. Ar ya a deserter?"

"I was not supposed to use magic out here. I don't want a Crow to find me," Nava whispered and glanced over her shoulder at the sea of faceless people. Coins were being slammed against surfaces and tossed to the floor. Nava straightened. Hopefully, if she voiced some of her real fears, her act would be believable enough.

"Haven't seen a Crow in years," the fae said and tapped her pouting lip with a long finger. "But the pricks usually use disguises."

The very thing Arkimedes and Devon were doing right now. Two ex-Society members who used the tactics they'd learned once upon a time when they were Crows.

Nava grabbed her drink with trembling hands and took a small sip. "I need a ship that can take me out of this kingdom. I heard I might find someone in this crowd? Perhaps you could point me in the right direction?"

The fae stood straight, her friendly expression dropping within an instant. She eyed Nava from beneath her long lashes. "Who told you to come here?"

"I heard it out in the streets. It was rather busy today, so I don't recall who said what, but the name of the bar stood out to me. Please. I really, *really* need to leave."

"Ya still got meat around your bones, which leads me to believe ya haven't been on the run for long." The bartender spoke with empathy. Nava hadn't expected that. "Have ya any clue how many deserters ask me that very question?"

Nava could not swallow past the thick lump that formed in her throat. Images of the family they'd found in the abandoned bakery weeks ago leaped to her mind's eye. Caden, the special boy who had the gift of the Sight, his brother the protector, and his sister who'd fed them broth. Children running away—unable to escape. Cameron and the way she'd had to leave him behind to protect his freedom when Devon came to her potion shop. "I'm well aware. But I'm not alone, and I have to leave."

"Another pint, Morgan!" someone yelled from the other side of the counter.

The bartender grunted a curse in another language and waved a dismissive hand toward the screamer. "For a price, I can pass yar information to the right *merchant.*" Her eyes said more than her words. A pirate, who was a lot more dangerous than a regular trading ship. "Like I do for most of those who come here asking the same."

"How much would that cost me?" A wave of annoyance rushed through Nava. Why would this fae prey upon the deserters when they had little to nothing left? When most, as she so gracefully pointed out, were only skin and bones?

"Twelve gold coins, and even if you pay, I can't guarantee that he will come to meet ya," Morgan said. The corners of her lips tilted down as she studied Nava's expression. She leaned forward, and her sour breath hit Nava straight in the face. "I know why yar looking at me like that, girl," she whispered. "But nothing in this world yar attempting to enter comes for free. This is not all for me. The merchants charge a hefty fee to even meet ya, and it won't be coming from me."

It wasn't worth getting into this argument. Nava would never understand what drove people to prey on the needy. But her main aim here was to find a magical artifact to save the kingdom from the Zorren. And the pirates were the only lead they had.

Nava reached inside her pocket and counted out fourteen round coins. Two for her overpriced drink and twelve for a meeting with a pirate. The uneven texture of the gold clanked loudly against the counter as Nava allowed it to drop from her hand. Greed was the downfall of all sentient species of this world.

28
NAVA

Nava rolled her shoulders to ease the ache that extended down her back from sitting too stiffly on that uncomfortable stool. How long had she been waiting for this supposed pirate to appear? A long time, if the lack of circulation in her legs was any measure at all.

Morgan had disappeared from behind the bar at least half an hour ago, and a younger server had taken her place. The new fae's shifty eyes kept flicking at Nava like she was trouble. And perhaps he was right.

Had she lost fourteen pieces of gold for nothing? Surely this was why Arkimedes had attempted to warn her about not trusting anyone in this place. Heat rushed to her face as she finished what remained of her drink and glanced discreetly toward the main area. Come to think of it, where was he?

His feelings were very much present and filtered through to her in waves, which could only mean he was in the room. He wasn't pleased, either, but hadn't approached her yet.

A sudden shadow fell over her before the largest man Nava had ever seen settled on the stool beside her. He smelled like the sea and the lingering scent of pure sunlight, but not entirely pleasant at the same time.

What a ridiculous thing to think—who smelled like sunlight? Clearly, that amber whiskey had some of the fae juju in it, and she was losing her mind, after all. Nava blinked rapidly and turned away from the man so she wouldn't catch his attention.

"Are you the mouse Morgan came yapping about?" He tipped his head toward the scrawny bartender, not sparing a look at her. The leathers of his clothes creaked as he leaned forward on the counter. "The magic-wielder looking to leave this fine piece of dirt?"

There was a healthy dose of sarcasm in his tone, and it bothered her. What did he have against her kingdom? No, not her kingdom. But even she could admit it had potential.

Nava looked at him and attempted to keep her features blank. He carried himself with the confidence of someone who had no troubles in the world. The complete opposite of how she felt because her nerves had returned with new vigor. This man wasn't human, although she couldn't quite place *what* he was.

He moved with the edge of someone dangerous enough that they weren't one bit concerned about her potential to harm them. "I don't have all night, mouse. Speak or this meeting is over."

Nava straightened, pushing down her bubbling temper. She couldn't afford to lose this lead. "I'm looking to leave…and have gold to buy me and my family passage." She kept her words simple and close to what she'd told Morgan.

The pirate faced her straight on, and the breath caught in Nava's throat as she noticed his missing eye. He studied her, not in a salacious way but with curiosity. A discolored scar ran from one end of his forehead, across his brow bone, and all the way down his cheek.

"The answer is no."

"No? That simple?" Her lips parted in shock. "You won't help me even if I pay you?"

He grimaced. "You have freaky eyes."

Nava fought the sudden urge to turn away and hide her face behind her hair, like she always did when people made negative remarks about her different-colored eyes.

"You're one to talk," she said heatedly and pointedly looked at his missing eye. She usually wasn't the petty kind, but she also wouldn't let this man walk all over her and insult her to her face. She had no time to waste. "I can't see what my eyes have to do with what I need."

The pirate grinned, revealing sharp, yellowing teeth. A shifter? What was he? "Neil! A pint of ale." He slammed his tattooed hand on the counter. There was a snake—or a dragon?—inked on his tan skin. It appeared to slither with the movement of his muscles. An optical illusion, perhaps?

The server, who'd been avoiding the area where Nava sat ever since Morgan had left, was with them in the blink of an eye. Up close, he was a mousy thing, shaking under his thin clothes. He picked up a clay mug and filled it with bubbling beer. "Here, Draken."

"Put it on the mouse's tab." He pointed at Nava but didn't turn to look at her.

"Excuse me?" Nava's lips parted in a silent gasp as she stood from her stool. "You don't get to decide whether I buy you a drink or not. Especially after you just denied me what I need."

"Sit. I'm not done with you," Draken ordered. "To answer your question, your eyes could easily be bad luck. In a world of magic, I'm not one to take risks." He took a long swig of his drink.

And what did that mean? Perhaps he'd had a premonition that warned him of someone with different-colored eyes?

Nava didn't sit. Instead, she gripped the pommel of her dagger, narrowing her eyes at him. "I'm not paying for your drink, but I have gold to pay for passage."

"No gold can get me to take you on my ship. It's not worth the risk. But I can give you information about who might—for a price."

All of these bastards were leeches. "If you can't take me, then I'm interested in a trade." She lowered her voice so the bartender and the surrounding patrons wouldn't hear her. "The Crows are trailing me and my family, and I need a weapon that will help me fight them."

"A weapon to defeat the Crows?" He laughed from his belly up, a genuine sound that even reached his shimmering eye. Perhaps he was curious about her. Or he wasn't used to anyone answering him so directly.

He was a scary-looking shifter, but Nava possessed more power than he gave her credit for, and she wasn't a damsel in distress. Besides, Arkimedes was somewhere in the room.

"How much gold are you talking about? It seems you already have a fine dagger strapped to your body."

He'd noticed. Had he watched her threaten the other man? He was so large, Nava couldn't imagine him blending too well into the shadows of the dining area. "I have enough to buy a god's artifact...with no one being the wiser."

Of course, that was a bald-faced lie. She had maybe ten coins left. He would never sell her an artifact for that little.

"A god's arti—" Drake sobered and looked around them, as if he expected someone to jump him from the shadows. Not that he was that far off with his fear. "I'm thinking you're a Crow. Hiding behind this act of a powerless mouse." His growl began in the very center of his chest, and his eyes sizzled orange and yellow, like the embers of fire. A dragon shifter. "Speak the truth or face the consequence of wasting my time."

Grit stuck in her throat, and she *felt* Arkimedes move toward her. His shadows floated around the tavern like cool mist that raised the hair on the back of her neck.

There were a few gasps in the distance, but Nava focused on Draken, unblinking.

She craved more of the bitter amber whiskey. They didn't need to add another foe to their growing list. Ari always spoke the truth, and it was what she longed for as well. She was tired of lies.

"I'm not a Crow, but I'm not a deserter either." She hesitated but didn't release the handle of her weapon. Her bees began to circle her body. Drake swatted at a few of them that flew too close to his hook nose. "I would like to purchase the item if you have one."

Dragon shifters were dangerous, according to legend, and Nava wanted nothing to do with them. The tavern darkened further. Undoubtedly, nobody was paying attention to her and the pirate because they were gawking at her soulmate.

The dragon eased onto his stool and regained the edge of curiosity he'd almost lost. "I commend you for being brave enough to tell me the truth, after all your lies. But even if I owned such an artifact, what makes you dream I would ever part with it? I kill for my treasure."

"We both know they possess great power—but also that they curse those who wield them." Nava pressed her lips together. That was an important detail they had avoided discussing while devising this plan.

Who was going to wield the weapon?

"I also know the emissaries of the gods have been tracking these artifacts across the world. So if you do have one, it's only a matter of time before you find yourself pitched against an immortal."

The dragon shifted his gaze toward the crowd in the back. The silence had finally caught his attention. He instantly paled. "A Dark One," he exclaimed and rose, his body growing hotter and the tattoo on his arm moving with light.

"He is with me. He won't hurt you if you don't hurt me..."

"You said you weren't a Crow. But I would recognize the Reaper anywhere. He's one of them." The dragon reached for Nava, his fingers turning to long claws covered in golden scales.

"Don't touch her," Arkimedes growled as he reached the bar, his hand on the hilt of his sword. He was almost a head shorter than the pirate but stood just as tall with the shapes of his shadows.

The tavern was so quiet Nava could hear her own ragged breaths as she racked her brain for something to say. "Let's go talk somewhere more private. I promise you we aren't part of the Crows."

"Fuck that. Like I'd believe shit you say." His distorted voice held nothing back, and the scales growing on his body had extended past his elbows. He smelled like smoke and fire, and the scent turned her stomach as she remembered the Zorren.

"Settle down, dragon. There are more of us than you right now, and we aren't looking for a fight," Devon said as he came up beside Arkimedes. Although they were all speaking in hushed whispers, everyone could probably hear them.

This was it, their one opportunity—and he was shifting to fight them. Nava's heart was in her throat, beating quickly as she dipped her hand into her pocket and held the sun stone, wanting Ari to give her strength. The sun stone beat inside her grasp, warm as a newborn chick. She had to get the artifact to protect Ari and Arkimedes and to avenge Illaris.

"I've got this." She withdrew the stone, light against her palm but hidden from view of the crowd by her lap. The dragon's eye snapped to the stone, and his scales retreated as he settled into his normal size.

"What's that?" His voice wasn't the same as before, but he suddenly seemed more interested in the treasure than even his fear of Arkimedes.

Nava pocketed the sun stone and raised her chin. "We want to talk, in private, about what I already told you. I wasn't lying then, nor am I now."

Drake glared at Devon and Arkimedes. "I don't like to be outnumbered. If you want a deal, mouse, then meet me at the night market. There, we can talk business." He reached for his clay mug and gulped down its contents, making sure he was taking his time—even though a minute ago, he'd been itching to leave.

Then he walked in between Ark and Devon, knocking the latter with his shoulder as he passed him.

Devon stumbled, barely catching himself against the counter. Ice traveled across the wooden surface, triggered by his temper. "That fucking bastard always pisses me off when he gets away. I told you, Arkimedes, one of them was bound to be up in the rooms fucking a whore."

Nava's lips parted, and she blinked rapidly as she caught up to what Devon said. "You've met him before?"

"Draken? Yes, he and his crew are always in trouble with the Corvus. His captain is vicious. That fucking snake is not who we should work with. He's dangerous." Devon coughed loudly.

He wasn't even a ship's captain? Given his size and how alpha he acted, Nava had assumed he was in charge and used to make demands.

She looked at Arkimedes, who was staring daggers at the door through which the dragon shifter had disappeared. Both of them were soaking wet, as if they'd been standing outside in the rain instead of waiting inside for her to arrive.

It didn't take long for the patrons to resume their chatter, although uneasy tension lingered in the room.

Nava patted her pockets to make sure she still had her sun stone and the leftover gold, and followed them to the front door. "You didn't see Draken before I arrived?"

"No," Arkimedes said. "Everyone here isn't anyone we recognize—but everyone knows him." Arkimedes opened the swinging door for her and Devon to exit.

The cold evening air enveloped her like a thick, unwanted hug. She wasn't wearing warm enough clothing for this kind of weather, and she cursed her own stupidity for leaving her coat at the inn.

The server caught up to them before Nava could fully step outside the establishment, gripping the billowing sleeve of her dress. "Miss! You may not leave until you pay for Drake's drink. We won't welcome you back if you don't."

The nerve of him.

Nava yanked her arm away. “I never ordered that drink, and I won’t pay for it. Next time, ask the person to see if they agree instead of ignoring them the entire night.”

They left the round-eyed fae and loud place behind. Nava doubted she would ever step foot in there.

“Is there such a thing as a night market?” she whispered to Arkimedes. Devon was leading the way, a mere silhouette in the dark street before them.

“The guards often spoke about it, but I haven’t been to it myself.” Worry was etched onto the lines of Arkimedes’s face. Even though they were outside and had the information they’d come for, something was wrong. “Speaking of the guards, two of them have been following us ever since we left the safe house.”

29
NAVA

The whereabouts of the night market cost them another five gold coins, given to a drunken shifter they encountered while walking down the old port road.

How could Nava focus on the magical market around her and the pirate they needed to find when the king's guards were lurking somewhere in the shadows?

Arkimedes had filled her in on everything that had happened while they'd been apart. Was this the reason the bees had been around her at all times, even after they'd escaped the castle?

Nava shook her head and wrapped her arms around her body. She'd been wearing Arkimedes's coat for the entire walk here, and it almost swallowed her whole. The bottom edge fell right below her knees. Besides keeping her warm, his scent eased some of her nervousness.

"Do you think Leela sent the letter to Cameron?" she asked.

"You know what I believe."

She did. He'd told her that he believed Leela had provided a roof over their heads while informing the guards of everything that had taken place inside the house.

"She didn't seem to know that we are...you know."

"If my father believes it's a spell, then he wouldn't use a word the entirety of Caztian reveres to describe our relationship."

That made sense. Soulmates were rare and coveted by so many, supposedly designed by a higher power. Many had stopped believing they even existed. At one point, Nava had been like the king. She'd hated that she had no choice but to love Arkimedes.

But the reality was so different from the pictures painted by folklore and fairytales. When they met, his beauty had overwhelmed her. But love had grown gradually, born from trust and friendship. And, of course, there was the intense chemistry neither of them could deny.

Devon glanced at her with pity in his eyes. Nava expected a scathing remark about Leela to hit at any moment. "I hate to advocate for her," he said instead, "especially if she betrayed us, but the guards would've killed her, had she not agreed to do their bidding. Just like they almost killed us on the night we escaped."

"I agree." Arkimedes nodded, and hot air billowed out of his lips with a sigh. Dark circles were smudged beneath his eyes, an exhaustion that ran deep—like hers. "If Leela has been working with my father, then she had no choice in the matter. She is a victim here. Let's not forget that and lose focus on what's truly important."

Nava sucked in a breath and held her words. Of course they were right. Their words were for her, not for them. But it was hard to keep on fighting when everything good in her life kept being torn away. Her family, her home, her friends, her potion-making skills, her father. It was selfish of her to burden Cameron with the truth of it all when he couldn't do anything to help her. But it mattered to her—that he would know she'd never meant to leave him behind.

The scent of spices and magic permeated the air, and the distant chatter of strangers distracted her from the suffocating feeling. "I've only been to one magical market before, on Grey Island, right before Devon attacked the village."

"You had to bring that up, didn't you?" Devon said, although his tone lacked his usual mockery. He dodged around a cart, which held massive gourds in rust and green colors, and adjusted the lapels of his coat so they hid his grimace.

It was far too easy to forgive him for the disaster he'd caused then, especially now that he'd stopped being nasty to her. It was a terrible disaster not to hate him. If only the remorse didn't taste so bitter as it churned in her stomach. Nava forced her eyes away and hoped Gavin and

Violet would forgive her. Hopefully, they would be understanding at the very least. She didn't know if she could lose another person she trusted, not right now. Not when the list of foes by far exceeded their friends.

"This won't be the same," Arkimedes said. He kept glancing up at the metal balconies of the narrow townhouses around them with a growing frown.

Did he remember that day? He'd been regaining his memories, and it was unclear how much he'd truly lost in the spell. He felt a lot more like his old self than several weeks ago.

The market spilled onto the narrow street that had brought them here from the tavern. When they entered, it was as if they were transported into a new world entirely. Wooden carts rested under a canopy of draped silks, illuminated by the soft glow of enchanted lanterns that swayed gently in the sea's breeze. Fae and humans wandered about, carrying their loot in carts or burlap sacks.

Nava itched her nose as the exotic spices blended with the briny tang of the ocean. "How are we supposed to find Drake in this chaos?"

Just as the words left her lips, Arkimedes's arms wrapped around her torso, and he pulled her out of the path of a small running creature.

"Stop the thief!" a woman with strange clothing and wiry wings screamed, chasing the small shape out of the alley and into the street.

Nava's heart hammered as Arkimedes let her go. "Was that a child? Should we help him?" she asked in a high-pitched tone as the three of them watched in horror as the two figures disappeared around the corner of the building.

The vendors, who had quieted after the commotion, continued as if nothing had happened, traveling from stall to stall, carrying baskets with trinkets, strange-looking plants, or bugs bottled in small potion jars.

"I want to help him, Nava, but we can't do that and find the artifact. We have to keep moving," Arkimedes said. His jaw clenched tightly, as if the words burned his tongue. "What we have to do will save them all."

It was true, but it felt wrong all the same.

"You two go ahead. I'll make sure she doesn't hurt him. I'll find you back at the pirate's den," Devon said in a strained tone. Darkness flashed behind his gaze as his aura deepened around him, and the air around them seemed to grow colder. Then he dashed toward the exit of the market, following the woman's footsteps.

"I'm sorry, Ark. I'm just not cut out for this kind of job. My heart is too soft." She'd been so ready to drop everything to help that child, and to hell with their actual task. She turned her head away, her cheeks growing warm. "I don't think it's a good idea for us to split up."

"This is a tough job, and your soul is beautiful. It's good to know what's happening here, especially because of who we are." Arkimedes reached for her hand and dragged her through the narrow path in between stalls. His grip was firm and kept her grounded. "A pirate's den is the term we used in the Society of Crows to refer to the black market stalls the pirates set up in places like this."

"How can we find it?" Her eyes darted around the narrow, busy space. The cries of the sellers advertising their wares made it hard to hear, their shouts echoing off the labyrinthine alleys.

"Their contraband usually contains magic, much like the artifacts. Most humans, fae, or shifters can't detect it because they don't have magic like me and you."

"Does that mean we will sense it when we come close? That's how Devon can find us later?"

"Exactly."

They walked in silence after that, surrounded by displays of curiosities she'd never seen before. Pools of light spilled onto the slick, rain-soaked ground, coming from the lanterns strung above their heads. It didn't take long to sense it, the gentle poke to her subconscious that warned her of the presence of magic.

Nava's skin prickled. This was similar to how she felt near a place haunted by Neems, and yet different somehow. This time she didn't want to run away—she felt drawn toward the sensation.

She craned her neck to look at the passersby. A year ago, she could not see things like auras or wards, much less sense the old magic lying dormant in an object. Especially in a place like this, where a myriad of impressions overwhelmed her senses.

And yet there it was. Clear waves of magic radiating in shades of green from a tent made of thick canvas. Nava approached with tentative steps, driven by her burning curiosity.

"Is that the place?" she whispered and pressed her body against the wall of the building beside them, allowing people to flow through the riverlike alley with ease. Arkimedes didn't need to answer her, regardless.

They were almost at the end of the market, and she could spot the street beyond the pitched ceiling of the tent.

"You can feel the artifact in there as much as I do. What remains to be seen is whether the gods crafted it or if it was made by a Caztanian." Arkimedes pointed at the street, empty this late at night. Or this early, really—the first glimmers of sunrise marked the bottom of the clouds with hints of orange. "This is a pirate's den. Usually, they set up their stalls in a place where they can escape easily."

"Should we wait for Devon?" Nava asked. They'd been walking through the market for at least an hour, and her legs ached just as much as her body demanded rest. Having Devon's help inside the pirate's den couldn't hurt.

"No, we shouldn't stay here for long. I haven't stopped feeling uneasy this entire evening, and I'm not sure if it's because of the guards that are following us." Arkimedes glanced to the rooftops, tracking the shapeless shadows.

Worry churned in her gut.

Nava nodded and moved toward the thick canvas flap that served as a door. But before she could enter, Arkimedes's hand grabbed hers, making her pause.

"Are you sure you want to part with the sun stone?" His words rose clear in her mind, much like they had back at the safe house. This connection gave them an immense advantage when the walls could listen.

"No, but we have nothing else to offer." Ari had given her the stone so she could maintain a connection with him. Even now, it gently thrummed inside her pocket, a reminder that he was out there, alive and well.

A wall of smoke greeted them as soon as they crossed the threshold. Nava's heart leaped, and the image of a Zorren floated from the depths of her mind, of nails made of iron digging into her skin. The phantom ache of her old wound became a sharp throb as she gripped the pommel of the dagger strapped to her leg.

"No weapons in our shop," a man close to the door said. He pointed at a wooden sign that hung crookedly from a rusty hook jutting out of the canvas wall.

Sweat beaded on her temple as she took in the enclosed space. Logically, Nava knew this wasn't the smoke of fire, but her mind continued to spin, and nausea racked her body, making her wheeze.

"Breathe, Bee." Arkimedes's voice was a gentle whisper and helped bring her back to reality.

She took a deep breath and tried to focus on something that could anchor her to the here and now.

There. The two narrow tables on either side of the shop, and the three men waiting for them inside. Drake was sitting on a stool, casually leaning on his knee as he smoked a long wooden pipe.

"I told you, captain, the magic-wielder is small like a mouse." He rose and pointed in her direction with his sharp jaw.

"And she walks with the Reaper." The second man—the captain—picked a random trinket off one of the tables with a gloved hand. He didn't turn to meet them. "You aren't welcome here, Crow. Not after Aliyah."

The town of Aliyah in the Iron Kingdom? Nava turned to Arkimedes with a raised brow.

"That was a long time ago, and I was doing my job," Arkimedes said. "You should have known better than to sell contraband in the city. The ports are always crawling with Crows."

"Yes, it was a long time ago, but a dragon never forgets..." Heavy tobacco use had roughened the captain's voice. He took a long draw from his pipe and blew the smoke in their direction.

"We didn't come here to fight. We came to trade," Nava said, hoping to derail the conversation from old vendettas.

The captain wore very few clothes for someone managing a shop, as if he were ready to change into his animal form at any given moment. He'd rolled up the legs of his trousers, revealing muscular calves and ankles marked with scars. A leather vest did little to cover his tattooed torso, where a silver necklace hung, contrasting with the deep shade of his skin.

"Drake said you know about the emissaries? How did you hear about them?" he asked.

Aristaeus had told her the emissaries were hunting for the artifacts, and he'd lived for a long time. He'd watched the world go around the sun more times than one could count and all that happened within it. Nature whispered to him, sharing the truths of what he couldn't see.

But of course, the pirates would know about emissaries. They had probably encountered them many times before and undoubtedly feared them. It had to be why Drake had agreed to even consider this exchange.

Arkimedes glared daggers at the captain. "We don't have time to discuss our sources, Emir. If you have the artifact, let us see it and be on our way."

Emir's eyes were more beast than man when they landed on Nava again. "You know I have an artifact, Reaper. It's how you magic-wielders find us, no? But I haven't seen the stone the mouse wants to trade us for it. Show it to me."

Nava exhaled slowly and pulled the stone from her pocket with a sweaty hand. It flickered with the same warm light it had in the cave, illuminating the dark interior of the tent. They all went quiet. She couldn't even hear their breaths as they took it in.

If the market had been warm, standing inside this tent, so close to three dragon shifters, was like being back in the burning forest.

"What's that?" the third dragon asked.

"A sun stone made by a Beekeeper." Nava closed her hand around the glowing stone, hiding it from view. All three dragons tracked her hand as she shoved it inside the pocket of Arkimedes's coat.

"I have never heard of a gem made by the keepers of life. How did you obtain it?" Emir's voice rumbled in his chest as he blinked away the daze of utter desire from his face.

Aristaeus was going to kill her for trading away his creation, but perhaps he would understand that this was the only way to protect him from the evil immortal trying to kill them. "Now you've seen mine. It's your turn to show us the artifact."

"How do I know this supposed stone is even real and not a spell you're trying to trick me with?" Emir's eyes flashed to Arkimedes, who stood beside Nava. Her soulmate's wariness continued to bleed through their bond.

"It's real, and I can prove it," Nava said.

No one here knew what she truly was, so they wouldn't understand the stone was irrelevant to what she was about to do. Nava raised her hand and called to the bees that had been crawling this place ever since she'd entered. She asked them to fly, and all at once, they listened.

Her insects circled the bright stone in a cloud of dozens, drawing surprised gasps from all three shifters.

The spectacle lasted for a few seconds until she lowered the stone and the bees settled down. "Is that proof enough? If you aren't interested, we will leave with our stone."

"Let's take that little trinket of hers. It's just two of them against three of us." The third dragon shifter, who seemed younger than the rest, took a step forward, and his features elongated as he slowly changed into something inhuman. Nava took a hasty step away from the captain, who stood unmoving in front of her.

"I would like to see you try," Arkimedes growled, and his aura all but exploded around him. "She is mine to protect, and you'll keep your distance, or I won't blink before killing you all."

Nava's skin prickled with gooseflesh at the menacing tone Arkimedes used. He was deadly serious, too. And she didn't want her soulmate to carry these souls with him for the rest of his life.

The younger dragon laughed as if Arkimedes's warning was the funniest thing he'd heard in a while. It was likely the young one had never seen how quickly Arkimedes could kill. The captain, on the other hand, paled and lifted a hand, which stopped the man's cackle. "Drake, bring the table so we may begin the assessment."

Out of the corner of her eye, she saw Drake lift one of the wooden displays as if it weighed nothing. He carried it toward them, the few items on it rattling across the surface as he placed it in between the captain, Arkimedes, and Nava.

"When my man came back from the tavern and told me about your Beekeeper's stone, I returned to my ship to retrieve this," the captain said and removed the necklace hanging around his neck.

Drake slid a polished, wooden box in front of Emir, who used the pointed corner of his necklace to open the ornate lock. He picked up a small vial that rested on a deep purple velvet cushion.

A potion, really? Nava glanced around the table, hoping to find something a bit more...impressive. She focused on the green liquid sloshing against the glass walls of the vial. It stuck to them like a thick substance—the same color as the magic that had called her here. The vial vibrated faintly, like the flutter of her bees' wings.

This wasn't regular magic woven into the fabric of this object, but something much stronger and older, like the Vulcan the Crows kept in the safe house.

Made by the gods for the gods.

"You don't strike me as someone who trades illegal contraband often," Emir said, bringing his hand to his lips and slicing the skin of one finger open with his canines. Drake placed a dirty brass cup in the center of the table. "This is a blood oath. It protects the two parties from fake claims."

She brought her hand to her chest in response to his words. So they wanted her to bleed in that cup and make some sort of oath she had no protection against? No, thank you.

"The Reaper will testify. This is the way we do it. After the oath, we will tell you the truth of what we know of our artifact. Then you'll place the stone on the table and do the same. We can inspect it, and you may do the same with ours."

"If we choose to enter this trade. So far we have shown you we are indeed telling the truth," Arkimedes said, pushing the words past gritted teeth. A split second later, his voice filtered through to her mind. *"He is right, Bee. The blood oath won't bind you to anything other than speaking the truth about what the stone is. That's all. We have nothing to hide."*

Nava met Emir's expectant gaze, and sweat beaded on her temple as she brought her dagger out and pricked her hand. She allowed a couple of drops of blood to drip into the cup.

The scent of rotten flowers sitting in stagnant water drifted through the tent, although she wasn't sure if it was the oath or something else. But when she placed the sun stone on the table, her skin crawled with an odd numbing sensation that gripped her by the throat.

"This is a sun stone, made by the Beekeeper. It makes light and produces warmth. I don't know what other powers it has, but it gives me energy," Nava said. Her eyes opened wide as the words slipped from her lips. What the hell was happening to her? She glanced at Arkimedes, horrified but glad she'd said nothing that might give her away.

"Where did you get it?" the young dragon said from the back, just as Emir reached for the sun stone.

"In the forest." Nava pressed her lips tight, willing herself not to speak another word.

"She doesn't have to tell you anything else. The artifact is what we claimed. Now it's your turn." Arkimedes extended a hand to Emir for his artifact, and his misty aura wrapped around the vial as soon as it hit his palm.

"We discovered ours at a temple in the Gold Kingdom two years ago.

The scriptures claimed it used to be a spell of auspices—or whatever. We don't have an excellent translator in our crew." Emir scratched his bald head and sneered at the wooden box. "I don't like you two, but I feel I should warn you. All of my men who dared to open that vial are now gone."

Auspices? What did that even mean? "Did it kill them?" Nava asked.

"It drove them mad, and that's what killed them."

Arkimedes glanced at her, probably reading every single one of her thoughts. "What else can you tell us about it?"

"We know nothing other than that Alera, the Goddess of Life, crafted this spell."

The Goddess of Life...? That must be why the magic waves had called so strongly to Nava, why they reminded her of her winged insects. Was the goddess somehow related to the Beekeepers?

"So it's a spell?" Arkimedes's flat expression gave away how unimpressed he was with this discovery. "Do you have anything else, like a weapon?"

"What do you think happens when we are out there searching for these, Reaper?" Drake scoffed, but he didn't move an inch from where he stood. His eyes were those of someone who'd spent too long out on the ocean. "Why don't you open it, Dark One, and tell us? You're a magic-wielder, no? You ought to know more than us." Drake spat to the side.

Arkimedes's lips peeled in a feral expression she rarely saw. Whoever these people were, her mate didn't like them one bit.

A random spell they knew nothing about was useless and would likely cause more harm than good. What were they going to do with a potion that drove people insane? Force it down the emissary's throat? He was already mad.

"This is all we have got, and this auspice protects whoever is strong enough to use it. I bet it won't harm you as it did us," the captain said. He seemed to be realizing the trade wasn't going in their favor and was still holding on to her stone.

"We need a weapon, not this." Arkimedes offered the vial back, but the dragon did not reach for it.

"You used to be a Crow, Reaper. You should know there isn't a vast array of artifacts left undiscovered. One thing I can assure you of, we are the only traders currently docked in this city in possession of a god's artifact. I urge you to reconsider." The captain's voice had grown deeper, and now his nose extended into the shape of a scaled snout. "I very much desire this."

Arkimedes's entire body stiffened, and for a second, Nava thought he might fight the dragon. But then he spun toward the tent's door just as an explosion shook the ground.

Nava lost her footing, pushed back by an intense pressure that sent her flying against the wooden table.

"Nava!" Arkimedes shouted, running toward her. A cloud of dust and smoke blew the tent's door open, right as the screams began outside.

30
ORION

Orion's ears rang, and his vision blurred. Everything inside the tent rattled as the ground shook. He clutched the goddess artifact in his hand, while orange-tinted smoke poured in from the outside, smelling of sour tangerines. He would recognize the blinding spell anywhere. Now, it numbed his skin. Soon, his limbs would follow.

Disoriented, he knelt beside Nava, hoping she hadn't hurt herself in her fall and was still mobile. She looked dazed and coughed into her elbow, shielding her face from the bite of the magic surrounding them.

"Try not to inhale too deeply." He wheezed out the command and pulled his scarf over his nose with his free hand. But it was too late, even for him—he could feel his power dull beneath the effects of the spell.

The sound of ripping fabric drew his attention. The younger dragon was clawing at the wall of the tent, right before the three of them left through the back, shapeshifting into large, winged beasts.

The captain glanced at Orion, baring long teeth and still cradling the sun stone. He was escaping, taking the Beekeeper's stone with him and leaving this useless vial as a trade-in.

"W-what's happening?" Nava slurred. He would have gone after the shifter, but he couldn't abandon her. The effect of the stunning spell was twofold: it numbed the magic-wielder's power and their motor skills.

Even the bees crawled aimlessly over the ground, unable to find Nava easily.

"It's the blinding spell I mentioned before. Someone must have crafted it into a bomb of sorts. We have to go through the back." He dragged her off the ground and past the mess of trinkets the dragons had left behind.

"It couldn't be the dragons who did it—right? Was it the guards?" Nava asked once they were out in the alleyway. If anything, it was worse there than inside. People were crawling on the ground in a vain attempt to escape what they all knew was coming.

A couple of shifters stumbled past them, clinging to each other as they dropped bags of contraband that would land them in prison for a long time. Orion reached for Nava, pulling her under his wings for protection. His memories might have been patchy, but he knew she'd never experienced the Society of Crows in true pursuit.

Smoke clouded almost everything except for the shadows that approached, unbothered by the spell they were using to punish everyone. They wore gas masks with rounded glass eyes and pointed beaks.

It had been foolish not to think of them anymore after they'd escaped the safe house. All night long, the city had warned him that someone followed him around the streets as they prepared for the attack.

"It's the Corvus. They finally tracked us down."

Nava's stiff movements slowed as she looked over her shoulder. "They are here?" Her wide eyes barely seemed to focus on anything, and her aura flickered on and off as her ragged, panicked breaths intensified.

Out in the main street, where the air was clearer, he could finally think straight. The sooner they were out by the sea, the better they would fare. He moved them farther away from the alley, toward the pier and the ships with their hollering crews. "Try to calm your breathing, Bee. Put the coat over your nose."

He would have given her the scarf, but at that point, it was best if he kept a handle on whatever was left of his magic, for she had already inhaled too much of the bomb to have full control of hers.

"I can't feel anything. How am I going to fight them?" Nava asked.

Orion doubted the Crows had spotted either of them yet. They'd been lost in the throng of people who had fled from the market and into the streets. If they got away fast enough, they wouldn't have to fight them at all.

"Most establishments in town have basic protective wards. It prevents stun weapons—like the bombs—from being detonated inside the shops. My guess is the Crows waited to attack us once we were no longer under the tavern's protection."

Nava exhaled. "How long is the effect going to last? I can't feel my magic..."

Orion peered over her head at what remained visible of the night market. The Crows' silhouettes loomed clear against the bright light of the lanterns, stalking closer and closer to the main street.

They should keep moving. But something nagged at him. Some detail at the back of his mind that didn't allow him to continue.

The heavy beating of his heart nearly drowned the screams of the crowds. And then he spotted it: the Corvus were dragging someone behind them. A tall male figure tied with a rope, pulled like cattle into the open streets of the ports. The man stumbled with each step he took, his features hidden behind his messy hair.

Orion's heart jolted as panic gripped him. Even at this distance, there was no mistaking him. "They have Devon," he choked out.

This place had been vibrant with colors only ten minutes ago. A haven for illegal trade that was harmless in the grand scheme of things. But the Crows had burst in and released a bomb where a child had been running but a moment ago.

If they had Devon, what would they have done to the small thief?

Orion pulled Nava behind an empty flower stand and crouched down. Its wooden edge dug into his palm as he rested his weight on it.

"How many Crows can you see?" Nava asked.

"Six."

His wings were too large to hide behind a small cart, but putting them away would use too much of his magic, and he had little to spare.

"Do they normally send that many when someone breaks into a safe house?" Nava flashed a panicked look at him. Then she peered around the corner of their hiding place to where the Crows were gathering in the middle of the main road. "Or is this a routine task and we are in the wrong place at the wrong time?"

"They are here for you and me..." he said, fully focused on the hunched shape of his brother. Devon was clutching his throat, as if he was having a hard time breathing. Of course. He was far too sick to deal with the effects of the bomb.

"But how could they know it was us? We didn't hold the Vulcan. And this is a large city."

"They likely used the Vulcan to track whoever broke in," Orion said. "It might have shown them Devon, and when they found him..."

"They found us."

Tonight had been the first time the city had warned him that something was wrong. Aristaeus had been right—his connection to the land was strengthening more with each day he remained in the kingdom.

Nava's brows knitted together, and determination set in. "My mother taught me to fight without relying on my magic because she knew that when we left Willowbrook, I might run into one of these bombs."

"Yes." If only Celeste had allowed Nava to learn about the world of magic sooner in addition to that. She'd been a cunning creature and always kept her cards close to her chest. And just like that, his annoyance at Nava's mother flooded back, like an old foe that had never left him. He was still too angry at her for taking Nava away—for cursing him to become a crow for a decade of solitude.

Fuck, he hated her.

"They are going the other way," Nava said.

Devon's legs faltered, and he nearly stumbled to the ground as a Crow pulled him down the street, away from where they were hiding.

Nava let out a shaky breath. "We are going to have to fight them, aren't we? To free him."

The rest of the group remained close to the exit of the market, searching through the unconscious people who littered the street, prodding them with their booted feet to turn them around and get a better look at their faces.

"Yes."

There wasn't an argument he could come up with that would convince Nava to run and hide while he attempted to release his brother. What was more shocking was that he didn't want to do this alone.

Nava was powerful and adept in battle. Her ability to heal would likely make the blinding spell dissipate from her blood faster than normal. Together, they were more powerful than alone.

"The Crows use this tactic when they are breaking up a group. Often, it's magic-wielding families who are protecting their youths from the draft."

"What tactic is that?"

"Staying out here in the open to make sure that I see they have Devon. They will start torturing him next," Orion said and turned toward her. Shame weighed heavily on his heart. How could he have stood back and allowed them to do this before?

"Here, in the middle of the city?" she gasped. Her feelings were bitter as they poured into his gut from their bond. Panic and anger blended together, fueling his own dread.

"It sends a message to the rest of the city as well," he said. "Do you have enough energy left to transfer one more time?"

Nava nodded, although she was frowning. Perhaps she thought he was about to ask her to leave him behind. Which, to her credit, would have been his first choice if he dreamed she would do it.

"There's a possibility they don't know you're here with me, which could give us an edge."

"You want to be the bait?"

"I will distract them long enough for you to transfer to the guy holding Devon. He has walked far from the rest. They won't be able to get to you fast enough. Once you free him, there will be three of us, which gives us better odds."

"Three of us without the full use of our magic," she mumbled but shrugged. "I guess I don't have a better plan."

Orion grabbed her face with both hands and pressed his forehead to hers. Gods, he wished they had more time to heal what they had gone through before having to fight again. He wished he could love her without having to fear that this might be a goodbye.

The waves crashed hard against the rock wall that divided the street and the sea.

"I'd rather fight them alongside you, even with half of my magic, than without you with the full use of my powers," he said, caressing her chin.

Her lips trembled into a sad smile. "Me too."

Orion pressed his lips to hers, and then he stepped out of the cover of their hiding place, his wings shifting before settling on his back. He swept toward the Crows, who paused the moment they noticed him.

"Let him go," he demanded, advancing on the group while tightening his grip around the pommel of his sword.

"Reaper." The first cloaked figure laughed and inched forward. Waves of bright gray power swirled around his wrists as he readied himself for an attack.

The helmet he wore muffled his voice, and Orion didn't recognize the tone or way he moved. He sounded too young to be someone he knew from his days in the Society.

"I've heard so much about you, the *dead* Dark One who disappeared a decade ago. Imagine our shock when we found you alive and assisting our traitor. Which makes you the same." The Crow moved with the cockiness of a recent but powerful recruit. The rest of the group kept their distance from the reach of Orion's powers. Smart.

"I'm the heir to this kingdom, and if you attack me or mine, you'll be breaking the treaties between the Society and the Crown," Orion said. It was a long shot, admittedly. He sincerely doubted the Crows cared about the treaties.

And if they got him out of here and back to the Iron Kingdom, they might use the same memory spell his father had employed to continue to use him as a weapon.

Or they might just try to kill him and be done with the whole thing, with no one being the wiser. There was no chance they understood how the kingdom spoke to his kin.

"What treaties?" The Crow barked another laugh and pointed to what remained of the market. "We discovered you in an illegal trading post just now, which King Oberon allows to exist in his land. I see broken treaties everywhere I look."

His steps slowed down, but he was close enough for Orion's power to reach him. The rest of his group were allowing this poor fool forward to test if he had, in fact, lost his ability to do magic. The silent figures had most likely met him in person before.

Interestingly, there hadn't even been a trace of shock when he'd mentioned that he was a prince. How many of his old comrades had known who he was all along?

"Next time I ask, it won't be so pleasant for you," Orion promised. Not an empty threat and that was even worse. His body craved to be replenished after the bomb had taken everything from him.

"Can you believe this fool?" The Crow scoffed, his magic on full display now, pure energy buzzing in between his fingertips. "You have no power left in you and no one even knows you're alive…"

All the Corvus' eyes rested on him. They still seemed unaware of Nava moving in the shadows as she transferred close to Devon's location, using her last reserves.

"Let's feed upon his delicious soul and show him what happens when they challenge us," a voice in his aura called.

Orion's magic returned to him slowly in swirls of black ink. They wrapped around his body as he gripped the wisps of what power remained awake after being stunned.

The ground and the surrounding buildings had lent him the energy he needed, and he'd accomplished his goal of distracting them. He had enough magic left for a single blast—and now it was time to move.

"Sahir, stand back…" A whispered warning came from the group, even as the young Crow sent his first attack swirling toward Orion.

But it was too late for Sahir to change his mind. Orion barely dodged the spell, and it singed a few feathers on his wings. Anger bloomed hot inside him, and he lifted a hand in the Crow's direction and gripped his soul.

Sahir moaned and drifted forward on his tiptoes, tugged by the energy of Orion's curse. A song of laments pierced his surroundings as all the fragmented pieces of old souls swirled around Orion, greeting this new one.

The fresh energy he drew brought back his dormant power. His skin tingled as he fed on and on, until the Crow crumpled forward. It only left him hungering for more.

The Crow who held Devon lifted a trembling knife to his brother's neck. "Stop, Reaper, or I'll kill Black."

A second later, Nava materialized right next to him and stabbed him with her dagger. His scream pierced the silent night.

The ground trembled beneath Orion's feet. Was that Nava's doing or his magic? It didn't matter. They moved in unison, connected by a string of shared energy. Her skin glowed as she danced away from a Crow's spell and leaned forward to cut through the ropes that tied Devon.

Orion dodged another attack cast by one of the remaining four Crows who approached him. They were keeping a big enough distance that he wouldn't be able to pull at their souls. Four separate spells shot at him at once, and with his wings, it was near impossible to outmaneuver them all.

He rose up into the sky and flew toward the first, slashing with his sword until it cut through armor, flesh, and the bone of a ribcage. Then he pulled at the energy that remained to allow his magic shield to strengthen as he flew a few meters higher.

"Ark, watch out for—" Nava's words were drowned out by a battle scream. An arrow sliced through the air, striking his shoulder, followed by another that punctured his right wing.

He lost control and spiraled down to the ground.

Lightning illuminated the sky and struck somewhere nearby. Someone screamed, and the potent stench of singed hair and burnt flesh wafted up to his nostrils. Thunder boomed a second later as Orion landed roughly on the rocky ground, and the glass vial in his pocket cracked open, its gooey liquid seeping through his pants and onto his skin.

The god's spell took hold of his movements. For a moment, the adrenaline pumping through his veins dulled the ache from his rough landing and the arrows still jutting out of him. But the searing pain returned just as quickly. He needed to keep an eye on what was happening around him, dammit, but he couldn't. He couldn't breathe. He couldn't think.

Two blurred, winged figures touched down on the ground, chased by trails of shadows. The Dark Ones descended upon the Crows. Were there really just two of them? They looked more like ten.

Then his vision blurred as darkness claimed him.

"Ark, the guards are here."

Orion blinked. Nava was kneeling beside him. A magical rain fell on him, hot against his icy skin. There was a sound that didn't make sense until he realized she was repeating the same words again and again. "You are fine. You'll be fine."

Was she telling him or talking to herself? Even with his thoughts scattering like birds, he could feel the touch of her healing magic caressing him in spluttering waves that didn't quite reach him. At least the rain continued to fall. That meant Devon was still alive. Right?

"I need to take these out," Nava said, grabbing at the shaft of the arrow that stuck out of his shoulder.

"Leave them," he wheezed, lifting his body with trembling arms, chasing the warmth of her skin. Sometimes, the Society dipped their arrows in poison that was meant to slow down their victims. But he didn't think his body could handle the pain he was experiencing and the artifact at the same time. At least not without losing consciousness again. Even the blood pouring from the wound felt scalding. "The vial broke. The liquid is on me," he stuttered.

He tried to look over her shoulder to make out what was happening in the road, but all the shapes were blurry, and he couldn't tell friend from foe. He met her gaze and pressed his palm to her cheek, but the edges of his vision were already narrowing in.

"You had the artifact?" A brief look of comprehension flashed over her features, quickly replaced by pure panic.

"I do—did." He winced as everything continued to swirl around him. Tilting forward, he pressed his forehead to her chest, just as a spell cracked in the background, illuminating the wet street.

"Hold on, stay with me, all right? I can—I can use my magic to heal you. Just give me a moment."

Her arms wrapped around him, shaking with the effort to keep him sitting upright, but Arkimedes no longer possessed any control over his tired, aching body. He closed his heavy lids, chasing an odd sensation that began to brew inside his gut. It seemed to come from somewhere deep inside him and vibrated with power.

It felt similar to the warning he'd been getting all night but different somehow. While before, he'd sensed an enemy was tracking him, now he sensed a reprieve. The cavalry was coming, headed by the king himself.

How could he possibly know that?

"Bee, he…he is coming," Orion whispered, trying to swallow despite his parched throat.

And then darkness swallowed him whole.

31
NAVA

Enemies surrounded Nava, from the guards who had flown in minutes ago to the Crows who were fighting them from down the road. At least, they weren't paying attention to her and Arkimedes, which gave her a chance to get away.

"Wake up," she pleaded, choking as she gripped him by the shoulders. Arkimedes's eyes flickered under his eyelids. "Can you hear me? We need to leave now, Ark—please."

Tears blurred her vision as she struggled to pull air back into her lungs. She was teetering on the edge of losing what little composure she had left.

He is coming, Arkimedes had said before collapsing. His words ran circles through her mind as the urgency inside her grew. Who was on his way here? The emissary? She couldn't think of anyone else it might be. The two guards who had been trailing them were already here, and they couldn't have gone all the way back to the castle and warned the king of the Crows' attack. Right?

Nava hooked both arms beneath his armpits and pulled with all her strength, but she barely managed to move him a couple of feet along the bumpy road. No matter what, she needed to get Arkimedes out of the middle of the street and hide them away from further danger.

If she could catch a brief break, her body might regain some of its strength. Then she could attempt to heal him.

She wanted to puke as her arms slipped over the slick texture of his wet shirt and grazed the sharp point of an arrow jutting out of his shoulder blade. A moan escaped his lips, but he remained unconscious—and far too heavy for her to drag under cover.

He was too big, too badly injured for her to lift without the full use of her magic. She pulled harder, and the veins in her forehead throbbed with exertion. The scent of magic burned her nostrils, drifting across from the spells the remaining two Crows were shooting at the guards.

"What are you doing?" Devon's voice broke through her ragged breaths.

She jumped and nearly dropped Arkimedes to the ground. "Out of the rain," she answered. If she hadn't been so tired, she would have screamed with frustration. "And away from them."

"It's not raining anymore, Nava," Devon said. He looked far worse than when she'd last seen him. Too pale, with purple lips that matched the circles around his eyes.

She leaned forward and continued to drag Arkimedes away from the battleground.

"Where are you taking him, exactly?"

"Behind the flower cart." Dammit, why did he keep slipping?

"Going at that pace, you won't make it there before they finish killing each other and come to find us."

She glanced at the battle still raging in the street. The two guards were using their shadow magic against one of the Crows, all the while avoiding the arrows still raining down from a nearby building.

"Can you help me, then? Or are you just going to criticize my handiwork while you stand there like a statue?"

"I don't think there's any way you could call *that* handiwork. Move over, Cat. I'll carry him from behind, you hold his legs. We'll go faster that way."

Nava pressed her lips tightly together so she wouldn't tell him where to shove his commands. Then she let Arkimedes sink to the ground. His skin felt like it was burning through the wet layers of his clothes—and through hers. Yet his face was as pale as Devon's.

Together, they managed to carry him behind the flower cart, skirting the large puddles that had formed while it rained. Devon leaned Arkimedes against the weathered wall behind it.

"Can you heal him?" he asked, crouching beside Arkimedes and pushing his hair away from his forehead. Then he examined the arrows jutting out from his wing and shoulder. "The Crows sometimes dip their arrowheads in poison... That must be why he is out."

Nava had used every last ounce of her magic to transfer to Devon and defeat the Crow who had held him. Gods, she hadn't realized how much she relied on her power until the bomb had dulled it. Now a hole gaped inside her.

It wasn't the arrowheads or the blood loss. Arkimedes had told her the artifact had shattered right before he fainted, and in the midst of her panic, she hadn't even considered what that meant.

"It wasn't the Crows, or at least not just their arrows." She shoved her hand inside Arkimedes's pocket. Pain shot through her finger as the broken glass pricked her skin. She withdrew it and examined the thick drop of blood that beaded on the tip of her finger.

"What is that?"

Devon watched in silent horror as she carefully pulled bloodied shards of the small bottle from inside Arkimedes's pocket, taking better care this time so she wouldn't get cut by the larger fragments. None of the green substance that had previously filled the vial remained.

"I need to make sure that the artifact isn't harming him further..." How much of the spell had Arkimedes's skin absorbed? Maybe it had only soaked into his woolen pants? She debated pulling the garment off to examine further.

A cloud of pure magic assaulted her nose as the guards and Crows shouted curses at each other in ancient languages. The smell alone was foul and brought tears to her eyes.

"We were trading for the artifact when the Crows attacked." Nava tossed the pieces she'd fished out of Ark's pocket to the side, eager to fill in the silence. Best not to focus on the fight going on around them or that it was growing quieter by the minute.

"You found it—and it's all over him?"

Nava sucked in a breath and pressed both hands to Arkimedes's chest. His rapid heartbeat was palpable beneath her touch, too fast for an unconscious person. Sorrow sank its claws deep inside her. If she still had the sun stone, it would have amplified her energy, and perhaps she would have been able to help her soulmate. But now it was gone, lost to the grimy hands of those dragon shifters.

"The pirates called it a spell, though it was a potion and not the weapon we were hoping for. I didn't even know Arkimedes had taken it until right before he fainted."

A curse slipped past Devon's lips, and he slammed his open hand against the cart's side. "I shouldn't have gone after that kid. I wasn't able to help him either way, and it distracted me from the Crows approaching." He frowned at Arkimedes's unmoving body. "If I'd been there with the two of you, perhaps it wouldn't have gone this way."

It was far too quiet all of a sudden. Not a single sound traveled toward them from the street.

As if reading her thoughts, Devon peered around the edge of the cart, then pulled back quickly. "There are two Crows left, and they're checking their dead. We don't have long until they search for us."

Nava swallowed and tried to grasp at whatever sliver of magic lay dormant within her. But there was nothing left for her to heal Arkimedes, let alone fight with. "Are the guards dead?"

"I don't see them. They might have gone after the archer." Devon sighed, pressing his body to the building behind him. "What a team we make..."

"Even the best team wouldn't be able to hold out against such odds," Nava said, forcing the words through the knot in her throat.

Soon, steps echoed through the empty street. The Crows were drawing closer, their words still muted by the crashing of the waves.

"More useless deserters and pirates. I don't see Devon Black, the Reaper, or the girl."

Too close. Devon pressed his finger to his lips, and Nava held her breath, waiting.

"They couldn't have gone far. The archers got the Reaper."

Nava slid the dagger from its sheath and tightened her sticky hand around its pommel. They could still fight and make it out of here alive, right? Surely this wasn't the end. She was tired, but so were the Crows.

A bell rang from a nearby rooftop, echoing over the two-story buildings that lined the boardwalk, and a sudden rush of shadows dropped from the sky. Nava counted at least twenty guards. They landed on the road with a rustle of flapping wings.

Looked like the Crows' lives wouldn't last long.

She peered around the edge of the cart. They all wore shiny metal armor in warm copper tones with brass details. She'd seen that same armor many times when they'd stopped her in her tracks in the castle. The final Dark One who descended had the longest wings, black like the shadows that wrapped around him, shrouding him in darkness. Why had the king come all the way to the ports when he could send out his people?

There weren't that many Crows left, right? Not unless there were many more archers than she'd originally thought. Nava glanced down at Arkimedes and pressed her hand harder to his chest. He'd known and tried to warn her. Not that it would have made a difference.

"Line up all the Crows on the street and find me my son—and *the girl*." The king's voice deepened on his last two words. Goose bumps rose on Nava's skin as she drew closer to Arkimedes.

His hot breaths were fleeing his lips in ragged puffs, hitting her face like burning coals. What was worse—to face the Crows or the king?

Fear paralyzed her, gluing her to the spot. How were they going to escape when they couldn't defend themselves with magic?

The next time she dared to peek, the guards were dragging the two remaining Crows across the cobblestone and toward the stunned bodies of the passersby. They fought against the guards' hold, no longer wearing those weird, bird-like helmets that had protected them from their stunning spell.

The king moved like a shadow, silent, although his shimmery metal armor should surely have made some noise. His silver hair stood out in contrast to his immense black wings. Like Ark, his aura billowed out angrily as he stepped closer to his prisoners.

"To kill a Crow is forbidden by the gods," one of the prisoners muttered. The same words she'd read in that book at the safe house.

"Is that so?" King Oberon drawled, looking over his shoulder as laughter rippled through the ranks of the guards behind him. "Are they here to protect you now?"

"We haven't broken our treaties. You agreed that we may seize the black markets."

"I remember the treaties I signed better than you, and I cannot recall where I gave you permission to harm the heir of my kingdom—my only son?"

"I saw no prince here." The Crow peeled his lips back to reveal jagged teeth stained with blood.

"You dare lie to our king?" The guard who held the Crow shoved him to the ground, nearly forcing him to kiss the puddle he knelt in. "Need I show you what we do to those who harm our royals, prick?"

"We're terribly sorry and meant no disrespect," the second Crow said in a shaky tone. Clearly, he was much more afraid than the first, or at least showing it more. "It was an accident, Your Majesty—we didn't know the prince was here. We've been hunting deserters, not Dark Ones."

She pitied them both—and herself, for soon she would be kneeling alongside Devon on that ground, ready to be killed. Or worse. "Do you think we can escape now?" she whispered, briefly turning to Devon. But he shook his head almost imperceptibly. He didn't have to say a word, for his emotions were written all over his face.

"You believe you can fool me? That I don't know exactly what happened here? I have eyes all over my city." King Oberon's steps grew louder. Was he moving away from the Crows and closer toward them? Could he sense Arkimedes?

Nava peered into the street, just as Arkimedes's father raised his hand and called upon the Curse of the Fallen. Not a second later, the first Crow crumpled onto the ground. Dead. The king turned abruptly, and his cerulean eyes met hers, and then he took the second Crow's soul.

32
NAVA

Nava's ass hit the ground as she jumped back behind the cart. Hopefully, it was all in her head, and the king hadn't seen her.

Of course, she wasn't that lucky. Not a minute later, King Oberon was standing four feet away from them. His face, barely visible behind the swirls of his power, twisted with ire. "Is Orion alive?"

She nodded, at a loss for words.

Devon's sword caught the light of the moon as he stood up, stepping between Arkimedes, Nava, and the king.

"Before you strike, consider if you want to die right now or live to see another day," the king said to Devon. "I know my son cares about you, but I've lost my will to care."

"I'm already dying." Devon gripped his sword with frosted, white knuckles. "I'd rather die right here than watch you hurt them."

Did Devon think he had enough magic left in him to actually harm King Oberon of the Dark Ones? Or was he stalling?

The king's brows knitted together as his lips twisted into a deep grimace. "I don't care if Orion can't forgive me for killing you, Crow. I won't warn you again."

Even through Nava's panic, her mind sharpened at the king's words and his hesitancy to strike. It didn't add up. He claimed not to care, but

Nava got the impression that he cared a lot more than he would ever admit out loud. Was that why she'd remained alive back at the castle, even though he'd clearly seen through their lies at the time?

If she'd stayed inside her gilded cage like a good little prisoner, King Oberon would have had to devise a better way to get rid of her. Perhaps that was why he'd made her go to that horrid seamstress before the masquerade ball. To taunt her, make her hate this kingdom, and in hopes that it would drive her to leave.

It had almost worked…

Now that she thought about it, perhaps the king had always hoped that she would try to escape so he could kill her without having to hurt Arkimedes further.

But then her dress had changed from the customary blue all the guests in the castle wore to black, the color of the royals, and the king had realized she was more than just a thorn in his side. She was the future queen in Arkimedes's mind.

Devon stayed rooted to the spot, though his face turned toward the nightmare of black shapes that morphed out of the shadows of the buildings. She'd been so worried about the king and his reasons she hadn't noticed the flying fae approaching them. They were closing in from every direction.

Nava shot to her feet, lifting her short dagger with a steady hand. Unlike Devon, she had no resources left; all her magic was depleted, and she needed the sun or plants around her to regain some of it. But she wouldn't make it easy on them either.

"I don't want to fight you," she said in a trembling voice. "But I will not let you take him so you can erase his memories again."

The fate of the world depended on their success in defeating the emissary. He was letting the Zorren in, and the demons wanted to kill the Beekeepers. Without them, there wouldn't be balance in Caztian for a long time. She was a human blessed with the strange gift of being a Beekeeper, but it was Aristaeus they needed to protect the most.

He'd once told her it was up to them to keep the world of plants thriving, for dark creatures—like demons—intended to burn it all to ash. Together, they could travel the world like pollen and dust, flit from forest to jungle to make sure new seedlings would sprout when a large natural disaster took it all away.

If Arkimedes lost all his knowledge about his connection with Ari and Nava again, they wouldn't be able to defeat the evil coming into this land. She hated to admit it, but this went far beyond their love for one another.

"I can offer a healer who will help him, and you staging this little... performance is harming him more than I ever would." The king gestured at Arkimedes's unmoving shape.

Her heart ached at his words. He was right. She couldn't help Ark right now...

King Oberon took another step forward, ignoring Devon completely. Nava believed her initial assessment about the king not wanting to hurt him, but she also believed his warning. Did Devon not care whether he lived or died?

Whatever his wishes were, his life wouldn't be on her hands.

"You can't take Orion's memories again, Your Majesty, or your kingdom will suffer. We are working against something much bigger than politics," she said in an unwavering tone that conveyed her conviction. "I am a healer, and I can make him better. I just need time."

The king tilted his head and paused. His face softened, and so did his shadows. "Humans lie constantly, yet I sense you're speaking the truth. I have allowed you three to run around my city, searching for things I can't claim to understand. But I also know you went into the forest when new fires rose up. To fight the demons, I presume."

"Yes."

"My men couldn't find a trace of the Zorren when they got there." The king spoke more quietly than before and glanced around the wide-open street. On one side, the dark waters of the Leona Sea crashed in wild waves against a rocky wall, and on the other, two-story-high buildings shielded the view of the castle in the distance. "I don't intend to harm you today, sorceress, but you will come with us, and I recommend you comply."

A part of her wanted to fight him, to tell the king to go to the shadow lands himself. But when she looked at Arkimedes, all the fight left her. If she didn't come willingly, she would get hurt—or worse yet, he might command his guards to kill her. It seemed unlikely, as he probably suspected they were soulmates by now. But that didn't mean he wouldn't use Devon as a bargaining chip. Besides, while Nava possessed the gift to heal, she had no idea how far or how fast it would work with his kind of injury.

On Grey Island, when Mortimer stabbed him, her healing powers had worked remarkably fast. In a day, Arkimedes had been fighting Devon's army.

Nava glared at the king and shot Devon a look while she lowered her weapon. To think that this man had been her enemy a year ago. And now she was here, ready to comply with her other enemy so he wouldn't get hurt. Her softness knew no bounds.

The king stepped to her side, crouched down, and picked up his son from the ground as if he weighed nothing.

"Do you have to be the one taking him?" Nava returned her dagger into its sheath, her hands clenched into fists. She wanted to scream in frustration. And to fight him.

"Inar, Liure, and Olli—take our wounded civilians to the nearest healer. Kane, send a message to the Society of Crows and tell them that if they set foot in my kingdom again, we will kill them all," the king said.

Of course he'd ignore her question completely.

"Wait," she said. What did he mean by that? Surely he wouldn't hurt Devon, right?

King Oberon's blue eyes met hers for a long, suspended moment. "Eris, take the future queen back to the castle. She only gets to speak to you until I give permission otherwise."

Nava's lips parted as the king's words registered in her mind. He'd called her the future queen. Her heart hammered inside her chest so fast that it hurt. Arkimedes lay unmoving inside the king's arms.

Her hair blew into her face as the king flew away without another word. Debris scattered around them as most of the guards took off after him.

Unlike the time she'd arrived in the kingdom months ago, when all the guards had treated her as if she was the scum of the world, this time the guard approaching her from the shadows took off his helmet and dipped his head. A sign of reverence. Nava blinked, confused.

She recognized him as one of the two who had been fighting the Crows before the rest arrived alongside the king. He brushed his wavy, blond hair away from his face, revealing the sharp angles of his cheekbones and smooth skin, now covered in a thin layer of dirt and sweat. Blood dripped from a deep gash on his chin.

"Are you the sentinel that's been trailing us?" she asked. What was she meant to do with this? Was it all an act, a trap, or was he truly showing her respect?

"I am Eris," he confirmed. "The land compels us to obey and protect our royals. King Oberon commanded us to keep you safe, and we did so, gladly." The fae placed his open hand over his armor, right in the spot where his heart would be, and dipped his head once again.

Nava could only gawk at him. Surely she had spilled some of Alera's spell on herself and gone mad.

"Horseshit," Devon said, stepping forward, closer to Nava. He lifted his sword with the smooth motion of a trained warrior. "You almost killed her back at the castle, multiple times. And you called her a witch."

Faster than Nava could register, the fae scooped her up in his arms and lifted her off the ground before she could protest. She screamed, tightening her hands around the guard's wide neck and shoulders as they rose into the sky. The street below became smaller and smaller.

"Nava!" Devon screamed, and his hands brightened with his magic as a spell shot from the ground, grazing the long feathers of Eris's right wing.

"You didn't have to leave like that. Devon is part of our group!" Nava complained. She'd better not move too much. She couldn't transfer away from his arms and into a safe spot if he were to drop her.

If she survived this disaster, she would have to have a proper conversation with Devon about his inappropriate use of magic. Shooting at the wings of a fae who was flying away with her in his arms was hardly going to help her.

"The king commanded that no one should speak with you, milady, until further notice." Eris looked away—but she didn't miss the pained expression flashing through his features. He held her tighter to his body, as if that alone would prevent him from dropping her.

"Except you, apparently." She pressed her lips together, trying to spot Devon in the small city below.

"I'm your royal guard, madam," Eris said. Then he focused on the castle that loomed in the distance. "After what happened with Fael, your last guard, the king didn't think he would be the correct guard to protect you—or the prince."

"I'm aware of who Fael is, Eris. He betrayed Arkimedes's trust. He hurt him back on Grey Island. Kidnapped him and lied—" Which apparently the fae couldn't do but kept doing repeatedly.

While Nava had never been someone to opt for aggression first, she would do anything to protect Arkimedes from those who had betrayed him. She didn't understand the fae or their politics, but what Fael had done was wrong. He had hidden behind the mask of a friend when he had been a foe all along.

At least Devon never lied. When he wasn't a friend, he made sure Nava knew it. Even the king had the decency to be truthful about his intentions.

"Are the guards going to hurt Devon?"

"The king commanded us not to harm the prince's fake brother."

Ha. What a funny—and untruthful—way to refer to an adopted sibling. Clearly, they had no clue how strong their bond was. Admittedly, she hadn't really grasped it either a few months ago.

"Are you going to hurt me?"

"I would never harm the future queen of the Copper Kingdom. And if I did so before, it was because I didn't know who you were."

"How about the king?"

Eris was quiet when his eyes, blue and vibrant with light, met hers. "Be careful with the king, madam."

So much, so vague.

They'd been stuck near the port for a couple of hours at most, but it felt like an eternity. Nava glanced at the ships sailing in the orange-speckled seas, one of them carrying her precious sun stone. Hopefully, whatever the artifact was that had seeped into her soulmate's skin, it wouldn't hurt him.

Even if right now it had gotten them captured.

33
NAVA

The staff in the castle welcomed Nava as if she hadn't left as a fugitive. Even the maids who awaited them outside in the gardens, wearing their long orange dresses, beamed at both Eris and her. None of them said a word, though. They simply bowed as they walked by.

Their welcome wasn't the oddest thing to greet her, however. What truly shocked her was the strange burst of energy that instantly filled her depleted reserves and the gentle probing sensation at the back of her mind. Not entirely unpleasant, just odd.

Not even the creepy white flowers in the garden felt like they were spying on her. They had once frightened her, but not today. Right now, they were only offering to help.

From all around her, long tendrils of yellow energy reached out, moving like wispy fingers over the stone path. Being near the castle felt almost like being inside Ari's cave. The power running through each marble brick and every blade of grass knew who she was.

It didn't take long for the bees to find Nava once they'd stepped inside the actual building. They flew and crawled over the castle walls, demanding an explanation for her prolonged silence in their small voices. But through her exhaustion, Nava could only think of Arkimedes's well-being.

"Where is Orion?" she asked, turning toward Eris, who walked a couple of steps behind her. He hadn't said a word about the strange behavior of the staff, nor about what was going to happen to her now. The king hadn't specified where she would go once she was here.

"He might be in the infirmary or his chambers."

Was that where he was taking her? Their surroundings looked familiar. She'd been through these halls before.

Nava's shoulders tensed when the green room she'd stayed in before came into view. She'd never wanted to see its huge double doors again.

Eris had brought her here through a different route, expertly avoiding crossing in front of Arkimedes's room, which lay beside it. Nava understood why he had done it. Could he sense that the castle was returning some of her magic to her? She had enough now to transfer away a few times, and damn the consequences. But perhaps it was best to allow him to think she was still under the king's mercy. She could transfer to Arkimedes's room later.

The king's plans for her weren't her biggest worry at the moment.

Eris pushed the green room's doors open for her. "This will be your room. I'll be waiting right outside the door. If you require anything, just ask."

Nava didn't move. A sudden dread held her hostage. She couldn't bring herself to step right back into the cage she'd been a prisoner in for weeks on end. "I don't want to go in there," she said, breathing harshly as her palms dampened. "Please take me to see Orion."

"I'm afraid I can't do that," Eris said, shifting from foot to foot. He was clearly uncomfortable with what he had to tell her. "He is being tended to by the best magical healer of our kingdom. You have nothing to worry about."

Nava tapped her worn boot against the polished floor, trying to mask the panic that twisted her stomach into tight knots. "He will heal faster if he has me by his side."

It was common knowledge that soulmates benefited from being near each other. Which was probably why they'd brought her here, instead of to the dungeons downstairs—that was, if the king intended to imprison her again. It seemed doubtful when he had called her the future queen in front of his guards and whoever else was observing the fight outside.

"Right now, you're tired and could use some rest." Eris pointed at her clothes.

Nava looked down and gasped as her heart leaped. She'd been expecting to find the filth of the wet streets marking her dress or Arkimedes's blood staining the fabric. What she hadn't envisaged was for her previously maroon dress to have shifted to black, the color of the royals.

There it was. The real reason Eris did not whisk her away into some unknown tower in the castle to never see Arkimedes again. The citizens, guards, and workers knew of her. She hadn't caught a lot of good luck lately, but this she would take with a smile.

"I know it's hard to stay here," he said, gesturing to the dark room beyond. "But you mustn't be afraid. I was told by the king's women that you can shapeshift into something magical—" Eris's voice faded into a breath, but he didn't look afraid of her. His expression turned reverent. "And that you can move through space without us being able to stop you. So why not go in and wash off? Rest. Later, you can see the prince."

Was it true that a guard wouldn't be able to stop her? The Zorren had cut through her in the middle of her transferring. Nava wrapped her arm across her wounded rib, feeling the ghostly pain of the demon's claw digging into her. "So don't stop me. Take me to see him now. I will wash off in his bathing chambers."

"The king commanded you not to speak with anyone," Eris said, shaking his head. "It's not you who will get punished if you go there, madam. It will be the healer and the nurses. If you ask them questions, they will answer you. It will seal their fate."

And just like that, her good luck vanished. The king was always one step ahead. "What about you? Will he hurt you?"

"I accepted my destiny when I offered to be your guard."

She wouldn't trust his words, not like she had trusted Fael. Yet it was hard to ignore how he pulled at her heartstrings.

There was no lie hiding in his expression. Still, the fae were cruel manipulators. "Why would you and the rest of the staff in the castle heed my command if the king has told you to do something different?"

"Because of his sickness. It's why we came to get the prince back on your island. Our allegiance changes as his health worsens."

Ah. That was why the castle felt different. "Fine," Nava said. "But I won't stay here for long. I'll bathe and change, and then you can take me to him."

Eris opened his mouth and then shut it again, standing rigidly against the door as she crossed the threshold.

A bath wasn't a bad idea. It was one of the few luxuries she'd enjoyed while being a prisoner here last time. And she was filthy.

The flames in the fireplace burst into life as she strolled in, warming her chilled body. The fine tapestry that hung behind the four-poster bed was new and depicted a white horse with a horn growing from its head. A new rug lay beneath the bed, handwoven to perfection in beautiful patterns of turquoise shades that reminded her of the Leona Sea.

Nava turned to thank Eris—and caught a look of pity flashing over his face as their eyes met.

Then the king's words rang through her mind. *"She only gets to speak to you until I give permission otherwise."*

When Eris mentioned the healer and the nurse, he had withheld Orion's name from the list. But the king wouldn't allow her to speak with anyone but Eris. Not even with Arkimedes.

"Wait, Eris." Her heart jolted as she rushed toward the door, reaching for it as a spike of magic surged through her fingertips. Her body became air, but the weight of her aching limbs held her back.

Eris slammed the door shut with such force that the glass panes of the balcony doors trembled. Nava slammed her entire body against the wooden surface that prevented her escape, trying the handle. Of course, it was locked.

They had imprisoned her in this hole, even though Arkimedes was hurting.

The brass heated under her grip, but the doorknob didn't move. "Eris!" she shouted, banging against the door with all her strength, until pain radiated from her hand to her elbow. "Let me out this very instance."

At first, it didn't seem like the guard would answer, but she waited, breathing heavily. If only she could force the door to explode into a million splinters and let her out.

"Try to rest, madam," Eris said. "It's been a rough day. I'll bring you breakfast in a while."

"Fuck you!" she shouted, slamming her body into the door again, until the pain traveling from her arms to her shoulders brought tears to her eyes.

These pricks wouldn't keep her locked inside this room ever again, as if she were a doll to be toyed with. Nava was a keeper of life and a magic-wielder, mate to the prince of the Dark Ones. She wouldn't be caged again.

The heat of her fury made her skin tighten and then loosen, and Nava transferred quickly in the air, heading toward the sliver of air beneath the door.

She hit a hard wall that prevented her exit.

It was transparent to the naked eye—which was why she'd missed it when she first entered. It had to be a spell that was triggered by the door closing. Otherwise, she would have felt it.

Hard air formed an invisible bubble, sealing off every crevice of the room. Now that Nava had hit it, she could see the markings of finely woven magic, crafted with tight black threads. Like a spider egg.

She couldn't allow this.

For the next several hours, she attempted to leave through every nook and cranny that appeared big enough for air to weave past. But the king had hermetically sealed the room from the inside.

Tremors raced through her as she reached for her dagger's pommel, gripping it so tight she lost the feeling in her fingers. Not that it did her any good here. "If you don't let me out, Eris, and take me to Arkimedes right now, I will kill you."

There was promise in her voice. She wasn't bluffing.

A cry tore past her lips. How stupid was she not to have seen this coming the moment the king appeared somewhat friendly in the ports?

It all made sense now. He'd let Arkimedes, Devon, and her roam around his city while the sentinels made sure neither Arkimedes nor Nava left the kingdom. Meanwhile, he'd crafted the perfect spell to keep her trapped in here.

Silence descended upon the room as she allowed her body to collapse against the smooth surface of the wall and onto the cold floor. She pressed her head to her knees and let her tired mind drift.

"It's not personal, madam," Eris said in a cautious tone, as if he didn't want to be overheard. "If I let you go, the king would kill me, and I would be a disgrace to my family. So you understand my predicament..."

She wanted to tell him that he'd lied to her, but then again, if she recalled every word he'd used carefully, he'd only told her she would get to see Arkimedes *later*.

Not at a specific time. Later could mean an hour from now or two years.

"You can't keep me away from him," she said, her voice trembling. "I told you, we heal better when we are together. You're harming your kingdom by keeping us apart."

Perhaps she could talk some sense into this fae?

"He is next door, madam, so you're very close." If Eris meant to make her feel better, he failed miserably. "The healers are with him, and the prince will survive," he continued, undeterred by her silence.

Sniffling, Nava wiped her face with the filthy sleeve of her coat. There was no use in crying. Tears wouldn't help her or Ark.

No, she had to come up with a better plan.

She focused on the webs of the king's spell right outside the balcony. Beyond it, the brown bodies of her bees crawled over the outside of the door, trying to get to her.

Unlike the last time she'd been locked in here, Nava now knew what her role in this family was. She was the future queen, and the gardens belonged to her. The plants outside had welcomed her. The castle had even restored her power.

It was as if it had known she was about to become a prisoner and wanted her to understand that she wasn't out of options. Slowly, she rose, the numbness in her body dissipating as she approached the doors and peered at her insects outside. There were so many of them she couldn't count them all.

Nava pressed her hand to the cool glass, and the threads of magic that were woven onto the surface reached toward her. The sensation was unfamiliar but welcoming, the same low voice that had whispered to her when she first arrived.

When Nava arrived here, a maid had told her the castle provided what people needed, as though it was alive. And right now, a whispering voice welcomed her home. *Home?*

Nava shut her eyes and focused on the strings of power that surrounded her. They were similar to the magic webs she often saw draped over plants, and that was something she could work with. She tugged on the soulmate bond but met only silence. Arkimedes was alive but sleeping.

But her connection to him would hopefully help her. *I can't be a pris-*

oner in my own home, she thought. If the castle was indeed a sentient being connected to Arkimedes, then it should hear her.

The glass trembled under her touch, and the bees accumulated where her hand rested, although they remained outside. More and more swarmed, so many that they obscured the bright daylight outside.

If you're the castle and you're happy that I'm here, then let me know, she thought, encouraged by the answering vibrations. The walls could hear her.

Once, when Leela had been fixing her hair, she'd spoken ill of the old queen. The room had gone cold and dark that time. Leela had been afraid to speak of Arkimedes's mother, as if the king had forbidden it. But now Nava wondered… Had the reaction been the castle all along?

Or perhaps she'd gone mad. *Why are you allowing the king to lock me in? I'm the queen.*

It was a stretch, and she could sense the magic threads of the walls as they pulsed in defiance. Was it aggravated by her questioning the king? Or at her referring to herself as the queen when she wasn't quite yet? But the tree was alive, and that had to count for something.

This was her only way out of there and to Arkimedes. Every fiber of her body told her as much. The glass of the door vibrated faster, ringing as if a storm were shaking it.

At any moment now, it would shatter.

"Madam?" Eris called from outside. He'd probably heard the tremble of the doors and felt the walls vibrate. The doorknob rattled as he tried to enter. The door cracked open an inch, and Eris's mane of blond locks came into view.

"Don't let him in," Nava said. "I need to go to my soulmate, castle. Let me out."

The door slammed shut in front of Eris's face, and his panicked gasp filtered through the door, making her smile.

"Won't you leave us if it lets you out, queen?" A voice, sweet and strange, rang inside Nava's ears. *"Won't you leave us and take the prince with you if it lets you out?"*

Nava's throat constricted, and she took sharp breaths at the intrusion in her head.

This didn't feel like it did when Arkimedes or Aristaeus spoke with their thoughts. That felt natural, like breathing. This, however, felt like an intrusion in her mind. Like the castle shouldn't be speaking to her so directly yet.

"You aren't the queen yet," the castle said with a touch more menace in its tone, and Nava's ears rang painfully. Like she shouldn't listen to its words, even if its energy felt warm and inviting.

"Let me out of this room so I can heal my mate, your future king, before the emissary gets to us."

"Madam, let me in at once. I don't want to call the others," Eris called, trying the doorknob again, but the door remained shut.

"Then don't," she responded, closing her eyes to fend off the pain that filled her skull. Gods, it hurt. "Are you going to take me to Orion?"

Eris grunted in frustration. "I… I can't."

Wrong answer.

Nava looked at the door. Her bees pressed on the balcony door, and a hairline crack crawled up the glass. Inside it, a fragment broke loose. The hole was so small she could barely see it, but it was there.

"Will the future queen leave if it helps her?" the castle asked.

"I won't leave the kingdom," Nava promised. And for the first time, those words didn't feel like a betrayal of herself.

"Then…it's time. The princeling of darkness is alone."

This didn't feel like home yet, but the kingdom was something she could learn to love. She wanted to help the citizens who were barely scraping by. She wanted to prevent people like those children in the bakery from ever having to suffer like that again.

Arkimedes had been right. Together, they had the power to make changes. To address the issues that others ignored.

The weblike black spell retreated around the hole. It was tiny but big enough for Nava to escape.

She reached for her bond with Arkimedes, but it remained empty. Panic seared through her, her body tensing as she looked over her shoulder.

"I don't want any guards in his bedroom, only the healer and the nurse," she said out loud to the room. Her ears were still ringing with a continuous high pitch from listening to its words.

Hopefully, this time, it wouldn't talk back.

No one stopped her as Nava moved through the humid air of the early afternoon toward her soulmate's room. His door was unlocked, and like the castle had told her, the room was empty.

Here, she didn't hear Eris's frantic knocks on the door anymore, and that alone brought her a semblance of peace. As soon as she'd crept past the balcony doors and into the darkness of Arkimedes's chambers, the weight of a thousand stones dropped from her shoulders.

She ran toward him across the expanse of the room, grinding to a halt beside the bed.

Arkimedes was fast asleep, clean and out of his bloody clothes. His bandaged wings lay beneath him in an awkward position that didn't look comfortable. His eyes were closed, his long dark lashes kissing the top of his cheekbones.

Nava pressed her lips together and ran her fingers over the soft velvet covers of his bed. It was the first time she'd seen him looking this ill, and her worry for him only increased with each step that brought her closer to him.

The slick marble floors were cold beneath her bare feet. She had left her boots in her old cage. She inspected every dark corner for anything odd—a hidden fae waiting to ambush her, perhaps.

The castle said he was alone, but how could someone be truly alone in a place like this?

"Ark?" she whispered, perching on the bed and reaching for his hand.

A thick green salve covered the deep gashes on his knuckles from where he'd fallen after the Crows had shot him. He didn't move or answer, and if it weren't for his shallow breaths, she might have thought he was dead.

"I'm here now," she said. Was she reassuring him or herself? Could he even hear her?

Best not to focus on his pale skin or the dark circles lining his eyes. The parallels between Ark's and Devon's appearance were a coincidence, surely. He'd only used the potion once, unlike Devon, who'd held the Vulcan twice.

Arkimedes's lips twitched into a grimace. Even in his slumber, he seemed to be in pain.

Nava's body sank into the plush mattress as she crawled closer to him. Her touch was the only way she knew how to use her healing magic. Even if, right now, she felt so depleted physically and emotionally that she could barely hold herself up.

Her eyelids drooped as her adrenaline dwindled further. The intense night and busy day had finally caught up with her. Still, she couldn't allow herself to go to sleep. What would happen when Eris found out she'd left the room? Would he call the other guards, and would they try to break into this room to remove her?

What if he called the king? Even if the castle didn't allow the guards in, surely it would let *him* in.

With each blink, it took her longer to open her eyes. The ache in her body throbbed deep, resonating through every inch of skin and bones.

"With the king and prince asleep, you are the one I heed," the castle rumbled, and Nava's ears rang at the sound. *"Only those who intend no harm may enter until he wakes. When you wear the crown, then I shall answer to you."*

The mild pain dissipated quickly after the castle quieted. Or perhaps it had never spoken at all. Was she the one who had gone mad?

It didn't matter. Sleep claimed her.

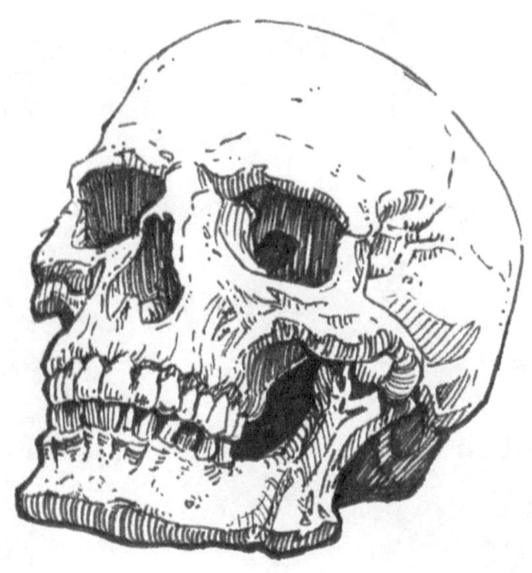

34
NAVA

A bang jolted her awake. Blinking sleep out of her eyes, Nava focused on the fae standing on the balcony outside Arkimedes's room.

Eris stared at her through the glass, his arms crossed, his blond hair whipped around his face by the wind. She turned to Arkimedes, who was still asleep, but at least he felt warm to the touch once again.

Good. Whatever the healer—or Nava—had done to help him must have worked a bit, although he was still unconscious.

She scooted across the bed and walked toward the door. It was clear Eris couldn't enter. Judging by the sun setting behind the castle walls, she'd slept for a few hours.

Once she stood in front of him, she mimicked his pose by squaring off her shoulders and lifting her chin in defiance, glaring at him. "What do you want?"

She'd not forgotten her promise when he hadn't let her out. But now that she was here with Arkimedes, her fury had dimmed, and she didn't see the need to kill him.

"How did you escape?" he asked.

The castle's magic thickened before her, floating over the door with strings of gleaming power. It was keeping its promise to her.

"The castle released me," she said, not seeing the point in lying.

Eris blinked, once, twice, thrice. His face lost all color as his lips parted. "The castle?"

"That's what I said." Nava took a step back. She was just about ready for that bath she desperately needed.

"Wait, madam. Don't go yet," Eris pleaded, pressing his hand to the door. A snap of energy popped him, and he quickly pulled his hand away, shaking it as he squinted at the wood. "You've got to let the healer in, madam. The prince needs him."

"If the castle is not allowing them in, then it must sense they are a danger to me," she said. "Is the king still sleeping?"

Eris's jaw dropped, the knot in this throat bobbed as he swallowed. "How did you know…?"

A hint of worry pricked at the back of her mind. How long did she have left until King Oberon woke up? How long until the guards barged in here and tried to take her away?

"You won't lock me anywhere ever again, Eris," she said instead, shaking her head as she retreated into the room. "I'll stay right here, besides Arkimedes, as I'm meant to. Any fae who is loyal to me may enter and help us until Arkimedes recovers."

"And that's not me?" he asked, frowning. "I swore to our king that I would protect you from any danger, no matter what."

"And yet the castle doesn't allow you in." She pointed at the door and turned around, walking away without another look back.

Nava lay down next to Arkimedes. She draped a leg over his body and her arms around his torso. Her magic wove around them with a gentle buzz as it worked to heal him.

It was their second day since returning to the castle. The few fae who had come in to help had just left. They had brought them food and potions. Most were maids, and there had been one nurse as well, who had seemed thrilled to meet her.

Nava didn't know how long she lay there with her eyes closed while thinking of nothing except healing his wounds. She couldn't sense the poison in Arkimedes today, and his skin was already looking less sickly than before.

She tightened her grasp on his naked shoulder and felt his breathing stutter where it washed over her forehead.

When she raised her head, his long lashes were rippling with faint movements. "Are you awake?"

Arkimedes's eyes cracked open, revealing his bright green irises. "Are we in my chambers?" he asked, his voice like gravel.

Her heart beat so fast she felt light-headed. "Yes, we've been here for a few days." A sudden thickness clogged her throat, and she swallowed deeply, trying to stop herself from crying. "How are you feeling?"

"Like a beast ran me down," he said gruffly, rubbing his face before attempting to sit up.

Nava pushed him down with one hand. "Don't you dare try to get up. We are in enemy territory, and I need you to be well so we can handle whatever the king throws our way."

Arkimedes lifted a brow. "What happened?"

And she told him everything. From him passing out by the docks to her being locked inside the green room and then escaping with the help of the castle.

He shifted about as she spoke, clearly uncomfortable with his wings scrunched underneath his body. But he also attempted to stay still, staring at the ceiling unblinkingly while he digested all the information. "I got the potion on me..."

"Yes. How are you feeling?"

"Strangely good," he said, "So, Eris said my father was indisposed, and then the castle told you he was asleep? Has Eris attempted to come back here?"

"Not since last time."

"How long have I been out?" he asked. "And have you heard about Devon?"

She shook her head, worrying her bottom lip with her teeth. "You've been out for a couple of days. I have no idea how Devon is doing or where he is."

"Fuck. I need to get out of here and figure out what's happening with him—and with my father." Arkimedes sat up, his face twisting with pain.

Nava opened her mouth to demand that he lie back down but shut it when he shot her a warning look. "Before he locked me away, Eris told me that the kingdom's allegiance has been shifting to you—and to me—

because your father's health is worsening. He said that's why they kidnapped you on the island. I guess that's why the castle helped me break your father's spell as well. I've been feeling like I've been going mad, because surely a castle can't speak, right?"

"Neither can bees, and yet they speak to you." Arkimedes reached for her hand and squeezed it tightly. "Like I said before, we have magical ties to this place."

True. She knew this, even if a part of her still struggled to accept it. The notion just felt so strange.

"I—I've been feeling the shift," he admitted, ruffling his hair with one hand like he usually did when he was nervous. "It's been building slowly. I sense things happening in the kingdom I didn't before. Like the city telling me the Crows were going to attack and that they were watching us. Or when I somehow knew my father and the guards were coming to aid us."

Just as she was about to answer, gooseflesh erupted all over her skin. A warning.

Arkimedes sat up straight, staring at the door. "Someone's coming."

If he felt it too, it couldn't be the bees warning her. It had to be the castle.

As if answering her thoughts, the walls trembled as the door handle moved. *"They have the king's permission,"* the castle rumbled in her ears. It sounded unhappy.

Pain shot through her head, and Nava scrambled to her feet, reaching for her dagger on the nightstand.

"The king is awake," she told Arkimedes. The doors swung open, and Eris stepped inside, along with two other guards. They paused, their eyes widening as they found Arkimedes awake and sitting on the bed.

"Your Royal Highness, we didn't realize you'd be up," one of the guards said. She'd never seen him before. His long copper wings matched his polished helmet.

The wisps of their shadows hugged their bodies, a reminder of the power they all possessed.

"No, you didn't," Arkimedes said darkly, shifting in bed with calculated movements. His aura deepened around him to match his low growl. "Were you planning to hurt my mate while I was unconscious?"

Their lips parted, and they retreated by several paces. Then they all dipped into a deep bow.

"The king commanded she shouldn't speak to anyone but her royal guard," Eris said, his skin shimmering with sweat. He looked at her with arched brows, and something shifted in his expression. Realization that she'd healed her soulmate as she had said she would—because Arkimedes was fine, even without the royal healer.

"He can't order her to stay away from me," Arkimedes said. "The laws of the gods demand that soulmates be respected." And he slipped out of bed in all his naked glory.

The three guards lowered their gazes.

"She was next door, Your Highness," the third guard said. The same ridiculous excuse Eris had given her.

"Did she request to come here?" Arkimedes asked, stepping dangerously close to the guards. Nava's stomach churned. His ire was spreading through their bond like a festering wound. "When you kidnapped me from my home and left her behind, you didn't know who she was to me, and therefore, you didn't break the godly laws. Now you do, and you will respect us. Or we shall leave."

Oh, he was angry.

These three fae were one wrong answer away from becoming a part of Arkimedes's aura. A couple of days ago, when Eris had first locked her away, perhaps Nava would have looked the other way. But right now, she had her head on her shoulders. She didn't want any of them to die simply because they were following a direct command from the king.

If anything, the guards' allegiance shifting to them faster would only help them. They couldn't fight the entire royal guard, the Zorren, and the emissary on their own. They needed allies, not more enemies.

The two guards near the back exchanged worried glances before one stepped forward. He passed his polished copper helmet from one hand to the other, giving away his nerves. "We wouldn't have come, sir. Th-the king sent us to get your mate so she could meet with him for a conference."

"My father wants Nava to come alone?"

"Well," the guard stammered, "we didn't know you were awake, sir. His Majesty wants to know how she could escape her chambers and what happened in the market."

"Shut up, Elliah." The third guard narrowed his eyes at him. "We can't divulge this information unless the king commands it."

He had white wings and was clearly incapable of reading the room. Or perhaps the other guards were feeling compelled to speak to Arkimedes more than he was. After everything that had happened, Nava doubted Arkimedes had the patience to deal with a disgruntled guard.

Nor did she.

"Well, I can tell you she isn't going anywhere near my father without me."

"His Royal Highness should continue to rest," said the guard with the white wings. "We won't harm her."

"And are you going to stop me from coming?" Arkimedes asked, and his shadows sneaked closer to the guard, who tensed visibly. Silence descended until only the sound of their heavy breaths cut through the air. "Where does he want Nava to meet him?"

"In his private library, sir," Eris said. "His Majesty isn't feeling well enough to come here."

"I see. You can tell my father that we are coming as soon as I've eaten and freshened up."

"And when will that be, sir? Your father is not a patient man."

"Tell him I'll be there after dinner." Ark paused, his eyes narrowed on Eris. "Send someone to the city to find my brother."

The three guards bowed in response and backed away one by one, leaving them alone in the room once more.

Nava's blood rushed in her ears. Gods, she felt light-headed, her palms damp with sweat.

"You two woke up at the same time. It seems strange, no?" she mumbled.

The hardness in Arkimedes's features softened when he took her in. She could only commend him for remaining so unaffected by standing naked in front of everyone. He'd resembled a statue.

"It's odd," he agreed and walked to the bed. For a moment, he sat, breathing heavily and pressing his hand to his forehead. "I wonder if me being ill affected him somehow?"

So many mysteries. It felt equally odd to grow used to another overwhelming connection to something else besides her bees.

"Why are you naked?" she asked after a moment of silence.

Arkimedes met her gaze. "The guards just came to bring you to my father, there is a building talking in your head, and you are wondering why I'm naked?"

Nava shrugged, her cheeks growing warm as she traced every hard edge of his body with greedy eyes. "I'm just a simple girl."

He huffed a laugh. "I suppose I've been secretly wondering the same thing. My guess is that the healer noticed there was a cut on my leg. He must have felt a remnant of Alera's spell on my trousers and skin and decided to strip me so he could examine it properly."

Ah. Well, that made sense and was a lot less nefarious than she'd feared.

"I don't want to go and meet your father," she said.

"I know, but now that we're here and have no artifact to speak of, we should talk to him about the emissary. We still have no way to kill him, and while I don't trust my father, we can't fight him and the emissary at the same time."

"Ari said that he might own an artifact we could use?" Hope seeped into her tone, but it was short-lived. No, that was stupid. How ridiculous of her to even dream that any good could originate from the king.

Arkimedes shook his head and lay down, covering his eyes with his forearm. "I doubt we're that lucky, Bee."

And while she preferred to be positive, she couldn't help but agree with him.

35
ORION

Seven guards came into Orion's chambers when the sun was setting. Perhaps the food they'd just eaten would be their last meal, although at least he had a strong feeling somewhere deep within that he didn't have to worry about most of these fae.

"You are well aware that I know how to get to my father's library," he said, by way of greeting. "Did he command all of you to come and get us? Seven against two? It seems unnecessary."

"No, sir," the guard nearest to him said. His glowing eyes shifted from side to side as he blinked rapidly. "All of us came just in case you needed our help. We thought a group of us could assist you with your journey. If His Royal Highness were to be in need of help."

"If it displeases you, sir, some of us can leave," Eris added from behind Nava.

Orion mulled it over. Other than the ache in his wings where the arrow wounds were still healing, he felt like himself. Sure, he was sore, but he had more energy than he'd had in weeks.

Nava's healing magic was working, though he wondered if, much like Devon, he would slowly deteriorate unless she helped him again. Poor Devon. Where was he right now? Had he left the kingdom? It weighed heavy on his heart to think of how he might be doing, as sick as he'd been when Orion had last seen him.

"No, it's fine. You may stay," Orion said, taking note of how carefully they examined him during his prolonged silence. Perhaps they expected him to collapse at any given moment, and that wasn't ideal. They had to believe he was at full use of his power so they wouldn't get any ideas about Nava.

Most of the group dipped their heads in a solemn bow, except for a couple near the front. The kingdom compelled them to obey the king, and yet Orion could sense some of their loyalties were slowly shifting. Like the castle and the city.

"Do you have any news about my brother?" He asked, as they began their trek to meet the King.

"No, sir," Cyrus said.

The tower holding his father's library was as grand as Orion remembered, but the closer they got to his room, the more trepidation Orion felt. His hands prickled with an unease that crawled over his skin, traveling up his arms and shoulders, all the way to his skull.

He spotted the ebony doors of his father's library at the far end of the hallway. The warm shades of the sunset spilled through the windows and caught the gilded patterns carved into the wood.

No fae waited outside to guard this place, so when they entered, it surprised him to see it wasn't empty.

Three wingback chairs stood in front of the marble fireplace. The king sat in one. Their eyes met, and Orion ground to a halt. This was the first time he'd seen his father ever since King Oberon had commanded his concubines to attack him.

The crawling sensation in his skull intensified as he forced himself to move forward, making sure his expression remained as blank as possible.

He'd been in this library many times before, but it had never felt as suffocating as it did now. Its tall, vaulted ceilings and stained glass windows closed in on him. He was stepping into a nightmare.

Orion tightened his hands into fists as his temper flared hot. Everything his father had done to him... Taking him away from his home with Nava. Almost killing her. Robbing him of his memories. Even if Orion could understand his father's reasons, it didn't make this easier. "You called?"

Two of his concubines stood unmoving by the bookcase, pretending to page through a book. Orion didn't think they were the sort to read. No, they liked to fight—to plot about how to remain in the influential position they held, whispering their thoughts into the king's ears.

Like the stories they had told Leela. They believed Nava had him under a spell, and perhaps that was what being a soulmate meant to them. If his mother had been his father's soulmate, as the whispers traveling around the castle suggested, then the mere mention of their rare bond could be upsetting to his women.

The king crossed one leg over the other and draped his hands on top of his knee. His white hair shrouded his face as he narrowed his eyes at Orion. "I don't recall asking *you* to come, son," he said in an icy tone. "But the guards informed me of your demands to join your mate. If you must be here, then sit down. I won't be looking up at you."

His father gestured at the two empty chairs, just as one of his ladies placed her book on the shelf and went to fetch wine from the cart. Orion glanced at Nava, who had been quiet since they'd left his room.

Where were the rest of the concubines? Hiding in the shadows, readying for an attack? Orion inspected every corner, expecting to see the dark, oily energy shifting in the air, but there was nothing there.

Much like him, Nava was perusing every shadow in the room. It was difficult to miss the insects that crawled around her.

"Can you blame me for wanting to come?" Orion pointed at the concubine Orna as she placed a carafe filled with burgundy liquid on the small table next to his father. "Last time I was here, they attacked me, and you commanded the guards to kill Nava, too. You knew we were together before you even kidnapped me."

"So you think you remember everything?" the king asked. "The real question you need to ask yourself is: are you going to put aside your own selfish desire to hate me for the good of our people?"

Manipulation didn't sit well with Orion, and realizing it was happening didn't make it any less difficult. Self-doubt crept in as he recalled his earlier promise to Nava: they would leave if she wanted to. He resisted the urge to fidget, unwilling to show vulnerability in front of his father. That would only give him what he wanted.

"That doesn't change what you did."

The king gave a dismissive wave. "I knew you'd recover from their punishment." He sounded far too lively for someone who looked as ill as he did. "It was the only way I could ensure that you wouldn't use your gift on one of them."

"You know full well I don't use the curse if I can help it." Orion pushed the words past gritted teeth. "And I don't forgive you for hurting Nava and me, not even if your reasoning was that you feared I would hurt them."

How could his father call something so wicked—stripping away the pieces of a soul—a gift?

The king reached for the wine and filled a crystal goblet before bringing it to his lips. The wine wasn't poison, but the alarming speed with which his father gulped it down made Orion wonder if he was using it to dull his pain. "I didn't know who she was to us then. You never told me you had a soulmate. Had I known, things would have been…different."

"Perhaps I would have said something if I could remember a damn thing." Orion sank into the chair, and Nava followed his lead. "You don't look well. Why have you become this ill so quickly?"

"I didn't get an explanation from the gods, Orion. It may be because magic is dwindling in our world and the kingdom demands more of me." The king waved his hand again and placed his empty glass on the table. "I'll be better by morning. Going to the ports earlier took its toll on me."

That had been on Orion's mind ever since he'd woken up. Why *had* the king come all the way to the west side of the city when he could have simply sent the royal guards?

As if reading his thoughts, his father continued. "The treaties clearly specify the Crows can raid the night markets to search for deserters. However, they can't take one of mine. No fae, no guards—much less my son."

"So you came all the way because of the treaties?" Nava scratched her forehead. "I don't understand how that works."

"What is that you don't understand?" his father asked. The bite of his condescending tone made Orion's gut twist. Clearly, a civil conversation was *not* the king's aim.

"Why does the Society of Crows even exist?" She raised her arms above her head and stretched.

"I thought you magic-wielders received a special education on the subject from your prestigious schools. Aren't you all supposed to serve the Crown from youth? It's the first thing they teach you there."

"My parents did not send me to the army," Nava said. "And my mother shielded me from the Crows and the Crown. She was part of the Society, but she didn't agree with their methods."

The king tapped his chin, studiously watching Nava as she spoke. "The ignorance of humans never ceases to amaze me. It's unacceptable in a future queen."

"If you can't be nice, Nava and I will leave." Orion rose from his chair.

"Sit down, Orion. We have to talk about what happened in the market. To answer your question, *Nava,* when the gods nearly obliterated our world, it was because of the wars between humans and fae." The king continued to speak, undeterred by Orion's glower. "The destruction of the natural resources and the gods' favorite creations set them off. A few magic-wielding humans and fae managed to hold them at bay—for a time. But we were losing, so my family and those of the founders made a deal to pay the tithes in order to pacify them."

Orion hadn't heard this tale from his father before. Undoubtedly, the version that the Society of Crows taught their recruits wasn't quite the same. King Oberon was likely closer to the true source of this ancient knowledge, since his father's bloodline was directly connected to the fae founder.

"They also created the Society of Crows, who maintain balance in the world. Their primary purpose is to avoid us upsetting the gods again. But they have a secondary task, and that is to keep magic from disappearing, so if the gods were to strike us, we could fight back."

"But…?" Orion prompted.

"The Crows ceased to care about the fae and the balance held in the Copper Kingdom a long time ago. Everyone knows they favor the Iron Crown over the rest." His father's frown deepened. "To answer your previous question, I came to the ports because only the king can overrule a direct command coming from the higher-ups in the Society. No guard could have demanded that they release the three prisoners they found in the black market."

"Not even him?" Nava asked, pointing at Orion.

"You tell me, girl. The Society hid my only heir in a kingdom made of iron, knowing full well the fae can't visit a place like that. Now, I've answered your questions. It's your turn. Why were you at the night market?"

Nava and Orion exchanged a look. Could they trust the king? Did they even have a choice?

"We were looking for a god's artifact," Orion said.

The king reached for the carafe of wine again and refilled his glass. "The healer mentioned you had the markers of an artifact's poisoning. Why would you need one to defeat the Crows?"

"I don't care about the Crows—not right now, at least. We know who is letting the Zorren into the kingdom, and the only way to stop him is with an artifact. We were in the middle of striking a deal with the dragons when the Crows ambushed us." Orion let his weight sink into the chair with a heavy sigh. The ache in his wings became more prevalent the longer he sat. "But all the pirates could give us was a liquid spell. It cracked and soaked into my clothes and skin."

"Who is allowing the demons in?" the king asked, leaning forward slightly.

"An emissary of the gods. He has been opening portals to the forest and attacking the Beekeepers." As soon as the words left Orion's lips, Nava tensed all over. He would not tell his father what she was, but speaking of this at all with someone like him—it felt dirty.

Yet with the useless artifact broken, they didn't have a way to defeat the emissary.

"How could you possibly know that?" the second concubine asked. She'd been standing by the bookcase in complete silence. Orion had almost forgotten she was there.

Judging by his father's jolt, he must have, too.

"I know because he attacked me in the forest. He has a vendetta against our family."

"Did he look like me?" the king asked.

Orion sat unmoving in his chair, his lips parting as he looked from the king to Nava and back again. "Do you know him?"

"All of you. Leave the room. Now." His father pointed at the door. The guards hesitated but obeyed after making eye contact with Orion. The concubines hovered nearby, still watching their every move and overhearing every word. "That includes the two of you."

"Your Majesty can't be considering staying here alone with them..." Orna stepped forward, worry etched deep into her features. Out of all of his father's companions, she looked the oldest. Full fae seldom showed their true age, not until they were ancient. How long had she been serving the royals? She seemed the boldest of them all.

His father sighed, shooting her an exasperated look. "Do as you're told, Orna. I might be sick, but I'm not powerless. Now go."

The guards waited for the two concubines by the doors. The silence grew charged as they trailed from the room, an uncomfortable energy hanging in the air that was hard to tolerate.

As soon as the doors closed behind them, his father spoke again. "My twin brother has been a thorn stuck in my side for a long time. Ever since he went after my queen."

What?

Orion had been expecting them to be twins, but he'd assumed the fight must be about the right to the throne, not his mother. Shock rendered him speechless, and cold crawled up his body, numbing his mind. He suddenly struggled to think, unable to weave the disconnected strands of information into a cohesive whole. "W-what do you mean?"

"That before I realized what was happening, Leir had seduced Briar right under my nose."

Leir, his father's twin and the messenger of a god. Orion couldn't hear anything other than Nava's sharp intake of breath. He attempted to swallow, but even that seemed impossible.

"Why would an emissary care to seduce the queen—or bring destruction to your kin?" Nava asked.

"Jealousy drives those with weaker minds to madness. You can't reason with someone like that. No crime of passion warrants the destruction of an entire kingdom. But he is an emissary of the gods. It's not the first time they've attempted that."

What was his father trying to say? Jealousy, a crime of passion? Who'd committed it—him, her, or the emissary?

Nava's wide eyes and trembling lips told Orion that she was also putting together the horrible puzzle that he desperately longed to ignore. "Was he jealous because you and the queen were soulmates?"

Thunder cracked, rattling the stained glass windows. A storm was brewing.

The king's eyes skittered away from them, focusing on his drink instead. "She said we were soulmates at some point, but I never quite understood the bond she kept referring to. I have a connection with this castle—with my duty to its citizens." He paused and took a sip of the wine, which stained his lips deep red, like blood. "I loved her in my way, but she was always ill, and it was hard to connect."

They hadn't been soulmates, for there was no way to deny the pull that tied them together. But if his mother had believed them to be...had Leir been her true soulmate all along? Perhaps she had seen him in passing and assumed they were the same person?

Either way, Orion wouldn't like the answer. His mother's death looked more and more like an execution the longer he sat in this room.

Past the king's chair, a piece of wood hung from the wall. Orion had spotted it months ago when he'd visited here to obtain the key to unlock the magic-canceling bracelet Nava was wearing.

His father glanced over his shoulder, following Orion's line of sight. His face twisted as he realized what Orion was looking at. "You asked me once what that was..."

"And you said you like to collect art."

"I do, although I guess it was not the entire truth. The carvings were once part of the throne room's door, gifted to my father by a skilled soothsayer. They formed part of a prophecy that heralded he would have twins and lose one of them to the gods. I kept it here because I like to remind myself who is supposed to rule and claim the queen, and who is supposed to stay a servant."

The tithe. The royals of the Copper Kingdom parted with their secondborn to Dargan as payment for his forgiveness. "When did you remove the panel? When you discovered they were having an affair or after she died?"

"I had it removed after Briar stole you from your crib and took you away from me."

"How did she die?" Orion pressed his body into the chair. His heart beat in his ears like a drum.

Thump, thump, thump.

"I don't like to repeat myself, Orion, and I've told you already. Your mother died in a fire, and as you know, the west side of the library was obliterated by one."

And there it was, the carefully concocted lie that hid behind half-truths. Months ago, when Orion first began to ask questions about his mother's fate, the king's answer had rung like a falsehood. But now the actual truth could only reveal how truly evil his own blood could be.

"You claim you want us to work together? Then stop lying to me!" Orion slapped his hand against his thigh. The stinging sensation grounded him in the present, pushing away the vivid memories the ghost of his mother had shared with him.

"Why are you so sure I am lying?" His father's sudden stillness was so absolute, so unnatural that it sent a shiver down Orion's spine.

Orion shot to his feet and strode around his chair and toward the fireplace. Nava continued to sit quietly, hands folded in her lap as she stared wide-eyed into space. The bond was a confusing cacophony of emotion, and he could no longer discern who was feeling what.

If Leir had been his mother's true soulmate, then he would never have hurt her. His motivations were becoming so crystal clear that Orion felt like throwing up.

"You never mentioned you had a twin who was an emissary, let alone that he was out for your blood. Instead, you sent me to the forest for weeks on end to track down the humans who were supposedly burning it down."

The king's pale skin was mottled with pink and red patches. He bared his teeth. "How was I supposed to know that bastard had anything to do with the fires? I haven't seen or heard of him in decades."

"If you care for the kingdom as much as you claim to, stop this deceit. I already know what truly happened."

"Full fae can't lie, and you know that. I don't have human blood like you." His father's eyes shone with a wickedness that would make most people cower. He wasn't technically lying—he was expertly avoiding and changing the subject.

"When I arrived at this castle, you insinuated that my mother died in that library. Gave me some clues and allowed me to fill in the blanks. I assume you gave the rest of the kingdom the same treatment. Yet I know it's not the truth." Orion's vision tunneled in on the king as he pushed away from the fireplace and strode back toward Nava. He needed to remain by her side, in case his father used his power to hurt her.

"How would you know where it happened? You were but a babe, and she abandoned you in another kingdom that hates our kind."

"I've seen her die," he growled. Those horrid dreams and how he longed to escape them. He'd never wanted to piece together the gruesome reality of what had happened to his mother. But now it all made sense. And he felt dizzy with it.

She'd taken Orion away because the king realized she had slept with his brother. Had she known they were two different people? How could she not? They were almost identical, but their eyes were different. While his father's were blue, Leir's had been blood red.

Then his father had burned her alive in that tree. Her final thought had been that the one she'd loved most had killed her. Even with her dying breath, his mother had believed he was her soulmate.

But that was impossible. Orion and Nava couldn't feel that strongly for anyone other than each other. She must have known.

"The queen thought you were going to hurt Orion, and that's why she took him away," Nava said, digging her fingers into the layers of her skirt, while her skin glowed bright yellow. "It had to be."

"Perhaps," the king said. "But I told her many times that I would never hurt my son. Even when I thought *Orion* was Leir's. I always intended for him to remain my heir."

Had the king become violent when he believed the baby was another's? Scared her enough to take him away to another kingdom—one he couldn't reach?

"Can immortals even have children with mortals?" Nava's voice held bitterness as she glared at the king. "Because I doubt they can."

"Orion didn't have pointed ears or the wings of our kind. Only a weaker fae could have produced such offspring. Not I, who possessed the Gift of the Fallen." The king stood on wobbly legs, leaning heavily against the chair.

Even now, the broken child inside Orion worried about this monster. But he would never refer to him as father ever again.

"The midwives told us that your lack of fae traits was an effect of mixed blood. That, since she was a magic-wielder, there was a possibility your fae traits would present along with the human magic."

Which was precisely what had happened when Orion turned five. The Crows had found him and whisked him away at a young age to become their weapon. "So you told everyone she had taken your heir, so no one would question how she died and know that you killed her."

King Oberon remained silent, still gripping the furniture hard enough for his knuckles to turn pale. He hadn't cared enough. Not about his queen, nor his son. To him, their union had been a transaction to obtain an heir and keep the kingdom alive.

"You never searched for me because you thought I was a bastard."

"What are you going to do, Orion? Kill me?" The king leaned forward. He didn't appear the slightest bit afraid to die. "Go on, I'm sure our people will believe you. After all, you didn't abandon them for more than a decade to chase after a woman."

The manipulative bastard...

"Then you also demanded to come here when I requested to speak with your soulmate, alone." The king circled the chair and dropped into it unceremoniously. Perhaps he'd thought Orion would do something rash, like actually kill him. "I have given you everything, even after you abandoned me. The knowledge to control your gift, power, gold..."

"Who would our people believe?" the spirits of Orion's shadows wailed in his ears, loud and clear, although the king had left the words unspoken.

"What if I don't care if they believe me? I don't need to be their king. I can live anywhere inside the kingdom to maintain whatever magical balance our ancestors bargained for. This castle can crumble into dust once you're gone for all I care."

The lie burned his tongue like acid rolling down the back of his throat, searing his vocal cords. Orion nearly choked, struggling to keep his arms stuck to his sides, to not grab at his throat and give the monster the satisfaction of watching him struggle.

It didn't matter, for the king's lips tilted up into a faint smile. "I always wondered if you were more human than fae and could lie, just like Briar did. It turns out you cannot."

Nava jumped out of her seat and rushed to Orion's side, her brows drawn together as she stroked his arm. The warmth of her magic soothed the pain.

"Ark?" Her voice came into his head, trembling with emotion. He couldn't tell where the anger that pulsed deep within him began and where the sorrow ended.

"If you're done trying to lie to me and yourself, we can both move past this setback—"

Setback? Was that all that burning his mother alive was to this bastard?

Orion flew forward, ignoring the pain that flared from his injured wings, and collided with the king in a pile of legs and arms. His fist met the king's jaw with a loud crack.

Then he punched him again and again. Blood splattered his knuckles from a deep cut in the king's lip. His wide blue eyes met Orion's right before the next blow rained down upon him.

Memories of his mother struggling against the burning tree flared inside him like wildfire. How much she'd suffered. How angry her spirit was. Darkness crept over the edges of Orion's vision, and the mist of his power crawled up his fingers slowly.

"Take him," a voice whispered in his ear.

"He deserves it," another goaded.

He pulled on the king's energy as he attempted to push him back and get Orion off him. But his efforts were a weak wisp of nothingness compared to Orion's rage.

"Ark, let him go. He doesn't deserve your humanity." Nava grasped Orion's hand and gently pulled him away. Her voice was a warm blanket in a sea of ice. He blinked away the haze of tears that clouded everything, and the room came into focus again.

Her hands framed his face, and as he focused on her features, illuminated by the flickering candlelight from the walls, his heartbeat slowed, making space for the true feeling—a sorrow so raw he nearly collapsed with it.

"You're pure evil," he heard Nava say. "I never understood Arkimedes's fears of what he would become if he let his darkness consume him, but I do now." She glared at the king, who lay groaning on the ground. "Even though you speak so righteously about sacrifice for your people, all you are is a monster."

The doors of the library swung open, and the seven guards and his father's women poured in, rushing to the king. Still, no one attempted to arrest him, not even the concubines.

"Thank you," he whispered to Nava through their mind bond, unable to gather the strength to say it out loud.

"I bet he wanted you to kill him. He would have died a martyr if you'd done so," she said.

Worse, still, a fragment of the king's soul would have stuck to him forever. Wouldn't the bastard have loved that—an easy way out but not a permanent end. To whisper in his son's ear and torment him for the rest of his life.

"I've not dismissed you, Orion. We must devise a plan to kill Leir!" the king slurred, hanging crookedly from the shoulder of one of his guards.

Orion paused by the door, resting his hand upon the gold handle. "My name is Arkimedes. After what I just learned, the name you gave me means nothing."

Nava had been right. In his attempt to hold on to the family he'd never had, he had pushed away the man he'd become on Grey Island. He regretted that he'd allowed this kingdom to suffer during his absence, but he wouldn't have changed it for the world now. Those precious years in seclusion had made him more human.

Months ago, when the king offered him the chance to take the name he'd been given at birth, to fill the role of prince, he'd been eager to impress. To be wanted by the father who he thought had abandoned him.

He'd wanted to forget all the crimes he had committed in the name of the Crows. Orion was a fresh start. A fit name for the ruler of a kingdom.

But his mother hadn't abandoned him. She had saved him and given him a chance to survive, to become a better man away from this. And for that, Arkimedes would be eternally grateful.

"He is bringing the demons in," the king urged. "We have to talk."

"Not tonight," Arkimedes said. He didn't look over his shoulder. What was there for him to see? Nothing. "We will meet tomorrow and discuss how to handle the villain you've brought to our doorstep."

He curled his fingers around Nava's hand and drew her out into the frigid hallway. The king had little time left, and Arkimedes would not be a part of his life any longer than necessary.

36
ARKIMEDES

Arkimedes needed to be as far away from the king as humanly possible, for the darkness within him still craved retribution. It was hard to silence the spirits of his aura when anger blinded him like it had back in that room.

He and Nava went down a set of long, wide steps until they reached a spacious hall. In the absence of daylight, its towering ceilings made him feel like the tiniest speck. The only illumination was wall sconces holding individual candles on either side and the promise of windows at the far end.

Nava's breaths came in short, quick puffs that gave away her exhaustion. She hadn't complained about his punishing pace so far, allowing him a moment of respite as they moved down the king's wing and toward—

Where were they?

He slowed down, taking in his surroundings, from the warm gray walls mottled with age to the tall columns and cobwebs that had accumulated in the corners.

"Do you know where we are?" Nava's voice had turned soft as her brows pinched together in the middle.

Arkimedes shook his head to clear his numb mind. "I don't think I've been here before," he admitted, dragging his hand over his face.

The space was unfamiliar and cold. Other than being built of the same stone as the rest of the castle, there were few similarities. It was desolate. There were sculptures but no wall tapestries or furnishings. Now that he thought about it, their steps had been echoing down the hall because of the lack of runners.

"Are these your ancestors?" Nava trailed a finger over a marble pedestal that supported an unfamiliar bust of a fae. This male wore a crown of thorns, molded perfectly to his thick, wavy hair with an impressive level of detail that depicted every last crevice of each sharp thorn. It looked very much like his own crown, so this must have been a prince from long ago.

Beside him, the statue of a female fae stood proudly. Both of them appeared young—perhaps in their twenties, although age showed differently in fae than humans.

"I suppose so," he said with a shrug, looking down the infinite hall. "It makes me wonder if all my family were as conniving as the king or my uncle. It seems to run in the family."

"Not you," she said.

Arkimedes nodded, feeling a weight lift off his heart. This time, he believed her. He was definitely not as wicked as them. Even in the Society, he'd never burned his wife alive, the woman who'd birthed his child. Much less threatened to kill an entire city for the sake of vengeance.

"I think you'll be a great king when the time comes for you to take your place here. We will show this kingdom what true soulmates can do when they work together instead of against each other."

Arkimedes sucked in a breath. After all that had happened with the pirates, the emissary, and the king, he had never expected that Nava would want to stay in this castle and assume their roles as monarchs. Of course, he had hoped she might, but even though this life called to him, he was ready to leave and never wear the crown again. So this meant a lot. "We are staying, then?"

"Why would I ever want to leave this cozy, lovely place that speaks to me?" She gestured at the creepy hallway with a quirk to her lips.

A laugh escaped him, and he shook his head. "Are you changing your mind because you know the castle is sentient now?"

"I admit, I'm curious." She shrugged, clearly doing her best to distract him from the awful truth that lay hidden within this place. It worked, somehow. "Does the castle speak to you?"

"Not like it does to you, apparently," he said. "But in this kingdom, the queen is the ruler of this place, which is why there is a tree that lives when a queen is here. It might have a stronger connection with you than with me—and even with the king."

Nava bit her nail, her eyes darting from dark corner to dark corner. "It's kind of overwhelming," she admitted. "Why do you think this area is so dirty?"

"I don't recall the last time I could roam the castle without a tail of guards behind me," he said, and they continued past the statues. If he really thought about it—had that ever happened? No. His fa—the king had tracked his every move from the moment he'd arrived in the kingdom. But now things had changed.

"There's nothing here." Nava's skin became a beacon of light in the darkness. Her nose wrinkled as she sniffled. "I don't think anyone has been here in a long, long time."

He reached out for her hand, and her warmth enveloped his cold skin. Tonight had been terrible, but being with Nava made it somewhat tolerable. Even when grief overwhelmed him, she anchored and guided him. He looked away, unable to find the right words to express himself. He would probably not make much sense if he tried.

His spirits were quiet now, eerily so. They moved to the end of the hall, where two stained glass windows let in long streaks of light, casting a myriad of colors onto the floor. His gaze fell on a single mahogany door within the wall. Painted black and decorated with gold accents, it seemed to shield a lonely room, surrounded by nothing.

A shiver ran down his spine, causing every hair on his body to stand on end. The castle didn't speak to him like it did to Nava, but had it guided him here, somehow?

His heartbeat sped as he inspected the familiar filigree adorning the entrance to the room, similarly designed to the ones in his father's room door. A cool breeze seeped under the layers of his clothes as he took in the marble statue standing on one side of the door.

He would recognize his mother anywhere. This bust was much like the ones of the fae they'd passed earlier. She wore the same crown of thorns, and her hair, long and billowy, covered her round ears.

The storm of his feelings matched the weather outside. He focused on the gentleness in her eyes and the smile that made her look so young.

She was almost the mirror image of the full statue beside the king's room.

"I think this was my mother's room…" His voice shook with emotion. Moving away from Nava and the sculpture, he blinked as his vision blurred.

It was idiotic to feel this overwhelmed and sad for someone he'd never even known. Except that the ghost of her burnt body had chased him for so long, and it was impossible to ignore the devastating truth of what he'd just learned. He'd been looking for answers about what happened to her when Nava arrived at this castle. Now he knew the king had killed her.

"She was beautiful," Nava said gently and stepped toward the door, allowing him time to collect himself.

She could read him like an open book and could tell he wanted her nearby but needed space. He didn't like to be coddled, especially when he felt vulnerable. "My mother was so young when she became the queen. She wasn't ready to be married to the monster inside that room."

"Nor was she ready to be mated to the other monster," Nava whispered.

So she had come to the same conclusion: the emissary had been his mother's soulmate, not the king.

She took a shaky breath and met his eyes. "Although if Leir is immortal and can't die, then he has been stuck suffering for all these years. I think if that had happened to me, I would have gone insane, too."

Arkimedes nodded. "My father said she was always ill. Maybe she was sick because her soulmate was away for so long, much like what would happen to the both of us if we were separated."

"...you will be dead before the day is over, and your bloodline will be gone soon. Then, and only then, will I be free," the emissary had told him the afternoon they'd fought in the forest.

Arkimedes had thought it meant that Leir wanted the crown for himself, but it had never been about power. He had no interest in taking the throne. He only wanted to die so he wouldn't suffer anymore. This was about revenge and loss.

"Do you think she knew the king wasn't her soulmate and lied to him?" Nava asked.

The same question had been running through his mind ever since his father had told them the truth. "I don't know how she wouldn't know." He clasped his hands loosely and let his gaze drift over the edges of his mother's statue. "The first time I met you back at the manor, I didn't know you were my soulmate right away, not until I saw my mark later. I suppose it's possible that if she saw Leir first, got the mark, and then saw my father, she could have assumed they were the same person..."

But—that didn't add up, did it? They had different eye colors.

"I don't know. She wouldn't have found the soulmate mark on the king's body either... Not unless he never allowed her to see him naked."

He definitely didn't want to think about *that*.

"Leir's a blurred memory to me, but I remember his eyes were red." Her breath billowed from her lips, giving away the chill in the air just as thunder rolled over the castle, shaking the windows behind her. Her brows dipped low, and her expression turned serious. "We both know how lies can fester if they go on for too long, but someone is hiding the truth here."

"As I did back on Grey Island, when I didn't tell you we were soulmates."

"And then I did the same." She looked away, and her cheeks turned red.

Perhaps his mother hadn't been particularly bright and unable to tell the difference for that reason. A harsh thing to think, but how else could she not know?

Love made you blind to certain things, but even taking that into account, it didn't make sense. If she felt something special for Leir when he was toying with truths, then she might have looked the other way when she didn't feel the same for the king. Especially if she'd been as young as she appeared from the statue.

"Your mother showed me the moment before she died and what she said to the king."

"What did she say?"

"She told him she loved him."

Arkimedes had to prop himself up against the base of his mother's statue. It was as if the ground was dropping out from beneath him.

"I didn't remember everything she shared with me until your father was talking to us." Nava shook her head, anger ringing through her words. "But I thought his voice sounded familiar. I should have known earlier—"

"The memory she shares is a lot to take, Nava. Particularly the first time you experience it."

"What if the emissary actually *is* your father, Ark? Perhaps we can speak with him. Make him stop this madness before it's too late."

Arkimedes sympathized with Leir. He wouldn't survive with an intact mind either if someone tied Nava to a tree and sentenced her to die such a horrible death.

Still… He didn't think Leir was his father. Not that it mattered, because they were both evil. Even though the queen might have been his mate, she had also been with the king while he was away. Arkimedes had inherited the Curse of the Fallen, and only the king and Arkimedes possessed the power to strip souls from the people around them.

"Even if he is, there's no way we'll convince him to change his plans. He's out for blood because he can't die otherwise. He's willing to kill both you and Ari. He doesn't care about the thousands of innocents in this kingdom who will die if our bloodline disappears. He's neither a fatherly figure nor a lost soul."

"Which brings us to our initial problem," she said. "We have to stop him, and the only advantage we have is whatever godly magic you absorbed from Alera's potion. We don't even know what that is."

He'd be damned if he knew. Other than poisoning him at the docks, the spell had done nothing.

"I know." He rubbed his chin, studying the curve of his mother's round cheeks, made from polished marble, sculpted so exquisitely. "We can use her against him."

"How? Can you call on her spirit to come and beat some sense into him?"

"I would love to see that." He squashed a smile and cleared his throat. "We can't predict when or where she will show, but perhaps we can distract him if we find something of hers that she might have worn back in the day. Or a letter, a diary—a gown?"

Arkimedes opened the door, revealing a grand, yet bleak room shrouded in darkness. Someone had hastily draped blankets over its furnishings, and a fine layer of dust had accumulated on every surface. Spiderwebs covered the broad windows, the bedposts, and the end tables.

They tiptoed inside, taking in the abandoned chambers that had once belonged to his mother. Painted in light colors, they were the complete opposite of his father's. Blankets were piled up on the four-poster bed, and the drawers of the dresser by its side looked as if they had been closed in haste.

No one had bothered to come in here to make the bed. A wave of emotion rolled through him, starting in his gut and traveling up his body, taking hold of his throat and choking him. He drew an angry breath just as the fireplace sputtered to life, burning dust and sending fragments of old, ashy logs dancing into the room.

Nava jumped away from the fire with a scream. "That always scares me," she said, placing a hand over her chest as she took deep gulps of air. Then she glared at the ceiling, as if the castle had personally wronged her.

"At least it'll get warmer now." He wandered over to the dressing table and rubbed his fingers over the dusty surface, picking up a silver hairbrush with white bristles. "Leir is a skilled fighter, and his sword is unlike anything I've ever seen. He has been doing this for a long time, and he heals quickly."

Wait a minute. That was it. They had been going around in circles trying to find an artifact to defeat Leir—when he had been holding the perfect weapon the entire time.

"And there will probably be demons everywhere." Nava wrapped a protective arm around her stomach, gripping the fabric of her dress over the side of her ribs, where she'd been gored.

"We can steal his weapon," he whispered.

Her eyes widened as she met his gaze. "Of course. His sword is an artifact."

Arkimedes nodded slowly.

"So…we distract him with something that belonged to your mother and that way we can get close enough to steal his weapon?" Nava crept deeper into the room, pulling at the half-open drawers.

Every hair on Arkimedes's body stood on end all of a sudden. There it was again—the sensation of being watched. Frigid air seeped under his trousers, a touch of death in the little warmth they had gained. He dropped the hairbrush on the rug and glanced up at Nava, who was clutching the garments she'd plucked from the dresser to her chest.

Her mouth hung wide open before she screamed, and her skin had turned several shades paler. On the other side of the room, his mother's spirit floated, pointing at the settee by the fire.

Arkimedes jerked away, and pain shot through him from his healing wounds. He lost his balance and fell onto the carpeted floor. His heart thundered against his ribcage, and it took him a long moment to breathe past his panic.

The spirit was frightening but safe, and she was here to show him *something*. He checked to see where she was guiding him, then got to his feet and headed toward Nava first.

"She's not a Neem and won't hurt us." He touched her face, shrouding her vision of the ghost with his body and wings.

"How do you know? We're in her space, and she looks angry," Nava whispered. But she relaxed inside his arms. Her fear was almost too much as it poured through him from their bond, paralyzing him all over again.

"I know she is frightening, but ever since I arrived at the castle, she has been leading me to clues about what really happened." He stepped away from Nava and glanced over his shoulder. The ghost was still there. "When you'd just arrived at the castle, I was in the main library, trying to find some answers. She showed me a book, which I took to Devon to be translated, and we discovered an old prophecy."

"Was that the one Devon spoke about back at the Society's safe house?"

"Yes. *The child of royal blood came to this world sick, poisoned by evil, and was taken to the world of shadows, away from our land and our people,*" he recited. "I thought it referred to me, but it was always about Leir, and my mother must have known that."

"Even though the king killed her, she still wants us to stop her soulmate." Nava dropped the clothes she'd been clinging to for dear life and followed him across the room to the fireplace, skirting his mother.

Their steps left marks on the dusty ground, and for a good while, they searched behind the cushions of the sofa, only to come up empty-handed. Arkimedes flattened his lips and examined the mantlepiece, but other than the resident spiders, it was empty.

"There is something here that she wants us to see, but I can't seem to find it." He glanced at the ghost, who continued to point in their direction, unmoving. No matter how often he saw her, the image would never cease to upset him.

He frowned and glanced at Nava. She was kneeling on the floor, peering below the sofa. "Nothing— Wait... There might be something under here."

They pushed the settee aside. It didn't take them long to find the tile on the floor that had jagged edges, as if someone had repeatedly picked at the mortar. Arkimedes stepped on it, and it shifted under his feet. Nava sent him a charged look, and he opened his palm, his magic pouring from him in a burst of black ink. The tile moved aside, leaving behind a shallow hole carved into the stone beneath.

From a pile of rock debris and dust, he pulled out a rectangular wooden box that had lost its luster. Almost too large to fit in the hole, it had slumbered there, hidden for the past thirty years.

Settling on the ground, Arkimedes dusted off the top and found her name engraved in mother-of-pearl and gold. Briar. He looked for the ghost, but she had vanished. He swallowed and took a breath, hoping it would give him the strength to push forward. It was easier to keep going when anger drove his actions, and right now, he needed that focus to get her the revenge she deserved.

Inside the box was a small diary. Its leather binding had twisted with moisture and age, its parchment pages faded into a multitude of shades of browns. He withdrew it and placed it in Nava's expectant hands. Then he rummaged through the contents again, finding a small bundle of golden hair, wrapped in blue ribbon with a small tag with his name on it.

Orion, five months.

"I don't see how any of this will help us." He cleared his throat and placed the strands of his hair back into the box. He couldn't use it for anything other than to make himself spiral into sorrow at what the twins had stolen from him. Most of the remaining items weren't useful at first glance, except for the intricate ring made of silver. Symbols he didn't recognize were carved into it, and it was decorated with green emeralds.

"The ring—it says here that her soulmate gave it to her when they first met," Nava said, calling his attention to her. She was paging through the diary with a frown, her face an inch away from the pages. "It's very hard to understand her writing, but she drew a picture."

Arkimedes glanced over her shoulder as she continued to read.

"He told her that wearing it would ease the discomfort when they were apart, that it would call him back to her, except..."

"Except what?"

"She saw him again a few days later at the royal masquerade ball."

"And let me guess, he didn't remember who she was?"

"No." Nava's gaze cut to him, and he fell quiet, allowing her to continue uninterrupted. "He seemed to follow along with her story, though he didn't recognize the ring, so she didn't bring it up again. She wrote that the king told her he liked to change his eye color with magic."

They'd been right. His mother had met Leir, her soulmate, before she'd met the king. Probably when he was out on a mission for Dargan, and she was here traveling. Then he had been forced to leave, and she'd told his father about them being soulmates, sparking his curiosity.

Arkimedes brought the ring closer to his face, inspecting the designs carved into the band. If he closed his eyes and focused, he could sense the subtle vibrations of magic emanating from it. An artifact, although not one with a lot of power.

"Ark—your mother knew the king wasn't her soulmate." Her face shifted with an emotion that was hard to place. Disappointment—or anger? Her eyebrows pinched in the middle.

"What?"

"It's written here." She closed the diary and handed it to him. Her fingers were icy when he touched them.

Arkimedes put the ring aside, flicking to the page Nava had read last. His mother's writing was the finest calligraphy, elegant swirls written in deep green ink.

The twins believe I'm a naive idiot if they think I haven't figured it out. And perhaps at first, I was for believing their lies. I suppose being seventeen will do that to a person, not that they would understand, with time holding such different meaning to fae.

I curse my heart for loving them, for having a soulmate who hasn't even shared his name with me. I shouldn't love Oberon, as he isn't even my mate. But here I am, a fool—lovesick and wondering when my king will decide to see me instead of one of his whores.

He insults me by bringing his female guards into his

chambers while I rot in this room so far away from him. They are healthy—when I'm not. I hate him for even mentioning it, far more than I love him.

I never cared for a sacred love, even if at first it sounded like such a wonderful escape. What I long for is a family. My mate won't give me a child, for I know he isn't of this world. He's one of them—a messenger of the gods—at home somewhere I can't ever follow. So I must take matters into my own hands if I, too, want a home.

If fate is as cruel as binding me to a soulmate I can't ever be with, then I shall use my spare moments of health to carve out my own destiny. A child, a baby that will love me no matter how ill or how human I am.

His vision blurred. No matter how hard he tried, he couldn't seem to swallow the fresh surge of grief. He shut the diary and shoved it inside his coat pocket, unable to meet Nava's eyes. Of course, she could feel his emotions, regardless.

Arkimedes grabbed the ring from where he'd dropped it inside the box, and its magic buzzed in his hand. He cleared his throat, trying to steady his voice. "We can use this to call Leir to us. I believe what he told her was true. If my mother had worn this ring when she wanted to see him, he might have made it all the way here to save her."

"She loved you, and she saved you." Nava reached for his hand, and the warmth of her magic seeped through him. He fell into her sad eyes. "Leir had the upper hand all this time. He killed Illaris, tried to do the same to Ari and me. Now it's our turn, and when he comes, we will be ready."

37
NAVA

The king summoned Arkimedes and Nava to a meeting the following afternoon. They met in a room she hadn't visited before, which was decorated with dark murals. In its center, a bulky wooden table stood. It could easily seat forty people, although only four awaited them.

The sound of the heavy chairs scraping the floor welcomed them as three of the fae stood as soon as they entered.

"You're late, Orion," the king complained from his seat, the black of his wings and aura shrouding most of him. Yet the bright shades of his self-illuminating eyes cut through the haze as they burned into her. "The emissary might strike our kingdom at any moment, and you've been taking strolls around the city all morning."

Arkimedes pulled out a chair for Nava, his jaw tensing as he met her gaze with quiet fury. She sat in silence. The black velvet fabric of her seat was soft and warm.

"The guards conveniently left my brother back at the docks, and haven't located him. He's ill, and we were trying to find him," Arkimedes said. "But being out there this morning made us realize that there is a possibility the Zorren's next attack will spill over into our city, and I would like to open up the castle grounds to the citizens. The wards will keep them safe until we can defeat the demons."

"We can invite the high fae to seek refuge within our walls, Your Highness, but there isn't a way for everyone in the city to fit," a male sitting beside the king said. His skin was a rich brown, and his golden eyes were striking even from a distance.

"I don't care how, but you will find a way," Arkimedes said through gritted teeth. His dismissive tone held no room for argument.

The male opened his mouth as if to protest, but the king raised a hand. "That's enough, Finian."

"We can work on how to prevent the demons from getting to the city, but if we have to ruin the gardens to save our people, then we should," Arkimedes said.

"If our primary concern is the Copper City, we could send some of our people to our other major cities. In the meantime, of course," a female sitting to the king's right said. Her beautiful pale face grew pensive as her eyes traveled from Arkimedes to the king and then finally settled on Nava.

"Leir can open a portal anywhere in Caztian or the kingdom, but he'll likely target the city where King Oberon and Arkimedes are," Nava said. It wasn't the whole truth, given that Leir and the Zorren were targeting the Beekeepers.

The emissary had told Ark about it. Leir would help the demons kill Ari and Nava, and in return, the demons would help him burn the place down and kill the royals. It just so happened that, in this case, all of them were connected.

"While you were looking for your Crow, we've been discussing a way to stop Leir." The king gestured at the center of the table where a small jeweled dagger lay.

"Is that an artifact?" Nava pressed her hands to the polished table and leaned forward to study the hooked blade and the runes etched into the shiny black metal. Could it be? Although it looked ancient and clear traces of magic wafted over its surface, Nava was too new to this to sense the difference between a magic-wielder's power and something created by the gods.

"It's not," Ark said in an icy tone that matched his harsh expression, suffocating the hope bursting in her chest. She slumped into her seat.

"It's a *powerful* fae weapon and has belonged to our people for longer than I've been alive. It was crafted even before the gods waged war on our territory." The king's ire was plain. "Back in those days, our ancestors fought the gods with our own artifacts, and they even killed a few. My magic can and will defeat a god's *servant*."

Nava sucked in a breath and focused on the dagger and the magic flowing off it. Somehow, she knew with absolute certainty that this wouldn't be enough. This blade would never kill an emissary. They were back to square one, and their end was still nigh.

"You can't be serious and believe we can actually stop Leir with this knife. He won't let us get that close." Arkimedes reached for the weapon, touching the silk fabric wrapped around the hilt.

"Don't touch the artifact until you're ready to wield it, son. It may not look like much to you, but much like our power, it steals energy. It slows down our enemy's ability to heal and poisons their blood. But if there isn't a foe, it will drain your energy instead."

As if the king cared whether it hurt Arkimedes. Oberon poured himself some wine and leaned back like his fate didn't rest in the hands of his estranged son.

The nerve of him to assume Arkimedes would be the one to wield the knife. But then again, the king looked worse with each passing day. Right now, his face was an array of all possible shades of purple and red from the beating Arkimedes had given him the night before.

"I felt more magic coming from the useless potion the dragons gave us," Arkimedes challenged, allowing his hand to hover over the knife, his lips setting into a flat line.

"If you have a better way, I'm all ears."

Nava observed their interplay, much like everyone else in the room. How much of the advisors knew about Leir? Were they aware that the king had murdered the queen in a fit of jealousy and anger? If so, then they were keeping it quiet.

"When I fought Leir in the forest, I noticed he had a powerful sword. Nava and I have been talking about the possibility of stealing it."

"And how are you going to steal it if he is as strong as you make him sound?" The king's eyes glinted with curiosity.

"He won't know what's happening, and he won't see us coming." Arkimedes glanced down at the knife, pursing his lips.

"What did you find in your mother's chambers? I had it searched after she passed to discover where she took you, but there was nothing."

"How did you know…?" Blood rushed through Nava's head as she met the king's eyes from across the table. She had been extra vigilant of being followed, and her bees had been on high alert all night long.

"Don't be surprised, girl. The castle speaks to me. Soon enough, it will begin to communicate with you if you listen. It always prefers the queens."

Nava pressed her lips together. No need to reveal that the castle was already doing so.

"We found something Leir gifted my mother. It should call to him if one of us wears it. Our plan is to bring him to the tree my mother died on," Arkimedes said. "I do believe you know precisely where that is."

The king smirked, his eyes gleaming with something Nava couldn't decipher. But he didn't say a word.

Ark placed a hand over her shoulder as if the touch alone would soften the sorrow filtering in waves through their bond. It was hard not to empathize with the emissary's loss of his soulmate, not when they both knew how devastating that would be.

"Brilliant," the king declared. "And that's why you're my son."

"Indeed, Your Majesty," the male next to the king gushed, eyes bright with excitement. Instantly, the room darkened, and the scent of magic wafted through the air.

"These bastards know he killed her. I'm sure of it," Arkimedes growled through their mind bond, and his aura darkened further. The counselors sitting by his father shrunk back into their chairs with wide eyes, probably sensing they were one wrong word away from meeting Ark's power.

Her heart ached as she remembered the ghost of his mother and what she'd shown them. All her notes of how her life had spiraled due to her choices. How she'd tried not to fall for the king but had done so either way.

"What did you find in Briar's room, Orion?"

"A ring," Arkimedes said, steadying his temper. "You will wear it."

"Prince Orion, you can't be serious." The counselor laughed loud enough for the shrill sound to echo in the wide-open room, although his face showed nothing but panic. "His Majesty is ill. He can't fight an undying Dark One."

"Yes, he can. He is Leir's primary target. Leir will be too focused on his need for revenge to notice anything else, which will give us a chance to get close enough to steal his weapon."

"You won't need me as a distraction if you have a part of me within you," the king said. "Use that anger, take what's yours, and use my power to defeat him."

"You're mad," Arkimedes whispered, shaking his head in disbelief. Judging by his advisors' widened eyes, they felt the same. They had been right. All along, the king wanted to become a part of Arkimedes, to be absorbed so he could remain in this kingdom as a part of his shadows.

"The emissary's weapon will poison either of you if you were to hold it. A guard should do it instead," the female counselor said, calling their attention to her.

Nava felt numb. Why hadn't they even considered that?

"Miss Elina is right. The artifacts lose power the longer they remain in our mortal lands. Most artifacts will poison a person after they hold it only twice. I can only imagine what it would do to His Royal Highness if he were to steal it," Finian said.

"I agree as well. His Majesty should consider this." The last counselor indicated the guards standing by the door. "Neither of you two, nor the future queen, can be the ones to steal it. It has to be a guard."

Her life wasn't more important than those souls standing over there. This felt wrong, even if the gods had tied Arkimedes's life to the kingdom and Nava was a Beekeeper, tasked to maintain a balance in nature. They couldn't demand their lives, right?

Perhaps that was naïve, but she didn't care. The person who should get poisoned by that weapon was the king. He'd caused this entire debacle.

If she was reading Arkimedes's emotions right, he felt the same. "There is no need to sacrifice the guards."

"It's their duty to protect us, just as it's ours to protect their kingdom from collapsing," the king reasoned, glancing at the door where the guards stood, watching the hall. They hadn't moved an inch, although their shoulders had gone rigid as they'd listened in.

"His Majesty is right, as always," Finian said, dipping his head in reverence. "I'm proud to serve you and yours, and I shall protect you with my life, as my family has done for centuries as members of the royal guards. It's with great pride that I shall do my duty when we march to defeat the emissary."

Nava's throat tightened as her lips parted in shock. She studied all three counselors with renewed curiosity. At first, she had assumed they were merely fae who held influential positions alongside the king. She'd never seen a non-Dark fae wear a guard's armor.

And Finian wasn't a Dark One, even though his eyes glowed, making them appear like molten pools of gold. But his shoulders were wide, like those of a warrior.

"Finian, Elina, and Kaden have been the king's counselors for as long as he's held the throne. They served as royal guards when my grandfather was alive," Arkimedes's voice filtered into her mind.

"Well, they certainly don't look as old as your father," she grumbled in answer. While the king's features were breathtakingly similar to Arkimedes, his skin was cracking like dry mud. The other three fae looked young, much like Leela or even Fael.

Had the three of them helped King Oberon take the queen to the forest to burn her alive? Had they advised him to do so?

An additional guard entered from the hall, his breaths coming out in rapid puffs as he dodged the sentries guarding the door. He wore the polished copper armor most did and a long blue cape like the guards out front. He saluted rather stiffly before he spoke. "Pardon my interruption, but I come with an important message for Prince Orion."

He bowed, and his bright brown eyes traced every fae around the rectangular table, pausing for a moment on the king before settling on Arkimedes, who signaled him to approach. The guard tucked his chin into his chest and strode toward her mate, expertly ignoring everyone's disapproving gaze.

"Sir, a man is demanding an audience with you." The guard straightened and interlaced his fingers.

"Since when can random citizens request an audience with my son?" The king slammed his open palm against the table, making the poor guard nearly jump out of his skin. He opened his mouth as if to explain, then shut it as the king's frown deepened and his aura shrouded his sick appearance further. "You're already wasting our time. Speak now, for I also desire to hear what this is about."

"We tried to turn him away, but he kept talking about an emissary of the gods and insisted he had important information, for he believes the

Zorren will attack soon. We thought it prudent to come and inform you before we got rid of him."

Arkimedes's eyes cut across to Nava. "Was his name Devon Black?"

"Yes, sir. I believe that sounds right." The guard stared at the floor, as if Arkimedes might hurt him if he dared to make eye contact. "He is quite ill, so we didn't want to bring him here."

"Take me to him." Arkimedes stood so fast, his chair fell to the ground.

"I'm not done agreeing with your plan. Surely finding the way to save your people is more important than seeing to the Crow," the king said.

"Devon is my family, and he is here saying he has information we need. I'm going."

"I don't trust the Crow, Orion. Eris told me that when the Corvus imprisoned him on that market, they didn't hurt him. It seems rather convenient that he wasn't with you when the time came for them to attack."

He was attempting to plant a seed of doubt. Two months ago, Nava would have fallen for it, but not now, not after everything that had happened at the safe house. Devon had been trying to save that child because he'd identified with it. The king didn't know that she'd saved Devon from the Corvus.

"And as I've stated before, I don't trust you. We can iron out the details once we know what Devon knows about the Zorren. Until then, I'm done with this conversation."

Nava rose to follow her mate, her back protesting from sitting for too long. In truth, she couldn't get away from the king fast enough.

"Did you find anything else in her room, Orion?" The king's face twisted with a strange sort of desperation. "Did she say anything about me—about him?"

Was he still jealous? Did he want to know about the emissary's gift to the queen because of their plan to defeat him or because of their love triangle?

He looked sick, but deep inside, Nava wondered. Had the king loved the queen? Had her betrayal driven him mad?

Could anyone have two soulmates? Perhaps Briar had two. It would explain why King Oberon was dying, when other fae older than him were still healthy. Perhaps his hate for her and love for himself kept him alive.

It didn't matter. In the end, Ark's mother had died a horrible death, and he was still here.

38
NAVA

Devon had to be all right. It had only been a couple of days, and while his condition had advanced, he'd had a few more healing potions left the morning they'd been split up.

Nava took a deep breath, wiping a small bead of sweat from her temple. With Arkimedes's legs so much longer than hers, she had to use a spike of her power to keep up with him.

She glanced at the guard who was trailing after them with a serious expression. His vigilant eyes snapped to every open door they passed, as if he expected an ambush. "Are we worried that someone will attack us here in the castle?"

Eris tightened his hand around the rim of his helmet. "It's my duty to protect you at all costs. As I mentioned, our allegiance is shifting. His Majesty feels it, and so do the guards. To prevent unnecessary bloodshed among our ranks, the king commanded me to keep vigilant."

"Because I'm in danger?"

"Yes, my lady. There are rumors circling the castle about the prince being under a spell. One that will only be broken if you're gone."

Great. Nava pressed her lips together, and Leela's words echoed in her mind. She'd said Nora, Fael's sister, had claimed the same during her visit. Nava would have to be extra careful with the king's consorts.

Arkimedes's gravel tones floated into her mind. *"They will be dead before they can come close enough to hurt you."* It was a promise of blood—or, in his case, the fragment of a soul.

They walked past a group of maids who scattered as soon as they saw Arkimedes. Some smiled in their direction, bowing with an eagerness Nava hadn't seen from the staff other than the night before. The rest did so in a more restrained way, looking at them warily.

Arkimedes offered Nava the crook of his arm, gazing into the distance. "So the king thinks Nava might be attacked? Is that why none of his concubines were present during the meeting?"

Eris seemed to ponder his response. "It's for our future queen's benefit and for His Majesty's ladies. He fears for their safety from your mate—and from you."

"Fair enough," Arkimedes said.

A flare of anger rushed through Nava's body, and she swallowed the snarky response threatening to spill past her lips. She wouldn't hurt them unless she had to defend her life. This wasn't the time to make biting comments, though. Not when they were on the brink of a major attack and they had to work with the monster for just a little longer.

Two guards awaited them on either side of the gold room, the same place where Devon stayed when they were prisoners. Past its doors, a warm wash of air greeted them. A healer stood next to Devon, who lay on the bed looking paler than she'd ever seen him.

He coughed, and his black eyes met hers from across the room. "You're free," he breathed, and his expression softened with relief.

"How are you feeling, Devon?" Arkimedes asked, taking in his brother's condition with a growing frown. It was impossible not to notice the way his eyes had gone duller, how drab and thin his skin appeared.

"Your Highness." The healer bowed, stepping away from Devon and approaching them. The fae clasped his arms behind his back, not looking at his patient as he spoke. "Your...guest has a similar reaction to what I saw in you when you returned. I'm assuming it's the same poison. Except his runs deep within his body. I don't believe I have a spell that can heal him. I can only ease his pain and prolong the inevitable."

Devon's lips turned from a sickly shade of purple to lilac as he peeled them back to reveal his white teeth. "If you're going to tell my brother I'm dying, look at me while you do it. I'm very much still here."

How long had he been out there, exposed to the elements? Had he been walking the entire time while sick and hurting? Her heart ached for him.

Nava untangled her arm from Arkimedes and stepped forward, grasping the foot of the bed as she studied Devon's complexion. "Do you have any potions left?"

"No, but you can drop the concerned face, Kitten. I'm not dying just yet."

She cleared her throat and moved around the bed, doing her best to adopt a more neutral expression. Anything to set him at ease a bit. "How would you know? Have you been in this position before?"

"Have you seen someone who's dying look this good or have this cheerful a disposition?"

"I guess you've got a point." Nava smirked. She reached for his arm, knowing what she had to do. Her healing magic could help him as it had before, even though her body was still tired from using it so heavily.

Devon's face pinched as he inched away from her touch. "Don't waste your energy on me. You will need it soon."

Nava perched on the edge of the bed with a frown. It was soft and almost swallowed him whole. She heard the distinct steps of someone leaving the room, just as she sensed Arkimedes approaching slowly.

"What do you mean?" Ark asked. "The guard said you mentioned the emissary was coming. How would you know that?"

Devon took a deep breath and sat, reaching with a trembling hand for the carafe of water next to him. Nava stood up to help but paused when he glared at her. "As you two know, I'm able to change the weather—somewhat."

"Yes…"

"Well, after the guard took Nava, I was making my way here to ensure you were safe. I didn't know how I was going to get inside the castle, so I returned to the maid's home to ask for help. I overheard her neighbors say that the storms were unusual, much too cold for fall. It made me think, and it's true. They feel similar to the ones I'm able to conjure." He paused to cough.

Arkimedes's breaths quickened. "And you think it's a spell?"

Devon drained the glass of water as if he'd been thirsting for days. Then he refilled it and took another long drink before he spoke again. "It seems a strange coincidence that they happen every single time the

Zorren attack. Before every fire over the past months, there has been some weather event. When you two left for the forest last time, it was coming down for days. I don't believe in coincidences."

Nava's breath caught in her throat. She looked down at the bees adorning her dress, their brown bodies standing out against the dark fabric. "You're right. After we arrived in the kingdom, I had a dream of Ari during the fires, but it had also been storming. It's odd that the fire demons should come when there is rain."

"Unless they don't have a choice but to come during a storm. As if it's a warning spell brought on by an emissary crossing a portal, perhaps." Devon drank the rest of his water and placed the glass on the table. "I believe the emissary is in the kingdom already. He's hiding away until he can bring the Zorren without hurting his chances to destroy this place, as he promised you he would."

Nava stood, her skin prickling as she broke out in sweat, her skin suddenly cold and clammy. "He might hunt for Ari while he's alone in the forest." Her body began to shift into air and pollen, the bees taking flight, coalescing into a swarm.

Arkimedes's eyes widened, and he stumbled forward, trying to catch her. "You can't go without me!"

But she could, and she wouldn't wait here and do nothing while Leir killed her Beekeeper. Had she known deep down he was here all along? Was that why the bees had been following her the entire time?

"We have run out of time."

"Nava!" Arkimedes lunged for her, coiling his arms around her disappearing body. His magic bloomed black and enveloped her like a cocoon, shrouding everything around them. He was shaking. Or was it the ground beneath their feet as the very castle shifted in displeasure? "The only way to defeat him is by working together."

She breathed, her heart racing, although his muffled words made it through her fuzzy mind. "He doesn't know I'm coming."

"Remember when we went to the forest, when we thought Aristaeus was in danger, but then we got there and he was fine?" Arkimedes searched her gaze, and his resolve seeped through their bond. "Close your eyes and focus on your connection to Aristaeus, to the kingdom. To the forest."

Her eyes watered with the intensity of being contained while she was mid-transformation. The air tasted spicy, but Arkimedes's magic was relentless. He would not let her go. And would she, if their roles were reversed?

Her body collapsed back into her human form, cool inside Arkimedes's warm embrace. She closed her eyes and focused on the quick beating of his heart and then, beneath that, the fluttering of wings. Hundreds of thousands of bees were all whispering in small voices. All calling to her.

The headache was a gentle throb that built in her temples as she dug in deeper, following their whispers. It wasn't a human language; it had no words, only feelings.

Her body trembled, and in the darkness, she tugged on the trail of the gold ribbon that connected her to the castle and the gardens beyond the walls. To Aristaeus, beyond the trees, so far her body levitated from the ground.

"Nava…" Ark's tone was pure awe.

"Dearest one?" Ari's voice drifted into her head, and even Arkimedes tensed. Could he hear him? *"You're here, but far, too."*

There wasn't any panic or pain coming through Ari's bond. He was fine, likely inside his cavern, awaiting her return. So Nava returned and asked for the forest instead.

"Leir opened a portal last night." She repeated the strange thoughts of the trees, and her body shook harder as a sudden cold rippled all over her. Ark's hold tightened around her, and his nose pressed against her neck, his breaths burning fast and hot against her skin.

"Come back to me, Bee." His voice carried enough panic to pull at her. She retreated down the hills of the forest, over mossy ground, and past fallen branches.

She descended along the golden rope of magic that connected her to the kingdom. Her nose prickled as something wet dripped down to her lips. She blinked her eyes open into the bright, golden room, and although the fireplace was roaring, she shivered inside Arkimedes's arms.

"W-what happened?" Her teeth clattered together, but her mind was too full, fuzzy around the edges. What was she doing here? What was going on?

"I could hear Aristaeus through our connection. You reached him. How?"

"I don't know." She lifted her heavy eyelids and raised her face to meet his worried gaze. He swiped a finger under her nose, and it emerged covered in crimson. Blood.

Nava had bled while she'd been between planes, out there following magical ribbons that wrapped around things. Whatever power she'd tapped into was something new. Except—it wasn't. She'd always been able to see the strings. She'd just never attempted to follow them anywhere before.

"How do you feel?" Arkimedes whispered and tucked a strand of hair behind her ear.

Her mouth was dry, her body weak and still shaking with how much she'd drained herself, but she had her answer. "He's back."

Arkimedes already knew this. She was sure he'd heard her words through their connection. The sorrow, fear, and anger that filled her belonged to her and him in equal measure.

"Leir doesn't know *we* are coming. Let's set the trap."

"What trap?" Devon asked from his bed. He was leaning against the headboard, his eyebrows raised high as if he'd observed the entire spectacle in silence. "And who the fuck is Leir?"

39
ARKIMEDES

The armory wasn't as large as the golden room they'd left Devon in. Nor did it have sufficient ventilation, judging by the pungent smell of oil and the tang of metal that nearly suffocated Arkimedes as he strolled around the place.

He wiped his sweaty forehead with his handkerchief and watched closely as the armorer measured Nava's waist, the length of her torso, and the stretch of her arms, muttering subdued comments that not even Arkimedes's enhanced hearing could discern at this distance.

The armorer, Gallon, was an unassuming Dark Fae. He had a lithe build and smaller wings than the guards. His magic hadn't presented as strongly as most fae of his kind, yet his true gift lay in crafting protective spells for the armor he built.

"I don't have enough time to make the right chest plate for Miss Nava, Your Highness," Gallon said, shaking his head as the corners of his lips tilted down. His tone was harsher than most would dare to use with Arkimedes. But he'd visited this dungeon enough times to like the male, sharp edges and all.

"Do what you can, Gallon. The most important part will be to deflect the Zorren's claws and guard against the heat."

Nava's skin turned a few shades paler with every word he spoke.

Sucking her lips in between her teeth, she traced her small hand over her ribs.

Gallon's eyes shifted from him to Nava, before he spoke with a softer tone. "We haven't had a queen in thirty years, sir. I won't send her there with subpar armor. This is not the Iron Kingdom. We have standards here."

Arkimedes's lips twitched, and it took all his restraint to beat his smile back into submission. This was not the time to find something funny. In fact, they probably wouldn't return, but he wouldn't voice those thoughts for Nava to hear. Last time they'd met the emissary, only luck had saved them.

The armorer shuffled away in silence, taking with him all his parchment scraps of notes and scribbles. He selected a new chest plate from one of the floor-to-ceiling cases on his way out.

Now that they were alone, Nava's frustration and fear came through their bond with increasing intensity. He reached for her hand. "Is this the first time you're getting proper armor fitted?"

Nava grabbed his hand with clammy, stiff fingers. "Yes. I-I've worn armor before, usually when I trained with my mother, but it's been a while." She tried to smile, but the expression didn't reach her eyes. "Wouldn't metal make the heat of fire worse?"

"Gallon has a gift for casting spells onto metal. Earlier in the year, he created a special spell that helped us while investigating the fires." Arkimedes touched her cheek and caressed her soft skin until the pad of his finger met her bottom lip.

Her breaths stuttered just as she met his eyes, and the world around them fell away.

Arkimedes didn't need to read her thoughts to know she feared the same thing he did. They had no way of knowing how many demons Leir would bring through the portal this time around.

He swallowed against the suffocating pressure building in his chest and stepped closer to her. These were the last few minutes of peace they would have in a while, and the intensity of his need to be near her, to touch her, was as great as the fear that threatened to paralyze him.

"Don't look at me like that," she whispered and placed her hand over his heart. But the thick copper plate blocked the warmth of her touch.

"Like what?"

"Like we won't return."

If only he could lie to her. But the weapon they had to steal from Leir had disintegrated trees with each of his swings. None of the guards would be able to wield it long enough to kill the emissary. And if either of them managed to steal it instead, the poison would probably kill them within a few days. That was, if they even survived the fight that followed.

But going into battle without hope was a surefire way to seal their fate, and he wouldn't bring that upon his soulmate. No, he would fight for her with everything he had.

"What you did in the gold room was a marvel to witness, Bee. Your power goes far beyond what we imagined. I can't believe you could contact Aristaeus from the castle."

Nava narrowed her eyes, her lips tightening into a small pout. "You're changing the subject."

"I can't lie to you and claim we will be fine, but I can point out our strengths to give us hope," he said. A warm glow of pride spread in his chest, dulling the ache building there. "I believe you have untapped power. Let's see what it can do for us while we're in the forest."

Her lips parted with understanding. She was so beautiful inside and out. Powerful. Everything he shouldn't deserve.

One of his shadows billowed out on his side, the clear profile of a male flickering in and out of view. *"And she is ours to protect."*

"Fuck those who try to take her from us," another whispered, and for once, Arkimedes couldn't agree more.

Gallon came into the room an hour later with a stack of armor pieces inside his arms and glistening with sweat. "I have adapted one of the consorts' breastplates. I believe this shall work."

Arkimedes stepped away, giving Gallon enough space to fit her properly.

Nava lifted her arms, as she'd been doing for most of the afternoon, while Gallon tightened a thick leather corset around her torso. Then he draped lightweight chainmail over her head that the fae had developed during their last war with the gods. Finally, he affixed the copper breastplate.

Nava touched the hammered metal. It was usually shiny, but in this case, Gallon had beat it into shape during the little time they had left, lending it a dull patina.

"It's not as heavy as I thought it would be," she said.

"Of course it's not. Only humans create novice metalwork that weighs down their guardsmen." Gallon inspected his handwork so closely he didn't see Nava's yellow aura spike around her, nor the insects flying in waves, diving toward him. He swatted at a bee and hissed when he got stung.

"It seems you've forgotten I'm human, too," Nava said in an icy tone that cooled even the stifling humidity of this room.

The armorer hunched down to avoid another bee, and Arkimedes's lips curved into a smile. "I'd advise you not to upset my mate, Gallon."

Whether the fae understood that the warning was for his own protection against Nava's anger—not Arkimedes's—didn't matter in the end. Gallon voiced an apology that sounded sincere, and the bees ceased.

Eris entered the room not five minutes later, just as Gallon tightened the straps of the last gardebras. The guard's steps were every bit as loud as the screeching of his armor. He'd been waiting outside, keeping a watchful eye on the corridor. "Sir, madam, the king calls for you. He is out in the courtyard with the guards. It's time."

Nava tensed, then visibly willed herself to relax. She climbed off the pedestal she'd been standing on. "I guess I'm as ready as I will ever be."

They had gone over the plan multiple times. Even if Leir were to spot the guards heading into the forest, the ring should distract him enough to give them the upper hand.

By the time they made it out of the front entrance, the sun burned like fire as it set behind the castle and dipped past the horizon of tree tops.

The king walked ahead of the line of his guards, his armor made of a silver so light it appeared white in the distance. Only the chest plate was decorated with edges of copper and gold. "You're to remain out of sight until we can get close enough to the emissary to dispose of him."

Arkimedes tightened his hand around his mother's ring. He'd kept it hidden inside his pocket ever since they'd left her chambers last night. The metal was unnaturally cold, a clear sign that this jewelry wasn't of this world.

Nava strapped her long daggers to either side of her belt. "I don't think it's a good sign that it's stopped raining."

Arkimedes grunted in agreement and placed his crown-shaped helmet over his head. It was identical to the king's and a straightforward way for the guards to distinguish who was who.

Even with most of their features obscured, Arkimedes doubted anyone would confuse them, for the king stood taller than most, towering by a couple of inches over even his largest guard.

Nava reached for his crown. The pads of her fingers traced the edges of its pointed, thorny shapes. "The crown suits you."

"It was my father's before he became the king." Dammit, there he was, calling the monster his father again. He would destroy this piece of tin and never pass it down his family line if they were lucky enough to have children.

If they survived first.

"I will see you two in the forest. Good luck." Eris bowed to them, his features hidden by his helmet right before he, too, took off to the sky, following dozens of fae who were headed for the trees. Their wings and shadowy auras blended with the darkening sky.

The king remained, his braided hair billowing on the breeze. "Orion, if the time comes, you must take my power to defeat him. We can't let him destroy the kingdom. No matter if you hate me now, this is our duty." He nodded in their direction, his face strained before he took flight, not waiting for an answer.

There was no need to discuss where they would meet. Thinking about the tree his mother had died on clogged Arkimedes's throat and made him want to kill King Oberon all over again.

But tonight wasn't the night.

"Are you ready?" he asked.

"As ready as I will ever get." Nava held on to his shoulders as he wrapped one arm under her legs and the other around her back. He lifted her with ease, and her magic soared through him, warm and gentle. It dulled the ache flaring from the arrow wounds in his wings.

"Hold on tight, Bee," he said and rose into the rainy sky.

They flew in silence to a part of the forest he knew well. While he usually avoided it, he seemed to end up at the tree more often than not, as if destiny itself pulled him there.

Tonight, they would use the power of grief as a weapon to save thousands of innocent lives. To defeat an evil that festered in this kingdom, brought about by lies and jealousy.

The burnt tree stood in the clearing, commanding the same familiar dread. Charred and lacking life, its naked trunks twisted up onto spindly branches that allowed the stormy sky to peek through. A sense of unease sank underneath his skin and twisted his gut as he inspected the area.

"The trees are angry, but I don't sense the emissary is close." Nava drew a shaky breath. The silence was almost absolute. No creatures or insects dashed about in the undergrowth. Nothing lurked in the shadows of this cursed place.

"I've avoided returning here ever since my mother's spirit showed me the truth," he whispered, studying the blackened, gnarly branches. "I doubt Leir would come to the place where the king murdered my mother either."

"It's why this is a brilliant plan, Ark. We will get under his skin. You've outsmarted him."

"*We* did." Arkimedes gripped her chin and dropped a kiss on her forehead. He lingered for a moment, closing his eyes and enjoying her warm scent and the spice of her skin. She wrapped her arms around his neck, pulled him down to her face, and kissed him with a desperation that he matched.

This could be their last chance to do this.

He wrapped both arms around her waist and drew her close to him, tasting the sweetness of her lips. They had no time to lose—the guards could arrive at any moment. But he didn't want to let go, either.

This was the reminder of why they needed to fight, of what they might lose. He withdrew, brushing the hair out of her face. If only she hadn't been so stubborn and worn a damn helmet.

"Nava…" He clutched her hand, trying to inhale around the tightness squeezing his chest. "I'm glad I got to fall in love with you two times. You're the best thing that ever happened to me."

"We aren't saying goodbye, Arkimedes," she said.

"Do you have the knife?"

"Right here." She patted the satchel hanging across her chest.

However useless the artifact the king had provided was, it would probably be better than a regular iron sword. They had decided Nava would wield it, as she might be able to transfer close enough to use it.

"Good. Now hide and don't come out until you see Leir is distracted, even if I'm struggling."

"Don't ask me anything you wouldn't do yourself." Nava traced his jaw with a single finger before tapping his cheek. "So it's best if you don't get in too much trouble."

One moment she was solid, and the next she was gone, transferring away with the evening breeze that rustled the canopy of leaves above them.

40
ARKIMEDES

The first group of guards landed shortly after the king. They crept into the clearing with quiet steps, listening for anything that might be amiss. Only the crunch of debris under their boots and their heavy breathing broke the evening silence.

The king strolled toward Arkimedes as if he didn't have a care in the world. Was the kingdom lending him the energy he needed for this?

"I'm here as you demanded." The king frowned as his eyes cut to the tree, and his features morphed into an expression that was hard to read. Anger, disappointment—sadness?

No. Monsters didn't feel remorse.

"I did as you told me and used my connection to the forest," Nava's voice came through their bond. *"The trees told me the emissary is slightly north of here, close to Ari's home."*

She had tapped into the power she'd used back at the castle and found them a location.

Arkimedes withdrew the ring from his pocket, a feat with all the armor he wore, and placed it into his father's outstretched hand. Here, amidst the darkness, where there was almost no light, the green stone at the center of the ring glowed with magic.

"This should call Leir when you put it on. Nava said he is north of here, so you and the guards have enough time to hide."

The king's eyes flickered as he clenched the ring in his fist and stepped toward the tree, the nut in his throat bobbing as he swallowed. "I didn't want her to die, Orion."

"You didn't want her to die when you tied her to this tree and set it on fire?" Arkimedes asked and fell away toward the trees that would become his cover.

"Briar betrayed me long before I forsook her," the king continued. His shadows swirled around him as he stepped behind the tree. "She cheated on me for years. I didn't even know about Leir's existence. Then she took you away. She broke my heart first."

If only that were true. But Arkimedes had read the diary and all his mother had written about her feelings for the king and how insignificant he made her feel. She'd been lonely in that castle while he slept with his concubines.

"I don't care about your woes. You killed her, and that's all I need to know."

A gasp came from the edge of the clearing. Perhaps some of the guards hadn't known the truth, but it didn't matter if they discovered the king's true nature.

Arkimedes studied the guards. Some had raised their shields and pointed weapons in his direction. Shifting on their feet, they hid in between the trees. Their auras bloomed much like his, and their solid bodies became part of the shadows.

Arkimedes rolled his shoulders to ease the strain that had built in his injured wings. Closing his eyes, he focused on the way the ground trembled beneath his feet, a gentle murmur that responded to his power.

"The forest is uneasy. It remembers Leir brings the demons and fires. He is coming toward us now," Nava's voice rang in his mind.

Arkimedes dug his heels into the ground and rushed to a nearby tree, gripping its rough bark to keep his balance. He tucked his wings behind his back. He hadn't learned how to blend into the shadows like the others of his kind, but he'd mastered a spell that would hide him from view for a time.

A shield popped up in front of him, and he pressed his body against the rough texture of the tree behind him, just as slow steps resounded from somewhere nearby. The task should be straightforward. He had to strike fast.

Leaves ruffled in the distance as a large shadowy figure wandered into the clearing.

"Briar?" Leir's voice shook with hope as he stepped toward the burnt tree. His face was visible from Arkimedes's hiding place, but seeing that expression robbed him of his breath.

The emissary's confusion wouldn't last long. It would become clear soon enough that this was a trap. Arkimedes's heart constricted inside his chest as he watched his uncle walk toward the spot where his mother had died. An expression of pure pain took over his features.

None of this was fair.

Then understanding flashed through Leir's pale features as he twirled in his spot. He widened his blood-red eyes with a snarl. "You make a mockery of my pain." Leir swung his weapon like a pendulum, and waves of static bounced across the ground, cutting down limbs from the tree.

The king's aura exploded into a black sea of spilled ink, and he stepped out from behind the tree, the ring still on his finger. The stone hummed with green light, like a heartbeat.

Thump, thump, thump.

Time slowed as dead twigs crunched under the king's feet, and here, in the cursed clearing where the king had murdered the queen, the twins finally met face to face.

Leir straightened in a slow, calculated movement as he faced his brother. His arms fell to his sides. "I should've known it would be *you*."

They looked like mirror images of one another, standing so tall their shadows stretched up to the trees. The only difference other than the color of their glowing eyes were their wings, for Leir's were misshapen.

The king planted his feet wide, his neck corded with tension. "Last time we met, brother, you should have learned your lesson to stop messing with what belongs to me."

Their voices were so loud it was as if Arkimedes were kneeling right beside them. He swallowed. When had the king last met the emissary? Had they fought? Arkimedes wasn't surprised that the king had kept more secrets.

The ring continued to beat louder in the silence.

Thump. Thump. Thump.

The king pulled his sword from its sheath. "You would think losing your wings would be enough to teach you that lesson."

"This?" Leir reached over his shoulder with one hand, right before a laugh tore from his lips. The sound was wrong, like a banshee's cry. He advanced toward the king.

It was almost time. The moment the emissary attacked, Arkimedes and Nava had to strike.

Arkimedes's heart clenched. Part of him didn't want to. In his uncle, he saw everything that he could have become.

"You fool, my wings heal every day. I burn them to remind myself of the torture Briar went through." Leir's eyes took on a crazed look that turned Arkimedes's blood to ice. Spit bubbled from his lips as they split to reveal pointed canines. "Now your kingdom will suffer the same fate as she did."

Leir was going to burn everyone who lived in the Copper Kingdom. His madness had reached a point of no return. The new information of how he mutilated his body only confirmed it.

Leir leaped toward the king, swinging his deadly artifact, which sucked the life out of the ground. Despite his illness, the king moved out of the way faster than anyone Arkimedes had seen. His aura enveloped the emissary in a cocoon of life-draining magic.

Leir stumbled back, his white skin recovering from the onslaught of the king's dark power, although blood trickled down from his tunic. The king hunched over with a pained expression, the façade of his strength vanishing quickly after commanding so much power to hold the emissary at bay.

Arkimedes abandoned his hiding place and ran toward the twins when his father's complexion turned even paler. With how sick he was, there wasn't a chance he would hold on for much longer.

Arkimedes lengthened his steps and beat his wings so he could cut through the space quickly. Thankfully, Leir hadn't spotted him yet. He was far too focused on the king.

"Allow me to bring the cavalry that will destroy your precious kingdom," Leir gloated. As he held his hand to the side, the first portal hummed with static magic. It looked like a small dot of petroleum suspended high up in the air, dark and shiny and thick in consistency. Its popping sounds became louder as it grew like a festering wound. Another one swiftly followed.

Arkimedes's steps faltered as he paused and stared at the portals. If the demons made it through, it would be impossible to steal the weapon. His aura burst around him, calling on the same magic Aristaeus had taught him, and the portal closest to him shrunk to nothingness before his eyes.

Then a dozen more appeared where the first had closed.

"Ark—" Nava's panicked voice invaded his head but quieted when the black dots appeared around the space, so many he couldn't count them all. They grew at a frantic pace, and the scent of sulfur thickened with each passing second.

The king barely ducked out of the path of Leir's sword, his eyes widening at the number of portals that had appeared. Amidst the commotion, a guard shouted something, but his words got lost.

Demons broke through the dark holes, wearing capes of fire. The temperature rose, and the drizzle of rain turned to steam, making the heat all the more suffocating. If it weren't for Gallon's armor, Arkimedes's skin would be blistering.

Leir glared at the armored guards who rushed out of the shadows and attacked the Zorren. Then he noticed Arkimedes.

Arkimedes dodged the emissary's attack that felled a tree ten feet behind him. Judging by the rage burning in Leir's features, he hadn't expected the guards, nor had he realized Arkimedes was also here.

A scream tore from the Emissary's lips when the king cut the side of his misshapen wing. The feathers melted away as soon as they touched the ground, like they hadn't been from this world to begin with.

"Now, Nava!"

She appeared right beside the emissary and swung the dagger into the cocoon of Leir's dark aura, slicing underneath one of his ribs. The knife should slow down even Leir's immortal healing, giving Arkimedes and the king a better chance to steal his weapon.

Inky waves wrapped around Nava's hand, and blotchy black veins rapidly extended up her arm. She pulled back with a pained scream. Her eyes cut to him before she disappeared.

Leir clutched his side with one hand while he swung his sword toward the king once more. A cloud of dry earth and ash billowed in the air, making it hard to see.

"Nava, where are you?" Panic rushed through Arkimedes, all-consuming like the fire. He couldn't focus on anything when she wasn't answering. *"Nava?"* he repeated, but only met silence.

He couldn't breathe. His eyes searched the clearing for a sign that she was all right. The air sizzled with such power it singed his lashes. He pulled at the bond in his gut, reaching further.

"Aristaeus, are you here?"

"Protector?"

The Beekeeper's voice shook him from his stupor. Now wasn't the time to get distracted, even if he wanted—no, needed—to make sure Nava was alright. If they didn't defeat Leir, no one in the entire kingdom would be fine. He needed to get a grip.

The air around the emissary seared Arkimedes's nostrils and burned down his throat as he approached. Blisters formed over the exposed skin of his body, and it took everything inside him not to take off in the other direction to find Nava.

He struck with his blade and cut Leir's hand off from his wrist. Leir's sword fell to the ground, much like it had done during their first fight.

The weapon steamed with black tendrils that wrapped around Arkimedes's fingers as he reached for it. He heaved as the sword scalded his skin. Bone-melting pain racked through him. Taking a sharp breath, he attempted to straighten, his ears ringing as Aristaeus materialized beside him.

A beastly snarl escaped the Beekeeper's jagged lips as he held a demon, shielding Arkimedes. *"Use our connection to nature to push through,"* Aristaeus commanded inside Arkimedes's throbbing skull.

Arkimedes breathed through the pain of holding the artifact, finding the strength to use it. *"Is Nava hurt?"* He hadn't sensed her in so long. *"Something is wrong."*

"Focus on the emissary and live." Aristaeus's voice was a growl, and then he disappeared.

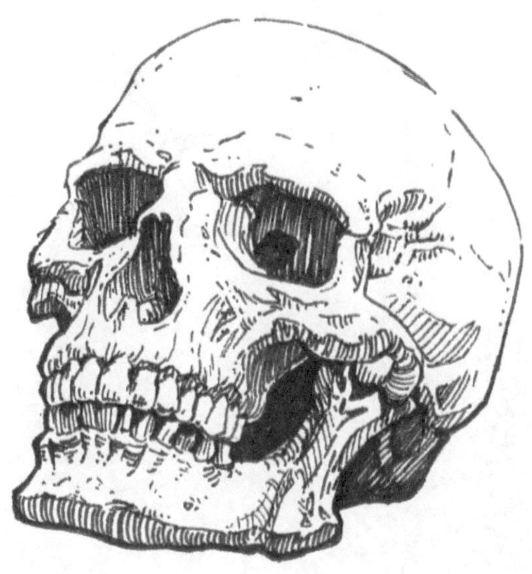

41
NAVA

Even as Nava transferred away, the burn from Leir's dark aura was immediate and it seared her flesh. Blood rushed in her ears, drowning out the demons' roars in the distance. Her body moved across the planes, barely evading a claw that reached up through the air and the sharp iron nails that scraped at her.

There were so many Zorren down in the clearing, Nava couldn't land anywhere as weak as she felt. She followed the call of the forest, and it led her to an area shrouded by tall bushes, untouched by fire.

Nausea bubbled up in her gut as she materialized behind one of the largest trees, not too far from Arkimedes. She could return to him once she'd neutralized the venom of the knife. She reached for the satchel hanging across her chest with shaking hands and pulled out one of the small vials Arkimedes had stuffed in there earlier.

The healing potion tasted of sweet lavender, and it immediately eased her pain. Blinking away her blurred vision, she inspected the cut in her hand. How had she managed to cut herself with the King's poisoned dagger during her attack? It hurt so damn much, and true to Oberon's words, the wound on her fingers oozed blood like it wasn't mending.

"Nava?" Arkimedes called to her through their bond. He was worried, and with reason. If the roles had been reversed, she would be looking for

him everywhere. She shoved the knife into its sheath, cursing her clumsy fingers and her stupidity at getting injured by her own weapon.

"She's alone," a female hissed from the shadows, her voice eerily familiar.

Nava's head snapped to the side just as a Dark One emerged from behind a tree, moving so fast she was a blur of feathers and black mist.

The copper armor caught the glare of fire in the distance, right before the heavy mass of a bony fist collided with Nava's cheekbone. She staggered with a hiss, eyes wide as five females appeared around her.

They all wore the Copper Kingdom's armor, their faces streaked with soot from the ash raining from the forest canopy.

The king's consorts who had tortured Arkimedes in his father's chamber.

Nava held herself up against the tree, her bad arm dangling limply by her side and her head throbbing from the punch.

Using the last of her energy, Nava attempted to transfer away, but unlike normal transformations, she became a thick dust cloud that was too heavy to move away. Her exhaustion pulled her out of her transitory state, and her body became human again.

"Why?" Nava hated that her voice sounded so weak. But truly, she couldn't comprehend why they were attacking her now that they were fighting a common adversary.

There was no way she could bring down these warriors with only her bees. Five Dark Ones against her without the full use of her power—the odds were impossible.

Their sneers grew more pronounced in response to Nava's question.

They were going to kill her, and she couldn't transfer. Nor could she call on her magic or on her bonds to her mate and Aristaeus.

Another fist collided with the side of her head, and she crumpled to the ground.

The side of her face hit a fallen branch, and her teeth dug into her bottom lip. The tang of blood coated her tongue. She reached for Ark, for Aristaeus, but the five of them descended upon her, their gifts draining her energy like vampires drew blood.

"If you think you'll sit on our throne, witch, you are *wrong*." One of them hovered close to her ear, her spit splattering Nava's cheek as her spindly fingers tightened around Nava's neck. She squeezed hard, digging them into her skin. "You have them fooled, but not us."

"Nava?" Arkimedes's voice was a whisper through a fog of sleep. He was teetering on the edge of his own worry. His voice brought solace, strength.

"Hurry, Nora," another hissed, though Nava couldn't see her from where she lay. "We can't be gone for long or the guards will suspect us."

"Step aside and let me handle it," another Dark One said, her voice oddly pleasant for the words she spoke.

Nava met her eyes. A fair-haired fae—she had been in the king's study a day ago. Nava's anger brewed beneath the layers of pain and despair, just as the energy of the forest glowed like a heartbeat, strings of magic shivering over pebbles, fallen branches, and dried leaves.

It urged her to move, to use her power and show these harpies who she was. Its song was a gentle reminder that, even though the venom from the knife had dulled her connections to Arkimedes and Ari, she wasn't alone. She wasn't powerless.

A Zorren's screech pierced through the roar of fire. The clanking of metal swords colliding with matter brought her back to reality.

Even in the heat of battle, a chill crawled into her bones as a Dark One's power slid through her. The concubines drew more of Nava's essence with each passing second, and black spots danced across her vision.

A metallic taste spread across her tongue, and she dug her fingers into a dry layer of ash that covered the top of the forest ground. She pulled at the strings of energy nature offered up to her, just like she had done at the castle, and her power awoke with a gentle hum. The bond between Ark, Aristaeus, and Nava was a faint whisper beneath the layer of suffering.

Suddenly, Arkimedes's panic burst through their bond, so intense that it took over everything else. He was in danger, and she needed to help him. The guttural roar that left her lips startled the concubines. Nava twisted away from her assailant's claws, her power a shield of gold as she rolled over the debris, ignoring the rocks that dug into her body.

Her mother would've been proud of her strength, even if her form was sloppy at best. Nava withdrew the ancient dagger and stabbed Nora between her shoulders and neck. She brought down the blade again and again, ignoring the gurgling scream and the warm blood splattering her fingers.

"Nora!" a Dark One shouted, and Nora's body slumped to the ground as Nava pulled more energy from the earth and limped to her feet.

With adrenaline rushing through her, the pain had faded into the background, although she couldn't seem to move her right arm. The remaining four concubines jumped forward with enraged screams, out for blood. But they hadn't expected the swarm of bees that descended on them like a cyclone.

While the bees wouldn't be enough to defeat them, they bought her time. Nava climbed over a fallen tree, dropping the poisoned blade and pulling her longer dagger with her left arm.

The fair-haired fool with a sweet voice rushed over to Nava in the next instant. Every inch of her armor was crawling with insects. Red bumps were swelling her eyes shut and covered most of her creamy skin. Had she kept her helmet on, it would have protected her from the bees.

An ill-advised move, but it benefited Nava. She swiped at her legs, and the fae tumbled to the ground. Nava moved to finish her off, but the bees' warning made her dodge right instead. She barely missed a black swirling spell that singed her hair.

Her skin burned where the spell had touched her. She turned to meet her attacker's weapon with her dagger, and her arm shook as she tried to hold off the concubine's much larger sword with her weaker arm.

"You'll die here," the female snarled. Nava didn't recognize her voice. Not that it mattered who this was or why they hated her. All she cared about was to be done with this so she could find Arkimedes. Hopefully, her absence had at least given him enough time to focus on Leir.

"Not tonight."

She could protect herself.

And she called to the surrounding trees, and while their voices had turned into moans of pain, they still answered her. The wood screeched, and the branches swept toward them, swinging low as they took the fae by the head.

"What are you?" the fae with the sweet voice asked from the ground, her voice shaking and her pupils blown wide. She stared at Nava as if she were a demon, worse than the Zorren.

Nava's energy dwindled again as the surrounding trees caught fire, and the damned poison running through her veins kept fighting the healing potion—and even her own magic.

She reached for her bond, trying to locate Arkimedes, to sense how he was doing, but she couldn't feel a thing.

The final two fae lunged at her but ground to a halt when a massive tree-like creature appeared in between them and Nava. She shouldn't be surprised to see Aristaeus. He'd likely received her position during the split second she'd sensed him. The two Dark Ones screamed, but it was too late, for Aristaeus was furious.

The moss and bark on his body were burned. He'd probably been fighting the Zorren and trying to find her at the same time.

For the first time since Nava had learned she was a Beekeeper, she couldn't hear him speak in her mind. But he came to her either way, his claws and sharp teeth tearing at the fae with such ferocity that Nava had to look away.

It wasn't as if she cared for their lives when they had tried to kill her only minutes ago. Yet her heart ached that even while demons invaded their kingdom mere feet away, they had come for her instead of fighting for their people.

When Aristaeus approached Nava, his gaze searched her face and narrowed in on her limp arm.

"I can't hear you," she said, knowing he must be trying to speak. "The poison of the knife has dulled my connection to both you and Ark."

And if she were honest with herself, she wasn't even sure how she was still standing upright. She began to trudge to the clearing with a wobble to her steps. Arkimedes was just across the way.

"I need to get back to him," she said, knowing Ari would understand who she meant. And perhaps it was actually a blessing not to hear his sarcastic quip about how unfit to fight the Zorren she was in her current state. Although, since her mind filled in the blank void so easily, perhaps it wasn't.

After a second, he nodded. Then he walked to her and pointed to a spot right across the clearing, where the forest lay nearly untouched by the surrounding chaos.

The yellow lines of energy were thicker, more vibrant, showing her a path to where she could regain some of her power. The two of them moved, fluid like water, and the deeper they went into the forest, the more like herself she felt. A caress of their bond touched her mind.

"Turn to the right here, dearest." Aristaeus's voice startled her. He ran a few meters ahead, removing obstacles from her path. Her panic grew when she couldn't feel Arkimedes.

She'd transferred too far from him. It was idiotic to separate. Perhaps she should have let him try to save her. They might be in better shape now.

What if he was badly hurt? What if he was— No, she couldn't think of that. He was alive, and they were going to be fine.

The burnt tree the queen had died on became visible in between immense tree trunks. Behind it, a fire glowed. She couldn't make out how well the guards were holding up against the Zorren through the thick layer of smoke.

Aristaeus and her bees swarmed around them, right before a black shape jumped out in front of them. A demon with clanking mandibles swung one of its claws at her, and Nava barely got out of the way. Transferring a few meters away, she studied the dark shadow of the forest.

"Go to our protector. I've got this one," Aristaeus commanded.

42
ARKIMEDES

Aristaeus was gone, presumedly to find Nava somewhere in the clearing. But it was hard to focus on killing Leir with the stolen artifact, when demons popped out of portals all around him.

Panic, anger, and determination settled within Arkimedes as he turned toward the emissary once again. Leir was cradling his missing limb, a new one already growing from the stump of his arm, forming a new palm and fingers.

Arkimedes's aura bloomed thicker, although the pain from holding the artifact didn't subside, he tightened his grip around the sword's handle. He let everything around him fall silent and leaped forward, cutting through the two-feet gap between them, and speared Leir in between the ribs.

His blade met resistance, the emissary's body attempting to heal and push the magical weapon away. But it was no use. Its power was too great, and it sucked the life out of everything it touched. One of Leir's hands coiled around Arkimedes's throat, squeezing hard.

Past the slope of his shoulder and mangled wing, Arkimedes saw the horrid shape of his mother's ghost materialize, right in front of the tree where she'd met her end. The sockets of her eyes were wet with tears, and flames lapped the ripped edges of her dress as it flowed in the air.

Arkimedes's magic stuttered, drained by the artifact and Leir's hold.

He pushed further, leaning his full body weight into the weapon, and the sharp point sank in a few more inches. A gurgling sound poured from his uncle's throat and their eyes met, frozen in time as warm liquid stained his fingers.

Leir's hand loosened just as an eerie moan escaped from his mother's lips. Then he crumpled to the ground, taking Arkimedes with him.

Arkimedes couldn't hear the warring demons and Dark Ones behind them. Nor did he know where the king had gone.

All he could see was the man underneath him.

"You're just like him. A back-stabbing monster that used my love for your own gain." Leir's blood dripped from his lips, trailing down his chin as he choked.

Tears stung Arkimedes's eyes. What could he say? This could so easily have been him if the same had happened to Nava. Losing her was the only thing he truly feared. "The king killed my mother, your soulmate, just as you tried to kill mine." Arkimedes tightened his burning fist around the handle of the weapon and held it steady.

Where was Nava? Her presence was stronger now. Was she coming to him?

Leir's eyes widened, his gaze drifting past Arkimedes's shoulder, up to the burning canopies of the forest. His lips parted and shut in a silent gasp for breath as comprehension flashed behind his uncle's red gaze. His expression softened. "The Beekeeper girl?"

"You shouldn't have come for her." And Arkimedes pushed the sword deeper. He didn't want Leir to suffer any more. The artifact clung to his fingers and wrist, seared into his skin.

Blood rushed through his head, numbing the sounds, the pain—everything.

"Arkimedes!" Nava's pounding feet brought her voice closer, her golden aura warm and beckoning him. But the tendrils of the magic emanating from the sword had taken over his body. He was cold. So cold and confused.

The land shook with tremors as more black shapes landed around the clearing. Zorren? Dark Ones? He couldn't tell anymore.

Nava scrambled past his shield and pushed him off the emissary's body. The chaos muffled her panicked screams as the demons continued to crawl out of the open portals. Was her face purple and bloodied?

“Stay with me,” he read her lips, but his vision was already closing in.

He swallowed the bitterness in his mouth and tried to raise his hand to touch her skin. To reassure himself she was truly here. But his arm was too heavy to lift.

Her healing magic was a warm embrace chasing away the cold. “*Ark.*”

Behind the blurry glow of Nava’s and Aristaeus’s combined power, darkness consumed his vision, and Arkimedes fell inside it.

43
NAVA

Nava reached for Arkimedes face—icy to the touch—and called on whatever power remained within her to funnel it into him.

She could feel Aristaeus's warmth coming from behind her before she heard his heavy feet settling on either side of her body. He loomed over them in a protective stance, looking out for attackers.

"Is Orion alive?"

She lifted her gaze and met the king's eyes. He lay on the ground a few meters away, supporting his body with trembling arms. His face was bloodied and burned, his hair a halo around his scalp.

Tears sprang to her eyes. She couldn't tell him that Arkimedes would make it. His skin remained too pale, and he wasn't responding to her touch. A sob tore past her cracked lips, and she sagged over his body, clinging to the metal chest plate.

He couldn't be dead. She would feel it in other ways, right?

"We need to take him to the cave," Aristaeus said, but he didn't sound as calm as he usually did. *"You're too ill to heal yourself, let alone properly help your mate."*

"But he is too weak to be moved."

Aristaeus shifted forward, the wood on his leg gracing her arm. *"There is something in his blood. An old magic that feels similar to the emissary's artifact."*

Old magic? Could it be Alera's potion?

Ari squinted at Ark's body, his face twisted with worry. *"He would be dead without it, but we need to go now. Can you transfer?"*

Nava nodded. Could she? She'd claw her way there if she had to. Aristaeus leaned forward and coiled his wooden arms under Arkimedes's body, lifting him up in the air. The branches above him blurred with her tears as Ari took one step and glanced at her over his shoulder.

"Meet me there, dearest, and don't longer here too long." And then he was gone, sprinting past the trees and away from her.

"Was that a Beekeeper?" The king stared at the spot where Ari had just stood. Nava looked at him, but there was no point in responding. She felt too numb to be angry.

She transferred away, back to Ari's cave and her soulmate.

"Our protector is lucky to be alive," Ari told her when they arrived at the cave. He placed Arkimedes in the same hammock they had slept in before. *"To hold a god's artifact charged with so much power would kill any mortal. He should be dead..."*

But he wasn't, and while they waited, Nava told Ari about everything that had happened since they'd parted ways. The pirates and their ill-fated trade that had turned into a terrible battle with the Crows—and what they'd initially thought was Alera's useless potion going to waste.

It had never been useless. It had saved Arkimedes's life.

In the cave's calm, Arkimedes's breathing steadied and grew gentle. While he rested in a magic-induced slumber, he was alive and well. He had even opened his eyes twice already.

Losing her sun stone seemed like a small price to pay, now that they'd defeated the emissary. It might have nearly cost Arkimedes his life, but they'd done it.

Nava never returned to the battleground that morning, even once Arkimedes was resting comfortably inside the relative safety of the cave. She was too badly injured to do much for him, and it took a while for the poison to leave her system.

Ari left the tree early in the morning and returned at night. He spent the day healing the forest and fighting the demons who'd escaped the king's army and were hunting for the Beekeepers. Thankfully, the Dark Ones had already taken care of most of them, and the portals eventually closed off.

"The portals only stay open if the spellcaster is alive," Ari explained when Nava worried about more Zorren sneaking up on him while he was alone in the forest.

Arkimedes woke up four days after the attack, although it felt more like two months had passed. Still, after the intensity of the battle, she welcomed the soft glow of the sun stones and the relative peace that came with the silence.

"So, are we going to stay in the Copper City, even though the king is still alive?" she asked, while they were eating breakfast. With a large part of the forest dead and the animals migrating north to higher grounds in search of food and untainted water, Ari had been eager to start the healing and for Nava to learn the ropes of her role.

"Or we could stay on the property I inherited down in the city of Milania," Arkimedes said with the rough voice of someone who hadn't spoken in days. He took a bite of his rabbit meat and met her eyes. "It's a dukedom granted to my mother's family while the king was courting her. I was never interested in it, but I would prefer to stay there rather than anywhere near him..."

"You have a dukedom?" she asked, blinking rapidly. "When were you going to tell me about this?"

"I honestly didn't think I would ever need to go there."

"Would we need to return after he dies?"

"I don't know, Bee, but if you want to stay there even after that, then so be it." He coughed into the crook of his arm and leaned back against the rocky wall with a strained expression.

"I would like to know the kingdom before I'm to become its queen."

"Me too."

Who knew how long the king had left to live? Either way, it would be good to enjoy this place when they weren't fugitives or prisoners.

"The monster will undoubtedly want to have a ceremony for me to claim the official title of a duke, thus making you a duchess," he continued.

Nava didn't want any more titles. Although it didn't hurt to know she wouldn't have to worry about money again, or how to get Cameron clothes, pay for his education, or keep food on the table for him and Laurie. She had been worrying about that her entire life since her parents passed away. Not anymore.

Nor did she have to be concerned that the Society of Crows might stake a claim on Cameron, since he would become part of the Copper Kingdom's royal family. This was an opportunity. It gave them a chance to fight for something good. Hopefully, Gavin and Violet would decide to join them as well when they brought Cameron back here.

"We will have to wait for Cameron to return before we can get married." She took a small bite of one of those strange fruits Ari was growing. "He's already missed out on enough. Besides, I don't have a ring."

"A ring, huh?" Arkimedes's eyes crinkled as a rakish smile tugged at the corner of his lips.

Nava looked away, her cheeks growing warm. In the grand scheme of things, it seemed like such a stupid thing to consider. A ring—who cared when there were crowns and talking castles? "I'm just nervous."

"The dukedom is mine, and we can go there tomorrow if we wish. We are soulmates, and that overrides everything else."

What would Cameron think of all this? His life was about to change drastically—again.

If one day for her on Grey Island had been four months to Arkimedes, how much time had gone by for Cameron, now that she had been here for almost two months?

"Ark—since time works differently here to the rest of the world, what if Cameron takes a month to get here, but it's actually years for us?" Her chest constricted with a sudden surge of fear.

"They explained it to me. During summer, when the days are longer, gravity or magic—whatever you want to call it—has a different effect on the kingdom. Time passes quicker here. It evens out after the summer solstice, and we fall into line with the rest of Caztian. Then, during winter, the effect reverses. One day for us is four months for the rest of the world." Arkimedes searched through their bag of supplies for something else to snack on.

"So, toward the end of the year, the same time passes as in the other kingdoms?"

"It's why merchants travel during fall and spring."

That made sense. Was that why the pirates had been in the city on the night of the Crows' attack?

"I feel recovered enough to go back to the castle. We need to make sure Devon is alive and well at least," Arkimedes said. "And then we can leave this place and not return until the king dies."

44
NAVA

It had been a month since the big altercation with Leir in the forest, and life had settled into a peaceful routine. It turned out that the dukedom was in an uninhabitable state, so they couldn't leave as easily as they'd dreamed. Still, they refused to stay in the castle again. There were too many bad memories there, not least of which the consorts attempting to kill Nava.

Only one of them was still alive—the blonde with the sweet voice who had seen Aristaeus that night. She avoided both Nava and Arkimedes as if her life depended on it, which, given how angry her soulmate had been when he'd learned of her actions, it probably did.

For a time, they rented a place by the sea, waiting for Devon to return. On their arrival at the castle, they had spoken to him briefly while Nava healed him—only for him to vanish into thin air without leaving a word behind as to his whereabouts. After her initial panic, Arkimedes managed to reassure her that he would show up again in no time. But then a day turned into a week and then a month. And then another.

Now they were set to leave the Copper City for their new home, the city of Milania in the Dukedom of Elara, and Devon was still missing. Where was he? Was he well? And if he was, how would he ever find them in their new home?

"I left a message with the castle's staff yesterday. If Devon sends a letter there, they will forward it to Elara." Arkimedes's voice shook slightly when he mentioned his brother's name. His hand tightened around hers as they walked along the seawall toward the ports. The streets were busy with vendors, and the heavy scent of freshly caught fish and seawater hung in the air. A hint of hope bloomed through their bond, and Nava had to swallow past the thick knot in her throat at Arkimedes's emotions.

"Devon will find us, Ark," she said with a tentative smile. "Just like he was able to track you to Grey Island."

By the time they made it to port, the sun was setting behind the horizon. A gigantic ship, unlike anything she'd ever seen before, had docked an hour ago. It could easily transport a thousand people. However, instead of sails, a giant, elongated globe hovered above it.

"What's that?" Nava asked, standing on tiptoes.

"It's an Iron City ship. They call them blimps, and they've been circulating the world more as of late. They're hybrids, so people can travel by both sea and air." Arkimedes wrapped his arm around her waist and pulled her toward him.

She sighed, enjoying the way her stomach fluttered at his warmth. A feeling she could only describe as utter delight burst through her chest. "Does it fly with magic?" The giant ball appeared to be made from canvas, and aged brass beams ran along its sides like metal ribs. It matched the ship's circular windows.

"All I know is that magical crystals power them." Arkimedes's eyes crinkled at the corners. "Once, the Crows sent me to shut down a tinkerer's workshop. Since they are powered by magic, the Society thought it entitled them to the blimps. The king canceled my mission after it caused an uproar with the citizens. Thankfully."

"Of course they wanted first dibs." Nava indicated the ship with her open palm, shaking her head.

She had received Cameron's letter less than a week ago. Despite the difficult circumstances that had led to her contacting him, he had sounded excited to be reunited with her.

Would she spot him as he came down the ramp of the ship? Had his hair changed while they'd been apart? For her, four long months had passed.

"Are you nervous?" Arkimedes's deep voice called her attention back to him.

"Am I that obvious?"

"You haven't stopped fidgeting since we arrived here, so yes."

"I haven't seen him in so long," she admitted. "Last time we spoke in person, we had a new home and Devon was our enemy. Then I went ahead and released him." She drew a deep breath and rolled her shoulders to ease the tension building there. "I hope he can forgive me, that's all…"

"I don't think Cameron will have a hard time understanding why you did it."

"Nava!" Cameron's voice cut through the space. He stood at the very top of the ramp, energetically waving his arm over his head. His voice was deeper than she remembered it.

Raw emotion clogged her throat, and she moved toward him with a smile.

Cameron's hair was a long mess of bright red curls. Even at this distance, his happiness was already contagious. The people ahead of him turned and smiled as her brother bounced on his feet, taking in the port with curiosity.

Nava practically ran to meet him at the bottom of the ramp, and his hug was tight enough to squeeze the air from her lungs. He smelled like the sea, like cinnamon and home.

"You won't believe all the things I've seen!" His warm eyes studied her, a crinkle forming in between his brows. "Look at you, so elegant. It suits you."

"Thanks, Cam."

Her brother turned to Arkimedes, and they both hugged tightly. With how much Cameron had grown, the top of his head was almost at the same height as her mate's. Would he turn out to be even taller than him in the end?

"Look at those wings! I don't remember seeing them before."

Arkimedes's cheeks tinted red, uneasiness dripping through their bond as he shifted on his feet. "I don't need to hide them here."

"I love them." Cameron reached out a hand toward the black and blue feathers. "Can you move them independently?"

She blocked her brother's hand before he made Arkimedes more uncomfortable. "Cam, Arkimedes is still recovering his memories. Give him time to get used to you before you start grabbing at him. How would you feel if someone were to touch you without asking?"

Cameron paused, his eyes flashing to her before he shrugged. "I wouldn't care," he said and sneaked his other arm around her to touch the feathers of Arkimedes's wing.

Arkimedes laughed, and his weary gaze softened. "It's okay, Nava. I don't mind it."

"I'm not used to anyone touching my wings, but he is my family, too," he said through the bond, and her heart soared.

"You see? It's fine. You're always such a worrywart, Nava."

Cameron seemed so grown-up now, even though his attitude hadn't changed much.

"I never expected we would end up here, but I like it," Cameron said, glancing around the docks with interest.

"Where is Laurie?" Nava stretched her neck, trying to catch sight of their old caregiver, but she couldn't spot her anywhere. A heaviness settled in the pit of her stomach. "Is she all right?"

Cameron's face drained of its color. "About that..."

"What happened?"

"She became ill back on Pearl Island, and Gavin didn't think the trip here would suit her health. She needs to follow us when she feels better, using a regular ship. Not a blimp."

"So you left her there?" Nava tried to find Gavin in the crowd. "Who is taking care of her?"

"They didn't tell me, but I overheard them talking when we got the letter. We couldn't wait until she regained her strength. Gavin had some healer friends there who promised to help her and send her our way when the time was right."

While she hadn't seen Laurie for a while now, the worry ate a hole into Nava's chest. Time moved differently in this kingdom, which meant Laurie could only travel during fall or spring. It might be a long time before they were all together again once more.

Arkimedes stroked her back in a comforting gesture, helping to ease her anxiety.

"We wanted to come here and help you with the—well, with everything. We left as soon as we could, but it doesn't seem like you're in trouble now." Cameron's red brows scrunched as he studied them.

True. Leir was gone, and Nava counted her lucky stars that Cameron had never been in danger.

"It's for the best. I wouldn't want you anywhere near what we went through," she said.

"That's it, no? You never want me to be there for you, even though you need help sometimes, too." Cameron's face hardened. He looked so much like their mother when he was annoyed.

"You came at the perfect time," she said and reached for him again. She needed to be close and remind herself they were together again. Finally. "I'm no longer a wanted woman, and I have a feeling you will like our new home. There is a drawing room, like we had at the manor. You were so young then. I doubt you even remember it."

Laurie would have loved it, too. Perhaps she would get to see it soon.

"And a weapons room? Violet has been teaching me to fight."

"Yes." Nava nodded. It was the first thing she'd requested from Arkimedes when they'd planned the refurbishment of the ancient estate. It was far from the city, a day's trip past the forest and into the mountains, surrounded by nature and lush, sprawling gardens.

Gavin strolled down the ramp next, his brown coat gaping open to reveal a loosely tucked-in white shirt. He stopped when their eyes met across Cameron's shoulder. A lopsided smile spread over his face a moment later, and then he dipped into the lowest bow Nava had ever seen. "Your Majesties!"

Nava burst into laughter, just as Arkimedes said, "We aren't majesties yet, Gavin."

"It's good to see you again," Gavin said. "However, I must warn you we got two letters from Roman while we were on Pearl Island. He's not pleased with you."

Nava had been worried about that. Sure, Roman had been her friend of sorts, but he'd been spectacularly unhelpful when the Dark Ones kidnapped Arkimedes. Of course, protecting the village he ruled would be his priority, but he could have at least told her something about what to expect in the Copper Kingdom.

"Well, I'm not happy with him either." Nava crossed her arms. "He could have told me Arkimedes was a prince before I embarked on this mission and nearly got myself killed."

"You still released the Crow that killed so many of us," Violet said as she stepped out of the crowd. Nava steeled herself for the predictable tongue-lashing. Undoubtedly, it would follow soon.

Her friend had cropped her hair short. Much like Gavin, she was wearing traveling clothes: a long tunic and worn brown boots.

"I meant to bring him back," Nava said, and the words tasted of the guilt that still churned in her stomach. "It just didn't work out that way."

"She gets to pardon a prisoner, Violet. She's a queen now," Cameron said.

Nava brushed her sweaty hands over the skirt of her deep charcoal dress, and the gems embroidered on her long billowy sleeves caught the sunlight.

Violet shrugged and walked toward Gavin, handing him a heavy brown bag, presumably filled with their belongings. "I'm guessing the bastard ran?" Her eyes settled on Arkimedes. "Or maybe you let him go? Weren't you brothers before?"

"Violet..." Gavin warned.

"*I* let him go, Violet, not Arkimedes. But I believe he was remorseful for his actions in the end, unlike some others we have met recently." Nava looked at the ground. "He helped me come here and save Arkimedes—and this kingdom."

Silence followed, and Nava bit her tongue so she wouldn't fill it with nervous rambles. Still, Violet's face softened, and while she wasn't a hugger, her tentative smile spoke volumes. "For what it's worth, I'm sorry we weren't there to help you. We can talk about it all when we aren't out here in the open. But we tried to get to you as soon as we could."

Of course they had. Nava had no reason to doubt it.

"I'm loving the way this reunion is going." Gavin took a loud breath of air, patting Arkimedes on the shoulder. "What do you say—should we get something to eat? I'm ravenous, and clearly Violet is, too."

"So where are these magical creatures I keep hearing about that only live in this kingdom?" Cameron strolled ahead, as if this wasn't the first time he'd ever been here.

"Be more specific. There are many magical creatures in this kingdom." Arkimedes lengthened his steps to catch up to her brother.

"A fae on the ship said they looked like bulls—but bigger?"

"The orrus?"

"Yes! Those."

"You are in luck. We have some ready to take us home."

They walked across the dock's wide planks, bleached silver by the unforgiving salty air and the sun. Their carriage awaited them by the street, and its two guards and the driver promptly bowed as they approached.

"Do they always do that? Bow to you?" Cameron whispered into Nava's ear, his breathing loud and excited as they climbed inside.

No matter how many times Nava asked them not to, they always treated her like the queen they believed her to be. "Yes. I'm getting more used to it now."

"So where is home?" Gavin settled down on the squeaky leather seat, his long legs bent as Violet squeezed in next to him, while Cameron wriggled in between Ark and Nava. They'd stuffed the carriage to the brim with two large men, a muscular woman, a gangly teenager—and her.

"As far away from the castle and the king as possible," Arkimedes whispered, almost more to himself, although everyone heard him. No matter how much time had passed since they'd learned the horrible truth, it didn't make it any easier. Arkimedes battled daily with his darkness and the need to avenge his mother in a more ruthless way.

This wasn't something Nava wanted to talk about here, though.

"We are heading to the city of Milania. It's in a valley surrounded by beautiful mountains and nature," Nava said, hoping to lift the heaviness that had descended on the carriage. "We will tell you everything that happened once we are there. I promise."

45
NAVA

One year later

Nava pulled hard on the stem of a tomato plant, ignoring the small hairs that pricked the pads of her fingers. The cold temperatures last night had killed her crop, but it wasn't much of a surprise. Aristaeus had chastised her days ago when she'd mentioned she had been extending the plant's fruitful season.

"We don't go against nature's course," Ari had said, and she was rolling her eyes even now. What good did it do for her to have the power to grow things if she wasn't able to wield it in here?

She sighed at the wilting leaves and the young fruits that were too small to pick and glanced to the side, meeting the eyes of her fellow gardener. The fae waved at her and continued working.

Urlah wasn't talkative, but he kept his uniform impressively clean for someone who worked with dirt all day. He loved to teach Nava about native crops that grew in this part of the Copper Kingdom.

Tossing the tomato plant aside to the pile she had been working on the entire morning, she studied her very dead vegetable garden. She would have to wait until later in the spring to get her favorite crops blooming again.

The thundering hooves of a horse on the gravel road drew her attention. The ornate copper gates of their estate swung open as a gray stallion galloped toward the house. Its rider was a large male, wearing a black coat with a wide collar that matched his beast's shiny fur.

He jumped off the saddle before the horse stopped moving. His wings popped out from his back, casting a shadow over the stone steps that led to the entrance of the dwelling.

Nava dusted her palms off on her raw linen apron and rose to her feet. He came up the steps, two at a time. His clothing hugged his wide shoulders and a thick belt cinched in his narrow waist. Watching him approach made her heart soar.

Arkimedes's gaze dropped to her bare feet, then traveled upward as he studied her choice of clothing until their eyes met. "You must be the gardener," he said. "Do you know if anyone else is home?"

Nava's lips curled up into a smile, her stomach swirling with a mixture of nerves and anticipation. "I'm afraid they have all gone to the market. It's just me—and Urlah."

"I see." Arkimedes reached for her, but Nava swatted his hand away.

"Keep your hands off me, sir. While you're dashing, I'm a married woman."

Arkimedes peered at her from under his long, dark lashes, returning her smile. "I see no ring on your finger, milady…"

"He keeps me here with something much bigger than a ring."

Arkimedes choked on a laugh. "How big are we talking about?"

"I meant our soulmate bond!" Nava's cheeks warmed, and she fought the urge to fan her face. "You've a naughty mind."

"When it comes to you, I do." He reached for her again, so fast this time that Nava couldn't slip away. Then he pulled her close by her apron's front pocket, his face hovering a mere breath away from hers. "Perhaps you should wear the ring I gave you. It will ward off unwanted suitors."

"But it comes off while I'm gardening, and I don't want to lose it," she said, right before his lips descended onto hers. As if they hadn't seen each other in ages, when they had been a tangled mass of two bodies this very morning.

Arkimedes's kiss was soft but demanding, keeping a rhythm that made her blood sing. She wrapped her arms around his shoulders, pressing her body to his while tracing her tongue over his bottom lip before deepening the kiss. His hands traveled up her arms, across her shoulders, finally settling against her lower back.

Then he pulled away, his breath whispering over her well-kissed lips. "What do you say, should we get you out of these clothes?"

"Shh! Urlah is going to hear us…"

Again.

Nava should feel embarrassed that the poor staff kept stumbling over them in heated moments. However, with the rumors that they were soulmates, their insatiable desire for each other didn't appear to bother most of them.

"I think it's too late for that, Bee," he said, peering over her shoulder. She could hear the gardener's quick steps fade away as he made himself scarce. Arkimedes didn't wait. He dipped swiftly, wrapping one an arm underneath her bottom and the other behind her back, lifting her up with ease before he took off into the sky.

The crisp air bit her cheeks, and Nava smiled as she looked down on their home. The golden sunlight kissed its clay rooftop, and beyond the magnificent old edifice made of gray stone and climbing roses, the lake's water caught the light with a twinkle, like stars glimmering in the night sky.

"I hate that the meeting took me away from you this morning," Arkimedes said, and dipped his face into the crook of Nava's neck. A soft, approving noise left his lips. "Your scent is intoxicating, and it's driving me crazy."

Perhaps they were getting close to the winter solstice, and their primal nature was already taking over. Or perhaps this was how they always were.

His lips grazed the sensitive skin of her ear as he breathed her in, tightening his hold on her as they approached the house. Her core tingled with her awakened desire, and she dug her fingers into his scalp, kissing the side of his jaw and down to his lips. The longer they lived together, the more she was discovering Arkimedes's animalistic fae side, and she loved it.

They landed on the balcony. The stone beneath her bare feet was warm, and the view from here—she would never tire of it.

The beautiful, manicured gardens sprawled before her with their tall golden grasses, white winter honeysuckle bushes, and bright bursts of pansies. Each season brought a new delight. The entire estate took her breath away. Gods, she loved it here.

For the first time in a while, she felt at home. Sure, these walls didn't speak to her like the castle back in the Copper City had. But the flowers weren't spying on anyone either, and no spirits haunted the halls. Not unless one counted her nosy teenage brother amongst those.

Here they had a fountain with turquoise water and goldfish that glittered under the moon. No portals bled demons to allow them entrance, and no Neems guarded the doors. They were safe to grow old and love each other.

"How did the meeting go?" Nava asked, pulling away from Arkimedes to get a better look at his face.

One of his father's councilors came every three months to deliver important information about the kingdom as the king could no longer travel. Nava didn't want Oberon to spy on them here at home, so instead Arkimedes held the meeting in the city center.

It was always the same dark-skinned fae she'd met on the day of their battle with Leir. A little more than twelve months had passed, but it felt like a lifetime ago that Leir had let the Zorren in.

"We have a few months to continue enjoying our home here in Milania," Arkimedes said, but his face looked strained.

"But...?"

He took a deep breath and met her gaze. "But he is bedridden now, and he has summoned us to return for the coronation. He claims the citizens should see that we are still in the kingdom. That we should take up residence in the castle for a few months of the year."

"Months?" Nava pursed her lips while taking a hold of his hand. She pulled him back into their room, seeking the warmth of the house. "And the concubine?"

"She has been exiled. He set her up with a small residence on Rust Island, and she isn't allowed back in the Copper Kingdom." Arkimedes locked the balcony doors behind them.

Then he tugged off his coat and tossed it over a leather chair in the room's corner, leaving him wearing a fitted black shirt tucked into fitted trousers.

Her mouth watered just from looking at him. Who cared about the concubine or having to see King Oberon again when she had this in front of her now? The king's demands didn't matter. In the end, Arkimedes and Nava got to decide how to build their lives together. Sure, they had to bear their wider destinies in mind, but they were the ones who would choose where and when to go.

Still, it would be nice to make sure the situation with the deserters was improving. That had been their focus during the last year. They'd set up a funnel of funds to help the humans who were running away from the other kingdoms and offered them jobs to clean up the west side of the city.

They were also giving away grants to encourage businesses to return. But now it was her turn to visit that place where so much of her life had changed again. It was odd not to feel dread about the possibility of returning to the Copper City's streets, but to feel a prickle of excitement instead.

The manor sometimes felt too big for her. And still—never big enough to get the privacy they needed away from Cameron, Laurie, Gavin, or Violet.

"Hey." Arkimedes grasped her chin and tilted her face to him. His eyes shone with happiness and love. "Where did you go?"

Her heart squeezed tight as she shook her head, tracing her hands over his chest and over his soulmate mark. "I was just thinking about how much I like it here."

He grinned, and when he kissed her, the soft dance of their lips and tongues made her toes curl. When she'd arrived here in search of Arkimedes, she'd never expected that one day she would call this kingdom her home.

But time healed even the worst kind of wounds, and her anger toward everything that had happened had eased into acceptance, morphing into curiosity and love.

This place wasn't perfect. Far from it. It was occupied by creatures of raw power and an animal nature. But it reminded her of her mate. A place full of beauty and the dark magic that was only scary when misunderstood.

Nava had never expected this life, but here, in this beautiful place, beside the man she loved, she was grateful that destiny had brought them together. To call this manor her home until the day came when it was time for them to rule.

The End

EPILOGUE

DEVON

Nava and Arkimedes had left the room an hour ago, and Devon was feeling much better. They'd invited him to stay with them and travel to a city in the Copper Kingdom, but he already knew it was no place for him.

He'd stayed behind to help them fight the emissary. The guilt of everything he'd done on that useless island had demanded it. But now that they were off to live their happily ever after, Devon Black would not live and die in the shadow of their domestic bliss.

He scooted out of bed and picked out the best suit the damn magical wardrobe provided him. His hands ached as he popped the lapels of his coat, shielding his neck from the brisk air. Then he looked in the mirror and brushed his hair back, hating the sharp angles of his face and how fucking thin he'd become.

No matter how many potions he drank, every muscle in his body ached, and his energy dwindled far too quickly. He didn't have time to make sure he looked good. He needed to leave.

If he was going to die, he would do it on his own terms.

The tingling of his magic rose with his renewed energy, and a black portal popped into existence right in front of him, smelling of rancid acid and snapping at his skin with static.

Now that he'd learned the Crows had killed his family to get their hands on his rare magic-wielding abilities, he also knew he had something special to barter with.

A gift a god might be interested in. Especially since he'd just lost one of his emissaries.

He stepped forward and crossed into the portal. Blackness surrounded him. Here, Devon floated in air that felt thick and light at the same time. It was neither cold nor hot but the same temperature as his body, and the experience was—oddly comforting. Like he was floating in a dreamless sleep.

Devon had opened countless portals, ever since he'd learned to master the spell. It was second nature by now, almost like breathing. But never in his life had he actually seen the God of Shadows. He was always a deep voice in the darkness that demanded payment, but he never showed his face.

Today, it was different. Today, Devon heard the echo of distinct steps in the distance. When he turned, trying to locate the source, he found nothing.

He needed to keep his mind clear of any memories the Shadow God would grab and steal for payment. Instead, he thought only of his reason for being here.

To speak to Dargan himself and the deal he wanted to propose.

"You deny me my payment?" Dargan's voice was a velvet caress against Devon's skull, and an icy chill crawled up his back as the god finally came into view. "The deal is simple, human. You cross through my world and give me a memory, or I shall take something else. Your eyes, perhaps? Or your tongue?"

He was incredibly tall, with long, silky black hair that got lost in his fitted suit jacket. A glowing crown hovered above his head, casting yellow light over his sharp features and wide shoulders.

Fear clawed at Devon's throat. Nothing illuminated their surroundings, and Devon's body grew heavier, as if he was about to touch the ground.

But even with the fear growing like a sickness through him, he kept his mind blank. He'd been training his entire fucking existence not to let his mind wander. He could do it for a little longer to get what he truly wanted.

The god strolled around Devon, clasping his hands behind his back while he eyed Devon with growing curiosity. "You want to be immortal?"

"For a time..."

"For a time?" Dargan's dry laughter echoed in the cavernous emptiness. The darkness was beginning to clear, revealing an immense ceiling with stalactites hanging over them. Dargan's eyes shone brighter, and a cunning smile took over his features. "What makes you think I will release you once you're mine, pet?"

Devon recognized the look on Dargan's face. He was a god, but humans had descended from these beasts. He desired Devon's soul much more than a silly, insignificant memory.

"I don't owe you anything other than a memory, and my soul is mine to keep." Devon paused when the air caught in his throat. It was the same shortness of breath that had been winding him since he'd held the Vulcan that second time. But he couldn't dissolve into a fit of coughs right now, not when he was making a bargain with Dargan.

"Your soul is poisoned, and you have little time left to live," the God of Shadows said, and his magic moved in swirling shapes. It looked familiar. So much like Arkimedes's aura that it made Devon feel stupidly safe.

"I will manage. I have a friend who is a Beekeeper. She's fond of me and might keep me alive long enough for me to get my revenge..." Although Devon highly doubted that Nava and his brother were interested in following him to the Iron Kingdom to burn the Society of Crows to the ground.

Not when they'd just inherited an entire kingdom themselves.

"*Is* she fond of you, like you are of her?" Dargan questioned, inspecting his fingernails. They shone, black and long like claws. But it wasn't his inhuman hand that had Devon's heart racing.

Shame burned deep within his wretched heart as it ached with the feelings he'd been unable to shake for months.

"You look surprised that I know." Dargan stepped closer to Devon, and an intensity bled into his features that he couldn't place. "You think I don't know how much you *love* the Beekeeper?" Dargan chuckled. "Your brother's soulmate. You already know that those feelings are wasted, as she would never feel the same for you. Are you ashamed of your envy?"

He was. Devon had never wanted to fall for an untouchable woman. He hated being jealous of Arkimedes, who was his beloved brother. The bastard got it all, while Devon was stuck in here, making a deal with this devil.

He swallowed past the knot in his throat, digging his fingernails into the fleshy part of his palms. "You can read my feelings. Would you prefer that payment over my request? Because if you can take away my love for her, then be my guest."

Dargan tilted his head, looking more curious. "So why lend me your soul if you can live out there without my help?"

"Because I need immortality," Devon said. "Everyone has a reason to want something, and I'm not above bargaining what I have at my disposal to get what I desire. You're a god, and yet you want my soul, sick and all." A cough rattled past his lips, and he could taste copper on his tongue. But he wouldn't allow that to hold him back, not when he was so close he could taste it.

"You won't be immortal if our deal has a timeline," Dargan reasoned. "Why not give me your entire soul and then no mortal can touch you for an eternity?"

"Because I don't want to belong to anyone," Devon said. The truth brought a lightness to his chest. His breaths became shorter, the itching in his lungs increasing the longer he held off on coughing. He reached for his pocket but found his arm was too heavy to even grab at the potion he had stuffed in there.

"You can cough if you need to." Dargan stopped so close to Devon that his face hovered mere inches away. It was rather perfect, with a straight nose exactly the right size for his angular face, golden eyes and unblemished skin. "I'll take your soul for one hundred years of service, and when you're free, you will no longer be ill."

A century away from Caztian didn't sound half bad. The Society of Crows still wanted and remembered him. He could only visit in brief spurts of time, much like Leir had done whenever he'd let the Zorren in, before the shadow world had pulled him back.

But what if Arkimedes was gone by then? What if…?

"All those years away will make it easier to forget your love for the Beekeeper."

"Get out of my head," Devon growled, and his annoyance spiked further when Dargan's smile widened.

"You came into my land to bargain with a god, Devon Black. I'll do as I please."

Devon craned his head to make full eye contact with this giant. "Fifty years."

"One hundred years and not a day less." Dargan extended his hand to Devon, and what had once been black swirls like his brother's aura were now golden streaks dancing around him, like the light coming from his eyes.

"No," Devon said, and the portal somewhere behind him fizzled. He was running out of time, and he needed that potion. "Unless I get to return to Caztian and won't be brought here until you need me. I intend to use my immortal years to destroy the Crows."

"You will do as I command if we make a deal," Dargan said. His careful words wouldn't undo whatever spell of a treaty the gods had struck with the founders so many years ago. "What you do with your free time is not my problem. I don't meddle in the Caztanians' affairs, as long as they respect what I'm owed. One hundred years and that's my offer, pet."

"One hundred years," Devon agreed, and his knees touched hard ground. He couldn't see much around him, but the air grew crisp, full of a scent Devon couldn't place. "But I get to stay in Caztian if I choose to—until you call for me." Devon paused, and he slowly inched away toward his portal.

"Fine," Dargan said, and everything around Devon took on a solid shape.

The cavernous walls resolved into an enormous dome, as if he was standing inside a human-made throne room. Its interior was carved from dark onyx, and underneath him, a floor of polished, rounded stones spiraled into the center of the room where Dargan stood.

"Welcome home, Crow."

SIGN UP FOR MY NEWSLETTER!

A Court of Beasts and Ruins
A new series of standalone novels, featuring a couple per book. Think gothic fairytales, yearning, slow burn romance and more!

Unraveled: A Beauty and the Beast retelling where SHE uses a forbidden spell to stop a monster from killing her people, and he steals her soul.

The Wicked Kingdom Series:
If you love fated mates, a shadow daddy and a slow burn romance:

The Curse of the Crow (BOOK 1)
The Curse of a Kingdom (BOOK2)
The Curse of the Fallen <- This BOOK
The Curse of the Shadow God (Prequel)

Go to
www.abbeyfox.com
To learn about the Kingdoms, see mood-boards and other fun stuff!

ABOUT THE AUTHOR

"Abbey Fox has always loved storytelling. Ever since she was little, she created characters for fun and got immersed in their life stories, worlds, and magic systems. This naturally progressed onto writing. Her first story being a cringe worthy teenage high school Romance, which she wrote at the age of thirteen in a notebook that was half falling apart by the time she wrote the end.

As time has gone by, she has dived into writing other genres, from YA Fantasy to Mystery Romance, Romantic Soap opera Sci-fi. Now she focuses on her love for Adult Fiction in the Fantasy Romance/ Paranormal Romance genres.

Her debut novel is coming out later this year. It is part of an enthralling series set in a magical world where soulmates are real and power corrupts the kingdoms.

When Abbey is not writing, she enjoys spending time with her husband and her four-year-old son. She also enjoys tending to her indoor tropical jungle and painting fun characters with watercolors. "

ALSO BY ABBEY FOX

A Court of Beasts and Ruins:

A new series of standalone novels. If you love dark fairytales, tortured heroes and a slow burn romance try:

Unraveled: A gothic Beauty and the Beast retelling, where she uses a forbidden spell to stop a Beast to hurt those she loves and he steals her soul.

The Wicked Kingdom Series:

If you somehow read this book before reading the rest, and want to read the other two, or the prequel featuring Gavin and Violet's romance:

The Curse of the Crow (Book 1)

The Curse of a Kingdom (Book 2)

The Curse of the Shadow God (Prequel)

www.ingramcontent.com/pod-product-compliance
Lightning Source LLC
Chambersburg PA
CBHW020451310726
48979CB00016B/2611/J
* 9 7 8 1 9 6 0 2 7 9 0 7 1 *